Requiem for a Rock Star

I0672488

Book Two of
The Rock Star Records

Barbra Best

Requiem for a Rock Star

Book Two of
The Rock Star Records

Dragon Breath Press, LLC
Ridgeland, Mississippi
ISBN: 978-0-9990692-6-4

Other Books by Barbra Best

Rise of a Rock Star – Book One of *The Rock Star Records*
http://amzn.to/2Xd7ke1

DISCLAIMER

All entities in this story are purely fictional. Any resemblance to anyone, living or dead, is coincidental.

The time frame of this series spans several decades in which "free sex and love" were the norm without realizing the emotional and physical dangers of leading the promiscuity of the times.

As Book Two of *The Rock Star Records* comes into play, we are introduced to the era of the 80s where STDs and AIDS prevailed.

DEDICATION

In my last dedication, I thanked those who were a part of my life when I began to write *Rise of a Rock Star*. This time, I have to give a shout out to my family and other close friends. My cousin, Xavier Figuerola, and Jesus Estarellas who put together an amazing gathering of friends at their home and family for the release of *Rise*. My friend, María Figuerola, for the beautiful cake with the book cover and poster. She has always been my rock in good times and bad. They went all out to make sure I had a wonderful evening I will never forget. We spent a large part of the night, talking music and singing "California Dreaming." Family is everything!

Must also dedicate this and the rest of the series to my readers, who helped me plow ahead with the remainder of the series thanks to their comments and praise.

Friends from childhood and Florida friends, along with a few surprises I've met along the way on this journey.

Last, to my husband, Gus. My other half and soulmate. Thank you for your love and for understanding this "crazy" lady.

ACKNOWLEDGEMENTS

I can never write an acknowledgement without first mentioning my friend, mentor, teacher, editor and publisher, Janet Taylor-Perry. She is the owner of Dragon Breath Press. She is the author of *The Raiford Chronicles, The Legend of Draconis: King Satin's Realm* and *Spirits' Desire, Wilted Magnolias,* the first *April Chastain Intrigue.* She recently published *Homegrown Healer,* from her *Hillbilly Hijinks* collection, my favorite series, and *Head Count*, Laura Beth Copeland's first misadventure. Without her encouragement and help, *The Rock Star Records* series would never exist. I must also acknowledge her authorship of "No More Motion without Emotion," the lyrics for The Warriors' hit song. She reserves all rights to republish in a poetry collection or singly.

I also acknowledge Patricia Ann Yaeger Hauge, who reads my work before publication and Rob Finney who serves as a proofreader.

I must give credit to Christopher Chambers (juroddesigns.com) for his design of the cover. A particular acknowledgement to a special person who "discovered" the photo we used on the front cover and who chooses to remain anonymous, "witchy woman." Thank you to the photographer, Miss J, for the beautiful photo that graces the cover.

REQUIEM FOR A ROCK STAR

REQUIEM FOR A ROCK STAR

"Agnus Dei, qui tollis pecata mundi, miserere nobis"

CONTENTS

1
THE GRIM REAPER RETURNS

JANUARY 1987, NEW YORK

The black Lincoln stretch limousine that carried Karl Engels pulled up to the side entrance of Brendan Byrne Arena at the Meadowlands Sports Complex, minutes away from the heart of Manhattan. He glanced at his Rolex. *Three more hours to go.* The chauffeur opened the door, and Karl stepped out onto the curb. Black ostrich leather boots crunched the ice on the sidewalk.

Furious, chilling wind slapped at his cheeks. He pulled the black cashmere coat close to his body and stopped for a moment to admire the interesting architecture of the building. *Five consecutive nights sold out.* In the summer, they would have booked Giants Stadium where he was sure they would have sold just as many nights. The strong winter sunlight caused him to squint despite the sunglasses.

He looked up at the cloudless azure January sky. The taste of bitter bile rose to his throat and burned. Though Karl loved the cold, he shivered. His bones felt the raw chill in the air. The chauffeur interrupted his musings. "Mr. Engels? This way, please."

Karl followed the man through a door marked "Private" and into the massive concert hall. He walked to the dressing area where a bottle of his favorite Remy Martin awaited him. His cold fingers opened it and poured a hefty shot into a snifter. He removed his sunglasses and threw them on the table without care.

The room was warm, but the bitterness of frost was ever-present in the air and throughout his body, so he left his coat on. Picking up his drink, he ventured onto the stage to watch the roadies set up.

Karl strolled out across the stage and stood dead center. All around him frenzied men worked, some so young he could have been their father.

Shouts of "Karl" or "Mr. Engels" greeted him. The tour photographer, accompanied by a reporter from *Rolling Stone Magazine,* approached him. The photographer snapped his Nikon FM away as the reporter and Karl spoke for a bit.

The Warriors—together for two decades. The secret of their continued success lay in the talents of their leader, Ron James, and Karl's ability to produce lyrics on subjects that ranged from broken hearts and lost love to nuclear war. Every time Karl wrote a song, it was as if a large, unknown mystical force pushed the pencil along the paper. He had a unique way with words and an excellent command of a language understood by fans worldwide. Jim Haley, their rhythm guitarist and keyboard player, contributed to their songs as well. The three could come up with a new hit in minutes.

The players remained the same Vladimir Vavilov, the Russian drummer; Mike Evans, the shy bass guitarist; Jim; Karl himself on lead guitar and vocals; Susan Michaels, Karl's fiancée and Ron's ex-wife on keyboards, vocals and of course, the leader of the infamous group, Ron James, one of rock and roll's sexiest and raunchiest men.

Karl took off his coat despite the ever-present nip that lingered within his bones. He threw it over the stool behind the drums and picked up his Gibson double-necked guitar to check its tuning.

"Karl," the technician called out holding up a bright red Fender Stratocaster. "Open tuning on this one too?"

Karl nodded. "Yup." He returned the Gibson back to its polished chrome stand and thrust his icy hand into his pocket. He strolled around, sipping his Remy.

The staff secretary, Jessica, called out to him from the left side of the stage. "Hey, handsome! I didn't know you were here. Can I get you anything?"

Karl flashed her his award-winning smile and held up his empty glass. "One more, no ice." He sat behind his comrade's drum set and stepped on a pedal, causing the high hat to bounce up and down.

He got up like a child playing with new toys on Christmas morning and turned on the Yamaha DX-7 keyboard, and his nimble fingers played a few chords then fell right into the introduction to one of their first masterpieces, "Forbidden Love." A keyboard intro that could only have been composed by their master keyboardist, Jim Haley. Memories of a seedy club in Hamburg called the Cosmos flooded his mind.

He clicked the power off and walked again to the center of the stage. His green eyes scanned the huge arena. *One hundred thousand fans.* Their last tour before a three-year hiatus, The Warriors would be taking a long, well-deserved break after their "Savage" tour.

The "Savage" tour. Karl took a long gulp from his drink. It felt different from the beginning. Wrong. The vibes negative, Karl shuddered as another chill ran down his spine. Goosebumps rose on his flesh. *Maybe I'm coming down with something.*

Jessica returned with a fresh drink and picked up his luxurious coat. "Karl, are you all right?"

"Yes, I'm fine, why?"

She shrugged. "I don't know. You look a bit pale. By the way, Kathy is in the dressing room if you want to get started. You know that once Susan gets here, all hands will be on her."

"Are you going to help me dress?" he asked, laughing.

"You wish," she teased back.

Karl's emerald eyes scanned the arena again, and standing among the empty seats on the second promenade, he saw a man in his early twenties with stringy, chestnut hair that hung to his shoulders. He wore a dark military-type jacket. Their eyes met for a split second, then the man turned and walked toward the stairs that led to the exit.

Karl thought the eyes seemed menacing, and he was probably part of security. But there was a certain look about the stare. It frightened Karl, as if madness lay behind the glare. Karl felt the hair on the back of his neck rise. *I must be going crazy.* Fear was not a part of his life…not ever.

♫

The stadium filled with eager fans. The final moments approached, and it was time to take their places on the stage. The first half of the show went as well as only seasoned performers could deliver.

During the second part of the show, Karl switched places with Mike and took his place beside Susan to do background vocals. Her duets with Ron were over, and now only Ron became the center of attention.

An overzealous female fan jumped onto the stage, only to be dragged away by security guards. Ron continued as usual, untouched by the pandemonium and the broken hearts of female fans surrounding him. Never missed a note.

While the security people tried to control the screaming female fans jumping onstage to touch their idol, a young man seized the opportunity to hop onto the stage. For a split second, his eyes and Karl's clashed again, and Karl noticed the mortifying and crazed expression on his face.

He raised his arm slowly and pointed a 9 mm Makarov. *BOOM! BOOM! BOOM! BOOM!* All but one shot hit one of the targets.

A different shooter emerged from another direction, a silencer attached to the PSS-2 in his hand. Many bullets hit their designated target that night.

It was a blood bath.

2
THE PAST RESURFACES

LAST WEEK OF NOVEMBER 1985, FRANKFURT, GERMANY

The final class before the semester break and Christmas holiday at Oxford ended. Alexander Edwards hurried out in search of his brother, Niall. Naturally, he wasn't in the dorm room. Alex checked his watch. Three hours until their flight and a long-awaited reprieve from school for a few weeks. Their passports lay on the dresser next to their tickets.

"Damn him!" Alex swore. He looked forward to going home this holiday. There was something he wanted to discuss with his mother.

Niall dashed into the room, out of breath. "Sorry, just a small last-minute good-bye with Stacey."

"Thank God it was a quickie."

Niall chuckled, flashing perfect white teeth. His dark-chocolate eyes sparkled. "It wasn't. I cut class today. I don't do quickies, especially with her. Just let me take a quick shower."

"We're going to be late."

"No, we're not."

He was out of the shower swiftly. He pushed his long dark-brown hair back into a ponytail and topped it off with a dark-blue cap sporting the NY Yankee logo. "Ready?" he asked Alex.

Suitcases in hand, they took a taxi to Heathrow; barely allowing a few minutes to pick up a scone and tea before the first-class flight headed for Frankfurt.

"How were your finals?" Alex asked.

"Good, I'm sure I passed everything. You?"

"I think mine went well, too." Alex knew his music teachers were thrilled with his expertise at composition. It came naturally.

"And Miranda?" Niall asked.

Alex rolled his sapphire eyes. "A pain in the ass."

"I guess I shouldn't have asked."

"No, you shouldn't have."

Niall and Alexander Edwards, less than two years apart, were virtually joined at the hip. Alex was a toddler when his mother married British international banker, Lord Byron Edwards. The tall, stoic grey-haired banker was the only father Alex knew. He adopted Alex legally and gave him his last name, but Alex knew Lord Edwards was not his biological father. His mother didn't speak much about his biological father, but her eyes twinkled on those rare occasions when she did mention him. Alex knew he was the result of a year-long relationship when she was a teenager, and his mother became pregnant. Somehow, Alex couldn't imagine his mother having an "affair" with anyone. She was too proper and elegant no matter how old she might have been.

Alex looked out the window. The plane broke through the clouds, and sunlight fell on his blond hair. He needed change in his life. Miranda, his girlfriend of two years, was pushing him to get engaged. She wasn't the one. She came from a good, well-known British family. She was attractive and intelligent; the sex was good, but something was missing. Music in his veins played too loudly.

♫

The family chauffeur waited for them outside the airport. Alex watched the scenery pass by while Niall tried to prod the older man for gossip about the family during the ride.

"Niall, no matter how much you want to hear gossip, you know that your family is quiet and sedate. The twins are a bit of a ruckus these days, but your mother handles them well. They are growing up and have discovered boys."

The twins, Anneke and Anneliese, recently turned sixteen; rich, spoiled and got everything they wished for. Brats.

"And how are you, Alex?" the chauffeur asked.

"Fine, just thinking of taking a semester off and traveling."

This was news to Niall. "You didn't tell me!" he said.

"Just decided."

"Where would you go?"

Alex shrugged his shoulders. "Maybe America."

"I'd love that!" His brother shouted with excitement. "Care for some company?"

"My true partner in crime. I wouldn't dream of going without you.

Let's see if we can pull it off without hearing the Riot Act. Take a semester off."

Alex laughed as the car pulled up to a massive mansion nestled in a secluded wealthy suburb of Frankfurt. Alex got out and looked around. The house was decorated with miles and miles of holly, lights, and garland for the holidays. A tall blue spruce stood to the left of the house, lit with bright colored lights. His mother went all out every Christmas.

The door swung open, and Eva Edwards ran out to greet her sons. Alex smiled at his mother, still a stunning blonde. Her elegance and style made her appear taller than her five-foot-six frame. She had always felt petite next to Alex's father who was over six feet tall and at the time, thin as a rail.

Eva reached up to kiss her first born and looked at him proudly. He resembled his father more as time passed. She then reached up to kiss Niall. She put her arms around theirs and stood sandwiched between them.

"I'm so glad to see you both. I don't get to see you enough anymore."

Alex bent down and kissed his mother's forehead. Eva had done well with her elder son. He never felt out of place and was an important part of the family.

Niall kissed his mother's cheek. "Where's Dad?"

"He's in the hospital again, but the doctors expect him to be out tomorrow."

Lord Edwards suffered a stroke the previous year and struggled to bounce back. He was in and out of the hospital since. His health started to deteriorate, and Eva knew it was just a waiting game.

They entered the house and Anneliese and Anneke ran down the stairs, shouting out their brothers' names.

The twins were exact replicas of their mother when she was young, long blonde hair and dazzling blue eyes. The butler took the bags and disappeared to the boys' respective rooms. They followed their mother into the formal living room where they remained for several hours, sharing a few refreshments and small talk until dinner was announced.

Eva smiled and studied her children. She adored them all but always carried a special soft spot for Alex, almost feeling sorry for him at times being deprived of knowing who his biological father was.

Dinner was loud as both Alex and Niall related stories of their mischief at school. They were both in the top ten of their classes. Niall studied criminal law and looked forward to an internship at Interpol. The offer could not be taken lightly; it was the chance of a lifetime. Alex was another story. Alex showed signs of slacking in his studies as music blared throughout his veins. He leaned toward an interest in contemporary music and loved the hard rock sounds of the "hair" bands. It brought Eva memories of another happier time in her life. Her lips turned up in a sweet smile, her mind going back, way back to a young man who changed the course of her life forever. She thanked God for every minute they spent with each other and regretted none of it. She had a life she would have never come to know if it hadn't been for a simple mistake and the curiosity of a young woman who fell for a teenager with sad blue eyes. She was now fulfilled by her children, and her husband was sweet and loving until the unexpected illness shattered the marriage and the family.

Alex noticed the look in his mother's eyes. Her mind was far, far away. The time was right.

Niall excused himself from the dinner table to go with Anneliese and listen to some new music she wanted to play for him. She recently "discovered" a band who had been around for a few decades and was fascinated by them. The Warriors.

This was his moment, Alex thought. Anneke was on the phone with a boy she just met in school, and his mother was all his.

The help cleared off the dining room table and Eva stood. "Let's go sit in the garden for a bit," she said, putting her arm through his bent elbow.

"Marcia, Alex and I will take our tea and dessert outside."

Holiday decorations lit up the patio. Alex welcomed the chill in the air. It was a bit cool, but his mother sensed his need for privacy. She wrapped a cashmere shawl around her shoulders. He wanted to speak with her and thought it best to sit by the fireplace outside. There was no doubt in her mind about how the conversation was going to turn.

She took his hand in hers. "Something is bothering you, Alex."

She knew him too well. Alex braced himself and wondered if it was indeed the right time. He stood, all six-feet-one-inch of him. He looked like his father, walked like him, the posture and gestures identical.

"Please know that I would never want to hurt you in any way, and if this is tough for you, I understand and forget this conversation ever happened."

Alex paced in eerie silence for a few seconds. Marcia came out with a tray of freshly baked scones and Earl Grey tea. He took a sip of his tea and let the hot fluid warm him.

Eva stood and put her arms around his waist. "I know what you want to ask me about, Alex. His name is Ron James. He is the rock star that has broken all the music charts worldwide."

His blue eyes met his mother's. "How did you know that's what I wanted to speak to you about?"

"A mother knows, and it's time you knew the truth."

"Ron James, *the* famous, legendary, musician is my father? The leader of The Warriors? Does he know about me?"

"No, I never got a chance to tell him. He left the orphanage where I was teaching before I found out about you."

"You didn't know where he went?"

"I couldn't go in search of him. He was beginning to make a name for himself in the club and music circuit. I was going to have to face a harsh reprimand from the convent."

His arms were still around her shoulders, and he let go for a moment so that he could look into her eyes.

"Convent?"

"I was a postulant at St. Mary's Catholic School and Orphanage. I was going to be Sister Eva if I went through with my vows."

"Really? You and a rock star? One like *him*? I can't imagine that at all."

"It's a long story for another day."

He looked at her with sympathy and love in his eyes. God, he would have never imagined! He didn't know what to say.

Alex took another sip of tea and picked up a scone. He bit into one of the corners of the deliciousness and picked at a cranberry to savor its tart sweetness.

"He was a good, young man, and I fell madly in love with him during the time we were together, but it wasn't meant to be. I like to think he loved me too."

"Would it be wrong of me to try and contact him after all this time?"

"No, Alex. I don't think it would be wrong, but I don't want to see you hurt. He's a mega star, and I don't know if he would take this lightly. He's had a rough life. I've read about him in the papers and tabloids over the years. He served some time in prison for drugs and other things. He was supposed to marry a famous music producer, Susan Michaels, and he was arrested at the altar. They eventually married years later and just a month ago, I read somewhere that she filed for divorce. He was near death from a drug overdose not too long ago. I don't know the kind of man he is now, but under the rough, hard carapace is a sweet, loving man who never got a chance in life."

"What are you talking about? He's rich, famous and loved throughout the world!"

"His eyes were always sad, and he covered the pain with anger, but he has a good heart. He just never learned to be good. His childhood was shrouded with pain. I will try to contact him for you. I think he'll do the right thing."

"Does Dad know who he is?" he asked, referring to the only father he'd known up to that moment. *Ron James, well, I'll be. That explains a lot.*

She nodded. "He's always known, but he loves you like you were his own. We both knew this day would come; we prepared for it. Ron lives in Los Angeles and yes, Alex, I know that music runs through your veins. You are his son in every aspect. Your walk, stance; the similarities are endless."

"Is this going to hurt you?" he asked, sitting on the bench beside her.

"Absolutely not, dear. We'll just have to wait and see what his reaction is to this unexpected news, but we'll deal with it. I don't want you to expect much just in case. I don't want you to get disappointed."

He put his arms around his mother again and hugged her tightly. When he let go, he smiled. "A nun, Mother? You were going to be a nun?"

"Yes, until a very nefarious night."

"Please spare me the details."

"I joined the convent when I was sixteen, never imagining I would fall in love. I will try to reach him through their manager, Richard Stone."

He kissed her cheek. "Should I tell Niall?"

"I think he should hear it from you."

♫

Alex and Niall went out that night, not in search of girls but as the two brothers who shared a deep, strong bond. Alex was not quite two when Niall was born. Neither boy could imagine his life without the other. Inseparable. He was thrilled to hear about Alex's father and looked forward to meeting him.

"Well," Niall said, "if we hang out at one of their concerts, can you imagine how much pussy we're going to get?"

Alex laughed. "Your mind is only on one thing, Niall."

"Always and rightfully so."

♫

Eva waited until two the next afternoon when Richard Stone, The Warriors' manager, promised he would have Ron call her. He didn't know what it was about, but she had been insistent. Richard didn't think it was a hoax or a fan, the sincerity in her voice convinced him of that. She asked him to check her background. Eva Edwards's history was as clean as virgin snow. She was one of Ron's teachers and the wife of a prominent banker.

She went into the den and sat by the telephone, reading the newspaper and waiting.

It rang at 2:30 German time. Eva picked it up on the second ring.

"Mrs. Edwards?" a female voice said.

"*Ja*, this is she."

"Please hold the line. I have Mr. James on the phone for you."

"Thank you," Eva said. A slight tremor coursed through her body, and she prayed she was doing the right thing and that the result of her sin would not backfire on her. Tiny beads of perspiration dotted her forehead, and her hand shook slightly. Her usual composure always disappeared when it came to Ron.

"Mrs. Edwards, this is Ron James; you wanted to speak with me?"

She pictured him as the young man she had fallen in love with. She recognized his voice, although he sounded more mature and polite. The rough edges more polished. She thought of the ruthless, angry young man who became the perfect lover. Her heart pounded.

"Mr. James, I'm not sure where to begin or if you even remember me. I was one of your teachers at St. Mary's."

The face of a beautiful, young and vibrant nun with a contagious laugh flashed in his mind.

"Sister Eva?"

"Yes. I'm Mrs. Edwards now."

Ron wasn't too sure where the conversation was headed or why she contacted him, but any doubt that Richard had of her telephone call being that of a groupie or a fan could now be put to rest. *What the hell is she calling about?* Was she suddenly pissed at him for taking her virginity that night in the confessional? Hell, she could have said no, and he would not have insisted; wasn't his style. Nevertheless, it was a triumphant moment in the life of a teenager with raging hormones he never forgot.

"It's been a long time. How are you?"

"Two decades."

"Wow!" He exclaimed, suddenly at a loss for words. *What can we possibly talk about?* He was glad to hear a voice from his past. *Is she going to ask me about the last time I went to confession? Does she know about my sordid life? She has to know.*

"You didn't go through with your vows, then?" he asked.

"I couldn't. I was thrown out of the convent shortly after you left."

"I'm sorry to hear that. Did someone find out about us?" His tone showed true repentance.

"No, I was pregnant."

He was silent for a few moments. "I'm sorry. I didn't know."

"I know you didn't. You left St. Mary's before I could tell you. I was already pregnant when you left."

"Eva, listen, do you need anything? How can I make it up to you? Do right by you?"

"Yes, I do need something," she replied.

"Whatever you need." Ron said, a lump forming in his throat. He'd done damn wrong, and it was payback time. He could picture those statues at the chapel laughing at him now. Blackmail, probably. She would go to the tabloids and cry rape. *Fuck.*

"I'd really like it if you would please agree to meet your son."

The lump grew, he could barely swallow. "My s-s-son?" he whispered into the phone.

"Yes, Ron. You have a twenty-year-old son who is studying music at Oxford and looks just like you. Can you agree to meet him? I wouldn't ask anything else of you. He has everything he needs; I just want him to meet his father. I know that he is a stranger to you, but it's important to him. This is just a mother's plea to her son's father."

Ron collapsed back in the leather chair he was sitting in. *A son?* Stefani, his only daughter and supposedly first born, would surely kill him now with her jealously. She was insanely possessive of her father.

"Of course, Eva. I would be more than happy to. I have some free time until our tour starts. I can fly him to Los Angeles and get to know him or fly there. Whatever you think is better for him."

Her eyes filled with tears of happiness for her son. "Thank you. I appreciate it. You won't be disappointed; he's a fine young man."

"I'll have my assistant contact you with the information. When can we meet?"

"Well, he's here on his Christmas break now. I wouldn't be too angry if he missed Christmas at home to spend it with you. I've had him for twenty Christmases. I'll share him this one time, Ron. It's for a good cause," she said laughing.

What a delightful woman she turned into! Thank God, she did all right.

"Do you prefer that I come there or have him come here to L.A.?"

"It doesn't matter, Ron."

Ron laughed nervously. "I think it's time I went to Frankfurt again. I lived in Hamburg all my young life and never saw much of Frankfurt, just the inside of cheap hotel rooms. Forget I said that, Sister. I should come to him, not him come here to meet a stranger. I'll have my secretary call you back with the details. Besides, I would love to see you again."

"Thank you. This is the best Christmas present you can give our son. I won't tell him, and you can surprise him. I'd like to see you too."

"I'm looking forward to meeting him."

"You can have dinner with us, break the ice. And stop calling me Sister. I'm the mother of your child, and if you remember correctly, you had to remain pure to become a nun at the time. We certainly put an end to that." Her familiar laughter made him smile.

Ron didn't have any doubt that Alex was his. He had been her one and only lover at the orphanage until he became emancipated and set out to find his parents. A sad mistake he didn't want his son to go through.

♫

Ron picked up his glass of club soda. He stood and walked to the window of the office on the Penthouse floor of the 611 Place building in downtown Los Angeles where The Warriors had their offices.

Most of them were on their way home to be with their families and significant others a long time ago. The holidays were coming, and they were all shopping, putting up Christmas trees, going to musicals, dance recitals with the children. He was having dinner with his kids on the weekend.

Ron stared out over the city. How easy it would be for him to drive into the rough neighborhoods where they knew him so well and look for his old friends in order to score. It would ease the pain of having to face another failure in his life. He missed out on the opportunity to have done the right thing for his first child. His hand shook, and he took a deep breath; but he would not to give in to the urge. He touched the crucifix Eva gave him before leaving the orphanage that he never removed. He never wanted to believe, to pray, but he certainly knew that Eva coming back into his life was no coincidence. She'd kick his ass if her son's father strayed in the wrong direction.

3
THE WRATH OF A REDHEAD

1st WEEK OF DECEMBER 1985, NEW YORK

Michelle Bujold-Stone returned home from the salon where she had her hair done and a manicure and pedicure for an event at an art gallery in SoHo that evening. Afterwards, she stopped by the Chanel boutique and Bloomingdale's before heading north along Fifth Avenue. Although it was winter, the weather was mild, and the sun, dazzling. She loved New York almost as much as Paris. She delighted in big cities where she could walk and relish the sites, step into small shops and eateries. Her mind travelled back to when she and Jim Haley, the keyboard player and rhythm guitarist of The Warriors, had travelled to the most picturesque cities in Europe. Eight wonderful years in which all they did was travel and enjoy the hell out of each other. They were two peas in a pod, inseparable. A smile touched her lips as she remembered those times. He'd been her first lover. An unwanted and unexpected pregnancy shattered the near-perfect relationship, and they went their separate ways. A drastic mistake she was guilty of. She became mortified of her feelings, feelings that consumed who she was to the point that she lived and breathed for the man.

Over the years, they encountered each other and found themselves thrust in each other's company because she married The Warriors' manager. She always watched him furtively on those occasions, and their eyes met from time to time, causing her heart to pound uncomfortably. Yes, the feelings were still there and stronger than ever. He smiled, and she smiled back, but neither had the nerve to approach the other about their feelings. She had also made vows that she took seriously. She wondered at times if he felt the same way, if he thought of all the years. Though he had relationships and was a father, he was still a bachelor, and they rarely spoke privately. The times they crossed paths were limited to concerts and functions that required The Warriors' presence. Every now and then, it meant dinners or parties at each other's homes.

Her best friend, Susan, knew how she still felt. Despite the decades, they remained as close as sisters, keeping no secrets from each other.

Her marriage? What else was there to say? She suspected that Richard was having an affair. He moved out of the marital bed a year before and filed for a legal separation without an explanation. She didn't ask why, didn't need to. *A woman knows.*

"Bonjour," she greeted the doorman as she entered the pre-war landmark apartment building across the street from the Metropolitan Museum of Art. Her friend, Susan, owned the penthouse apartment. She and Richard owned the floor below that. They travelled to New York so often that when the two huge apartments became available, they purchased them and extended their living space to spread out throughout the entire floor.

She opened the front door to silence. The twins weren't home from school yet. She walked into the master bedroom and couldn't believe her eyes. Richard lay on *her* bed, naked as the day he came into the world. His supposed love interest sat on top of him, moving and panting. They were so engrossed in the lovemaking that they didn't hear her.

Red-haired ire exploded. She raced toward the bed and slammed her Louis Vuitton bag against the woman's face and head knocking her off. She rolled to the edge of the bed and tumbled onto the floor, blood pouring from her nose and a gash above her eyebrow. The handles flew off the costly bag.

"How dare you? On *my* bed?" Her scream caused Richard to flinch. She jumped on top of him and began to pummel him. He grabbed her arms.

"Michelle, stop!" he shouted.

"I knew it! No one moves out of his wife's bed unless he is getting pussy elsewhere. Get out of my house, both of you, or I will call the *police.* And get that *prostituée* out of my face."

The woman who must have been half Richard's age stood and pulled a sheet over her, pressing it to her face. Michelle looked at the girl. Her features hardened with disgust. "Look at yourself. You are a nauseating example of a woman. He is a married man with children. Do you think you will get rich from this? One half of his money belongs to my sons. Thankfully, I don't need a fucking thing from him. He's been divorced and will be again as soon as I can file divorce papers. He did it once, and he will do it again. All you young women after these *ancient* men. There will always be another one, younger and prettier because no one will ever make these men happy. He lives for his ego and his fame. The sex? He's not that good! I've had better."

Richard stood angrily. "Michelle, stop!"

Michelle pointed at the girl. "Get her out of my house...NOW!"

"I'm sorry, Michelle."

"Sorry? Are you fucking kidding me? I want both of you out of here."

"We still have an engagement we need to be at tonight. We just can't not show up."

She walked up close to him and pushed him away with a bright red nail. "And I will be there, but it will be the last time I am seen in public with the likes of *you.* I am repulsed by you."

He started to put on his pants. "Because you prefer to be seen and photographed with the ambassador's son?"

She raised her hand and slapped him as hard as she could. "And don't you ever *dare* to mention Jim Haley in my presence! You are unfit to lick his shoes. To think I gave up any chance with him for YOU! He is someone you manage professionally, but never refer to him as anything else. You are not good enough and will never be good enough to compare yourself to him, *especially* in bed. Piece of *merde*!" She wheeled around and began snatching the sheets from the bed.

He placed his hand on her shoulder. She turned, ready to punch him, fists clenched. "Don't you ever touch me again. Asshole. Go look for that slut. I don't want her roaming around my house and have *my* sons see the piece of shit their father traded their mother for."

"I will leave for a hotel, and I will meet you at the gallery at seven?"

She spit on him. "Seven, it is and never again!"

4
THE LAST OF THE BACHELORS

1st WEEK OF DECEMBER 1985, NEW YORK

Michael Evans, bass player for The Warriors, managed to remain unattached for decades. He loved women as much as his music, just not as flamboyantly as the other band members. He was content, when after all the years of touring, he could finally move back to the United States. He owned an apartment in the Wall Street area of New York. He liked it there, a madhouse during the week but quiet on the weekends. He played the rock star role for too long. He grew more distinguished looking as he aged, like Jim Haley as they began to sport their hair a bit shorter but still unruly and dressed the part—torn jeans and leather, a diamond in one ear and a small hoop in the other. His body bore several tattoos here and there.

The drummer of The Warriors, Vladimir Vavilov, the rebellious and mysterious Russian still wore his hair longer than any one of them. Mike chuckled, thinking that his friend might have a Peter Pan syndrome, but then he remembered seeing Vlad's girlfriend entangling her fingers in the man's dark tresses. Mike sighed.

As Mike walked down the narrow, almost hidden street where he lived with a cup of coffee in his hand, a teenager on the sidewalk offered him a flyer. He smiled at the young man and took the paper just to be polite, folded it and stuck it in his jacket pocket. He opened the front door of the building and inserted the key into a private elevator. The doors opened into an eclectic expanse of modern space and light. He loved New York and the loft apartment he purchased a year ago. Fortunately, the magnificent designer who decorated all of The Warriors' homes and who was seen with Jim Haley from time to time, finished the work right before the end of the last tour. He dropped his gym bag on the floor.

The telephone rang in the background as Mike hurled his jacket onto the sofa. He sat on a stool at the kitchen island as he rifled through his mail when he answered, cradling the receiver between his shoulder and ear. "Hello?"

"Hey, got plans for tonight?" Jim asked.

Both well-known musicians remained bachelors and kept each other company at functions and visited new clubs, bars, any place to meet single women, being that they both lived in New York. Vladimir, the drummer for The Warriors, was single up to a few years ago, when he got involved with Susan Michaels's sister, Leslie.

"Nope. Wanna do something?"

"Yup, could use a quick one-night stand."

"I got a flyer announcing an opening of something; hold on." Mike pulled the flyer out of his jacket pocket and looked at it. "There's a gallery near here that has an art exhibition tonight; we can go hit some jazz clubs in the Village after that."

"Art and then we'll see what else?" Jim chuckled.

"Sounds like a plan."

"Let me have the information, I'll meet you there, say eight?"

"Works for me."

♫

When Jim arrived, Mike waited anxiously for him. "There are a ton of gorgeous women in there. Models, actresses…I've died and gone to heaven."

"Good," Jim said. "Maybe you will finally find that special woman."

"You too." Mike's eyes turned to long, shapely legs stepping out of a cab. The wind gently lifted the hem of the pencil thin skirt revealing a well-defined thigh. *Elegant and classy!*

"I'm not looking," Jim replied. "You know I'll only love one woman in my lifetime, and I can't have her. Need to get laid sometimes; just the motions not the emotions."

"I like that; we need to use that line in one of our songs—'Motion without Emotion.' Think I'll write it and let you guys spruce it up. Let's go inside."

The exhibition included a list of who's who…not only models and actresses, but also executives from Fortune 500 companies, musicians and artists. The gallery was huge, and there was plenty of champagne to go around.

Scarlett Williams, the interior designer linked to Jim in the tabloids, was the first person Jim saw when he entered. *Not the one I love, but she'll do fine. Pretty decent in the sack, just tries too hard.*

With his charming self, he leaned over and placed a soft kiss on her exposed neck. "Fancy meeting you here! What are you doing on the East Coast?"

"Getting you a painting?"

"Can I pick it out, or is it a surprise?"

She smiled up at him. "Whatever you want."

A waiter walked by with champagne flutes, and Jim took two glasses from the tray and handed her one.

"What have you been up to? You haven't called," she asked.

He shrugged. "Flying out to the West Coast to see my girls, putting the finishing touches on the next album, and getting ready for the final tour. Terribly busy. We'll be taking a well-deserved break after the 'Savage' tour."

In the distance, he caught a glimpse of Richard Stone, The Warriors' manager, and his wife, Michelle Bujold. They seemed to be arguing about something. Michelle frowned and seemed to be saying something through clenched teeth. He looked away, didn't need to see what he sensed the last time he encountered them together. *All is definitely not well in the Stone household.* He looked at Scarlett and smiled.

"What about you?" he asked.

"Too much work and not enough fun."

"Tsk, tsk. You always need to take time out for fun."

Richard headed in Jim's direction. He held out his hand, and Jim shook it.

"Hey," Richard said. "I just bumped into Mike in another room and he told me you were here. You guys buying art?"

"This is my decorator, Scarlett. We're looking at some artwork for my walls."

Jim's gaze fell on Michelle. He placed his hand softly on the small of her back. She immediately tensed, and his lips twitched in a barely noticeable miniscule smile as he leaned in to kiss her cheek. The scent of Chanel No. 5 overwhelmed him in the same way it had since the day he met her. His chocolate eyes ravaged her icy blues. He winked.

Michelle took a deep breath as her heart pounded in her chest. She never imagined seeing Jim at the gallery and much less in the company of a female, although the tabloids were having a field day with the relationship between one of The Warriors' most desirable bachelors and the well-known decorator to the stars.

"You are looking quite beautiful this evening, Mrs. Stone."

"*Merci.*" Her smile lit up the entire room, and her lower lip quivered.

"I have to get together with you guys in the next few days. There's something I have to tell you," Richard said.

Jim shrugged. "I'm here until the weekend. I'll be flying out to see the girls."

Michelle turned to Richard. "Why are you stalling? Tell him the truth, how I found you this morning in our house on our bed."

Richard shook his head and closed his eyes. "Because this is not the time, and don't cause a scene here."

"God, I would love to."

Jim let out his breath. He hated seeing her with Richard and the fact that they ran into each other constantly because of their business liaison. After decades, he still couldn't get over her. *Too many years together...too many wonderful times...too much love.* He addressed her for the first time in months. "Michelle, he'll tell us when he's ready."

Michelle rolled her eyes and walked away. Richard followed her.

Scarlett smiled. "Do you want to go to your place?"

"Not really. Some other time. I'll call you."

"How long were you and Michelle an item?"

"We weren't just *an item*. Not open for discussion." He became annoyed by her question. *None of your business.*

He didn't want to bump into them the entire night, and he certainly didn't want to take Scarlett home with him. As Jim readied to step into a taxi to go home, Michelle emerged from the gallery.

"Can I give you a ride home?" he asked.

She nodded. She couldn't speak because she was so angry. He held her arm and helped her into the car.

"I'm going to Susan's." Her voice quivered. "Please come with me."

"Sure."

"*Lui et moi avons fini!* I found him in my bed having sex with a young groupie. He left the marital bed a year ago, and I have an appointment to see a divorce attorney tomorrow. *Nous avons finis! Terminé! Plus de!*"

Jim looked out the window. He balled his hand into a fist and bit the knuckle of his index finger lightly. His blood boiled. *How dare he hurt Michelle that way!*

He reached across the seat and took her hand. He squeezed it tightly. "I'm sorry, Red. You never said anything."

"I couldn't," she sobbed.

He moved closer so that he could put his arm around her and drew her near. He kissed her hair, her forehead. "I'm sorry, *poupée.*"

5
AN END AND NEW STARTS

1ˢᵗ WEEK OF DECEMBER 1985, NEW YORK

Michelle's boys were at Susan's, and she wanted to talk to her best friend. She and Jim took the elevator to the penthouse. Sisters from another mother since their teen years, she needed to share the good news about her filing for divorce.

Susan gushed with gladness at seeing her. "I was just going to call you." Not quite ten yet, apparently, the evening ended early. She was surprised to see her best friend and Jim holding hands. "You and Jim? Did I miss something?"

Karl joined them in the foyer. "Hey, how good to see you! Come on in. Susan and I were getting ready to have something to munch on and share a few drinks."

They followed Susan and Karl onto the terrace. Karl poured an apple martini for Michelle and made a gin and tonic for Jim.

Michelle sipped her martini and sighed. "I found Richard screwing someone in my bed this morning. We've technically been separated for a year. We don't sleep in the same bed. He wants out, and I do too."

"Mike and I went to an event at the Angem Art Gallery and bumped into Richard. The daggers were flying between him and Michelle. She was leaving as I was flagging down a cab," Jim added.

"What a piece of shit!" Susan said and refilled their martini glasses. She took a finger sandwich and popped it in her mouth.

"I thought things would work out for the kids' sake, but it didn't happen. I have an appointment with a very famous divorce attorney tomorrow."

Jim looked at Karl. "Did you know about this affair?"

"Not a clue."

The four adults sat for another hour, talking about the upcoming tour and what they were going to do for the next few years while they took a long breather from music and touring to concentrate on their lives. They had been doing it since they were young, and it was time to take a break.

"How about a couple of rounds of poker?" Karl suggested.

"Strip poker?" Jim asked.

Susan pursed her lips at Jim. "The kids are in the house, Jim. You are worse than a teenager!"

He snickered. "Haven't seen my redhead in her sexy, lacy underwear in a long time. Going through withdrawal."

Karl laughed and pushed Jim into the apartment.

They sat at the game table in the den. Karl made another pitcher of martinis. Michelle took off her boots and rolled up her sleeves. Jim's eyes fell on a large bruise on Michelle's forearm. His eyes captured hers and he scowled. He reached out and took her hand. He pulled the arm closer. "What is this, Michelle?"

"It's nothing. In this morning's struggle, he grabbed my arm a little too hard, I guess. Don't worry, Jim; I got a few punches in myself. Think I broke the bitch's nose."

"I'll fucking kill him! You know, I never liked the asshole." Rage spewed from Jim's dark eyes.

Karl interrupted. "Let this pass, Jim. She's already said she was filing for divorce. Think of the twins and Michelle."

"If I see another mark on you, I will *not* be responsible for my actions," Jim reiterated.

Michelle took the cards from the table and began to shuffle them, refusing to meet Jim's glare. "It won't happen again. He's out of the house."

"It better not, or I *will* step in."

They played poker for a few hours.

"I need to get going," Jim said, standing up and stretching. He was angry but elated about the news of the divorce. *Richard is out of the house, and she is free. Not tonight, though. Too distressed.*

"I guess I should leave too. Make sure those kids let you sleep." Michelle stood, but she toppled a bit and Jim steadied her. "Too much alcohol," he said.

She shrugged and leaned so close their lips barely touched. "Yes, but I'm feeling *so* good."

"Come on, let's get you home."

When they reached her floor, Jim held her hand as she stepped off the elevator, and they stood in the hallway. "I'm serious, Red. I don't want him hurting you."

"He won't."

She sighed and reached out to put her arms around his neck. Her fingers touched his skin, and she drew him close. His soft warm lips slid over her cheek, and she closed her eyes. Her breath quickened and her lips softly kissed the corners of his mouth. She sighed and held on tight. Her blood thundered through her veins, and tremors invaded every muscle of her body. His mouth came crashing down on hers. She parted her lips and let her tongue slip into his mouth in desperate search of his. She savored the taste of the man she loved. The familiar taste of gin, tonic, and fresh lime. The kiss was long, full of passion. Her nails dug into his back, and she crushed her breasts up against hard chest. She pressed her lips against his neck and took a deep breath, having missed his scent. She licked the warm skin and placed a tiny bite mark, branding his flesh. A reminder of the night. Their love was still frightening…stronger than anything they ever encountered.

It took every ounce of willpower for Jim to step away. His heart pounded in his chest as he tried to still the overwhelming rush of emotions. "You taste the same, hot and fiery…and damn delicious."

He leaned his forehead against hers and took a deep breath. "Go on home. Call me after you meet with the attorney and if you need anything."

6
A SPANISH QUEEN

1st WEEK OF DECEMBER 1985, NEW YORK

Mike's eyes drifted to a beautiful woman staring at a painting with black and white stripes of different widths. In the dead center of the canvas was a red circle.

He watched her as she concentrated on the red with a slight frown. She was tall and thin dressed in a tight navy skirt, a white blouse and a navy leather blazer. *She's the one stepping out of the cab when I arrived.* Her hair was styled in long, soft waves. As if sensing his presence, she turned, and dark mysterious eyes met his.

"What exactly do you see in that red circle?" he asked.

She flashed a perfect smile with beautiful white teeth. She shrugged. "I don't really 'see' anything. I'm trying to make a decision on how to advise a client I'm meeting with tomorrow. I don't see my answer in this painting at all. I prefer the Old Masters. I don't quite understand this modern art much." She laughed softly. Her eyes were bright. She had a sense of humor that attracted Mike.

"Mike Evans." He introduced himself.

"I know." She acknowledged that she knew who he was. "I'm Julienne Costa."

"Julienne, gorgeous name! Not boring like Mike."

She dipped an eyebrow. "I'm not sure Mike Evans is a boring man with a boring name. I was at the last Warriors concert. You pack a lot of energy."

"Glad you noticed. Your name is French and Spanish, right?"

"Mother is Parisienne and Papa is from Barcelona."

"And I guess you speak all three languages."

"Of course."

"Are you a reporter?" he asked.

The mischievous laughter was back. "No, not even close."

"Photographer?"

"Lawyer," she replied.

"Ahh! That explains the client tomorrow."

"Yes."

"I'm starving," he said, touching his stomach.

"Me too."

"Join me?" he asked.

"I'd be honored."

He stretched his hand out. "After you, Counselor."

His eyes skimmed over perfectly shaped buttocks. *Yes, my other half!*

She turned suddenly. "When we get to the restaurant, it's my turn to ask questions."

He opened the door for her. "Fire away."

Mike and Julienne stopped outside the gallery. "What do you like to eat?" he asked, having just met her.

"Do you like Spanish food? I mean authentic food from Spain?"

"To be honest, I've been to Spain dozens of times while on tour, but all we really get to see of most cities is the inside of hotel rooms. Where are you taking me?"

"Sevilla, downtown in the Village."

"I've been meaning to go, and it never happens." He walked off the curb and flagged down one of New York's finest yellow taxis. He opened the door and let her in.

♫

Much later after a paella fine, Spanish wine, they were ending their meal with hot chocolate and *churros*. It was a Spanish tradition she enjoyed sharing with non-Spaniards.

"What kind of law do you practice?"

"I do very high-profile divorces and family law, domestic violence...all that fun stuff that goes on when the music dies."

"Do you think that all relationships end in divorce, custody issues, and violence?"

"Not necessarily. My parents are still married."

"You've never been married, I take it."

She shook her head.

"Why? You are a beautiful woman, intelligent..." He let his words float away.

She looked at him and shrugged. "Just haven't found the right dude, I guess. And…I need to get to the office tomorrow by eight-thirty, and I take a brisk walk to the park and back around six-thirty, so I try not to get to bed too late.

Mike paid the bill. "You live uptown?"

"Eighty-fourth and Park."

"Nice."

"My parents' gift for graduating law school."

"Colombia?" he asked.

"Harvard."

"Of course. I'll ride in the cab back with you and have him bring me back downtown."

"It's not necessary."

"I insist."

Traffic was light. They stood on the sidewalk in front of her building for a few minutes.

He put his hand on her waist. "You know something? Jim lives a few blocks away from here. Susan, Karl, our manager Richard and his wife live in the same building across the street from the Met. I'm the only nutcase who lives downtown."

"Well, maybe you need to move uptown with the rest of us and keep us all company."

"I had a wonderful time, Counselor. Do you think we could do this again?"

"I think so. I enjoyed myself, too."

He placed his hand on her arm. He kissed her cheek softly. "I'd like to call you tomorrow if that's okay."

She searched in her pricey, designer bag and took out one of her business cards and a Mont Blanc pen. She wrote her home number on the back.

"Good night, Counselor," he said and winked.

"Good night, Rock Star." They both laughed out loud.

When he got back into the taxi, he read her card. *Costa, Vargas, Stein and Glass, Attorneys at Law, Fifth Avenue and 43rd Street.* He released a long, thoughtful breath. *Beauty, class, elegance and brains…what more could a guy want?*

He'd waited a long time, but he was certain she was the one.

♫

Julienne smiled as she took the elevator up to her eleventh-floor apartment. She liked Mike…a lot. Was she willing to take a chance again? She was so tired of the dating scene. *You date someone for three months, six months, a year and then out of nowhere, pow!*

Her life had been a steady row of men who didn't deserve the time of day. She became engaged at the age of twenty-four only to be practically left at the altar. He disappeared several weeks before the wedding. Didn't have the decency to confront her. After that, she didn't date until she graduated from law school. No man was worth losing her career to.

After graduation, she joined a large law firm in New York and made managing partner two years later. She was the best in New York and just recently, passed the California Bar. That was her dream to be bi-coastal. She could never leave New York but wanted the flexibility of living in or near Los Angeles, and there were plenty of high-profile divorces in Tinsel Town.

She took a shower and went to bed, tossing and turning all night, as Mike Evans invaded her thoughts.

♫

When the alarm clock went off the following morning, Julienne felt as if she had just gone to bed. She glanced at the clock one more time as she went into the bathroom. It was 6:30. Late nights were not common in her life anymore.

After brushing her teeth and splashing cold water on her face, she put on some sweatpants, sneakers, and sweatshirt. She grabbed her keys but stopped by the kitchen to glance at her calendar before leaving for her walk. As the elevator took her to the lobby, she realized that she didn't set up the coffeemaker so that the precious dark liquid that would jolt her into gear for the day was ready by the time she came back. She shrugged and walked out the door.

She stretched her legs for a bit and then set out on 84th Street toward Fifth Avenue. It was an unusually warm morning for the first week in December. Had it been warm the night before or did the temperature have something to do with Mike? Did she not notice how cold it had been?

She enjoyed the brisk walk for forty-five minutes. Her first appointment at the office was not until mid-morning, so there was no reason to rush. As she neared her building, she saw Mike who was holding a cup of coffee in his hand and signing an autograph for her doorman.

He saw her approach the building and held out the coffee container. "I didn't know how you took your coffee, so I just guessed."

She took the cardboard coffee container with the Greek emblem…the typical take out cup of New York. Blue and gold…"We are Happy to Serve You" written in Greek text…The Anthora Cup, lately almost extinct, replaced by Styrofoam.

"Thank you. Would you like to come up?"

"No, I just wanted to bring this to you, thank you for the wonderful company last night, and to ask you to dinner again tonight. I'm an excellent cook and would be honored if you would let me cook for you. I've never cooked for a woman in my life, nor have I invited them to my place. You're pretty special, Counselor." He wiggled his eyebrows, and his smile lit up his hazel eyes.

"I am flattered. Let me know what time and where."

"Seven too early?" he asked.

"No."

"I'll send you a car, okay? I'll be too busy cooking."

"Perfect."

He leaned over and kissed her cheek.

"Thanks for the coffee. I'll bring wine and dessert."

"No dessert, I got it."

Mike turned and flagged down a taxi. He blew a kiss as he entered the cab. Julienne pretended to catch the kiss. She turned quickly and went into the building.

She sipped the coffee as the elevator took her to her floor. She jerked her head back and stared at the coffee cup. *Perfect. Exactly the way I like it. Did I just catch a kiss from Mike Evans? Is this really happening?*

Thank God my first appointment is a new client scheduled, and then I don't have anything else until 3:30. She wouldn't have time to change before her dinner date. She put on a navy gabardine suit with a knee-length skirt. The jacket was double breasted and tailored to her perfect body. She put on navy leather pumps and grabbed her navy Chanel bag and left.

7
AN ULTIMATE DECISION

1st WEEK OF DECEMBER 1985, NEW YORK

Julienne was in the midst of reading a legal brief submitted by one of her associates when her assistant announced the arrival of the morning appointment, Marie Anton, and that she was in the larger conference room with the lovely view of Bryant Park. Before the appointment, she tried to see if she could find out more about the mysterious client who preferred to remain anonymous. The woman didn't leave a call-back telephone number but confirmed her appointment.

The lawyer had seen too many of these cases. *Probably coming to see me while her husband cheats on her or even worse, mentally, emotionally or physically abuses her.* She picked up her leather covered note pad and gold Cartier pen. She stopped by her assistant's desk and reviewed the messages for the afternoon calls.

She took a deep breath and entered the room. A well-dressed woman with long red curls stood at the window looking at the view. She turned when she heard the door open. Her black Chanel jacket was impeccably fitted to a thin but curvy body over black wool pants. The woman smiled, and Julienne noticed a certain familiarity. She had seen this woman before…newspapers, fashion magazines…she couldn't remember where.

The woman walked closer and shook Julienne's hand. "I apologize for using another name, but I didn't want this visit to become public knowledge…not yet. I'm Michelle Bujold-Stone."

Of course, Bujold, the fashion empire, Bujold Wines and coincidentally, wife of Richard Stone, music mogul and manager for several mega groups, which includes The Warriors.

Julienne smiled. "Have a seat, Mrs. Bujold-Stone. Have they offered you coffee, tea?"

Michelle took a deep breath. "Yes. I'm fine. Call me Michelle, please."

Both women took a seat facing each other. Julienne wrote the date at the top of a page in her legal pad and used the initials MBS to take her notes. Michelle smiled.

"I want to file for divorce and would like your direction as to your opinion on venue because I have a several addresses. I have a home on the outskirts of Paris, an apartment here in New York, and a home in California. I know you are licensed in New York and California, and that's one of the reasons I came to see you. You come highly recommended."

"Thank you," Julienne said. "Any children?"

"Yes, twins."

"Where do you spend most of your time?"

"Mostly New York and California. I wish I could say France, but New York and California are more reasonable places as a home base. The *idiot* has offices in Los Angeles. The children go to school here."

"Citizenship?"

"Dual, I'm French and American. My husband is British and American, and my children are French."

"Where were you married?"

"Here. In New York."

"I will need to go over your financials, which I believe are in the multi-millions. What do you want from your husband? Alimony? Child Support?"

"I want my children to get what is due them, but I just want to end the marriage. He's been unfaithful, and I'm not willing to live with that. I walked in on him having sex with someone. "

"Ouch!" Julienne bit the end of her pen. "You know that the moment I file the documents, your divorce will become public record. Any chance that he will contest to the divorce?"

"Not at all. He wants out more than I do. We've been legally separated for a year. It's time."

"Michelle, the grounds of adultery can be difficult and probably very expensive to prove unless he signs an affidavit admitting to the adultery."

"I think he'll sign anything, trust me."

"Any pre-nuptial agreements?"

"Yes, but we agreed that what is his is his and mine is mine. Right now, my fortune still belongs to my father. My father provides me with a substantial distribution that is in a trust for my benefit from the Vineyards."

"I have to play the devil's advocate, no pun intended, and I must tell you that he can make this a difficult divorce."

"Julienne, may I call you Julienne?"

"Of course."

"Trust me, he will not contest. There's too much at stake for him."

"I have something for you to read and some forms to fill out. I always urge women to think about this and make sure it's the right decision."

"It's the right the decision. The only thing that would keep me from doing this right now is my children. They know, and so far, they haven't mentioned the separation. Children are sensitive to the world around them. They'll be fine."

Both women stood and shook hands. Julienne accompanied Michelle to the elevator. "Please feel free to call me if you need help filling those out."

She nodded. "Thank you."

♫

Michelle took the elevator to the lobby. She sighed. She thought she would feel awful, but she didn't. Divorce was the only solution. The children would accept the truth. She would fill out the documents and send them to Julienne via courier to file her divorce the following day.

She held her head high, put on her Chanel sunglasses, and walked through the glass revolving doors. She called Susan to join her for lunch and then Bergdorf's to do some damage! *Jim Haley, I'm all yours!*

8
A BACHELOR NO MORE

1st WEEK OF DECEMBER 1985, NEW YORK

By the time Julienne called Mike to tell him she was ready and to have the car pick her up at the New York Public Library, she was exhausted. She worked for three hours researching The Warriors, their members, their beginnings.

The limo stopped in front of a building well-known for its eccentric and pricey lofts. Julienne got out with her briefcase and a bag with two bottles of wine.

The scent of authentic Italian sauce reminded her that she skipped lunch.

He took her in his arms and kissed her. "Welcome to my humble abode."

She smiled. "Humble my ass. Smells great." She handed him a bottle of red wine and a bottle of white. "I didn't know what you were making so I brought one of each. A Barolo and a Pinot Grigio."

"I made something simple—chicken parmesan, pasta, salad, bruschetta as an appetizer, trust me you'll gain a few ounces after this meal...and for dessert, tiramisu. Mom's Italian."

"You made all that?"

"From scratch."

His eyes studied her. "You look beautiful. Long day?"

"Interesting day. I think I've landed a new client who I like a lot. Then, I went to the public library to do some research on The Warriors, so I don't sound dumb when you speak to me."

"You? Dumb? No way, Ms. Harvard."

She held up her briefcase. "I brought something to get more comfortable if you don't mind."

"Not at all." He motioned toward a door. "Bathroom is over there."

She returned a few minutes later in black slim pants. She kept her white silk blouse on and Chanel flats.

Mike smiled as he handed her a glass of red wine. He'd waited all his life to find the right woman, and here she was!

"I had to take those damn heels off; they were killing me." Her smile was sweet, enchanting, and touched his heart.

The table was set with candles, white square bone china plates and sterling cutlery. She helped him with the salad.

After dinner, they sat back in their chairs, drinking wine.

"I don't remember the last time I had such a wonderful homemade meal. I'm stuffed. I love cooking too, and you should let me cook for you sometime in return."

"Gladly." He put his elbow on the table and his chin in the palm of his hand and just stared at her natural beauty. "So, are you going to tell me who your famous client is?"

"I can't. As a matter of fact, I have to turn her over to one of my partners. She's associated with you guys."

"You don't have to say more. I know who it is."

She rose to help him, and they stood side by side in the kitchen as they waited for the coffee to brew. The tiramisu melted in her mouth.

"I'm going to have to walk home after this wonderful meal and dessert. Even the coffee was amazing."

"Cinnamon is the secret."

They talked about their upbringing and how he connected with The Warriors being an American. She told him that she had a brother, Craig, who lived in Spain and the U.S. and was a bass player as well.

He took her hand and turned her so that they faced each other. "I like what I feel when I'm with you."

She scrutinized him. "Me too." Her voice was a seductive whisper. Warmth spread over her body. Her heartrate doubled, and her chest was about to explode.

He brought his lips to hers and she opened her mouth to taste him. She caressed his shoulder and his arms, loving the feel of his firm muscles. His fingers unbuttoned her blouse and kissed her chest while he undid the front clasp of her bra. He slipped the blouse and the bra straps from her shoulder.

Her fingers undid the buttons of his shirt and their hot flesh molded into one. He picked her up in his arms and walked to the bedroom. He laid her gently on the bed while he undid her pants and glided them over her hips. He slipped his clothes off and joined her on the bed.

His fingers burned her skin as he traced circles around her nipples and his tongue lightly licked her, arousing her.

She slid her hand lower so that she could feel him, hot and erect. Her gentle caresses caused him to take a deep breath and groan. Her tongue slipped over his neck.

His hand snaked lower, and he found what he wanted desperately to possess. Her body jolted at the soft touch of his fingers. His tongue continued to play with her nipples and his hands moved her legs apart so that he could take her wetness and make her his. He slipped on a condom. Times had changed from the Hamburg days.

She sighed as he entered her and moved her body to accommodate him. Their movements, perfectly synched. She moaned as her body shuddered when he brought her to a quick orgasm before his own overcame him.

They lay quietly catching their breaths for a few minutes, then she turned to face him "I've never slept with anyone on a second date." Her nails raked over his chest.

He chuckled. "I wish I could say the same thing." He leaned in and his lips captured hers. "Will you stay the night?"

"I guess, another first for me...my first appointment is at eleven tomorrow. I don't have to be in the office until 10:30."

♫

Mike had an invitation to Susan and Karl's home for the weekend. He invited Julienne. They were adults, she wasn't a groupie, and he was sure about what he felt. Julienne was at the office that morning when Michelle returned her call from the previous day.

"How are you?" Julienne asked.

"Fine, I guess. I'm in California because I'm meeting with some friends this weekend and my husband stayed in New York. I understand he is looking for an apartment to move into with his girlfriend."

"That's what I want to talk to you about."

Michelle looked out the glass doors of her Malibu home. She watched the waves as they crashed against the shoreline. She drew her eyebrows together.

"Oh?"

Julienne sighed. "I received your documents this morning, and we can file them today. Unfortunately, I will have to turn you over to one of my partners. I'll be here and will oversee your case, but I technically can't represent you. I've met and am seeing Mike Evans, and I will be attending the same event that you will be at this weekend."

"That's wonderful. I definitely want your firm to represent me. I know the divorce proceedings can take up to eighteen months. Wow, the love bug finally hit Mike. He's been single forever, and he's a *superbe* guy."

"Mike and I will be leaving this afternoon, and I'm looking forward to meeting the whole group."

"Julienne, one of the members of The Warriors, Jim Haley, and I dated for many years when we were younger. We have a very close relationship, and I just wanted you to know that. He and I will probably begin seeing each other again."

Julienne smiled. "I know. When you left my office the other day, I took the liberty of going to the library to do research on all of you. First of all, I had just met Mike, and then you came into the office. I just wanted to know a little more about all of you. There were plenty of articles on your relationship with Jim and the fact that you rubbed elbows with royalty and were part of the European elite in the late sixties. I loved the pictures of you two when you were young. I could clearly see the love in both your eyes."

Michelle smiled; *another ally.* "I guess we'll have plenty to talk about when I see you this weekend."

"I'm sure we will. Looking forward to it."

"Me too. Welcome to the craziest family you ever met."

"No way!" Julienne shouted. "In my line of business, I've had my share of crazies."

Both hung up, and Julienne leaned back in her chair. *Interesting!* She was going to enjoy the weekend.

7
REVELATION

2nd WEEK OF DECEMBER 1985, LOS ANGELES

Ron James, drove to the home he lived in before the breakup with his ex-wife and onstage partner, Susan Michaels. He looked forward to seeing his children, Stefani and Ronnie, and having dinner with them; but he was not too happy about the news he would be sharing with them. Susan and lead guitarist of The Warriors, Karl Engels, invited him for dinner to discuss the upcoming tour. They needed to agree on song sets, choreography and lighting, and pyrotechnics. Final rehearsals began right after the holidays.

He entered the kitchen and kissed Susan's cheek. Luscious smells drifted throughout the house.

"I guess Karl is cooking," he said, teasing. The fact that Susan couldn't even boil water for the longest time was common knowledge among her family and band members.

"No, he's out on the patio barbecuing, and I made everything else."

He slipped his arm around her waist. "Why do I find that incredibly hard to believe?"

Susan rolled her eyes. "Your daughter is on her way home, and Ronnie is in the backyard driving everyone crazy."

"Good, I need to talk to her, and I'm not sure how she's going to take some news I have. I'm getting ready to make a major announcement here tonight."

Susan's eyes captured his with apprehension.

"Are you okay?" she asked.

He pulled her close. His lips brushed her hair. "Yes, I'm fine."

Karl came in from the backyard. "Hey, bud, how're you doing?"

Ron paused for a moment before replying. He still couldn't get used to the idea of his best friend and Susan together. He sighed. His relationship with her was doomed from the onset.

He looked at Karl and grinned. "I'm fine. Wait until you find out who I spoke with recently."

"Who?"

"My lips are sealed until I can break this news to everyone at the same time."

Stefani, Ron and Susan's daughter, entered the backyard with her boyfriend, Josh. She had dated him for the past few years but neither Ron nor Susan thought it would ever amount to anything. *He is such a disgrace to the male race*, Ron thought, shaking his head. As Stefani's father, he knew that when a real man came along, it would be over for Josh.

Stefani threw her arms around her father, her favorite man in the whole world. She adored him, especially since he now led a clean life free from drug addiction, alcohol, and violence.

She kidnapped her father away from the others, leaving Josh behind, and sat at the edge of the pool with him, their legs dangling into the water. He reached out and caressed her cheek. "I want you to know that you are the best thing that's ever happened to me."

"I know, Dad." Her smile was her mother's smile, but her coloring, the blue eyes and flaxen hair she inherited from Ron.

Susan stood beside Karl, holding a platter while he made a pile of steaks. She watched him as he turned over some hot dogs and burgers for the kids. Every inch of her reacted to his presence even after so many years. He exuded sex, charm, and every other adjective that could be used to describe a man. His presence never ceased to make her feel like an innocent virgin. He leaned over and kissed her cheek. Even with the smell of smoke from the barbecue, he unnerved her. The man oozed sensuality.

"I love you," he whispered in her ear and bit her soft earlobe.

She moaned under her breath, closing her eyes and reveling in the moment until her ten-year-old, Ronnie, walked up to them with a glass full of water from the pool and dumped it at their feet; then laughed out loud and ran away before either one could grab him. He jumped in the pool and managed to splash his father and sister in the process.

Vladimir Vavilov and Leslie Michaels frolicked in the deep end of the pool like two teens themselves and acted as if no one else was around. Susan snickered at their behavior, but she was happy her sister found a man she trusted, and she had to admit her worry about Vlad's intentions proved unfounded. She recognized the true love she saw in both their eyes.

Jim Haley played with his daughters, Jenna and Karla, in the pool. The first weekend they were spending with their father but that night a sleepover was planned for the children at Susan's house. Dad was getting them the following night. His separation from Karl's sister, Vera, was amicable; they never truly loved each other. He started to date Vera in haste, but his two beautiful girls were the best thing in his life for the moment. He and Vera should have never dated. A hopeless relationship from the start. He would always love Michelle. There were a few he dated here and there over the years, but not one of them captured his heart. Now, knowing she was getting divorced, he was sure he would never let Michelle get away again. Droplets of water dotted his day-old stubble and his dark, pushed-back hair.

As he thought of Michelle, she arrived in the tightest shorts he had ever seen. She maintained her body better than ever after the twins, Antoine and Sébastien. No matter how thin Michelle got, she remained curvy and voluptuous. *So damn sexy!* Still invaded his dreams and sexual fantasies. *One of a kind.* Her full breasts were pressed up against a white t-shirt. He was certainly looking forward to throwing her into the pool later in the evening to test the transparency of the cotton. He grinned to himself. Her long red curls were swept up in a twisted and frayed bun. He was free to look all he wanted without being caught. Richard was no longer in the picture.

Jim got out of the pool and strolled to her side. He shook his head. Droplets of water fell on the front of her shirt. The outline of her white lace bra showed, and two slightly darker circles peeked through in a subtle way.

He bent down to kiss her cheek. "*Ma trésor*, it's good to see you."

She looked up at him. "Why can't I even get mad at the fact that you have just wet me?"

He laughed and threw his arm around her shoulders. "Because you love me?"

They exchanged a look that entranced her every time. "Probably."

"Still? You still love me, Red?"

She tilted her head and stared at him from behind the Chanel sunglasses. A suggestive smile revealed perfect white teeth. "Never stopped."

He winked at her. "I still love you too. Damn, Michelle. Those nipples! Soft and pink and want to lick them until they stand at attention."

Michelle's cheeks flushed as her nipples reacted to his words, and she shook her head as her twin boys handed her their clothes and jumped into the pool, splashing her from head to toe. "So much for trying to stay dry," she said.

"And not aroused." He chuckled.

Jim reached out and slipped the sunglasses from her face. He pulled the bottom of her t-shirt toward him and used it to dry them. She felt the warmth of his hand on her stomach for a mere second. It took her breath away. He put them back on her face. "You look amazing, by the way."

She was silent, couldn't respond. Heat coursed through every part of her body.

God, I love him! Her blue eyes locked with sable eyes and she reached out to slip her fingers through his hair. The touch of grey at the sides made him sexier, irresistible, that facial hair he wore so well. The closeness of his body took her back to the years they shared too much of each other. "I like this new look, Mr. Haley. Makes you quite desirable and elegant."

"Are you game for strip poker tonight?"

"You still haven't forgotten that, have you?" Her laugh was back. The sadness she wore throughout her marriage was gone.

"No way. Been having 'wet dreams' about it."

His fingers gripped her wrist and squeezed. A silent language passed between them, and she sighed.

She walked away to hand Susan several bottles of French wine for dinner. She didn't miss the rock star tattoos on his upper chest and arm. She didn't want to look too closely. *Those are new.* She strolled to the outdoor kitchen area and kissed Karl and Susan. Her hair was wet, and her face flushed.

"You okay? How are you holding up?" Karl asked, draping his arm around her shoulders and kissing her moist cheek.

"Fine, now that I saw Mr. Haley," she replied with a smirk. She took his hand in hers and squeezed. She considered Karl and Susan her best friends, and their love for each other grew stronger as the years passed.

Karl pulled her close and whispered in her ear. "I think that tonight, after everyone is gone, you, Susan, myself and Mr. Haley over there are going in that big pool after we have been drinking most of the night, maybe we'll go skinny dipping. Remember the hot tub?"

Her heart stammered. "You think I still have it?"

"Oh, I'm sure you do."

She picked up a glass and poured some wine for herself. "By the way, the divorce may take to the end of next year to be finalized. Coincidentally my lawyer is dating Mike, so I'm looking forward to you guys meeting her. She is a lovely person and beautiful as well. She's going to fit in just right."

"I heard. I'm glad Mike has finally met someone special. He's crazy about her." Susan added. "You should go look at the poem he faxed me asking that we put it to music. 'No More Motion without Emotion.' It's about his new love. It's going to be a new hit for The Warriors. It's downright awesome, and I've already put some music to his lyrics." She hummed a melody and added the words:

> Motion without emotion,
> Just sexual relief,
> No feeling, no care,
> No regrets, no grief
>
> Until my eyes met yours.
>
> Now...
>
> No more motion without emotion.
> Love finally struck.
> Now the movements mean everything.
> Can hardly believe my luck.
>
> I waited so long never thinking it could be true
> Then I was blessed by the gift of you.
> Your touch, your scent, your eyes of darkest hue
> From the moment I saw you, there was nothing I could do.
>
> No more motion without emotion.
> Love finally struck.
> Now the movements mean everything.

Can hardly believe my luck.

Like me, you felt the pull, the draw
Though heartache had left your soul raw
When our eyes met, all ice began to thaw
One word spoken left feelings of awe.

No more motion without emotion.
Love finally struck.
Now the movements mean everything.
Can hardly believe my luck.

Yes, you are what I waited for
My one and only that I adore
All those who slithered though my life before
Lay forgotten and desired nevermore.

No more motion without emotion.
Love finally struck.
Now the movements mean everything.
Can hardly believe my luck.

You are my everything
Can hardly believe my luck
You have my undying devotion
No more motion without emotion.

"Still have to get all the instrumental parts, but this will be a chart-topper."

"It was time. The last of the bachelors." Karl said and refilled the wine glasses. "And the song is great. It's a perfect end to our tour."

Susan walked away from Karl and Michelle, sighing. She hurt for her best friend, she but knew it would all turn out well. Jim adored her. She put the platter of steaks in the middle of the table and called after Ronnie, trying in vain to coax him and the other kids out of the pool. He pretended he was coming out of the water, and just as he was about to grab a hold of his mother's hand, he turned around and jumped back in the water, splashing everyone sitting near the pool. The ten-year-old was still a handful. His hazel eyes sparkled with mischief. Jenna and Karla, ten and eight years old, Jim's daughters, followed his example as well as Michelle's twins, also ten.

"Ron!" Susan shouted. "Tell him to come out, please. Honestly, he doesn't listen to me. This kid is going to be the death of me."

Ron laughed and got up from the edge of the pool. "Come on, buddy, time to eat, and we still have to dry you out."

The child eventually climbed out, followed by the rest of the kids. He was a born leader. He listened to his father way more than to his mother.

Ronnie looked at Ron with a silly grin on his face. He purposely shook the water from his hair and droplets of water fell on Ron's face, soaking his father's cheeks and t-shirt. Ron threw his arm around his son and pulled him close. Jim's daughters and Michelle's twins complimented Ronnie's behavior. The five were a handful.

Susan and Karl watched Ron with his son, a pleasant sight after all the ugliness of the past. Karl put his arm around her bare waist. "Let's go eat, I'm starving and looking forward to having you as dessert. Besides, I'm anxious to hear Ron's announcement."

Esmeralda, who had been with the family for years, poured iced tea into tall glasses.

"So," Karl said. "Who did you speak to recently that's so mysterious? Are you going to tell us or leave us all in suspense?"

"Eva," replied Ron, calmly cutting into his steak.

"Sister Eva? From St. Mary's?" Karl asked, eyes widened.

"Yup."

"What did she want? How did she find you?"

"Well, she contacted Richard, and she mentioned that she knew me from the orphanage. She's married to some British lord. He checked her out and asked me to call her back."

Karl put his silverware down and wiped his mouth with his napkin. He picked up his iced tea. "I'll be damned."

"I'm going to Frankfurt in a few days. Want to come along? I could use your support."

"Why? What happened?" Karl asked.

"It appears that when I left the orphanage, Eva was pregnant."

"Ron!" Susan shouted. "A nun?"

"Eww!" Stefani added. The reality of her father's words hit her. She looked at him. "You did it with a nun, and she got pregnant?"

"She was not a nun! She was going to be a nun, a postulant, a novice, whatever they call them. I'm not so proud of it after the telephone call." Ron said in seriousness although a naughty twitch touched his lips.

"You were real proud back then if I remember correctly, Ron," Karl said, laughing.

"She gave birth to a son." Ron looked at Stefani with caution. "I'm going to meet your older brother in Frankfurt."

Stefani rolled her eyes and slammed her hand on the table. "Dad! Ugh! I thought I was your first born! I used to be your favorite until the little dwarf Ronnie came along! Now I have an older brother too?"

"You are the first-born girl, the first I knew about, and you will always be my 'little girl,' and don't call Ronnie the little dwarf. I'm going to teach him to defend himself and kick your ass from now on when you call him names."

"You are still sick, Dad! Don't change the subject."

Ron didn't know what to reply but he burst out laughing. Karl stepped in, "Stefani, hormones usually got the best of us in those days. Everyone looked good. Actually, Eva was quite pretty."

Susan raised an eyebrow at Karl's comment. "Is *that* right?"

"Wanna come with me?" Ron asked Karl. "I'm supposed to have dinner with the family the day after tomorrow. I would really hate to go alone, and you know her."

"Sure. I wouldn't miss this for the world. Liebling, want to go to Frankfurt? Christmas shopping?"

Susan put her hand up. "I think I'll pass. Before you leave, you and I are going to have a long talk about everyone looking good to you guys, Mr. Engels."

Karl's laughter broke the seriousness of the situation. One more piece of the past caught up with Ron.

"Well, if Richard hadn't checked her out, she could have been a stalker."

At the mention of Richard's name, Michelle rolled her eyes. No one caught the gesture except for Susan and Jim.

Jim leaned back in his chair and picked up his strong Tanqueray and tonic, loaded with limes and ice. His dark eyes captivated Michelle. "Looks like the holidays around here are going to be quite interesting," he quipped.

She shook her head. "The quintessential manager."

Jim laughed. "Of course."

♫

After dinner, Ron saw Stefani sitting by herself and called her over. She squeezed in beside her father. He put his arm around her.

"I'm sorry, Stef. I didn't know about Alex."

Stefani put her head on her father's chest. "I was just teasing you. I'd love you no matter what. You've led quite a colorful life."

He kissed the top of her head. "I'm not proud of all of it, but I'm glad I have you."

Stefani kissed her father's cheek. She and Josh were meeting some friends at a club, and she had to get ready.

Jim's two daughters and Michelle's boys loved spending the weekend at Susan's with Ronnie. They played in the pool until it was close to ten, their bedtime. Vera stopped by for a moment to bring Karla and Jenna some clothes for the highly anticipated sleepover at Susan and Dad's. Jim and Vera's daughter Karla just turned eight years old and seemed to be going on fourteen. The child was way ahead of her time and had a mentor in Ronnie. The two were inseparable. Jenna had just turned ten as well and was beginning to mature. She was open with Vera and had mentioned to her mother how "cute" one of Michelle's twins, Antoine, was. They were growing up quickly.

Vera arrived just after dinner. "Sorry I'm late," she said kissing Karl, Susan, Michelle, and finally, Jim. She worked for the Michaels Studios owned by Susan's parents as Assistant Art Director. Her degree was paying off. She tore a piece of Jenna's hot dog and ate it.

"Come and eat," Susan said, leading her to the table.

"I can't stay. I just came to drop these off."

She handed a duffle bag filled with clothes and hair accessories to Jim. The young girls were staying with their father alone for the first time. Vera laughed. "Do you think you can tackle this?"

They stayed friends and got along well. He was one of the world's most desired bachelors. Vera remained unattached, dated here and there but no one special. She concentrated on additional credits and attended evening classes to specialize in film and theater, as well as being an accomplished cellist.

"I can try. Susan or Michelle can help out." Jim said taking the bag and looking through it. *Bows and shiny hair clips, glittery stuff.* He shivered and laughed. "I certainly don't know what half of this is for."

Vera put her hand on Jim's upper arm and whispered. "I heard about Michelle's divorce, and I'm very happy for you."

He kissed her cheek. "Thanks, that means a lot."

"Don't feel bad, Jim. It was great while it lasted."

Esmeralda started to gather children to go inside to take showers and get them ready for bed. The boys had a room and the girls another. Karla loved being the youngest among The Warriors' children.

Mike and Julienne finally arrived. Susan went up to them. "What happened? I'm Susan by the way. Heard some good things about you."

"Likewise," Julienne replied. "You are more gorgeous in person. Flight was running late and then the traffic but we're here." She handed Susan a bouquet of assorted roses. "I was told to be careful what colors to pick."

Susan laughed. "Old joke I will tell you about someday. Come meet the rest of the crew. I heard Michelle hired your firm for her divorce. Oh, Mike, the song is splendid."

He grinned, never having actually written lyrics for the group.

"She actually hired me but because of my relationship with Mike, I can't take the case. She's in good hands, though." Julienne looked in Jim and Michelle's direction. "That's Jim, I presume."

Susan smiled as she saw them laughing at some private joke. "Her soulmate for life."

"You can see the love in their eyes, spectacular."

Michelle saw Julienne, and she took Jim's hand and walked in their direction. She leaned in and kissed the attractive attorney on the cheek. "This is Jim Haley, *ma moitié.*" Turning loving eyes to him, Michelle proudly introduced them. "This is the woman who is going to free me from my marriage."

Jim took the Julienne's hand and leaned in to kiss her cheek. "Can't happen soon enough."

She smiled. "It will. Just be a tad careful."

"I wouldn't jeopardize her reputation for anything in the world," Jim added, laughing.

Michelle punched him affectionately on the arm. "You certainly jeopardized my reputation in my teenage years."

"You didn't stop me."

Susan's eyes met Julienne's. "I told you—two of a kind."

Julienne arched her eyebrows. "So, it seems."

Susan waved it off. "Come and meet everyone else." She caught Karl's arm as he walked by. "This is my soulmate for life, Karl Engels."

"Glad to have you," he said, and kissed her cheek.

"Thanks."

They made their way on toward to pool. Susan said, "Everyone, this is Julienne, the lady that has snagged Mike." With a slight point she went on, "Ron James, Vlad Vavilov, and my sister, Leslie."

In turn, each kissed Julienne on the cheek, welcoming her warmly.

Mike came up behind her and presented her with a glass of wine. She smiled and slipped her hand into his. *I really do feel at home. I fit with these people.*

♫

Freshly showered and in pajamas, exhausted children said good night to their parents.

Ronnie kissed Ron, Susan, and Karl and dragged his feet toward the house. Karla hugged and kissed Jim. Jenna had just breezed by her father, pecked him on the cheek and said good night with a peace sign. Antoine watched her. He thought she was so cool and pretty.

"Are you coming tomorrow for breakfast? Esmeralda makes the best pancakes with chocolate chips and whipped cream. Sometimes she adds Nutella," Karla said as she sat on the arm of the chair where Jim sat. The mere mention of Nutella sent Michelle into a fit of laughter. Jim grinned and closed his eyes remembering a time he and Michelle had very kinky sex involving Nutella; it had never tasted better to him.

"Yes, behave yourself. I'll try to be here when you get up." She kissed her father again. "Dad, we're staying in your house tomorrow. I don't have to go back to Mommy's until Sunday night."

"Yes, you are." Jim hugged and kissed her. "Night, baby."

She was already walking away, but she turned suddenly and pointed at him with her little index finger with the hot pink painted nail. "I'm *not* a baby."

Jim tightened his lips. "That's right. I'm sorry. Night, young lady. Better?"

"Yes, better."

Jim shook his head and said to Vera. "She's eight years old and thinks she knows it all."

"She's really funny, has your warped sense of humor, and she does know it all."

He sipped his drink. "I like that." He loved both girls, but Karla managed to get under his skin from day one.

Michelle's twins bid everyone a good night, kissed their mother, and high-fived Jim. They liked Jim; he had been a part of their lives just like Karl. Michelle didn't think there would be any objection to her and Jim seeing each other in the future.

Ron was mentally drained and emotional from the day's events; he left unusually early. Vlad and Leslie departed for their own home while Mike and Julienne left for a hotel suite. Karl and Susan changed into their swimsuits. Michelle didn't bring a bathing suit.

"I'll just go in with my underwear and t-shirt. It's not like there's a shortage of t-shirts in any rock star's house."

Karl brought out a bottle of Jose Cuervo and placed it in the middle of the table with four shot glasses, salt, and lemons and limes. He poured the first four shots and turned on some soft jazz. They talked about the upcoming tour, their plans, and Ron's announcement. The conversation turned to Ron and Eva.

"That little nun kept him in check while he was at the orphanage. Too bad she's married," Karl said.

"Yeah, she sure did. In line and out of trouble." Jim added. "Ron's a good person; he's just never had the chance to be good. Always had to be tough. Life was never fair to him."

"He never slept well, tossed and turned all night, afraid something would hurt him." Susan's voice turned sad, remembering when his demons controlled him completely.

The topic of conversation turned to old times.

"That week that Karl and I spent in New York. Seeing you girls crossing 59th Street and Susan giving the cab driver the finger was hysterical. Who knew that weeks later we would see you again at the Cosmos of all places?" Jim sucked on a lemon slice, then downed a shot of tequila.

Karl refilled the tequila shot glasses and took Susan's hand. He squeezed it. "If that wasn't Karma, nothing was."

Jim took another shot of Cuervo. He crossed his hands behind his head and sighed. "That first trip we took to my parents' house in the French Alps was magical."

Michelle sat back in the chair and propped her feet up on Jim's lap. "That was an amazing weekend, that first time we all went. There *was* something magical about that trip other than Susan and me losing our virginity." She laughed loudly. "Although *that* was special *and* magical."

Jim's hand unconsciously caressed her soft tanned leg as they spoke. His fingers kept going higher and higher. She put her hand over his to stop his movements. He sneered.

Karl sat up. "What's everyone doing for the holidays?"

"Richard is taking the twins to Turks and Caicos. He's building a huge place, like a bed and breakfast for all of The Warriors and their significant others and a state-of-the-art recording studio. They'll be back right after the first of the year to return to school. I have them next year. I know it sucks, but it's fair. He *is* their father."

"The girls are with Vera on Christmas Eve and Christmas Day, but I have them for New Year's." Jim added.

"Ronnie and Stefani are with Ron for Christmas and back with me for New Year's Eve as well." Susan said.

Jim leaned forward and covered Michelle's hand with his own. "And I think you and I should spend Christmas in New York. We've never been there for the holidays together. I've spent too much time without you, *cheri*."

Warmth spread to Michelle's cheeks and her heart jolted in her chest. Her eyes remained riveted to Jim's, and she put her hands on his cheeks. Tears streamed down her face. "*Merde*, what did I do? I love you so much." Her lips captured his softly, and she turned to Karl and Susan.

Karl's green eyes glimmered, and he chuckled as he refilled the shot glasses. "What? You want our permission? Knock yourself out. You've been miserable for too long."

Susan stood behind Michelle. She placed her hands on her friend's shoulders. "Go, Michelle. Have a good time."

Michelle closed her eyes and shook her head.

Jim took her face and turned it to his. "I have a special surprise for you. Don't say no Michelle. We *both* need this."

♫

Susan and Karl were at the other end of the pool. A full moon cast a soft glow. Karl's hand rested on her waist, and from time to time, he slid his hand over her buttock and drew imaginary circles with his finger. He kissed the side of her mouth.

"Just how many women were you guys with?" she asked.

"Plenty. We lost count after a while."

Susan's hands caressed his chest. He still turned her on as much as the day they met. "Did you sleep with the nun, too?"

Karl grinned. "No, liebling, only Ron; she seemed to keep him civil during the time they were together. They saw each other every night for a while, and during that time, Ron never got into trouble. He just lived to get through school, and at night, they spent time with each other. Weekends he spent with me, but I think that unbeknownst to him, he was pretty taken by the cute nun. She was an attractive young thing and too sexy to be in a convent."

"Call me stupid, but how did they manage?"

Karl kissed Susan's chin. "In a confessional, in the chapel, with the statues surrounding them. Ron was always afraid they would strike him dead. Besides, where there was a will, there was a way. Believe me, we knew every hidden corner of that orphanage."

"You guys were amazing!" Susan said.

"You want to know about the night Mother Superior caught me with one of the schoolgirls in the barn, butt naked? She swore she would tan my ass red by the time she got through with me. When I stood to get my pants on, all she could do was stare boldly at my erection. I think she was more impressed than angry." Karl laughed.

10
JUST LIKE OLD TIMES

2nd WEEK OF DECEMBER 1985, LOS ANGELES

Jim got out of the pool. He handed Michelle a towel and drew his breath in when she stepped out. The white shirt stuck to her flesh, and erect nipples teased him. Maturity made her more exciting and beautiful if that could be possible. Damn, they hadn't been with each other in over a decade, yet he still thought about her every day. Without a doubt, she was the love of his life. Always would be.

Jim shed his towel to put his shorts back on. Michelle slipped her shorts over her hips. She snatched her underwear from Jim's hand and wrung it. "I guess I will have to go commando. I can't believe it. I came here tonight for a pleasant evening with some friends, and I'm all disheveled. No underwear, my hair is wet..."

Jim leaned, licked her earlobe and whispered, "And the evening is not over yet." His tongue slid over her chin.

Her perky blue eyes stared up at him, and she swallowed the lump in her throat. She caressed his face. *I love him more than the day I met him! How could I have ruined such a beautiful thing? Things had always been perfect between us, not a harsh word until that one day, and I let my pride and immaturity destroy the best thing I ever had.*

She longed to taste those lips again...have his hands slide over her body.

Jim gathered their stuff and squatted at the edge of the pool. "We're going to leave. It's getting late."

Karl got out. "Why don't you guys stay? We drank more than our share. I don't want either of you driving. This way, you'll be here early for breakfast with the kids. It's not like we don't have the room."

Susan tied a belt around her robe. "Yes, please stay."

Jim looked at Michelle. "You have the farthest to go. Want to stay?"

She bit her lower lip. and already her heart hammered. He was right; Malibu was at least a forty-minute ride. Her eyes turned to Susan who burst out laughing. She took Michelle's hand and winked. "Come, I'll put you in different rooms."

Karl grinned. "If either one of you sneaks into the other's room, you make sure you lock the door and get up before those kids do and go back to your rooms."

Jim gave Karl and Susan an innocent look. "I would never do that."

Karl put his hand on Jim's shoulder. "I've known you for too long, Jimbo. You're not fooling anyone."

Jim entered his room. He closed and locked the door behind him. He took a shower. *Do I want her? Shit, yeah! Not here! Soon! I held out this long. Another few weeks won't hurt, and it will be so worth it.* He lowered the temperature of the water.

Michelle showered and changed into a black lace teddy. It was time. She'd waited for Jim for too long. She sprayed some of her Chanel No. 5 on the white linen pillowcases and sheets.

She lit a scented candle on the nightstand and checked herself in the mirror. She opened the door to the room slowly and looked both ways. Quietly, she tapped her nail on the door to the guestroom where Jim was. No response. She tapped again. No response. She tried to turn the knob. The door was locked. It took all of Michelle's strength to walk away instead of banging on the door. Defeated and angry as hell, she walked back to her room. She closed the door *and* locked it. She tossed and turned the entire night.

♫

Susan and Karl woke up before the children did to make sure all was in order.

Karl poured strong hot coffee. He handed a mug to Jim. "Looks like you could use this.

"I sure can. I am so fucked, so in love." Jim shook his head. "More than ever."

Jim sipped his coffee silently, hiding behind sunglasses.

"Did you sneak into her room last night?" Karl asked laughing.

"No. I've waited this long; I want to do it when we go away. Nice and slow. She thinks we're going to New York—and we will—but I want our first night to be like that weekend. Let's talk when she and the kids leave. I have an idea."

Michelle came out to the patio and purposely ignored Jim. She was seething. She poured herself a cup of coffee and greeted her sons. Karla loved Michelle and stood between the twins

Jim smiled to himself. She was mesmerizing. He remembered that whenever Susan and Michelle entered the Cosmos when they were teenagers, every eye turned to watch them.

He looked in her direction again and took a deep breath. "She's the most amazing woman in the world to me."

"No woman deserves what she walked into, Jim. Susan and I have been together for decades, and I will never tire of her. I never wanted anyone else after I met her."

"Because what you have is real. Decades here too. I never got over that redhead."

Karl patted Jim's back. "I know. Let's just give this some time. When the divorce is final, don't hesitate. "

Jim took another sip of his coffee, his eyes never leaving every move Michelle made.

He stood and made his way to where she stood, talking to Susan. He put his arm around her and nuzzled her neck and sucked on her skin softly leaving a tiny red mark. He kissed her cheek and chuckled.

The look she gave him could have killed anyone, and she placed her hand on her neck. "What did you do? Did you leave a mark?"

"Of course, I did! What are you so bent about this morning?"

"I waited for you last night. To come to my room. I'm so pissed at you, Jim."

"Are you on birth control?"

"What?" She scrunched her face.

"It would be disastrous if you got pregnant. I didn't have condoms. We all know how fertile you are. We both are."

She walked away. "Don't talk to me."

Jim raised an eyebrow. "Does this mean we're not spending Christmas together in New York?"

"No, it doesn't mean that at all. Just don't talk to me for a while."

He crossed his arms and grinned. "So, you are willing to go away with me for Christmas, but you don't want me to talk you?"

She placed her coffee cup on a table. "I'll have birth control by then. Let's not play that game about babies again."

He winced and took her hand. "Michelle Yvette Bujold, you know you can't get pregnant now. Once that divorce is over, we'll have all the babies we want but not one moment sooner."

♫

Michelle followed Susan into the house to get some juice for the children. Esmeralda was making them chocolate chip pancakes and some with whipped cream and Nutella swirled on top.

Susan poured herself another cup of coffee and handed one to Michelle. "Did you sleep alone?"

"Yes, that stupid *idiot*." Michelle stuck her finger in the Nutella and walked out of the kitchen. She motioned Jim into the house because the children were all outside for the moment.

He and Karl entered the kitchen. "What's up?" Jim asked and placed his warm hand softly on her waist.

"*S'asseoir*," Michelle said as she patted one of the stools at the huge slate island in Susan's kitchen. He sat, and Michelle stood between his legs. She slid a dab of Nutella over his lips and leaned in to lick it off. "Remember this?" she asked, her voice husky, sexy. She leaned over and licked the last of the Nutella. A naughty smile caused her lips to curl. Jim took her hand and sucked on each of her fingers, savoring the delicious concoction. She leaned closer and whispered in his ear. "Was it the cabana in my home? Yes, I think it was. The Amalfi Coast was the sex on the beach at night, moonlight on our bodies…heavenly. And you know something? Two can play the game. I'm sure you are nice and hard now and would love for my tongue to do all kinds of things to you, but I won't."

Jim felt goosebumps running up and down his spine, and he looked at Karl. "I told you I was fucked."

11
THE RUSSIAN PRINCE AND HIS PRINCESS

DECEMBER 1985-MARCH 1986, L.A. & BALTIC SEA

Vladimir Vavilov, drummer of the Warriors strolled out of Tiffany & Co. on Rodeo Drive the day after the party at Susan's house. He touched the small signature turquoise box in his pocket containing a two-carat solitaire engagement ring.

It was time to marry the woman who stole his heart, when they encountered each other for the first time on the steps leading into a maternity hospital. He ran up the steps as she left with an elderly woman. As they passed each other, he noticed the gorgeous, flowing chestnut hair and brown eyes and caught a whiff of Anaïs Anaïs. He felt as if they were floating in slow motion. His lips curved into a smile and he winked. Her eyes gleamed as she returned the subtle greeting with a shy grin of her own. He could not have known that mere days after seeing her, she would experience the horror of rape that caused her to distrust men. Knowing now broke his heart every time he thought of it.

They had been together now for a few years. It was a trying relationship, but love seemed to prevail, and every time he thought of breaking up, it killed him that he would even think that way. His heart won every time. Their intimate moments improved more and more each day, and they were sexually satisfied, but they still hadn't consummated their relationship. Every time he got close, she clammed up and her eyes filled with tears, remembering a night when as a teenager she experienced the terror of date rape. She'd come a long way, and he was glad she trusted him as much as she did. He couldn't bear to lose her.

He got into his BMW and drove to their home. He let himself in. They lived in a well-guarded, gated community, a spacious modern home he bought for the two of them. She needed to feel safe when he was away.

His mouth watered as he entered the house and smelled pot roast. Leslie was an amazing cook. He dropped his keys on the table in the foyer and threw his jacket over the railing of the staircase.

"I am home!" He shouted, always letting her know it wasn't an intruder. It had taken a decade for her to become comfortable with being at home alone.

"I'm in the kitchen."

He watched her from the doorway for a few moments. She was wearing a t-shirt and her underwear. Damn he wanted her! She strolled across the marble floor and put her arms around his neck.

"I want you to teach me how to play the drums."

He pulled her away and looked at her. She was serious. "Of course." He took her hand. "Come, one lesson before dinner? Yes?"

They went into the room where he practiced every day. She sat behind the drum set. She picked up the tempo easily. She looked beautiful. As he stood behind her, he kissed her shoulder as he rolled a drum stick slowly and seductively up and down her arm causing goosebumps to rise to the surface.

"I want you to make love to me, Vlad. No more playing games. I want you to show me what I'm missing...now, before I change my mind."

He kissed her lips softly and picked her up in his arms. "Happy to!" He entered their bedroom and placed her gently on the bed. She knelt on the bed and threw off her shirt and began to unbutton his shirt. She slipped her hands over the tattoos she'd caressed a thousand times. She moved her fingers lower so that she could touch him. He was hard as a rock.

He took her lips and moaned as she slid her long fingers around his manhood. She wanted him, and he wanted her desperately. He fell on the bed on top of her. "Are you sure about this, Leslie?"

"Yes," she panted as his fingers entered her.

He slipped between her legs and looked down into her eyes. "Just stop me if you are not comfortable."

She closed her eyes and bit her lower lip. "I will." She placed her hands on his hips and pulled herself up to meet him. For a moment, she felt a slight twinge and then he moved slowly, holding her close and kissing her. He whispered words in her ear she didn't understand...didn't care. He continued to kiss her, wanting her not to fear him but be a part of him. Flesh and flesh...uniting as one. Her orgasm was strong, and she moved with him, bringing him to that place with her. He groaned and whispered her name. She felt wonderful, fulfilled...finally.

A little later as they lay side by side, he looked into her dark eyes. "I have a present for you."

"Where?"

"Be right back." He got up and ran downstairs to get the blue box from his jacket.

He fell onto the bed beside her. "Marry me. I want to marry you, Leslie. I love you too much."

She smiled. His English was atrocious at times. He spoke German better, but she didn't. It didn't matter, they had one language in common, love.

"Yes. Yes. Yes."

He took her hand and placed the ring on her finger. "Gorgeous, like you. I also have two tickets for a cruise; the Baltic Sea to watch the lights in the sky…what do you call them?"

She kissed his lips softly. "The Northern Lights. When do we leave?"

"I am sorry it is so quick. Tomorrow night we fly to Stockholm. We need to take the black eye to New York and fly out tomorrow from Kennedy."

She laughed and corrected him. "The red eye."

She stood and raced him into the shower. Once again, he made love to her, water cascading over them.

♫

They boarded a cruise ship in Stockholm. Vlad made arrangements for the Captain to marry them while they passed under the Northern Lights. They exchanged rings—hers, diamonds all around and his, a plain gold circle.

In the absence of family and friends, the first mate and the cruise director stood as witnesses. The other passengers reveled in participating in the dancing and feasting that followed.

The ship's photographer stood ready, snapping photos. Vlad in a black tux with tails and Leslie in a fitted velvet A-line skirt with a scooped neck ivory dress and white mink stole made a dashing impression. The photographer could not decide whose hair was longer, the bride or the groom.

They stood alone on the deck after the ceremony, him behind her, wrapping her in his arms and pulling her against his chest. They gazed up at the sky together for a while. He pointed to a tiny red light in the far, far distance.

"Those are the lights from Leningrad." His voice shook a bit.

She turned her face. "Are we going to stop there?" Her question was innocent. She didn't know the severity of his situation.

"I cannot step on Russian soil."

"Why not?"

"I left as a refugee—a defector. My grandparents smuggled me out of there."

"And your parents?"

He took a deep breath. He couldn't lie to her; she was his wife now. "They still live in Moscow." His eyes filled with tears. "I do not talk to them. I cannot."

Her hands started to shake. "Are authorities looking for you?"

"I do not think so. I am a very public person, too easy."

"Is your name really Vladimir?"

"No, it is the name on my German birth certificate and passport."

Soft lines dotted her forehead. "But you were born in Germany?"

He shook his head. "No. My grandparents smuggled me out of USSR when I was ten. They secured a German birth certificate and passport for me. How do you say—forged?"

"Oh, Vlad, I'm so sorry. We need to get your American citizenship as soon as we return."

"Yes. I would like that, but I love you no matter. My grandparents loved you."

"I'm glad I met them." She shivered. "I didn't think your life could be more tragic than losing them last year in the fire. Am I so self-absorbed I never asked?"

"No. You simply believe in me. That makes my world."

♫

Much later, bodies entwined with the afterglow of sex, Leslie cuddled up closer. "You are a very interesting bunch, The Warriors, I mean. Two orphans—one middle class, the other a drug abuser; a son of a US ambassador; the son of a secret service agent watching the US ambassador, and a Russian defector. Interesting bunch, and I am the sister-in-law to one of them and sister-in-law-to-be to another, but I love the defector the most!"

He turned and kissed her. "You better!"

♫

A month after they returned from the cruise, Leslie missed her period. She felt fine and had few symptoms to suspect anything was wrong. Vlad accompanied her to the doctor who confirmed that they were about to start a family. Leslie was thrilled. Not only because she was going to be a mother, but she yearned to give Vlad a child and grow their family. She wanted several children in order to give Vlad what he lacked during his childhood. A house full of children running around, screaming, causing chaos.

The doctor's news elated Vladimir. He was glad that after the Savage tour, they were taking a long break so that he can spend time with the family he and Leslie planned. He looked forward to enjoying his children.

Three weeks after the happy news, Leslie began to have cramps and some bleeding. The terror-stricken look on her face frightened Vlad more than he could remember ever being afraid, even on the run from Russian authorities at age ten.

A trip to the doctor confirmed that she had miscarried. Leslie wept uncontrollably. All Vlad could do was hold her in his arms and whisper comforting words in Russian. He was too distraught to think in English.

She was admitted into Cedars-Sinai for a day for a D & C. Once she was released, Vlad assured her that there would be others. He babied her.

Susan and Michelle showed up to pay her a visit and brought her flowers.

"When I lost my first child, I thought it was the end of the world. Years later, when I least expected, it happened again. Losing my first child devastated me to the point of my breakup with Jim. I didn't want children with Richard, yet it happened. Plenty of women have miscarriages." Michelle eyes watered as she mentioned her miscarriage. Losing Jim's child nearly killed her, but she never shared that with him. Someday, maybe she could tell him about it.

Susan returned to the bedroom and put the vase with flowers on the dresser. She took her sister's hand. "I was so wrong to worry about Vlad. He's is a wonderful man, and you have plenty of time."

Leslie nodded. She knew they were right.

♫

A few months later, Leslie became pregnant again. A month into her pregnancy, she lost the child. She didn't even bother to share pregnancy and loss with anyone but Vlad. Once again, she returned from the hospital without a child. Vlad consoled her but she remained depressed for weeks.

For the first time since he escaped Russia, Vlad felt helpless. He found a small Russian Orthodox Church and prayed, not knowing for sure if anyone heard his plea. But a strange comfort washed over him. He returned home with Leslie's favorite take-out, which at last brought a faint smile to her lips.

He took both her hands in his. "Leslie, once we are on our break after the tour, we shall talk to your gynecologist to see what can be done. Babe, if we cannot have a baby, there are plenty babies in the Soviet Union we can adopt, but we might have to smuggle them out. They need parents."

"But they wouldn't be ours, Vlad. I want a child with you."

"We shall plan after the tour. I shall be home for a few years."

She wiped tears from eyes and nodded.

12
REUNION

2nd WEEK, DECEMBER 1985, FRANKFURT, GERMANY

Ron and Karl fastened their seat belts for the long Transatlantic flight to Frankfurt. They had been on the same flight to New York as Vlad and Leslie, but they had no clue what their favorite Russian was up to. Vlad and Leslie often disappeared for weeks at a time. Karl put his head back in his seat and watched the plane taxi down the runway and lift off.

"I wonder what this kid is like," Ron said, slipping off his seat belt after the sign went off.

"He can't be that bad, if he likes music," Karl chided.

Ron smiled. "Who would have thought? Shit, life has surprises. I'm not sorry for the bad things in my life, Karl. I've learned a lot from my mistakes, and I'm glad I've gotten a second and even third chance. I wonder if she's still attractive."

"Eva was a cute little thing." Karl added, "She still could be."

"Too bad she's married. I liked her a lot."

"I know you were quite taken by her. She marry anyone we know?" Karl asked.

"Some British banker, and she has three kids with him."

The flight attendant came around to offer refreshments. Karl asked for cognac while Ron ordered club soda with a twist of lime. Karl sipped on his drink. His mind travelled back to their time at St. Mary's and having met Susan. Despite the years, he loved her as much as when he met her.

Both slept through most of the flight. The layover in London was brief and before they knew it, they arrived at the Ritz-Carlton in Frankfurt.

"Did we get a suite?" asked Karl.

"No," Ron replied. "I got us two deluxe rooms. Not sure if she may agree to a tumble for old time's sake. It would be nice if it wasn't in the dark. When I saw her in the daytime, she was always wearing the traditional convent garb. At night when we made love, it was pitch black. I'd love to see what she looks like nude for a change."

"You're merciless, Ron."

"I've changed in every way possible, but not when it comes to sex. As long as this sucker works, I'm going to take every opportunity that presents itself." He grinned and pointed to the spot between his legs. "I'm not married anymore, don't have to be faithful."

Karl put his hand up. "You made your point."

They put their bags in their room and had ample time before dinner. Ron called Karl's room. "Let's go walk around, check out the chicks. You can look, Karl, but you can't touch. I'll tell Susan." A familiar wicked grin flashed over his face.

Nothing had changed between them in twenty-five years.

It was cold out, and the city was dressed up for Christmas. Taking advantage of the few hours and being that as men they left everything to the last minute, they got their holiday shopping done. Karl suggested a few wines they could bring for their hosts.

They eventually left for dinner. Karl parked the rental car in front of the mansion, hesitating for a moment before exchanging glances and getting out. The two old friends walked to the huge wooden door decorated with a large wreath that had holly and red berries and a red velvet bow. Ron reached out to ring the bell, but let his hand fell back. His fingers trembled. He took a deep, steadying breath while Karl rang the bell.

Eva opened the door. There were a few seconds of silence as she and Ron studied each other. He faced a stunning woman. Her blue eyes shimmered, and her long blonde hair made her appear regal. It was pulled back in a ponytail tied at her neck. He admired the grey flannel slacks and white silk blouse. Her four-inch heels made her taller. His heart pounded loudly in his chest. *Wow, she's even better than I remember!*

Her face broke into a precious smile she always had on reserve exclusively for Ron, no stoic, religious looks for him...ever.

Ron held his breath for a second, taken aback by her appearance. He remembered her in black wool, wimple in place, and that damn rosary staring at him.

Karl smiled to himself. The obvious exchange had all the indications of having some sort of re-awakening for Ron, an epiphany.

Ron bent and kissed her lips softly. "Sister," he said.

"Eva, please," she replied, then turned to Karl. "Mr. Engels, I see you guys are still inseparable."

"Always will be." Karl smiled and kissed her cheek.

She hesitated for a moment, before entering her home. Her hand reached up and slid over Ron's upper arm. "You look good. Finally put on a few pounds."

Ron lowered his voice. "And you are more beautiful than I remember. Besides, I only saw snippets of you in the dark; outside of that, you were always in your habit."

"Come, let's not keep Alex waiting." Before she turned, Ron took her elbow. He squeezed it tightly.

"Are you sure about this, Eva?" he asked as his eyes studied her face. "Do you think we're doing the right thing?"

"Yes, we are. You are his father, and it's time."

Ron entered the huge foyer just as Alex descended the stairs. Ron looked up, and Alex stopped in his tracks. His mother had not told him she had spoken to Ron and that he was coming to Germany.

All the blood in Ron's body rushed to his face. His chest tightened. Neither made a move while they appraised each other for a few seconds.

Eva's voice severed the uneasy silence. "Alex, this is Ron James, your father."

Alex continued down the stairs, gripping the bannister, knuckles white until he stood in front of Ron. He politely stretched out his hand to shake his father's hand.

As their hands touched, Ron pulled the young man into his arms. There wasn't a doubt in Ron's mind that Alex was his. Their smiles were mirror images.

Alex returned the hug. It was a privilege to meet the main member of The Warriors and his father. Starstruck, he realized that Ron's persona was larger than life.

Ron held him at arms' length. "I'm sorry. I just didn't know."

"It's okay...*Vater*," Alex said, smiling to himself.

Ron smiled proudly at his son and the fact that he had called him "father" in their native tongue. Ron turned and motioned to Karl with his hand. "Alex, this is Karl Engels."

Alex broke out in a wide grin. "Great guitarist, man." He gave Karl a thumbs up sign before they shook hands.

"Let's go inside," Eva said.

She led them into the living room. Her home was beautiful, decorated with an elegant European flair. She introduced them to Niall and the twins who immediately broke out in nervous grins. *Wow, two of The Warriors in our own home, not just one!*

A nurse entered the room, pushing a wheelchair. The older grey-haired banker looked at Ron and Karl. His hands were twisted, and a blanket covered deformed legs, but he smiled at them. "It's an honor to have you as guests. Please have a seat. What can Marcia get you to drink?"

"I'll just have water, thank you." Ron's mouth suddenly went dry and perspiration dotted his upper lip.

Ron's and Eva's eyes met. He never imagined that her husband would be confined to a wheelchair. Eva took the wine from Karl's hand and handed the gift bags to Marcia. "What can I get you to drink, Karl?"

"Cognac?"

"Dinner will be served in a few minutes. I'll get your drinks," Marcia said.

They sat in the formal living room. Ron motioned Alex to sit with him on a loveseat. Looking at them from afar Eva realized how identical they looked. The only difference between them was twenty-one years and two gold hoops in one ear. Alex was also a few inches taller than his father.

"So, Eva tells me you were both her students," Lord Edwards said.

Ron's cheeks reddened, and Karl replied, "A tough young one, but a great teacher. Lucky for her, she only had one of us in her class at a time. Ron was younger."

"Not much older than you guys herself, but it's nice to know she managed the unruly teenagers of the times," he said.

Marcia came into the room carrying a tray with ice water for Ron and a small pitcher to refill the glass and Karl's cognac. She handed Eva a glass of wine. The kids helped themselves to sodas and some hors d'ouevres.

When dinner was announced, they were escorted into the formal dining room. Eva sat at the head of the table, her husband to her left and Ron to her right. Alex sat beside his father and the twins wedged Karl between them. Anneliese fell in love with the handsome guitarist of The Warriors. She hounded him about their music and concerts. Niall sat beside his brother. During dinner, Eva fed her husband. Her eyes and Ron's met several times. He'd had no idea what he was walking into when he agreed to come to Frankfurt to meet his son. Old feelings resurfaced and caught him by surprise. *It's only because I've been alone for too long. I can't be feeling this after so much time has passed. Besides, she's married.*

Afterwards, they shared dessert in the music room, where Alex talked to Ron and Karl about music. Ron looked over some songs Alex wrote. They were excellent; he couldn't have written them any better. Alex played them on the piano for his father. Eva excused herself, grabbing the handles of the wheelchair.

Lord Edwards smiled at Ron and Karl. "Thank you for coming. Mr. James, please feel free to visit with your son whenever you want, and take him to Los Angeles with you to meet his other siblings."

"I will, Sir. Thank you for your hospitality."

He looked at Ron and a secret message passed between them. "My time may be limited, Ron. I'm glad you've found Eva and your son after all this time."

Ron forced a smile. "I'm glad too, Sir."

"Good night, Ron, Karl."

Karl got up and placed a hand on the older man's shoulder. "Thank you for having us. It's been a pleasure spending time with you and your family."

"Please feel free to stay longer. I just have to get put to bed like a baby. I get tired easily."

"Good night," Ron said quietly. He was unnerved. Lord Edwards winked at Ron before Eva took him away. Ron and Karl were so close, no words were necessary between them. Karl was glad he wasn't in Ron's position. As Ron's eyes followed Eva's back when she exited the room, the feel of her hands on his body flashed through his mind. *Damn!*

He shivered, shook his head, and took a gulp of Karl's cognac. "Sorry, I needed that!"

♬

When Eva returned to the room, she placed a soft hand on Ron's shoulder. "Alex, would you mind if I borrowed your father for a few minutes?"

"Sure. We got Karl here. There's a lot we want to talk to him about too."

Ron looked at his son and grinned. "Maybe I can convince your mother to let you spend the holidays with your other siblings."

Alex's eyes widened. "I would love that. America, here I come."

"I'm going too!" Niall shouted, ready to go.

Eva turned before going to the back patio to sit by the fireplace. "Can I get you something to drink?"

Ron shook his head. "No, I'm fine."

She refilled her wine glass and led him outside. "It's been a long time, Ron. Thank you for coming."

"I'm sorry, Eva. I didn't know about your husband."

She turned away. Ron expected her eyes to get teary over her situation, but they didn't. It revealed her inner strength. "I don't want anyone's pity, Ron, especially yours. He gave me three beautiful children and some wonderful years. It's just been the past few years that he's been ill. He has rheumatoid arthritis, had a heart attack and a stroke. He never bounced back from the stroke."

He took her impeccably manicured hand in his. "What about love?"

She looked at him. "I only loved you, Ron. I know we were kids, but I knew what I felt," she whispered.

He ran his hand through his hair. "I don't know what to say, except I'm sorry for all of it, for running from the orphanage, for hurting you. I had to find my parents, confront them."

"I know you had to go, Ron."

"I'm so sorry, Eva. You weren't just one of the girls I slept with. I think...I fell in love with you. I've never stopped thinking about you."

Her silence broke his heart. *Why? She was supposed to be a diversion before I left the orphanage. Did I have feelings for her back then, but knew deep down in my heart that I couldn't have her? Maybe I didn't deserve her because I was such a bad seed? That I wasn't good enough for her? Why did I continue to meet her secretly in the confessional although I'd met other women—even Susan? Did I even know what love was back then?*

He took a seat beside her and turned to look at her. Her eyes seemed to bore into his soul. His heart thudded. He leaned over and his lips touched her cheek lightly. His hand caressed her chin and slithered over her neck as his lips met hers. He remembered the taste, her innocence.

"How long has it been, Eva?" he asked, his voice a mere whisper.

She placed her hands over his chest, loving the warmth that penetrated through his shirt. The warmth she remembered as if it were yesterday. "Too long."

He moved closer, and their eyes met. "There's never been anyone like you, Ron. No one's even come close."

He took her in his arms and crushed her against him. He kissed her hair, smelling her perfume. Even back at the convent, she had always been too feminine for her habit, perfumed, perfectly shaped but unpolished nails.

"I think we should go back inside. Would you mind if I took Alex and Niall back to L.A. with me for the holidays?"

"No, I only wish you could take me too."

He kissed her lips softly. "I wish I could."

"We need to talk about Alex, his school, his friends."

"Can we get together for breakfast tomorrow? I'm staying at the Ritz-Carlton. My flight is not until evening. I'll get him and Niall a reservation to come to L.A."

"What time?" she asked, her voice a mere whisper.

"Nine?"

"I'll meet you at the hotel."

They stood and faced each other. He leaned over and kissed her lips softly. He placed his arms around her waist this time. Their bodies touched slightly. Her form felt magnificent against his. *Man, I want her!*

They separated, eyes clashing. Ron ran his finger over her lips. "I'll see you tomorrow," he whispered. She nodded, speechless.

♫

When Ron entered the house, his eyes met Karl's. "I think it's time to go, these guys have to pack. I have permission to take Alex and Niall back with us. The twins will come next time, promise. I'll meet you guys at the airport, four o'clock. I'll give your mother the details and confirm that you can get on our flight."

Ron hugged his son. "You're going to love L.A. Tons of chicks for both of you."

"Thanks."

Ron smiled at Alex. He genuinely liked him. Eva walked them outside. "I'll see you for breakfast at nine. Good night, Karl, behave yourself."

Karl snickered and kissed her cheek. "Never."

"What a pair you were," she said, the memory making her smile.

"We still are," Karl said, breaking out into the same roguish grin he used to lure young girls years ago.

Some things never change, she thought, closing her eyes and shaking her head in exasperation.

Ron kissed her cheek. "I'll see you tomorrow." He looked at her for a minute and licked his lips. *Damn I like her, still!*

♫

When Karl got behind the wheel of the rented car, Ron put his hand up and said, "Karl, if you ask me anything, I'm going to punch you."

"I don't have to ask; I know."

Ron looked out the window and waved at Eva who stood at the front door waiting for them to leave. "Fuck," he muttered.

13
THE fNEVfTABLE

2nd WEEK, DECEMBER 1985, FRANKFURT, GERMANY

Ron sat at a small table by the window when he saw Eva crossing the street. Her loose hair fell in straight, blonde layers that framed her youthful face. As his eyes roved over faded jeans with a white blouse and navy blazer. S*he is still so damn incredible and sexy!*

He stood when she entered the restaurant and let out his breath when their eyes connected. He kissed her cheek and sat down.

"Thank you for meeting me. What did you think of your son?" she asked.

"You did an amazing job considering the circumstances. He is definitely my son. Thank you for such a beautiful gift."

Her smile lit up her eyes. Ron put the menu down and looked out onto the street. He watched the flurry of pedestrians rushing to work. *Shit!* His heart pounded like that of a lovesick boy! A waiter brought them coffee.

Ron sat back and took the linen napkin. He unfolded it and refolded it several times. "I really don't know what to say, Eva. You've caught me at a loss for words."

She placed her hand over his in an effort to steady his. "Then don't say anything. Can we have breakfast in your room?"

He nodded. Her touch burned. His eyes captured hers and a flash of lightning seemed to pass between them. *Is this an invitation?*

He put his cup of coffee down and took her hand. He intertwined his fingers with hers and brought her hand to his lips. He bit the knuckle of her index finger lightly, seductively.

Ron motioned the waiter over and asked him to deliver breakfast to his room. Karl entered the restaurant with a newspaper rolled up under his arm as Ron and Eva left.

Karl winked at her. "Good morning, Sister."

She nodded acknowledging his sarcasm. "Mr. Engels."

Ron's face was unreadable. "I'll catch up with you about three, Karl."

Ron nervously twirled the room key over and over in his hand as the elevator ascended. His other hand in his jacket pocket jingled change.

He got out and picked up his pace. He didn't want anyone to see her or recognize him. He opened the door and placed the Do-Not-Disturb on the brass knob. He locked the door.

He threw open the drapes and sunlight poured into the room. He turned to look at her. "I want to see every inch of you, Eva, and you're going to see every inch of me. No more dark confessionals or garments," he said removing her jacket and unbuttoning her blouse. He threw it on the floor and her white lace bra surprised him. He smiled to himself as he unsnapped it. "Sister, really. You are so damn naughty. I love it." He slipped his fingers through the front belt loops of her jeans and pulled her against him.

His mouth hungrily crashed against hers. Their flesh touched and it ignited a craving that needed tending.

Her hands desperately unsnapped and unzipped his jeans. They fell on the bed and he looked down at her face. "You are truly beautiful."

He tugged at her jeans and stood to pull them off. Lace panties teased him, and he pulled them down her legs. His eyes never left hers as he removed his clothes.

He put his hands on her ankles and pulled her legs apart. "Let me look at you, Eva. I've waited too long for this."

His lips traced a line to her navel and his fingers touched her. Her hips moved up to meet his caress in a desperate effort to find release.

He groaned. "Oh, sweetheart, you are so ready for me."

Her hands pulled him, and he slid into her softness. She moaned as he filled her. Her climax was quick and furious. He bit her lip as he felt himself meeting her release. He lay on top of her for a few moments, taking her tongue between his teeth.

"It's like we have never been apart," he whispered.

She placed her arms around his neck and raised herself to kiss him.

"I guess I can add adultery to my list of sins, Ron. You tempt me so much. You are like that damn snake in the Garden of Eden."

"I'll gladly follow you to Hell, Eva," he whispered, looking down and pushing her hair aside. He longed to see her face in daylight; the glow of her orgasm still on her cheeks, in her eyes.

He fell beside her. She rested her head on his chest. A single knock on the door jolted Ron out of bed. Eva ran into the bathroom. After a quick shower, she peered out. Ron, clad in his jeans button open, fly open, no underwear, winked at her. "Breakfast."

He walked past her and kissed her. "Mmm, you smell so good."

"It's sheer pleasure to see you in the light," she said, smiling up at him. He reached out and pulled her robe open. His fingers stroked her nipples lightly. His hand slipped over her hip and he drew her toward him so that he could kiss her again.

"I never get tired of kissing you," she whispered.

"I would never ask you to leave him."

"I wouldn't."

"It doesn't change how I feel right now, Eva."

He took her hand and led her to the table to have breakfast. She was all he needed to feel fulfilled. She spoke about Alex and his life growing up. She told Ron that Alex had a girlfriend, Miranda, who went to Oxford with him and was the daughter of Lord and Lady Hamilton, but Eva didn't think it was serious.

He buttered her toast; she refilled the coffee cups. They held hands, looked at each other, trying to make up for time lost.

"I don't think I ever realized how much I truly loved you, never told you how much I love you," Ron murmured, admitting the truth as much to himself as to her.

She looked away. Her lower lip trembled. He loved her, and there was nothing she could do about it.

She didn't want the moment to end, the day to end. He'd be going back to the States, a famous rock star with hundreds of women at his beck and call, and she to her beautiful home with all the priceless antiques and her two daughters who were never home anymore, to a painful and lonely existence caring for her husband. She didn't ask Ron about his life since leaving the orphanage nor about Susan. She didn't want to know. She only wanted the here and now. Her body glimmered with fulfillment after having been deprived of his love for too long.

She looked at him, tears filling her eyes. "I've waited so long to hear you say that, and if you had said those words to me at St. Mary's, I would have followed you to the ends of the world, but I can't now."

He hugged her. *I loved her!* It was impossible. He had been too young to ask her to leave the convent. He didn't have a dime to his name, no direction. Now, he had it all and at the same time, he still couldn't have her.

After breakfast, she dressed. "I have to go."

"Can I call you?"

"Anytime you want. He sleeps most of the day and night now."

"Make sure Alex and Niall get to the airport on time."

"I'll drive them myself."

He kissed her, their tongues playing tag in each other's mouths, their bodies responding to passion once again.

"I'll call you when we arrive in Los Angeles."

"Take care of the kids; those guys are a handful."

Ron smiled and tightened his arms around her. "Like Karl and Ron?"

She laughed. "Yes, just like you guys."

He accompanied her to the lobby. Right before she left, she turned and kissed his cheek. She walked through the doors and out into the street. Ron ran a hand through his hair and turned back into the elevator.

♫

Ron got off on Karl's floor and knocked on the door. Karl dressed in faded jeans with small holes near the knees and a black Warriors t-shirt.

Ron held up his hand. "No questions."

"There's nothing to ask, Ron. It's obvious."

Ron threw himself on Karl's unmade bed, his back against the headboard. He pulled off his boots, tossed them and crossed his legs on the bed. "Did you talk to Susan?"

"Yes, she knows we're all coming back to the States. Christmas is in a week and we'll all be scattered all over the place. Want some coffee?" Karl asked, pouring himself a cup. It was cold and he went into the bathroom to spit it out. "Never mind, it's ice cold."

"I need something stronger than that, Karl but not drugs, don't worry."

"Do you think you could handle some cognac?"

"Just a drop maybe."

Ron remained on Karl's bed. He lit a cigarette. "I have no idea what I'm going to do," he said running his fingers through his hair.

Karl took some ice and water to dilute the drink and poured some cognac. He handed the glass to Ron. Karl filled his glass with some ice but remained silent. With Ron it was best to let him vent for himself.

He got up from the bed and stared out the window. "What a fucking morning full of emotions. If I wasn't clean, I would have smoked ten joints, snorted five spoons full of coke, and injected myself with twenty CCs of heroin by now."

"And I would have found you in the bathroom again, probably not alive after all that." Karl remembered the time when he found Ron on the floor in his home, a needle protruding from his arm and damn near dead. Ron had come a long way. Karl hoped that finding out he had a son and finding Eva again after all the years didn't hamper his spirits so much that he turned back to drugs. He didn't think so; Ron was doing well. The demons appeared to have been laid to rest for good.

"I didn't learn too much about my son this morning, Karl, except that he has a girlfriend, doesn't need anything, and is at Oxford studying music. We were supposed to meet and discuss Alex and maybe his future as parents. I spent the entire morning in bed with his mother. Am I a shit or what?"

"No, I don't think so. I think you always had a soft spot for her. She was just unattainable, or so you thought. You were not in a position to ask her to leave the convent."

"Karl, I really think I fell in love with her back then. It's just that..."

"You don't have to tell me, Ron. I always knew, but Susan came along, and I guess that she took you by surprise. She has that knack. Hell, she did it to me, and Eva just wasn't available. You and Susan had the music in common as well."

Ron threw himself back on the bed. "Who would have thought? A nun and a rock star."

"Are you packed?" Karl asked.

"Yeah, I just have to go get my stuff."

"Go; we don't want to be late to the airport."

"Another chapter, Karl. Hope this one lasts forever."

"I hope so too, buddy. You deserve it."

Ron never sipped his drink.

♬

When Karl and Ron arrived at the airport, Alex and Niall already waited for them.

Alex hugged his father. "Thank you."

"We have plenty to talk about on the way."

"Will you tell me about you and my mother all those years ago?" asked Alex.

His father smiled. "I'm not sure I can, Alex, but maybe I can tell you enough to satisfy your curiosity."

14
GUILT

2nd WEEK, DECEMBER 1985, FRANKFURT, GERMANY

Eva started the car to return to her home as light snow began to fall. Her eyes misted as she drove. She deliberately planned on seducing Ron when she left that morning, and she couldn't help but feel the weight of the world on her shoulders. Her husband didn't deserve her betrayal. He was a good provider and father. Most importantly, he adored her. She'd grown to love him over the years, but not once did she feel the passion and love that she felt with Ron. She became unglued in his presence. She was a woman who had been taught composure and abstinence at the convent, yet when it came to Ron, her common sense disappeared.

As she opened the door, her tears fell on her cheeks. Guilt plagued her, yet she loved Ron so much. According to the church and society, she was now an adulteress. In her heart, she didn't sin. It had been several years since she shared a bed with her husband. She had needs, and having Ron storm back into her life caused her to become weak and fall under his spell again. She curled her fists in anger as she ran up the stairs to go to her bedroom where she could change out of the clothes that still smelled like him. As she walked down the hallway, Alex walked out of his bedroom, two suitcases in his hand.

He frowned. "Mother, what's wrong?" He dropped his bags.

Eva looked up at him. *Shit! I never meant for him or Niall to see me in this condition.*

"Nothing, Alex." She started to walk away from him.

He took her arm and stopped her. "Where were you this morning?"

She stared at her son. She'd never lie to him again. "I met your father to discuss your future and his place in your life."

"Did he say something to hurt you?" he asked.

She shook her head and closed her eyes tightly. "No, Alex, he didn't."

He didn't pry any further. He didn't want to know. He reached out and hugged her. "I love you, *Mutter.*"

When he let her go, Eva touched his cheek gently. "I love you too, *mein sohn.*"

"My father is sending a limousine so that you don't have to drive to the airport in this weather."

Eva nodded. She went into her room and closed the door behind her. She leaned her back against it and just let the tears flow.

♫

After Alex and Niall left, Eva and Marcia, the housekeeper, went into Lord Edwards's room to give him his dinner. She placed a tender hand on his cheek. "Darling," she called out softly.

He didn't respond. He didn't wake up. Eva sighed. Although her husband's death was eminent, she hadn't expected for him to pass on that particular day. Her eyes filled with tears and pleasant memories of her marriage flooded back and played out like a movie in her mind. She remembered meeting him after she was cast from the convent to fend for herself and her newborn son. She met him at a high-end restaurant where she worked, and for Lord Edwards, it was love at first sight. They married three months later. Tears streamed down her cheeks. Yes, he had given her three beautiful children and a few decades of happiness.

♫

Niall heard his name being called over the loudspeaker. He scowled and hoped it wasn't Stacey. He didn't like his women to keep tabs on him. He liked his freedom.

He walked over to a service desk and picked up the phone. "This is Niall."

He heard his mother's voice, sobbing into the telephone. "Mom, are you all right? What's wrong?"

"I'm so sorry. It's your father, honey. I need for you boys to come home."

"Another stroke?" he asked.

She was crying harder now. "No, I couldn't wake him up." Her voice hitched. "He's passed."

"We'll be right there."

He nervously walked to where Ron, Karl, and Alex stood, ready to board the flight.

He looked at Alex with tears in his eyes. "Dad's died."

Alex and Niall hugged each other. Ron put his arms around them both. "Come, Karl and I will go back with you guys."

The four men returned to Eva's house. She was in the study, making the funeral arrangements on the telephone. Ron walked in and put a hand on her cheek. "I'm so sorry."

She acknowledged his concern but continued speaking on the telephone. Karl entered the study, and when Eva hung up, he asked, "How can we help, Eva?"

"I know that I've been expecting this moment for a few years now, but you are never prepared," she said, wrapping her arms around herself. Her eyes met Ron's, and he knew she was feeling the guilt of having been with him that morning. He kept his distance.

Karl placed his arms around her, embracing her. "I know, Eva. Let us help you."

♫

The morning of the funeral, Alex looked out the window of his room as he slipped the cuff link onto his shirt sleeve to hide the silver bangles under the cuff. He buttoned his shirt collar, hiding his necklaces and hung his tie around his neck. The man who'd raised him and who was Niall and the twins' father was being laid to rest. Lord Edwards always treated him like a son and gave them a wonderful place to live and made him part of the family, gave him his last name. His death saddened him, and he would miss him.

Niall entered the room with a dark blue silk tie in his hand. His hair was pulled back in a ponytail. He wore a small gold hoop nestled between two diamond studs in his left. His shirt lay open revealing a new tattoo he had gotten the day he arrived in Frankfurt and several pendants hanging from leather cords. The sleeves of his shirt were rolled up and he wore three thin leather bracelets and a silver one on his right wrist.

"Do you remember how to do this shit? I can't remember the last time I dressed this way." He frowned and held up his tie.

"I'm struggling with mine, too. Mom will probably know. New tat?" Alex was referring to the new tattoo of sun rays shooting away from his belly button.

"Yeah, you like it?"

Alex continued buttoning his shirt. "It's awesome; looks deadly, and I think you're going to be dead if Mom sees those bite marks all over your neck and chest. I hope you can cover them up."

"Fuck." Niall stated flatly, looking in the mirror.

"They're scars from the war...shrapnel," he laughed. "Don't worry, I'll try to keep my shirt buttoned and I'll put some of the twins' make-up on it."

"She must have been quite an animal," Alex said, smiling.

"Brought out the animal instinct in me as usual," he grinned.

"Doesn't take much, Niall."

"You know it."

Niall buttoned his shirt and tucked it into his pants. "Ugh, I can't fucking breathe in these clothes."

♫

After the long service and mass, they headed to the cemetery to lay Lord Edwards to rest. Eva and her children and some friends stood to one side and the rest of the Edwards family stood on the other; the casket suspended in the center of the grave divided the families. The twins stood on either side of Niall, and he placed a comforting arm around their shoulders. Ron and Karl stayed behind them in the background.

Niall hid behind mirrored aviator sunglasses and looked at the group of people standing on the other side of the casket.

The families were not close. His grandmother was a petite frail looking woman of eighty-five who was still feisty. Her body was deteriorating but her mind got stronger as the years went by. Nothing escaped her. When Niall looked at her, she was watching him from behind the dark veil that covered her face but that was light enough for him to see that she stared at him with her usual disapproving glower. She had never approved of his choices and often blamed Alex, which made him angry. He was more likely to lead Alex astray. He gave her his usual smirk and nodded. They hadn't seen in each other in ten years.

♫

After all the company left, they all sat in the living room minus the twins. Marcia brought drinks and when she went to hand Ron a glass of water, he smiled. "Marcia, thank you for remembering."

She returned the smile.

Ron stood and leaned against the mantle of the fireplace, cigarette in his hand. "What do you plan on doing, Eva?"

She looked down at her hands and shook her head. Her wedding band was still in its place. It wasn't time yet. "I don't know."

Ron sighed, and he looked around the room at all the faces that watched him as if he was going to dictate the direction their lives would take.

Karl watched Ron who was deep in thought for a few minutes. He took a deep breath. "Come to Los Angeles with me."

Her head shot up. Her eyes met his, and her heart started to pound. "What?" she whispered.

"Leave this place and come with me," he said, shrugging. "You don't need any of this. We can start all over again."

"My children do."

"I can take care of your children, Eva."

Eva bit her lip. "I don't know. I think I need to speak to them first. I need time, Ron. My world has turned upside down in a matter of days. You can't expect me to drop everything. My children were born here, have a life here."

Karl interrupted. "Eva, your children are old enough to understand; maybe the twins aren't but I think that Alex and Niall would stand by whatever decision you make."

Ron sat beside her. "You don't have to give me an answer right away or make the move. I don't have to tell you how I feel, Eva. I think you know."

She looked at Alex who threw up his hands. "I'll go wherever."

There was no problem with Alex, but Niall wasn't Ron's son. She was sure that the twins would have to adjust but would be thrilled to live with a "Warrior." Not only that, they would get to meet the entire band.

Niall didn't wait for his mother to ask him. "Mother, these past few years have been a little rough for all of us. Maybe we all could use the change."

"Your grandmother?"

Niall snorted. "Will still be in England, and we'll be as close as ever. She didn't even come back to the house, Mother. She was on the next flight back. She spoke briefly to my sisters and gave them hugs. She didn't even acknowledge your presence except for a perfunctory hand squeeze."

Eva held up her hand. "Niall…"

"She's always thought you tricked my father into marrying you." He cut his mother off. "Her only words to me today were, 'If you go off with that brother of yours, you will not be in my will. I don't need a damn thing she has."

Eva looked up at Ron. *It is too fast. If for no other reason than to not give my children's only grandparent more reason to hate me.* "Take Alex and Niall back to Los Angeles with you, Ron. I still need some time."

Damn that woman to think that of Eva. His blood boiled, and his jaw clenched. Ron nodded, and his eyes met hers. "You know how I feel."

"And you know how *I* feel."

15
U.S. AWAITS

3rd WEEK OF DECEMBER 1985, LOS ANGELES

A limo waited outside LAX. Alex scanned the scenery and all the beautiful "California Girls." Niall felt as if he had died and gone to Heaven. His eyes shifted every which way.

"Damn," he said to Karl. "They're all beautiful."

Karl laughed. He remembered when they were all beautiful to him until he met Susan.

"Yes, Niall, they are all beautiful until you meet that one who turns your life around. You won't know what hit you."

"Really? I don't believe that for a minute, Karl. I want a taste of them all." He turned around to look at a blonde that strolled by them.

Karl stopped and turned to Niall. "Believe it, young man. I thought that way, too, and one day, someone walked into a seedy club in the Reeperbahn of all places, and my life changed. She exists, Niall. You just haven't met her yet. Excuse me, I have to call her and tell her I'm home."

He found a public telephone to call Susan. "Your eagle has landed."

"I've missed you."

"Me too, liebling."

"I have dinner waiting for all of you."

"I'll let them know. I have so much to tell you."

"And I have so much to do to you." Her laughter was nervous with anticipation.

"I'm sure you do. Looking forward to it. Love you; see you soon."

An hour later, the entourage arrived at Susan's house. She and Karl still kept separate homes until they married after the upcoming tour, but Karl stayed with Susan most of the time. She met them at the door looking fabulous. Skintight jeans and the ever-present stilettos.

She hugged Karl tightly and kissed his lips. "Mmm, you taste damn good."

His hand squeezed her side tightly. "We have company, so behave yourself. You not only taste good, you look amazing."

Ron took her hand and kissed her cheek. "Susan, meet my son, Alex and his half-brother, Niall."

Susan's eyes widened. "I thought that no one could quite look like you other than Stefani, but I was so wrong." She placed a warm hand on Alex's arm and kissed his cheek, then kissed Niall.

Niall was smitten by Susan's beauty. He couldn't help but notice the perfect body. Beautiful women were Niall's downfall. His eyes assessed the gorgeous woman who stood before him. She was as tall as he was. Her jeans appeared to be painted onto her body. Her breasts pressed against a red silk blouse. No wonder Karl was so in love; Ron had been too. She was incomparable. Karl sure was a lucky man! Niall would love nothing more than to sleep with someone like that for the rest of his life.

Nothing in the world prepared Niall for the stunning, lithe blonde that came out to greet them. For a moment, she took his breath away.

"Where's this guy everyone says looks like me?" Stefani asked as she eyed Alex for the first time, and her mouth dropped open. Traces of Ron were evident in the young man, but Alex was way better looking than his father. She laughed inwardly. *I guess that Dad and that little nun made a pretty handsome baby. Of course, no one on the planet like me—I'm perfection made by Susan Michaels and Ron James.*

Ron laughed. "Alex, this is Stefani. Don't get her mad at you. She's extremely jealous when it comes to her father."

Stefani looked at Alex. "Oh my God! You look just like Dad, but I think handsomer."

Alex offered her his arms and she fell into them. "I didn't want to like you, Alex, but it's good to have an older brother around for protection."

Alex took her hand and introduced her to Niall. Stefani turned to the handsome young man with long, dark, neatly pulled-back hair; a sliver of hair fell across his forehead, caressing his cheek. His dark eyes bored into her. Stefani lost her voice. The blood rushed to her face and made it warm despite the cool Los Angeles evening breeze that was making headlines because of the unusually cold weather. Her heart pounded too quickly for her comfort. Afraid he would sense her trembling, she didn't offer her hand. There was a hint of a smile on his lips, but his eyes seemed to dance with an appreciation that travelled the length of her body.

Niall became paralyzed for a few minutes and tried to assess the damage Stefani made on his usually calm and cool existence around women. She was stunning! "H-h-h-i," he stammered in a deep and sexy voice.

Stefani tried to calm her nerves before she could acknowledge his presence. Her voice quivered. "Hi." Her greeting was barely audible to anyone.

Niall put a hand on her arm and leaned forward to kiss her cheek. His lips were warm, and she closed her eyes. She took a deep breath as he lingered against her skin, inhaling the faint scent of cedarwood and musk.

His eyes pierced hers. *Damn, Josh never made me feel like this!* She quickly turned her attention to Ronnie and to Alex, only too aware of the fact that Niall was still staring at her. She could feel the heat of his gaze on her back.

Susan's and Ron's eyes met for a moment, aware of the exchange between Niall and Stefani. They were, after all, her parents.

"This is Ronnie, the youngest. You need to watch him though because he's a real monster," she said to Alex.

Karl went up to the bedroom to put his bag away. Susan followed him. She put her arms around him. "Damn, I missed you," she said.

He held her in his arms and his thumb traced her lips. His mouth captured hers, and as her tongue touched his, her whole body ignited.

"I love you, liebling. I'm starving for food and you. If we didn't have a houseful of guests, I would take you first, then food."

Her hands caressed his strong, muscled arms. "I guess it has to be food first."

"I'll be right down," Karl said, trying to stifle and accommodate the hard on she had managed to give him.

"I can take care of that...quickly," Susan said, a mischievous smile on her face.

"I don't want quick; I want slow and delicious. Get out of here, Susan," he warned, eyes darkened.

"Oh, news on the home front—Got a telegram from Leslie. She and Vlad are married." She sashayed out the door.

Karl stood and took off his shirt to change into something more comfortable.

♬

Susan helped Esmeralda bring the food out to the patio. Karl shook his head and watched the scene play out before him. Ron was with all three of his children. Niall watched Stefani as if she would disappear if he took his eyes away. *Poor Josh, he is surely history now; serves him right, not man enough for Stefani.*

Karl poured himself a drink and sat on a chaise lounge. Life was full of surprises. Susan's home-front news wasn't one of them. He watched Ron laughing. He finally found peace. Karl looked forward to the final tour. The Warriors were considering some form of semi-retirement. His and Susan's wedding would take place the month after the final concert and they were going to take a well-deserved hiatus and start their own family. *Damn that Russian beating me to the punch. Bet Mike's next.*

Karl's lips turned to a smile at the thought. Their family. Susan had two children, Ron had three, Richard and Michelle had the twins, Vera and Jim had two girls, but he was still childless, not to mention that Susan's biological clock was running. He yearned to spend the rest of his life with Susan and their own children as well as hers.

16
BIRTHDAY CELEBRATION

3rd WEEK OF DECEMBER 1985, LOS ANGELES

Susan and Karl wanted to have a party for Michelle's birthday. Karl called Richard, although he didn't care to, but technically, he was still her husband and The Warriors' manager. Richard's suggestion was to find a very romantic and lovely place but not French. Michelle thought American French restaurants were a cheap imitation of the real cuisine.

Susan and Richard invited all the band members, although Vlad and Leslie Vavilov were still out of the country and could not be reached. Michelle's father, Stefano, flew in from Paris with a gown designed especially for his daughter. Richard was out running some errands and would meet up with Michelle before going to the restaurant.

Stefano's arrival from Paris cheered Michelle. He was, after all, the only blood family she had, and she felt that his trips to Los Angeles were dwindling. It was a long trip. The internationally famous designer was getting older, and Michelle hugged him with bittersweet emotion. Of course, Stefano spoke with Susan and Jim from time to time. No one on Earth loved his daughter more than Susan, Karl, and, of course, Jim. Stefano liked the man from the day he met him. He also knew that Richard was having an affair and that Jim and Michelle were trying to pick up their relationship. He handed her a black velvet jewelry case.

"*Ma petite chou,* this is your birthday gift from Jim. He asked that I hand it to you this evening because he can't himself. I designed your dress around this *magnifique pièce.* The matching bracelet is from me."

She sat with her father on the sofa in the den and began to open the black velvet case. The first thing she unwrapped was the bracelet from her father which was full of half-carat to one-carat diamonds cut in every shape in a platinum setting. She put it on and held out her arm so that he could fasten the spectacular one-of-a-kind piece. She looked at her wrist. "It's beautiful." She threw her arms around her father.

"Happy birthday, *ma petite,*" he said, kissing her cheek. "Open the other gift."

There was a card attached to the velvet flap.

I'm sorry I couldn't give this to you personally, but I hope you like it and will let me see you with nothing on but this necklace someday soon. I love you more than you can imagine.

Jim.

When Michelle flipped open the soft velvet, she gasped. The necklace was not quite a choker but wasn't long and it matched the bracelet. It must have cost him a fortune. Tears welled up in her eyes. "Papa, I love him so much."

Stefano sighed. "You people! How could you have ever left him? Married someone else, when you knew there was no one else on this earth for you but Jim? I tried to tell you as we walked down that long aisle in St. Patrick's Cathedral that day. You had plenty of time to reconsider, yet you didn't. Why, *cheri?*"

"I was afraid. The feelings were so much bigger than we could handle."

"Don't think too much, Michelle. Divorce that *idiot* husband of yours, and move on with a man who thinks you walk on water."

Tears came to both Michelle and Susan as they heard his words, knowing they had both made wrong decisions, but at least Susan was now happy with her only true love, and Michelle hoped she would get that second chance as well.

Michelle put the necklace on, it was heavy but lay beautifully on her neck. He certainly knew her taste.

Much later, she looked at herself in the mirror with the phenomenal gown her father designed just for his daughter. The gown was made of soft, lightweight black crepe with off the shoulder straps. The neckline lay straight across her chest, and the waist was belted. It clung softly to her curves. The left side had a slit practically to her hip.

Her father went on to the restaurant, and she was going with Karl and Susan. Richard came in and kissed her cheek. "Nice dress. Is everyone ready?"

She pursed her lips and sighed. *What an ass!* She was wearing a million dollars' worth of diamonds and all he said saw was the dress. He probably knew where they came from. Her face flushed with anger, and Susan whispered while Karl and Richard went to get the car, "Don't you dare cry, Michelle. Your makeup is flawless as is your body, your skin; you look gorgeous. Don't let that asshole ruin your day."

"I wish you would have spoken to me before planning this. I don't want to be with him tonight, and I would love to stay home in case Jim calls me. I haven't heard from him in a few days."

Susan took Michelle's hand. "Come, tonight you and I are going to drink and party because you deserve to have fun on your birthday."

♫

On the way to the venue, Michelle basically spoke of how her father was beginning to show his age. For the first time in her life, she realized that he was getting old, and he would have to retire from the business that he loved. He had kept its ownership to himself and never went public with the company. He owned it outright, and when he died, the empire would pass to his only heir, as well as the vineyards that had been in the family for centuries.

A valet waited for them outside, and they stepped into the gorgeous five-star hotel, The Montage. Dinner would be served in a private outside terrace reserved for the members of The Warriors and their significant others. As they approached the terrace, Michelle caught a glimpse of Jim talking to Mike and Julienne. It was a wonderful surprise that she would never forget. She was about to cry when Susan whispered to her through clenched teeth. "No crying! Happy Birthday to my best friend."

Her eyes met Susan's, and she was sure everyone could hear the loud pounding of her heart. "You couldn't have made it any better."

"I wanted you to spend it with him even if the closeness is limited."

Michelle shook her head and laughed for the first time that day. "What would I do without you?"

"Well, maybe Karl can keep Richard busy and you can go for a walk throughout the beautiful hotel…maybe get stuck in an elevator." Susan grinned and wiggled her eyebrows. Both cracked up laughing, remembering the "stuck" elevator holding Karl and Susan at Michelle's wedding.

Jim turned and smiled. Dressed in a dark suit and tie, he excused himself and walked in her direction. Hair combed back and that day-old stubble and his signature earring made him irresistible.

Michelle tremored from head to toe.

He took her hand and leaned over to kiss her cheek. "I think I've died and gone to Heaven. I've never seen a more beautiful woman. Did you like the necklace?"

"What is there not to like?" she whispered.

"Well, Susan made it her business to seat me this evening facing you so that I can feast my eyes on your beauty all night."

"Mr. Haley, may I add that you the most dashing man here. I only have eyes for you."

They were seated at a long table on the terrace with candles on the table. Richard sat beside her, and once he was in place, Jim reserved his glances at Michelle. Right after dinner, Richard excused himself for the evening because he would be leaving for Turks and Caicos early the next morning with his sons for Christmas. Jim took advantage of his absence. He slipped his shoe off and caressed Michelle's leg, sliding his foot up as high as it could go until his toes reached the triangle he missed more and more. Michelle tried to remain calm and when their eyes met, he smirked. "Too bad the table is so wide."

"I'm kind of glad it is," she added. His foot caressed one leg first then the other.

"You know you don't mean that." He picked up his wine glass and ran his tongue over his front teeth. She returned the gesture by licking her bottom lip.

He lowered his foot but as he did so, his sock got tangled with her ankle bracelet. Very slowly, he tried to untangle himself but couldn't. After several attempts he pointed at Susan.

Michelle looked at him giggling and turned to Susan. "We have a problem," she whispered.

Susan leaned in. "What's up?"

Michelle started to see the humor in what was happening and had to stop laughing before she could tell Susan. "Jim and I were playing, how do you say, 'footsies' under the table. Well, his sock is caught on my ankle bracelet, and we can't untangle it."

"Oh, shit!" Susan exclaimed. She leaned over and told Karl who looked at Jim and chortled.

"Karl!" Susan said. "Stop laughing, help!"

All Karl could think of was to throw down his knife so that it fell under the table. He pushed his chair back and crept under the table. He tried several times to untangle the sock without success; finally he slipped the sock off Jim's foot. He climbed from underneath the table but not before slipping his hand under Susan's gown. She jumped and looked at him when he returned to his seat. Karl grinned and leaned in to whisper to Jim. "Put your damn shoe on."

"You guys are awful!" Susan said.

Jim's naughty chuckle caught Susan's eyes. "Are we?"

It took a while for Karl and Jim to stop laughing. For the moment, they were back in Hamburg, upsetting the whole room and causing a ruckus. Ron eyed them curiously from a distance. Karl finally excused himself followed by Jim and motioned Ron to join them.

They took the elevator to the hotel lobby. On the way down, they filled Ron in on the mischief. He looked at Jim. "You are so crazy!" He lit a cigarette. Smoking was the only habit he kept.

Ron finished his cigarette, and they went back to the dinner area. As they neared the terrace, Susan and Michelle were headed to the ladies' room. As they passed each other, Jim winked at Michelle. She held her breath and kept walking.

When Michelle returned, Jim took her hand and asked her to dance. Richard was long gone and would not be returning.

Michelle's heart pounded as he pulled her close. "You look stunning tonight. I want you so badly."

She leaned away though their bodies remained tightly pressed together. She looked at him and rolled her eyes. "We keep playing games, Jimbo. We're too old for this. We know what we both want. We haven't seen each other in days."

He chuckled. "Did you just roll your eyes at me? You have a whole new set of nuances since you matured. You never used to roll your eyes at me. It's really cute; I like it. You scrunch your face, roll those baby blues…Woman, I'm loving everything about you even more. A different, more improved Michelle, if that could be possible. Soon, baby, we'll be together very soon."

His hand slipped over her derrière and he squeezed. Her nipples hardened from the soft movements against his firm chest.

She discreetly tucked his wayward sock into the pocket of his slacks and could feel more than his firm chest. She moaned slightly.

Once more, he didn't make an effort to spend some alone with her, make love to her.

And once more, Michelle became furious.

17
SWEET DREAMS

3rd WEEK OF DECEMBER 1985, LOS ANGELES

Michelle woke up with a jolt in the middle of the night. Her hand slipped to her chest to calm the thundering palpitations that caused her to pant and caught her breath. She stood to look out the window and slid her fingers through her curls.

The same dream came back to haunt her several times a week. It was always the same. She was back in Jim's parents' chalet in Mont Blanc-Chamonix. Two young lovers skiing, making love and promising each other a lifetime of love. Games in the hot tub. Chasing each other in the night; falling on the cold snow that melted under smoldering naked, flesh. The caresses, kisses, moans…all there night after night. She was in his arms again. The laughter, chuckles…every night the eight short years crept into her mind like a movie. The loss of their child. His fear of commitment…all there in vivid detail. In living color. The walk down the aisle of St. Patrick's Cathedral on her wedding day to Richard. The pain in Jim's eyes as he watched her give herself away in marriage to a man that he clearly knew she didn't love…a slow-motion horror movie.

The short, black, silk night slip clung to her chest as streams of sweat slid between her breasts. The clock on the nightstand showed 3:30 a.m.

Her children were with Richard in the Turks and Caicos Islands. Richard was meeting with architects and took the twins with him for a few days.

She walked to the kitchen and poured herself a glass of wine. The pounding in her heart didn't stop. She hadn't heard from Jim since the get-together at Susan's a few weeks earlier. She returned to the bedroom and sat on the bed, crossed her legs under her body. She placed the glass of wine on the night table and picked the telephone. Her hands shook as she dialed a telephone number embedded in her mind. *What if he is not alone?*

A baritone voice answered the telephone. "Hello?"

"Did I wake you?"

"No, I was watching some TV and kind of dozed off. It's good to hear

107

your voice."

"Yours too. Do your dreams ever wake you up?"

"When you're in them? All the time."

"Hmm, I thought I was the only one."

"We belong together, Red. Always did. I was very immature, and here we are. I guess 'I'm sorry' is a bit late, don't you think? You're on my mind every minute of the day."

"Tu es toujours dans mon esprit aussi," her voice whimpered.

"What are you wearing?" His voice was a mere whisper which dropped an octave.

"A silk black slip."

"Short or long?"

"Short, thin straps."

"Underwear?"

"Black lace."

Every inch of his body reacted to the visual image.

"What are *you* wearing?" she whispered.

"A hard on."

Michelle snickered. "You're so sleazy!"

18
SURPRISE!

CHRISTMAS 1985, CHAMONIX, FRANCE & NEW YORK

Michelle and Jim boarded the private jet at LAX a few days after her birthday. She was excited about spending Christmas in New York. She knew it was magical, but the last time she was in New York for the holidays was for her wedding.

The plane stopped at Kennedy Airport to refuel. Moments later, Michelle looked at Jim. "We're taking off again."

He nodded. "It's a surprise. Just relax and get some sleep."

She leaned back in her seat and smiled. She knew...they were going to Paris. He took her hand in his and intertwined their fingers. *She is finally mine!!! I'll never let her go. I'll fight for her if I have to!*

He brought their clasped hands up and kissed the top of her hand. "You'll never get away from me."

A hostess asked them if they wanted anything. "Just some sleep." Jim gave the woman a warm smile. The flight would be close to seven hours, from being on the phone with each other until dawn. The seats turned into a bed and they snuggled under a blanket after she left, turning off the lights and just leaving on tiny courtesy lights.

♫

Jim felt the jet begin its descent. He stretched and went to use the bathroom. He brushed his teeth and poured cold water on his face. He had that day-old stubble that was prevalent every morning since puberty. The same one Michelle loved. He grinned at his reflection in the mirror. *Time to start the game.*

He crawled back into the bed and leaned over to kiss Michelle. She took a deep breath. *Enfin!*

His kiss was slow and seductive, and her body reacted to the passion in his kiss. He kissed her chin, and his tongue slipped over her neck. She turned to him. "I thought we would never get the chance to..."

His lips silenced her, and he slipped his hand under her top and rubbed his thumb over her nipple. She moaned under his touch. His fingers slowly unbuttoned her top and he pushed it away from her shoulders. He pulled her against him so that he could unfasten her bra. His lips and mouth found her breasts.

"You taste more delicious than I remember. I never stopped loving you, Red. It's always been you."

Her eyes welled with tears. "Some people don't get a second chance, Jim. I will never let you go again. I swear." She slipped her hand lower so that she could feel him. He moaned as her expert fingers stroked him. She knew every move to make on him. He taught her too well. No woman ever came close. It was hard for him to hold back, but as he slipped his hand between her legs, the captain asked them to put on their seatbelts for the landing.

"Fuck!" gasped Michelle.

"Soon, Michelle, we'll be making love. Just wait a little longer. This has to be nice and slow…memorable."

She sat up and started to fasten her bra. "Did you do this purposely?" She was livid.

"I like this new feisty Michelle. You are turning me on more and more with all your new…the faces you make?"

"You did! Ugh, Jim. How could you?"

Instead of responding, he snapped his fingers and began to dance around the plane and sing the Thelma Houston song, "Don't Leave Me This Way."

She got up. He followed her and grabbed her hand and twirled her around. "Come, let's dance. Where are you going?"

"To the bathroom."

"I'm coming with you." Jim said, grinning.

Michelle spun around angrily, sexually flushed, nipples erect. He could hardly contain himself.

"Why? Are you going to control *that* too?"

"Wait." He put a black silk sleep mask over her eyes. Didn't want her to look out the windows of the plane.

"What are you doing?"

"Humor me for just another while, Michelle."

She couldn't see a sliver of light. "Are you really going to go to the bathroom with me?"

"As a matter of fact, I am." He took her arm. He led her to the back of the plane.

Although she couldn't see him, she turned in the direction of his voice. "Are we going to do this in the bathroom?"

"No, you're too anxious, Red." He opened the door and let her in. "I'll be outside...door open."

She shook her head. *What is wrong with him? He's changed so much that I don't know him! Though the blindfold seems like fun!*

The plane landed and he guided her down the stairs slowly, blindfold in place. "It'll just be another half hour, I promise."

She sighed as she tripped into a limo. They arrived at their destination. She heard him open a door with keys. He led her inside and took her blindfold off. Standing a few feet in front of her were Susan and Karl beside the huge glass and marble table in the foyer of Jim's parents' chalet in Chamonix.

Michelle's eye filled with tears and Jim kissed her lips. "Welcome home, Red. This is where I wanted to make love to you again, like the first time."

She kissed and hugged Susan and Karl. She took Jim's hand and led him away. "Excuse us, we'll be back...*peut être*."

♫

She walked into "their room" and pushed him onto the bed. "I'm not playing games with you anymore, Jimbo."

She tore her clothes off and lay on top of him. Her fingers shook as they unbuttoned his shirt and slid down to undo his pants. She slipped them lower and leaned in to run her tongue along the length of his shaft. He groaned and raised his hips thrusting himself into her mouth. His breath quickened and she knew that body better than her own. She straddled him and slipped him inside her, deeper; moving up and down, back and forth. He dug his fingers into her rear.

He rolled her onto her back and slipped her legs over his shoulders so that she was wide, ready for him.

She moaned loudly, knowing she was on the brink of coming. "Oh, Jim, yes, yes, yes!"

She dug her nails into his back as she bit his shoulder. Gasping for air as she gave in to the strongest orgasm she had ever experienced.

"Damn, if you are not the only woman for me, Red."

"I'm going to make love to you all night. I've missed your lovemaking. I'm so sorry for all the years we missed out on the kinky sex."

He silenced her with his lips. "Hush, that's water under the bridge. A new start and a new beginning and plenty of new positions to explore."

"And I think we need to get back to our guests." She whispered and placed her index finger over his lips. "I love you so much."

They joined Susan and Karl who were thrilled about the reunion.

Michelle winked and said, "Sorry, I had to take care of something."

Susan laughed. "Did you just sexually abuse Jim?"

She grinned. "He had it coming…literally."

♫

They flew into Kennedy Airport on Christmas Day. Susan and Karl went on to their apartment in the limo.

Jim took Michelle's hand and he kissed her lips softly. "One more surprise," he whispered. "We can go home, freshen up and I want us to dress up like we used to and look fabulous. I'm taking you someplace special."

She smiled. Her eyes were full of love for him. "Of course."

The limo dropped her off first at her apartment to get dressed. She was staying in New York to wait for the return of her children, and he was flying out the next day to spend some time with his girls.

She stopped by Susan's place for a few minutes. "What a wonderful surprise," she said as she hugged Susan.

"You deserve it, Michelle."

"I'm so happy, I'm afraid I'll wake up from this dream."

"This is real. Merry Christmas."

"We're going to have dinner and round up the evening. I'll probably stay at his place tonight, but I'll see you tomorrow."

"Brunch, here, promise me. Both of you." Susan took Michelle's hand in hers.

"Brunch for sure."

An hour later, Michelle walked out of the building where Jim waited for her on the sidewalk by a limo.

Snow flurries started to fall as he took her hand and kissed her cheek. "Very handsome." Her voice was a mere whisper. She had on a dark green velvet dress and matching shoes. The dress hugged her waist tightly and flared out to her mid-calf. A mink coat completed an outfit fit for royalty.

The limo dropped them off at Tavern on the Green. The restaurant was beautifully decorated for the holidays with lights and Christmas trees filled with silver, gold, red, and green ornaments. Plaid bows nestled among yards and yards of lights and garland. Jim had made reservations for a table in the back where they could be alone.

After consuming two bottles of wine, brandy with dessert and a delicious meal, he stood and held out his hand.

"Ready for your final present?"

"My presents are never final with you, Jim."

"Okay then, next Christmas gift."

She placed her hand in his and she squeezed tightly. There in front of the door was one of the famous horse-drawn carriages she had fantasized about as a young teenager visiting New York for the first time. Snow now fell heavier, and the lights of the restaurant glimmered. It was a magical scene. Everything about their relationship had always included moments of magic. Surreal.

He realized she would kill herself on the slippery snow with her high heels, so he picked her up in his arms. He climbed in and turned to her. "Merry Christmas, Red. I can't wait until your divorce is over and you are all mine."

She took his hand in hers and intertwined their fingers. "I've always been yours, Jim."

It was enchanted indeed. Snowflakes falling softly on their hair, caressing their faces.

He leaned over and they kissed as the carriage pulled away.

19
DANGER

JANUARY-MARCH 1986, LOS ANGELES

Alex and Niall moved in and settled into Ron's house like they had lived there all their lives. Alex was thrilled that he was going to write some music with his dad. Niall was going to France for an interview with Interpol in a few months and would move if it went well. He was crazy about Stefani, but a month passed, and he was still skeptical about getting too close to her. He acknowledged her presence and they spoke casually from time to time, but he hesitated to pursue any further conversation. Didn't want to cause a family feud. When they all got together, either at Ron's or at Susan's, he caught her looking at him. She, too, caught him plenty of times watching her. Her hands shook when she was in his company, and although they made small talk, she tried to sit with Alex and avoided Niall.

Stefani never met anyone who unnerved her like he did. She was jumpy around him. He was more than she could handle, a lot more. She'd only been with Josh, and he wasn't as worldly as Niall. As a matter of fact, Josh was quite boring, and Niall was sexy, exciting, adventurous.

One afternoon, he lay face down on a chaise by the pool at Ron's house while everyone was out. His eyes were closed, and Al Green's voice crooned out "Look What You've Done to Me" in the background. He heard the patio door open. It was Stefani.

She was radiant in very short, tight shorts and a white bikini top. She was all tanned legs and breasts. His presence startled her.

"Hey," he said.

"Hi. Alex told me to come over. Is he here?" she asked. She wanted to turn and run. Run for her life.

"He's on his way." He sat up and stretched. He held up his glass. "Want something to drink?"

"Sure, what are you having?"

"Margarita." He got up and went to the bar to mix her a drink. Stefani sat on a stool. His eyes strayed several times to her breasts. He couldn't help it. They were perfect round globes. She was gorgeous!

"So," she said, "how do you like L.A.?"

"It's different from Frankfurt and England. Every place has its own beauty. The palm trees, the beach, sand, beautiful women."

Stefani got up and walked around the bar to find a snack. Niall squeezed fresh limes into their drinks. She felt the warmth of his body when she stood beside him. She took a jar of peanuts and returned to her stool. He stayed on the other side of the bar, arms spread out and leaning against it. His lips had the slightest bit of movement and his eyes squinted from the sun. She'd never met anyone like him. He smirked a lot, a tiny crooked smile that was devastatingly sexy and lit up his dark eyes. His eyes smiled! He wore black swimming trunks that lay low on his slim hips. Stefani caught sight of a sun tattoo surrounding his belly button. The rays of the sun were actually eight small snakes with open mouths. The tips of their fangs were dripped with blood and droplets of blood trickled lower and lower until the drops disappeared under the trunks. It was a condensed work of art but big enough to see. Directly below was a thin line of dark hair daring her gaze to venture below. Count the rest of the droplets.

A blanket of warmth covered her body, yet she shivered. He caught her glare, and his eyebrows shot up in surprise. He flashed her a full smile. "Inappropriate staring, Miss James."

"Are they poisonous? The snakes?" She swallowed and tried to lighten the conversation.

"Lethal." He grinned.

"No anti-venom?"

"None." He shook his head very slowly, and his lips turned into a sexy smirk. She bit her bottom lip. Their exchange was too sensual. He crept under her skin. She couldn't breathe.

"I hear you and Alex had quite a reputation with the ladies at school."

He laughed. "Is our reputation that tainted?"

"Enough," she replied. Her lips trembled, and he chuckled.

"Well, you seem to be well accompanied. Josh looks like a pretty decent guy."

She leaned over the bar to grab a straw giving him a perfect view of her breasts and just a peep of the darker skin that surrounded her nipple. He held his breath as his body tightened at the sight, and he imagined her naked. "Looks are deceiving," she murmured.

His eyes captured hers. "Hmm, not all is well, then?" he asked, voice low, full of seduction.

Stefani looked away. *Is it? Why did I prefer to stay in L.A. when Josh and some friends had invited me to spend a week in Hawaii?*

She shrugged. "Not sure."

He leaned back and crossed his arms. "Well, maybe we can take in dinner sometime, and you can tell me about it."

He consumed her space, the oxygen she needed to breathe. "Maybe we can."

He motioned toward the pool. "Wanna go for a swim?"

"I don't see Alex getting here any time soon."

He smiled at her, a full-fledged smile and not that lopsided smirk that made her swoon. "Well, maybe you mind swimming with me. I may not be worthy of your undivided attention and company."

She looked at him trying to determine if he was kidding or being serious. He snickered.

"Stuff it, Edwards," she said and dropped her shorts, ran toward the pool and jumped in. She came up for air just as he dived in. She didn't see him under the water until he pulled one of her legs and knocked her off her feet.

He reached out to grab her waist and bring her back up. They stood facing each other, his hands remained on her thin waist. He pulled her a bit closer and their thighs brushed against each other's under the water.

Stefani tried to catch her breath and clung to his upper arm. Their eyes met, and he squeezed soft flesh. Her fingers delicately travelled the length of his arm, and their hands clasped together, fingers interlocked. His squeeze on her fingers was hard. Stefani parted her lips.

Her body burned despite the cool water. His fingers slid over her hip and under the tie that held her bikini together. He twirled the knot between his fingers. They moved closer; she could feel the warmth of his skin on her face. He pressed his cheek against hers and the blood rushed to her face. He smelled of cologne and shampoo and chlorine. The feel of his unshaven face against hers caused her legs to tremble. It tickled, it scratched, it felt so damn good!

Alex dove into the pool, frightening the crap out of them. Niall let go of her, but not before beckoning her with his eyes. She returned the gaze, and he winked.

She turned to Alex. "You said one o'clock, stinker. I've been waiting for you, and Niall here has given me a drink on an empty stomach that is killing me. I thought we were going to have lunch."

Alex put his arm around her shoulder and kissed her cheek. "Female trouble. I just put some pizza in the oven for all of us before coming out."

20
SILENT WEDDING

AUGUST 1986, NEW YORK

Mike and Julienne spent every night together when he was home. Depending on her appointment schedules, she either stayed with him downtown or he stayed at her place. He enjoyed staying at her place. He was close to Richard, Jim, and Karl. Ron chose to remain in Los Angeles, and when he travelled to New York, he stayed at the Waldorf as he had for so many years.

Mike slept late one Saturday, and he turned to watch Julienne sleep. She was beautiful, and he was fortunate and glad he waited so long to stay faithful to one woman. He pushed her long, brown hair away from her face and placed a soft kiss upon her cheek. She smiled and stirred in her sleep. *She is the one.*

"I want to marry you, Jules. Let's do it. We both know what we want, and I love you."

She reached out and pulled him close. "I love you too. We're not that young anymore, and I don't need all the hoopla of a big dress and huge party. Just you and me, both sets of parents and my brother, Craig, and his girlfriend."

"I think that's perfect. No paparazzi. Small private ceremony at a restaurant."

She slipped her hand between his legs and caressed him. He was already hard.

♫

Julienne phoned her parents to give them the good news. They were happy for the fact that their daughter finally fell in love again. Her parents made reservations for a private room in Delmonico's. Her brother, Craig, flew in from Madrid where he was living for the moment. His current girlfriend accompanied him. Craig was a musician in a Spanish rock band and a well-known ladies' man in Europe. Like Mike, he played the bass guitar and remained single. His slight European accent was sexy, and he used it to his advantage. He had a tiny scar under his cheekbone from his teenage years when he was training to become a bullfighter. The bull won that day, and he decided to pick up the guitar instead. It worked, and so did the scar all the women liked. A well-worn war wound.

Julienne's mother arrived at her daughter's apartment with the wedding dress. It was a beaded, off-the-shoulder midi dress designed by Oscar de la Renta in ivory. Her hairdresser did her hair in a stunning French twist. Her makeup was immaculate. She wore pearl and diamond earrings and a pearl necklace with matching bracelet.

Mike waited for them at the restaurant. The limo that carried her and her parents pulled up to the entrance and Mike strolled out to greet her.

He took a deep breath when he saw her. He waited a long time for the right one to come along, and it paid off with flying colors. His love for her was the stuff of romance novels and he looked forward to having children and growing old with her.

She smiled and kissed his lips softly. "You have to be the best-looking groom I have ever seen."

"And you are a stunning bride. I love you so much."

He clasped her hand in his, and he kissed her. He greeted her parents and was introduced to Craig and the "current" love interest. Craig liked Mike the minute he met him. He knew that he and the bass player of The Warriors were cut from the same mold.

Mike smiled. Craig would eventually find "the one." They were going to get along just fine.

Mike's parents had met Julienne and adored her. His mother was ecstatic that she would finally be a grandmother, or at least hoped to be.

A partner at Julienne's law firm, Evan Glass, who also served as a Judge in the New York State Court of Appeals was happy to perform the ceremony.

Mike recited his vows to Julienne. He was nervous and he faltered several times. He took a deep breath.

"I, Michael Anthony Evans, before our family gathered here, promise you, Julienne Marie Costa, to stand by your side, share and support your hopes and dreams. I vow to remain faithful and always be there for you, by your side. When you fall…I will be there. I will dry your tears and comfort you…when you cry. I will laugh with you when you laugh. No matter what lies before us…I see it as a journey we can only complete together. I promise to love and cherish you now and forever."

"With all my heart, I, Julienne Maria Costa take you, Michael Anthony Evans, to be my husband. I promise to be your lover, companion and friend. The mother of your children. Your ally in conflict and"—a soft laugh escaped her lips—"your greatest fan. I will be your strength in times of need. I will trust you completely all the days of my life."

Evan leaned in and whispered. "The rings, please."

"Oh, that's right." Mike nervously searched his pants pockets, and the rings were in the jacket. Julienne grinned. He was so nervous. He handed the officiant a ring with round diamonds all around and a plain gold one.

Mike placed the diamond wedding ring on Julienne's finger. "I, Michael Evans, give you. Julienne Costa, this ring as an eternal symbol of my love and commitment to you."

Tears welled up in her eyes and for the first time, her hands began to shake as she placed the gold ring on Mike's finger.

It took her a moment to collect herself. This was it. She was marrying this wonderful man she met a few months ago.

The sound of Evan's voice interrupted the pounding of her heart. "By the power vested in me by the state of New York, I now pronounce you husband and wife. You may now kiss your bride, Mike."

Their kiss was long, and Mike could feel the blood rush through them as they were now united and committed to each other. Julienne trembled as she held on tightly to Mike. When they finally drew apart, she whispered, "I don't ever want to wake up from this dream. I love you, Michael Evans."

They shared a delightful dinner with their families. The champagne flowed as well as the love between them.

Several hours later, they were on a plane for a two-week honeymoon. They rented a home in the beautiful Basque region of Spain for the first week and travelled to Paris the second week.

It was a trip that sealed their love for eternity.

21
GRIFFITH PARK

NOVEMBER 1986, LOS ANGELES

Susan, Karl, and Ron were throwing a farewell party right before going on tour. It wasn't going to be an industry affair, just the band members, their wives and kids, some close friends.

Stefani was out shopping with some friends. When she returned to the house, she went in search of her mother who had both Alex and Niall up on a ladder, putting up lights, a last-minute idea after the event decorators left.

Niall climbed down when he saw her. His dark brown eyes ravished her body and moved up to her face. She blushed as she caught him scrutinizing every inch of her. He glanced at her bare shoulder. *She's braless!*

Her eyes looked at him from behind her shades. His hair fell across his forehead and caressed his face. His biceps and chest glistened in the afternoon sunlight. A bandana was knotted around his neck. He leaned over and kissed her cheek. Her perfume dulled his senses and he longed to take in the scent of her neck, kiss and lick her there. "Sorry, I'm all sweaty. Your mom has us working to get this place ready."

"When is this little shindig?" she asked, laughing.

"Tomorrow," he replied as Alex followed him down the ladder.

Stefani placed her shopping bags on a nearby table. She picked up a glass and filled it with iced tea. Niall peeked into her Victoria's Secret shopping bag. "Are you modeling something for me?" he asked.

A warm flush rushed to her cheeks. "You wish."

"How about that dinner tonight?" he asked, finally finding the courage to ask her out. He wanted her too much to keep waiting. She was sexy, seductive, everything he loved in a woman.

The invitation surprised her so much that it caught her off guard. She shrugged. "Sure."

He wiped his hands on a rag. "Six okay for you?"

Stefani glanced at the Cartier tank watch. It was four.

"Yes, do you want me to meet you somewhere?"

"No, I'll pick you up. Not too fancy, I'm not a fancy type of guy."

"I didn't think so."

Alex waited until she was in the house and he high-fived Niall. "Finally, dude."

"I know she's your half-sister, but she is smoking hot!"

Alex laughed. "Yeah, Dad's made some awesome looking kids. Mom's pretty good looking."

"And we all know Susan is a fine-looking woman," Niall added with laughter.

"The dwarf is adorable too, but don't tell him I called him that. My dad would have my head."

♫

Stefani came down to the kitchen to wait for Niall to pick her up as Susan prepared dinner and Karl sat at the kitchen counter nursing a glass of wine and watching her work. He loved to watch her cook. After all the years, Susan became a gourmet cook. Who knew?

Susan admired her daughter as she entered the kitchen. Her hair was pulled back and she wore a short denim skirt.

"You look really nice, Stefani," Susan said. "Seeing Josh tonight?"

"No, dinner with Niall."

Susan smiled at her daughter and crossed her arms in front of her. "Well, well, do I see Josh as part of ancient history?"

Stefani walked to the refrigerator and poured herself a glass of lemonade. "Maybe. I need to talk to you about Niall."

"Oh?" Susan asked.

"Josh is not the world's authority on women."

Karl stood. "I'll be outside and leave you two to talk. I will tell you one thing, Stefani, if Josh doesn't take your breath away, he's not the one. This woman took my breath away the moment I saw her." He pointed his index finger at Susan who smiled and bit his finger playfully.

"You did too."

He picked up his glass of wine and went outside to watch Ronnie and a friend of his playing with a remote-control car, and to make sure they didn't cause a guest to fall. For the moment, all was quiet.

Susan poured a glass of wine for herself. Mother and daughter sat side by side at the huge, marble kitchen island.

"I'm all ears, Stefani." Susan said.

"I want your advice and thoughts on Niall."

"I know Josh is not for you, Stefani; but at the same time, I think Niall may be too much for you to handle. He seems pretty mature."

"Wasn't Karl too much for a boarding-school girl living abroad?"

Susan studied her daughter's smirk and couldn't help but smile. "Yes, he was. And I was a spoiled brat. Look what it got me. I made some poor decisions because of my immaturity. I love you with all my heart, Stefani, but I don't want to see you go through the same thing. My childhood ended before I was twenty."

"You were miles away from loved ones. I have you and Dad and Karl. I'm not on my own. I have your support and love if my heart is broken."

Her mother's eyes filled with tears and she reached out to embrace Stefani. They held each other for a few minutes. "I don't ever want to see your heart broken, Stefi. It would kill me."

Disengaging herself from her mother's arms. Stefani confided, "Josh does nothing for me, Mummy."

Susan kissed her daughter's forehead. "Just be careful you don't get hurt. And stay on that pill."

Stefani hugged her mother. "I will. Don't you think Niall is cute?"

Susan smiled pensively. "No, I don't think he's cute. Niall is gorgeous and sexy like Karl and your dad; you have good taste. Remember, though, looks are not everything. I trust you."

The doorbell rang. "He's here!" Stefani said, jumping up with anticipation.

Niall couldn't help but stare when she answered the door. She was the most beautiful woman in the world! He kissed her lips softly. "You look stunning, Blondie." he said.

"You cleaned up pretty well, Mr. Edwards," she said, returning the kiss.

He laughed. He wore jeans and a white long-sleeved t-shirt. A few bracelets on each wrist and two leather necklaces, one with a peace sign and dove, the other with the letter "N" accessorized the casual clothing. He opened the door to a white Mercedes sedan and waited until she sat.

"Where did you get the car?"

"Rental."

She arched an eyebrow. "Looks an awful lot like my dad's."

"There's no fooling you. Borrowed, then."

He drove to dinner at La Dolce Vita in Beverly Hills, a favorite of Ron and Karl's. They talked about their upbringing and school. He ordered a bottle of wine and was shocked when the waiter asked for identification. Blood rushed to his face. Stefani had to stifle a giggle. "I forgot the States have laws about alcohol."

The waiter assured, "I have just the thing for you, sir. I think you'll be pleased." He returned with sparkling cider and proceeded to serve it just as if it were wine.

Niall sat back and let Stefani talk. He loved listening to her, watching her expressions. He fell hard for her, too hard, too quickly. Karl's words resonated in his ears. He twirled some pasta and offered it to her. She cut her chicken piccata and held her fork out for him to taste.

He was so enthralled with her that the time just flew by. He looked at his watch.

"I can sit here and watch you eat and talk all night. I am hypnotized by you."

A drop of lemon sauce fell on her chin and he wiped it clean, then licked his finger.

By the time dessert rolled around, both felt pretty darn good without the aid of wine. They were euphoric with each other's company.

Niall watched as she dug into her tiramisu with gusto. She had no idea of the turmoil that played in his mind. He and Alex were living with Ron until after the tour when they would either get their own places or move in together. Both had brought one or two girls back to the house with them after a night of hitting the clubs, but for Niall it was just to release sexual tension. Something changed him. In Ron's house there were two side entrances so there was no need to enter the house and bump into Ron. Niall wanted desperately to make love to Stefani. She drove him beyond the brink of reason, but there was no way on Earth he could even suggest it.

He paid for dinner, then placed his arm around her shoulders as they walked to the car. He held the door open while she got in and sighed as he turned the key. He took her hand in his when they pulled out of the parking lot.

"You've never been to Griffith Park?" she asked.

"No."

"It's only nine and they close around 10:30. The best view of the city is from there."

"Show me."

Not long after, they were parked on the lookout, the lights of the city before them. "Isn't this beautiful?" she asked, getting out and standing in front of the car.

"Not as beautiful as you, Stefani."

He took her in his arms and pulled her close. Stefani placed her hands on his shoulders. She could feel the hardness of his muscles under her soft fingers. He cupped her chin and his thumb caressed her lower lip. His brown eyes pulled her gaze in. His hand caressed her back as he held her.

Their eyes met, and Niall leaned down. Very slowly, his tongue played with her lips. Stefani let out a sigh. She'd wanted this from the moment she met him. His kiss was smooth. Their tongues touched softly. She imagined Niall as a rough lover, but he was quite the opposite, a pleasant surprise. He teased her in a slow, seductive manner. His finger traced a line down her cheek, followed by the feel of his lips. He stifled the air around her!

His mouth travelled to her neck, and his teeth nipped her skin. He moaned. Her breasts pressed against his firm chest. He smelled delicious. They leaned against the car and she could feel the muscles of his thighs pressed against hers. His arousal teased her. His fingers undid the first two buttons of her blouse followed by the soft feel of his tongue. Her breath quickened. Josh had never evoked the feelings Niall did. He looked down at her face while his fingers pulled the pins from her hair, letting it tumble loosely. He buried his face in her hair, breathing in her sweet scent, her neck. He pressed himself closer and his hands slipped over her hips. She felt his erection itching to burst through his pants. His hands slipped underneath her blouse and she moaned as his fingers slipped over her breasts. She caressed his back; his lips and tongue grazed her chin.

He took possession of her mouth again. "You know what I want to do to you?" he whispered, the tone of his words sensual, exciting. "I would love to take you somewhere and make mad love to you all night.

Find out if you are truly a blonde. You unnerve me, Stefani. There has never been another woman in my life that has done that."

Her eyes captured him. "And?"

"And I live in your father's house. How messed up would it be if I took his own daughter into the bedroom, he so kindly offered to me?" Seduction flowed on his breath.

She leaned forward and kissed him passionately, her tongue waltzed with his. Her hand slipped over the front of his pants, and she stroked him. She bit his bottom lip. Her breath was hot. "And what makes you think his daughter would do such a thing on a first date?"

He looked at her for a moment, then closed his eyes and groaned out loud.

♫

When Stefani got home, she first took a cool shower to calm herself before she picked up the princess phone by her bed and dialed Josh's room in Hawaii, his second trip in a year without her—spring break and Thanksgiving holiday. Still, she couldn't force herself to care, didn't miss him at all.

A giggling female's voice, said, "Hello?"

Stefani cocked her head to the side and almost laughed out loud. "May I speak to Josh? Tell him it's Stefani."

She could hear the exchange.

"It's some girl named Stefani."

"Oh, shit!"

A moment later, Josh breathlessly said into the receiver, "Stef! What a surprise."

"Yes, I could tell from the background noise. I was going to be really nice about this and just tell you that I think we've outgrown each other and it's time to see other people. To hell with that. Josh, why don't you drop off the face of the fucking planet? I never want to see you again."

She slammed the receiver in his ear.

Lying back on her bed she smiled. *Hmmm. Niall Edwards. I think I'll have pleasant dreams tonight.*

22
FAREWELL GATHERING

NOVEMBER 1986, LOS ANGELES

Stefani looked at herself in the mirror before joining her parents' party. As she put on her diamond studs and diamond bracelet, she thought about Niall. Damn she liked him! He could break her heart in a minute. Her mother was right—he was experienced and a handful, and she needed to be cautious. He was also part of the family now, and if anything went wrong between them, it would be uncomfortable. She wondered if a man like Niall could love just one woman. *Could I be the one?*

She met up with her mother and Michelle in the kitchen, just before going out to the patio. Susan wore a short white strapless dress and sandals. She was like rare wine; the older she got, the more stunning her looks. Michelle, too, was more beautiful with maturity. She was dressed in a short black leather skirt with an original white chiffon blouse designed by her father, Stefano. She wore a white lace camisole under the thin fabric Her neck was adorned with numerous gold beaded necklaces. The gold, her vivid blue eyes and red hair made her spectacular. Her sense of style improved with time, not to mention that she was 100% French and the daughter of a well-known international designer.

"You look beautiful, Stefani," Susan said, holding out a tray of hors d'oevres to her daughter and friend. "How did it go last night?"

"Really well. I think I handled him in a way he didn't expect. He's probably used to getting into someone's pants on a first date; didn't happen," she replied, taking a sliver of pizza from the silver serving dish. "Oh, and I broke up with Josh."

"I'm proud of you on both things, Stefani. Don't give in until you feel the time is right. That type is used to just snapping his fingers and a bevy of women bow down at his feet. You need to play Niall smartly, until he falls so heavy, that he changes his entire lifestyle for you. It could happen; it's not impossible. Karl was a ladies' man at the Cosmos; every female knew him and had slept with him. That all changed in one night."

Stefani turned to her favorite *aunt*. "Did you change Jim's life?"

Michelle choked on her drink at the sudden mention of his name coming from Stefani's lips. She frowned, and her heart started to pound. She didn't want to bring up the subject, especially with Stefani. Michelle nervously took another sip. The young girl didn't need to know that Michelle made a huge mistake years ago and that sometimes love hurt more than anything in the world. She didn't know what to say.

The girl smirked. "Aunt Michelle, there were pictures of you guys all over the house, and I remember when I was little, he used to stay over a lot. What happened to you guys? I thought you were so in love. I *know* you were."

"We were, Stefani."

"Then why?"

Michelle stood beside Stefani and put her arm around her, a child that had lived with her until she was a young twelve-year-old before Susan moved to New York with her.

"You are starting a new life with a new young and very handsome man. Why would you want to burden yourself with why Jim and I broke up? Love can be complicated at times."

"Okay, maybe you can tell me someday, but did you change him? Were you able to tame him?"

Michelle laughed. "I'd like to think that I did. I don't think he was ever unfaithful."

"I think you did. You guys were together like forever. I'm glad you're getting divorced. Uncle Richard is not for you. Jim is and always has been."

The stunning redhead took her glass of wine and dumped it into the sink, then refilled the wine glass with a double shot of tequila. "I wouldn't go there Stefani."

"I don't trust Richard, never did."

Michelle rolled her eyes. "Susan, please get her out of here. When did she grow up and have so much wisdom?"

Stefani put her arms around Michelle. "Jim arrived a few minutes ago, and he looks amazing. That grey at the side of his temples…yummy! That day-old stubble and that hoop in his ear…scrumptious. Along with Karl and my dad, Jim has to be one of the hottest rock stars on the planet."

Michelle opened her eyes wide. "Susan, stop her!"

Susan laughed. "She's right, he does look remarkable—they all look better with age."

Susan put her arm around her daughter and best friend. "Let's go join the party."

Stefani stepped outside and was greeted by Alex. "I now have *three* beautiful sisters! Wait until you meet the twins! They are going to love you." He crushed her in his arms.

"I've known Niall my whole life, Stef. He's a great guy. He just needs to find the right one, and in his search for that special someone, he is screwing everyone that will allow it."

"I know, Alex. I've sized him up already."

Alex winked at her. "I hope he realizes that you are the one."

"I may not be," she said, shrugging.

"I've known him my whole life, Stefani. Mark my words—you are definitely the one."

♫

Stefani found her father by the tiki bar near the pool. He sipped his usual club soda with a lime. She kissed his cheek.

"Stefani, you look so grown up," he said.

She smiled up at her favorite man in the whole world and sighed. "You don't look so shabby yourself, Mr. Rock Star."

He put his arm around her. "You okay with Alex in your life?"

"Yes, I like him a lot, Dad. I admit I didn't want to, but he's really nice, and he looks more like you than I *ever* will."

Ron took a sip. "Your mom tells me that you went out with Niall last night."

Stefani's heart jumped in her chest. "Yes, I did."

He tightened his grip around her. "Be careful. He's a player. I don't want him hurting you."

"We just had a nice dinner."

He kissed her cheek. "Just looking out for you."

She took his hand in hers and squeezed it. "I appreciate it, but don't make a big deal out of it. Mum and I spoke."

"Now, I'm *really* scared."

Both laughed.

Just then, her eyes fell on Niall as he entered the patio area. She drew her breath. His hair was pushed back off his face and he was dressed in a casual black suit and white button-down shirt. The top two buttons of his shirt were open. Their eyes met, and he smiled. That sick, twisted, smirk-like smile that kept her from thinking straight, his eyes squinted in a most seductive manner when he saw her. Ron smiled inwardly but on the outside, he gave Niall a warning glower.

He leaned into whisper to Stefani. "What about Josh?"

"History."

Ron grinned and excused himself to find Alex. He stopped briefly to greet Niall. Some kind of joke passed between them, and they both laughed. Stefani let out a sigh of relief. Niall made his way toward her.

He smiled as he came nearer, and he shook his head. "You're killing me, Blondie. Look at you. Wow!"

He bent down to kiss her delicately. "And she feels good, smells good, tastes good..."

"You too. May I tell you that you feel good, smell good and taste quite delicious, too."

He took her by the waist and drew her closer. "What the hell are you doing to me?"

She shrugged. "Just being me, I guess."

"You're playing me right, Blondie," he said, his dark eyes serious.

He took her hand. "Let's get a drink. No I.D. required here."

They stood at the bar and ordered their drinks from the bartender. Niall leaned against the bar with the drink in his hand and faced Stefani. He couldn't keep his eyes off her. Her body moved slowly with the music. Marvin Gaye's "Let's Get it On" played in the background. He put his drink down and took her hand to lead her onto the small, crowded dance floor. She put her arms around his neck. Their eyes met and he pressed his hips against hers. She closed her eyes, and he led her away. She swayed to the music. He bent down and kissed her cheek. A slip of his hair fell on her face and tickled her skin. She held on tight, afraid to fall. She could feel the blood speeding through her veins. He was everything! She tightened her arms around him.

He kissed her lips softly, and she kissed him back, taking his upper lip in her mouth and running her tongue under it. She reached out to kiss his neck. He shivered and tightened his grip. He groaned into her ear. He whispered her name, biting her earlobe softly.

She teased him to the point of madness the night before, and she was doing it again, more so. He never spent so much time with a woman and not have her. There was no place he could take her, no place they could spend some time privately. He lived in her father's house; she, in her mother's house. His borrowed car was out of the question. He wanted her so badly, he couldn't think straight. He would have taken her right there on the floor. He was desperate.

He took her hand, and they returned to the bar in silence. She faced him and stood between his legs as he sat on a stool. She pushed the unruly lock of hair back from his face. He squinted his eyes in that maddening fashion and he licked his lips.

"I usually don't have to work so hard for it Stefani. If I do this time, I want you to know that you are worth all my effort. Let me tell you though, I end up winning, all the time, every time."

"I'm sure you do, and you will," she replied, winking and giving him the sexiest smile he'd ever gotten.

♫

The final preparations were done, everyone was packed, and the going away party was in full swing. It seemed that the young ones were enjoying it more, though. Richard ran through the checklist with the bandmembers. This was the final leg of the tour and it was a short one. Only a little more than a month. The fans knew that the Warriors would be taking a much-anticipated hiatus afterwards. They were going to lie low for a few years and then hopefully make a dynamic comeback. All were tired and had been working since they were teenagers. There was more than enough money to go around and plenty of talent to work with, like Alex.

Susan went into the house and Ron followed her into the kitchen. "Sugar, Stefani tells me she spoke to you about Niall."

"Yes, she did. I was a bit concerned. They went out last night."

"What do you think?" he said, pouring himself a glass of club soda. Susan stood next to him and squeezed a slice of lime into it. She looked out to the patio, and Stefani was sitting with Niall at the bar, immersed in conversation. They were holding hands, heads together.

"I think he's a little much for her maybe, but he's a fine young man. He's polite, *gorgeous*, intelligent, *handsome*, dresses well, *fine*, gets along with everyone, *sexy*..."

Ron put his hand up. "I get the message, too fine to ignore, and you're too old to be noticing *that fine young man*."

Susan laughed. "I think she can handle herself well and that she has to learn from her own mistakes. I just don't want her hurt by this guy; there are other circumstances to consider. Your son, his mother. At least, he was good enough cause to get rid of the schmuck Josh."

"Amen to that. Well, I'll give him the benefit of the doubt that he would know better. Kid's been offered a huge opportunity to intern at Interpol, so he's no dummy."

Susan nodded. "You're right. By the way, I'm not too old to notice, Ron. I am not blind. Besides, I know I could still give the kid a good run for his money if I were single. Don't underestimate me."

Ron laughed out loud and kissed her cheek. "I know you can."

She looked at him. "I'm so glad you're happy. Is Eva going to move to L.A. with you after the tour, or are we going to lose you to Hamburg again?"

"No more Hamburg for me ever. She lives just outside Frankfurt. I'd like for her to come here." He shrugged. "We'll see. She has teenaged twin girls, so she may not want to uproot them. I just want to get this final leg of the tour done."

"Karl feels the same way."

"Well, we'll be done in a couple of months."

♫

Leslie and Julienne came in to refresh their drinks and caught the last line of the conversation. Leslie had a screwdriver while Julienne poured lemon-lime soda because she and Mike were expecting a child.

"That will be one long month to be away from my honey," Julienne said with a mischievous grin. "Maybe I'll tag along. Wouldn't want to have to kill some groupie."

Ron laughed. "You have nothing to worry about. And neither do you," he added giving Leslie a kiss to the forehead. "I never thought Mike would ever settle down, but those two men are totally besotted."

Just like a child, Leslie stuck her tongue out at her former brother-in-law. "I dare you to go out there and explain what besotted means to Vlad. He'd kick your ass."

Ron looped an arm around Leslie's neck. "I'll never piss off that Russian. I've seen him fight." He handed the ladies their drinks. "Come on ladies. Let's rejoin the party."

♫

Susan and Michelle stood watching and enjoying the young crowd and new lovebirds. Thinking back to the time when it had been them.

Michelle shook her head. "When did Stefani get so wise?"

Susan sighed and watched her first born falling in love with one of the most dangerous young men at the party. "I don't think she's had a tough life, but a jaded one maybe."

"Well, I like to think she's done damn well under the circumstances." Michelle stirred her martini with the two olives on a toothpick and slipped the tip of her tongue over an olive to lick the alcohol.

"God, I wish I was one of those olives."

When she turned around, she stood face to face with Jim. He placed his hand on her back and leaned down and softly kiss her lips. "Been missing you, Red."

From a distance, Stefani's eyes and Michelle's connected, and the girl burst out laughing.

She looked up at him and smiled. He did look handsome in a white silk shirt and black jeans with boots, and the ever-present rock star for the night. His hair was shorter, spiky and unkempt, and his constant day-old stubble made him totally irresistible. Stefani was right, the bits grey at his temples made him irresistible, and the California sun streaked his hair naturally.

Michelle leaned in and kissed his cheek. "Mmm…I could eat you up right here."

His body stiffened. "Shall I undo my pants now or will you do it for me?"

"If I could, they would have been off by now, *cher*," she replied. Her eyes sparkled with seduction.

"Yowza!" The exclamation came a bit too loudly.

Michelle shook her head and closed her eyes. "You are so *Américain.*"

He placed his hand on her waist and leaned in. His voice a breath on her ear, he said, "I love you."

"Me too," she said as she kissed his cheek.

Ron walked back into the kitchen and caught the exchange. He rolled his eyes. "I am feeling totally left out."

♫

Alex and Stefani planned to surprise Ron by playing and performing a few Warriors songs for their guests. Alex gave the signal and all the band members began to disappear from inside Susan's home except for Susan and Ron.

"Where the hell did everyone go?" Ron asked.

Susan flashed him her beautiful smile; she was in on Stefani and Alex's plan. "Let's go outside." She wrapped her arm around his. She noticed the expression on Ron's face when he heard the sound of Karl and Jim's guitars with his own two children, Alex and Stefani, giving their guests the show of a lifetime!

The performance of The Warriors' songs being sung by Alex and Stefani was too much for him to bear. He put his fingers over his mouth to keep from crying and watched with pride. Tears came to his eyes as he witnessed their flawless performance. Ronnie stood watching his siblings and moved to the music.

Tears rolled down Ron's cheeks. *So, this is it. This is what it's all about, leaving a legacy. I've had it wrong for so long!*

Susan tightened her grip on his arm and wiped his tears away with her fingers. "You deserve to be happy, Ron. You're a good father; you have a wonderful heart. Despite your madness, you were a good and loving husband."

He put his arm around her and held her tightly. "When this tour is over, I'm going to take it easy. I'm going to enjoy my children more, get to know Alex better. Maybe even marry his mother. What do you think, Sugar? Do you think I deserve a nun?"

"You deserve a woman that loves you and that you can give all that love you have in your heart. You've buried it for too long. Ron, let it out."

Ron's teary eyes caught hers. "I love you, Susan. Don't ever change. I just love you differently now, but I can't imagine my life without you."

She returned his gaze. "I love you too, Ron. You gave me two beautiful children. Come on, let's go show those kids how it's *really* done."

Susan let go of Ron's arm and they joined their children on the makeshift stage to end the set with "Forbidden Love."

Niall stood at the bar and watched Stefani prance around on the stage and deliver a performance worthy of any one of the rock greats. She was a spitfire, and her body moved as if she were made of rubber. Her hips, her waist, every inch of her. Niall took a sip of his drink. There wasn't a part of her he didn't want to ravish with his hands, his tongue, his teeth. Well, he was going to bed solo...again.

Up on the stage, Jim, Karl, Ron, Susan, Mike, Alex, Stefani and Vladimir played song after song. Finally, it was time to tone down the music. Stefani walked to the keyboard and started the first few bars of Marvin Gaye's "Sexual Healing." Jim picked up the mic and winked at Michelle in the distance. His voice was smooth and sexually charged. He was inviting as he moved his hips suggestively. His eyes riveted to hers. Michelle trembled from head to toe.

"Shit, Michelle, if that man isn't making love to you from a distance, I don't know." Susan sighed.

"I think I've had two orgasms just watching him."

Susan laughed. They watched as Jim finished the song, put the microphone down, and strolled nonchalantly toward Susan and Michelle.

"I'm burning for you right now." His wink caused her to take a deep breath.

Michelle took a gulp of her drink. She unbuttoned the top two buttons of her blouse. "I'm feeling a little warm myself."

His loud laughter lit up the entire backyard.

♫

Ron returned to his home emotionally drained about the night. It was wonderful to see his children performing his songs and all the players there.

He entered the palatial house, grateful to be alone for a bit. Alex was out with some girl Stefani introduced him to. He didn't expect Alex home any time soon. He left Niall at Susan's with Stefani. He wouldn't be staying out too late, no place for him to try to get Stefani into bed. Ron walked into the kitchen and poured himself a glass of ginger ale. He laughed out loud. "Blue balls for you, Niall." Ron had seen the man's eyes rake Stefani; yet at the same time, he saw love in them.

Maybe Ron didn't want to admit it, but he liked the kid. He was a player, but he was a good young man. Stefani could certainly be the one woman who could put the brakes on Niall's lifestyle.

Ron went to change into some sweats and sat on the bed to call Eva. He looked at the clock on the nightstand, it was one in the morning, Los Angeles time and it would be about nine hours ahead of his time.

Eva picked it up on the first ring.

"Good morning, Sister," he said.

Eva stretched in her bed and whispered, "Oh, Ron! I am missing you so much."

"Me too, sweetheart. I leave in a few days. Do you think you and the girls could fly in for the final concert, or can you come sooner?"

"I'd love to, but the girls have school."

"You wouldn't consider a tutor?"

Eva thought about it for a moment. What was holding her back in Frankfurt? A marble tomb? It had been a year. Ron had flown back several times. She dreaded every time he left. Alex and Niall seemed to have settled in with Ron, and the girls made it clear to her that they would love to travel to Los Angeles, and desperately wanted to go to a Warriors' concert. She sighed.

"I guess they could have a tutor until the end of the school year."

Ron smiled to himself. "They could transfer to private school here next semester."

"Maybe."

"I need you, Eva. Please say you'll come."

"Let me know your schedule, and I'll try to meet you as soon as I can."

Ron paused for a moment. He realized that he had missed her words of wisdom all his life, he'd loved her all along. He couldn't deny it anymore, and he couldn't deny telling her the truth. "I love you. I think I always have."

"I know I always have, Ron. I'll see you soon."
"Can't wait, baby."

23
THE FINAL SAVAGE CONCERT

JANUARY 5, 1987, NEW YORK

The "Savage" tour broke all previous records. The final day was upon them and Karl was thrilled it was over. Something didn't sit right with him. *Feels too final.* He shivered.

Susan arrived at the Arena and kissed Karl.

"All packed and ready?" he asked.

"Yes, I thought I would never make it on time. Are you okay? You look...pale," she said, reaching out to touch his cheek.

He covered her hand with his. "I'm fine; just looking forward to getting this evening and this damn tour over."

"I have to go into makeup," she said, kissing his lips softly.

Susan put on a black leather body suit. Her body was still perfection, and she donned her outfit proudly. She zipped her boots and took a final look in the mirror. *It's showtime!*

♫

Right before the concert was due to begin, Ron summoned Alex, Stefani, and Niall to his dressing room. "Where are you guys staying after the concert? At Susan's?" he asked as the concerned parent.

"Yes, I have my car here. We're all staying at Mom's apartment in the city after the show. Do you and Eva need a ride?" Stefani asked, knowing that Eva and her girls would attend the concert.

Ron shook his head. "No, we'll head back with Karl and your mom in the limo. We have to go out through the exit designated for us."

He handed them their backstage passes. "Make sure you have these at all times. Otherwise, they will throw you out, and I can't come get you. Stay on the right side of the stage with Richard, Michelle, and Vera. We can leave the stage quickly after the encore; meet here so we can all leave together."

"Dad," Alex said, proud of his father, "you have this down to a science."

"You learn with experience. Karl has a ton of war stories. Ask him."
They turned to leave the dressing room.

"Stefani, Niall," Ron said, "I need to talk to you."

Somehow, both sensed the speech that was about to begin. Their eyes met. After Alex closed the door behind him, Ron stood and leaned against the door, making sure no one would enter the dressing room. He crossed his legs at the ankles and crossed his arms. His posture demanded attention and authority. "Although it took months, I guess you two are dating. Let me tell you something, Niall; she may be yours now, but she was mine first. You hurt my baby, and I will literally wipe the streets with you."

"Dad!" Stefani protested.

Ron held up his index finger. "You let me finish, young lady." He turned his gaze once again to Niall. "Unless you're willing to make a commitment, you keep that thing in your pants, or I will kick your ass from here to kingdom come, and I don't give a flying fuck who your mother is. Do we understand each other?"

"Yes sir, we do." replied Niall. No woman's father had ever spoken to him in that tone. He accepted Ron's concern for his daughter, especially after knowing that his reputation was as bad as Ron's had been.

"I can't believe you!" Stefani shouted, fuming with anger.

"Just watching out for you. You'll thank me some day." Ron opened the door to let them out and went to kiss Stefani's cheek as she left, but her hand pushed him away and she turned. Ron shrugged. He'd delivered the message.

♫

Each member took their place on the stage like chess pieces. Karl and Michael once more made sure that their guitars were tuned before plugging them into the amplifiers. Ron and Susan took their places, side by side, backs to the audience, standing center stage to begin the show. Richard spoke into his walkie-talkie, giving the lighting people the signal, and laser lights flooded the stage at the same time that fireballs of colored pyrotechnics blasted toward the ceiling of the venue.

Ron threw his cigarette down. He was ready. His whole body shook. Karl threw his head back, took a deep breath and struck the first chord.

It reverberated through his entire body. Jim's fingers complemented Karl's guitar introduction with his keyboard, the look of complete concentration on his face. No matter how many times they performed, their hearts still pounded nervously during those first few seconds. The music blared as the fans went into their usual frenzy.

Ron winked at Karl. Performing was the biggest thrill in Ron's life. Ron's back was still to the audience and he snapped his fingers to the beat of one of their biggest hits, "Sins of Lust," while the fans screamed out the words. He turned suddenly, mic in hand, and he pranced across to one side of the stage and Susan to the opposite side. The concert was in full swing!

After three songs, Ron and Susan greeted their audience. Ron joked around with the fans more than usual. This would be their last performance for a while, and it was only fair they gave their fans a show they could remember until their comeback.

During the brief ten-minute intermission, they stood together backstage. Karl pushed his sweat-drenched hair back and dried his face with a towel. Susan stood beside him, arm around his waist.

He kissed her lips. "I can't wait for the next forty-five minutes to be over. Tonight, for the first time, this feels like work and not fun. I'm not enjoying this at all."

Richard met them and congratulated them on the performance as one of their best. Jim and Michelle exchanged glances, and she took a deep breath. Richard figured out that Jim and Michelle were back together. He was okay with it, though there would always be animosity between them. He was happy with his groupie, but he had a hatred for Jim that went back to the days before they became famous. Jim was a privileged young man back then. The t-shirt was glued to Jim's chest and he peeled it off while the wardrobe girl brought him a towel and a clean, dry one. Michelle tried not to stare at the muscles or the tattoos she caressed with her fingers, but she couldn't help herself. She loved him too much. A tight smile touched his lips not wanting to be obvious. They continued to see each other whenever they could. Life was a bit more complicated now with children and the impending divorce looming over their heads.

As the bandmembers returned to the stage, Ron gave Karl a thumbs up sign. He looked to the sidelines and winked at Alex, Niall and Stefani. He blew a kiss to Eva who stood with Michelle, watching, mesmerized at the magic that surrounded The Warriors.

Ron spoke to the fans briefly. "As you all know, The Warriors will be taking a long break after tonight. But we want to leave you with an unforgettable gift. Our last release for a long time will come out at midnight, but you will be the first to hear it live. For a change, neither Karl, Susan, nor I wrote this one. This is a work of art from our bassist, Mike Evans." Ron pointed at Mike who gave the audience a cheerful wave bringing screams and applause. "Ladies and gentlemen, guys and gals, lads and lasses, I give you 'No More Motion without Emotion.'" The crowd went wild with crazed female fans storming the stage and being dragged away.

While the pyrotechnics went off behind the band and Ron belted the first line of The Warriors' destined hit, a man with stringy dark hair and a badge hanging from his neck jumped up onstage and pointed a gun at Ron. He fired three shots, all hitting Ron in the chest. Ron fell, to everyone's horror, and then he aimed his gun at Susan unbeknownst to all except Karl. It happened so quickly that Susan didn't have time to think. She stood horrified and speechless one moment, and the next she felt the weight of Karl's body upon her, shoving her against the floor; it knocked the air out of her. He fell on top of her, getting her out of the way of the bullet that was meant to kill her. The house lights of the arena went on just as Karl rolled off Susan and onto the floor. Ron lay motionless; blood covering his chest. A bullet had passed through Karl's shoulder and grazed Susan's upper arm. The last thing Karl saw before unconsciousness took him was the man he had seen earlier. He wore an all-access pass. He evaporated before Karl's eyes before he could take a shot at the rest of the members of The Warriors.

Shots continued from somewhere else. Mike fell to the ground, blood gushing from his chest. As inseparable as Karl and Ron, Vlad bellowed his best friend's name and ran to the bass player. Another shot spun him around with its force. He, too, fell. Screaming, Leslie raced frantically toward the stage and was grazed by a bullet on her thigh.

Pandemonium broke out in the arena and one of the shooters managed to escape the authorities, but security apprehended the one that had jumped on stage. In the utter chaos, it was unclear where the other shots originated. Susan crawled to Ron's still form, screaming. She knelt beside him and called out his name. She felt for a pulse. It was fading rapidly, and blood streamed out of his chest wounds. There was blood everywhere. On the floor, Karl's shirt and Susan's upper arm. Her face was splattered with blood. She felt for Karl's pulse, and it was much steadier than Ron's, but neither Ron nor Karl's eyes were open. She touched Karl's face and then turned to touch Ron. She wanted to wake up from the nightmare. *Oh God, noooo! Please let them live!*

Julienne and Michelle darted to the stage. and Jim tried to stop them, but Julienne slipped from his grasp and skated on the slick blood to Mike. She knelt beside her husband's body. She screamed. "No, Mike, no. Please Mike, don't leave us. Your baby needs you…I need you.".

Jim turned to Michelle. "Don't you dare move an inch from here. Stay out of sight!" Jim suddenly hollered, "Ah!" and grabbed his arm.

"No! Mon Dieux!" Michelle shrieked. "You've been hit!"

"Barely a scratch." Jim ground his teeth. "You stay back here. I *mean* it, Red."

He ran to where Julienne knelt, and he pulled her up and away from Mike's body. He walked to the exit door and reached out to take Michelle's hand. He placed his arms around them and took them to the side. His shirt was drenched in sweat and blood.

Richard didn't know who to tend to first. He breathed a sigh of relief as the paramedics arrived with stretchers and he, Alex, and Niall helped push people out of the way to clear a path.

Two paramedics tried to run but kept slipping. One of them looked at Mike, his favorite bass player, and tried to find a pulse. "He's gone; nothing we can do. Move on to the others."

Another paramedic covered Mike's body. Julienne screamed. "Oh, Jim, tell me it's not true." She placed her head on Jim's shoulder and wept uncontrollably.

Jim put his hand on Michelle's elbow. "You okay?"

She nodded and started to shake and cry. "You're bleeding and your shirt is torn!" He searched for Richard.

"Richard!" Jim shouted. "I gotta get these gals out of here."

Richard motioned to Jim to go. Jim put his arm protectively around Michelle and Julienne, but Stefani said, "I have to be with my mother." He nodded and let her go. Eva was nowhere to be found.

Michelle pushed Jim. "I have Julienne. You're hurt. Go. Please."

He nodded and sought a paramedic.

Susan sat on the floor, watching the paramedics strap Ron and Karl onto stretchers. She was numb. An ambulance attendant tended to Karl's shoulder, as it bled profusely. Susan watched Karl barely open his eyes and wince in pain. He grabbed his chest. Eva joined her on the floor.

Richard pulled Susan up and she fell against him. Alex and Niall both ran to help their mother who was screaming.

Susan was wheeled into an ambulance with Stefani and Niall. Karl in another ambulance. Ron yet another, and Vlad with Leslie refusing to leave his side into one more ambulance. Richard stood outside the arena and grimly watched each of them being tended to by paramedics. As the paramedics hurried to get the injured to ambulances, they walked swiftly but cautiously, trying not to slip on the puddles of blood. The ambulance that carried Ron was long gone. Karl lay on the stretcher in and out of consciousness. Mike lay covered under a yellow tarp on the stage. Nothing could be done for him. Vlad never regained consciousness.

The ambulances tore onto Route 3 and flew out of the Arena and Giants Stadium complex. Dozens of police cars opened the way for the emergency vehicles with their sirens blaring, trying to the get the ambulances with their precious cargo to Riverside General Hospital quickly. Three of their patients arrived close to death. One was dead. Two were grazed by the multiple bullets.

The ambulances that carried Karl, Susan, Vlad, and Jim screeched to a halt outside the hospital as Ron was wheeled into the emergency room and transferred to surgery immediately. Karl and Vlad both followed into surgery. Susan, Leslie, and Jim remained in the emergency room—their injuries superficial.

Richard, Michelle, Eva, and Alex arrived at the hospital. Michelle ran to the first nurse she found.

"How are they?" she shouted.

The nurse looked at Michelle, then her eyes met Richard's. "I won't know about their condition for a while; they have all been transferred to surgery. Mr. James has critical injuries as well as Mr. Vavilov. Mr. Engels is also critical, and Mrs. James is in the emergency room with Mr. Haley and Mrs. Vavilov. I don't have any more information. The roadie didn't make it. He died in the dressing room. We'll just have to wait and see. The doctors will come to see you as soon as they are done."

"What roadie?" Richard asked with a frown.

"The roadie that was found dead in Mr. James' dressing room. His didn't have an 'all-access pass,' and he was shot. We don't really know who he is. The policemen down the hall want to speak with you."

Shit! thought Richard. *That was one of the shooters! He shot the roadie in order to get the badge. He had "all-access" permission! That's how he got up on the stage and off the stage!*

Richard placed a hand on Michelle's arm. "I have to speak with the police."

Michelle nodded. "Go."

Julienne sat in the waiting room. Silent tears covered her cheeks.

Michelle sat beside her. "I'm so sorry."

"I don't even know what I'm doing here. They couldn't save him…oh, Michelle. I just need to be with you guys." Her body shook with her sobs and she placed her hand over the small bump of the child she was carrying. The child who would never know his father.

Stefani and Niall arrived.

Stefani joined them and heard the nurse speaking with Michelle earlier. It couldn't be happening! She couldn't lose her mother, her father, her aunt and Karl. Niall put his arm around her in an attempt to comfort her.

"I'm here with you, sweetheart," he said, softly kissing her temple. She buried her face against his neck, and he tightened his hold around her, trying to make her feel optimistic, trying to make himself optimistic.

While Richard went into a room with the police, Michelle wrapped her arms around herself and started pacing back and forth. Jim strolled quickly down the hall with several cups of coffee for everyone. It was going to be a long night. His upper arm was bandaged. Fortunately, one of the bullets merely grazed his shoulder.

She stood in front of him, tears streaming down her cheeks. "Oh Jim, what is going to happen?" she murmured. At that moment, Jim didn't care about anything but consoling her. He put his arms around her and kissed her temple softly. "I wish I could tell you that everything is going to be fine, Red. This is awful. Let me go see if there is any more news. Here, hold my coffee; I'll be right back." He kissed her cheek.

♫

The doctors emerged from surgery at different intervals during the night. The first doctor reported to them that Susan would be fine and that the bullet that pierced Karl's upper back grazed her shoulder. Susan had half a dozen stitches, and Karl lost a lot of blood, but the doctors were optimistic. Mike Evans was pronounced dead at the scene, and Vladimir Vavilov was pronounced dead at the hospital, succumbing to his injuries during surgery. Susan came out of the emergency room, her arms wrapped around herself, tears falling.

Michelle hugged Susan. "Oh my God, Susan. Mike and Vlad are dead. I haven't heard a word about Leslie." She took Susan's hand in hers and let her tears flow. Susan squeezed her hand.

"She's still being tended to in the emergency room. A bullet grazed her thigh, but she'll be fine. I have to stay with her. Where's Richard?" Jim handed Susan one of the coffee cups, and she turned to return to her sister's side.

"He's being questioned by the police. They will probably question all of us." His eyes were reddened from the tears he shed and the fear he felt for all of them. "Where's Julienne?"

"In the waiting room." Michelle said softly.

"I'll get her," Jim said. He started to walk off but stopped suddenly. He reached out and wiped some blood from Michelle's cheek with his thumb. His eyes were filled with tears, dark circles surrounding the chestnut eyes that lacked their usual luster for the moment, and he whispered, "I hope we can get through this."

"We'll never be the same," Michelle responded.

Jim saw a tall, huge black man in a white coat approach them. "Everyone here all right?"

"Good." Jim nodded. He couldn't speak any longer. For the moment, it was just him holding the group together. Ron and Karl hung to life by a thread. Mike and Vlad gone. His lips quivered and his eye twitched as he feared losing Karl or Ron or both.

The doctor continued down the hall and disappeared into a room. Another victim was wheeled out of the same room. A sheet covered the body. Long dark hair dangled over the side of the gurney.

Jim closed his eyes and shook his head. *Vlad.* He went in search of Julienne. She returned with him and fell into Michelle's outstretched arms.

♪

An hour passed before Richard rejoined the group, his face ghostly pale. "Karl seems to be out of the woods. The bullet punctured his lung; they're removing it now, but he's lost a lot of blood. No word on Ron yet."

Susan's eyes met Richard's. "The blood was just pouring out of Ron's chest. I don't see how he could make it."

She took Stefani's hand. "We need to be strong, honey. We don't know what may happen."

"Mummy, Dad went to kiss me before going onstage, but I was mad at him and turned away," Stefani sobbed. "I need to say, 'I'm sorry.' I didn't mean it."

Niall pulled her into his arms. He held her tight and kissed her tear stained cheeks. "Hush, Stefani. It wasn't your fault; don't blame yourself."

Niall surveyed the group. "Where's my mother?"

Richard said, "She's in the chapel."

Richard turned to Jim, a sardonic smile on his lips. "A pity you weren't the one under the yellow tarp, Haley."

"Fuck you, Richard. Now I don't *ever* have to deal with you again. The Warriors are no more as far as I'm concerned." He took account of all present. "Let's all join Eva in the chapel."

♪

Karl's eyes were closed but he could hear the commotion around him. He knew he lost a lot of blood. He felt weak.

A voice shouted with urgency. *"We have to stop this bleeding! Give me some pressure here!"*

"You, come around, we have to get this lung re-inflated. His breathing is too erratic. Damn it, hurry up, we're losing him. Increase the oxygen level. Shit!"

The nurse looked at the monitors. *"His blood pressure is very low 80/50, heart rate 200."*

"Somebody get me that X-ray. Make sure there are no bullet

fragments in the lung."

Karl's thoughts turned to Susan. If he died on that table, he was grateful that he had saved her life. Someone tried to speak to him, but the voice was distant. His chest hurt too much, and he couldn't breathe right. He heard the word "lung" several times.

"Mr. Engels, I'm going to give you something that will relax you and you will go to sleep."

He wanted to ask about Susan, but the words didn't come out. He couldn't speak. A tear escaped his eye.

♫

The doctors hovering over Ron were certain that they were at the point of losing their famous patient. One bullet missed his heart but punctured his right lung. A second shot went through his left side, just missing his left lung. The third came too close to his spinal cord.

Ron felt nothing, didn't hear anything around him. He was in a dark void, and his breathing labored.

24

WORLD MOURNS LOSS OF BELOVED MUSICIANS

JANUARY 6, 1987, WORLDWIDE

"Today the world mourns the devastating loss of two of the members of the renowned rock band, The Warriors," was the headline story of every newspaper and broadcast service worldwide the day after the shooting at the concert.

In a barbaric attack by unknown multiple assailants during their concert in Brendan Byrne Arena, two members of the band were taken from adoring fans, family, and friends; and the world still awaits news on the recovery of two others.

Michael Evans, bassist for the group was pronounced dead at the scene. He is remembered as being mild-mannered and the most introverted member of the band. Mike was born in New York, but he lived most of his life in different places around the world. In a recent interview he recalled the most memorable place being Hamburg, where he met the other members of The Warriors.

Michael is survived by his wife, Julienne Costa Evans, their unborn child and his parents, Paul and Catherine Evans.

Vladimir Vavilov, the dynamic drummer of The Warriors was rushed to surgery where he reportedly succumbed to his injuries during the procedure. Vlad was often viewed as a mysterious loner, having been a Russian defector. He, too, met the other members of the band in Hamburg.

Vladimir is survived by his wife, Leslie Michaels Vavilov, the sister of Susan Michaels, also a member of the band; a niece and nephew, Stefani James and Ronnie James, as well as the children of other band members who referred to him as "Uncle Vlad."

As the world prepares to lay these two men to rest, reports say that Karl Engels, Susan Michaels, and Jim Haley are recovering from non-life-threatening injuries, but family, friends, and fans request prayer and thoughts for Ron James, as his condition is listed as critical and possibly career-ending, if not fatal.

Also among the injured and dead at the mass shooting are Leslie Vavilov, whose wounds are reportedly superficial and Jamal Dolan, a trusted road crew member who was apparently murdered in order for the on-stage assassin to obtain an all-access pass.

This publication has also learned that the one shooter authorities apprehended apparently committed suicide while incarcerated and awaiting questioning.

The families have requested that funeral arrangements remain private. Fans may later hold a memorial for the fallen at the site of their demise.

In a final note, The Warriors' new release, "No More Motion without Emotion," debuted this morning in the number one slot on the Billboard charts, a fitting tribute to the loss of a legendary band.

♫

Three high-ranking officials sat in a small conference room of the KGB headquarters in the Lubyanka Building in Moscow. The eldest of the three looked out the window in silence for a long time before making a final decision. It was time.

"Sergei Sokolov had to die. We know he had classified information that he overheard his father talking about. The young man was brilliant at the age of nine when I saw him for the first time. Brilliant and handsome, like his father. Too bright not to remember what was said. He could have been a national icon and asset with his talent and mathematical genius. Too bad that even at that young age he displayed a streak of rebellion against our way of thinking, which was encouraged by his meddlesome grandparents. He *must* have known that his parents represent the deepest secrets of our existence and understood the implications of what he heard."

He turned to face his colleagues and picked up a newspaper. "Mirina Sokolov changed once her son disappeared. After almost two decades in a gulag, she still rages against what she once held dear. Even the brutal slaying of her parents did not faze her. I gave the order to kill her son, but you must kill *everyone* he came contact with. We don't know if he ever divulged any secrets to anyone. Move quickly and efficiently. All of them; do not leave anyone out. No more mistakes."

25
RECOVERY AND REALITY

2nd WEEK OF JANUARY 1987, NEW YORK

Susan stared out the window of Karl's hospital room at the view. The traffic on Route 3 flowed freely that Saturday morning. Beyond that, the Empire State Building and World Trade Center glimmered in the sunlight. *It must be really cold out*, Susan thought. Her eyes travelled over steam and smoke billowing from buildings.

She turned and placed a hand over Karl's. They had been waiting for the tour to be over to get married. Now, who knew what awaited them. She was still listed as Ron's next of kin and might and have to deal with Ron's estate, his heirs; she didn't want to think about it. She took his hand in hers and brought it up to her lips. Green eyes opened, and he looked at her. "Hey," she whispered.

He smiled. He lifted his right hand and pulled the oxygen mask away for a brief moment. "Hey to you too. I can move my right hand and arm; guess I can still play the guitar."

Susan's eyes filled with tears and she said, "Of course, you can." She took the mask. "You're not supposed to take this off."

"How is everyone?"

Susan leaned over and kissed him. "There's plenty of time to talk about that later."

A nurse came in to check on Karl and interrupted their kiss. "How are you feeling, Mr. Engels?"

"I want to make sure my friends are fine, and then I want to go home."

"Let's see," the nurse said. She looked at the monitors and took his blood pressure and pulse. "You're doing good. Mr. Engels, according to your latest X-ray, your lung is still not back to normal, it takes anywhere from forty-eight to seventy-two hours. A full recuperation will take several weeks. You're a strong man, and you should resume normal movement of your arm. Any questions?"

"Yeah. How are my friends?"

Susan widened her eyes at the nurse encouraging her to remain silent.

"Mr. Engels, we can take the oxygen away now. The doctor will be here in a few minutes." The nurse looked at Susan and, with concern, then left the room. Karl smiled and Susan laughed. "I think we've confused her."

Karl nodded, smiling, "She has no fucking idea what's going on. She knows you're Ron's wife, but you're here with me, and there is another woman sitting with Ron."

Susan and Karl waited alone for the doctor. "How is everyone, liebling? I have to know."

He reached out to take her hand and squeezed. "Please tell me. Don't keep it from me."

She lowered her eyes to the ground, tears falling silently over her face, and she glanced out the window. She crossed her arms in front of her chest. "Ron's life is hanging by a thread. Vlad and Mike didn't make it. A bullet grazed Leslie's thigh, no stitches, a bullet grazed my shoulder, six stitches, and Jim's as well, but just a flesh wound. After you fell to the ground, bullets started flying again."

Tears brimmed in Karl's eyes. "Vlad and Mike are gone?" *It can't be!* She nodded.

Tears spilled from Karl's eyes. "Oh, God, liebling. How is Julienne? Leslie?"

"As bad as can be expected. Jim and Michelle drove Leslie to the house, and they are with her. I don't want her to be alone. Grandmother Michaels is on her way here. Julienne is with her parents. Ron is still in an induced coma, but the doctors are not optimistic. I honestly don't think Ron is going to make it. Eva hasn't moved from his room."

The doctor entered the room and checked Karl, the chart, the monitors. He started to remove some of the instruments. "Ready to go home?"

"Yes." He sniffled and Susan handed him a tissue to dry his tears and blow his nose.

"I'll sign your release, and you can go home. Any pain?"

Karl shook his head. "When the meds wear off, it's excruciating."

"We need to keep that shoulder still. Come, let's get you up."

"Doctor, how long have I been here?" Karl asked.

"Two days, Mr. Engels, but you're doing well enough to send you home. It's better for you to recover in your own home."

With the doctor's and Susan's help, Karl got up from the bed for the first time in two days. The room spun for a moment.

"Do you want a wheelchair?" the nurse asked.

Karl motioned her away. "No, just let me get my legs back. I'll be fine." He took a deep breath and he put his good arm around Susan's shoulders. She held on to him tightly by the waist. She looked up at him, "You okay?"

"A bit shaky. Hold on." He took another breath and took his first step. It felt so damn good to get out of the bed although the room spun around.

As he and Susan walked down the hall. He held on tightly to her shoulder. His tears didn't stop.

"And we're not sure about Ron? Is he still in a coma?"

Susan nodded. She pushed the door to the room where Ron lay. Eva sat beside him.

Karl walked close to Ron's bed. Eva looked up at him.

Karl smiled and put his hand on her shoulder. 'How is he, Eva?"

She smiled faintly. 'The doctor just left. It's just a waiting game, Karl. Ron is strong, but his condition is very delicate. He lost a lot of blood, he was shot several times, and the bullets have left some damage."

Karl sat on the chair beside Eva. He looked at Ron; he looked worse than bad. Still, Karl didn't think his friend would die. Gut feeling. He hoped he wasn't wrong.

"How are you feeling, Karl?" she asked.

"I've been better. Eva, I don't know how long Ron's going to be like this. We were planning on leaving as soon as this tour was over. I don't want to stay here now. I need to forget this incident. I don't know who is responsible for this massacre, but I surely am not going to stay here and let the media have a field day with our sorrow. I know that none of us will ever be the same." Karl pushed his hair back. "I want to be here when Ron wakes up, but I don't want to be here if he dies." Tears formed in Karl's eyes again. He put his head down and sobbed. 'It was so awful. I didn't know who to save, Ron or Susan. He's like a brother to me…more."

Eva took Karl's hands in hers and she smiled tearfully. "You all did the best you could under the circumstances. I know he'll be fine, Karl. I just feel it. Ron's going to be a father again and I want him to know this child and watch it grow up. He wasn't there for Alex; he missed so much."

"He missed it with Stefani and the first part of Ronnie's life, too, Eva," Susan said softly.

Karl took Susan's hand and got up from the chair. As Karl and Susan walked down the hall back to the room. "Another child, just what he needs if he gets out of this."

"When are the funerals?" Tears slipped over Karl's cheeks. He couldn't stop them from coming. Two brothers, dead…his favorite, near death.

"I believe tomorrow." Susan said. Her voice quivered.

He put his arm around her and pulled her close. "Let's go home and get ready to leave right after the funerals."

♫

Jim and Michelle waited for Karl and Susan at their penthouse. Jim and Karl hugged each other and for the first time since that fateful day, and they let their tears flow freely. Their bodies shook with loud sobs, uncontrollable body tremors, wailing.

Michelle and Susan could do nothing but let them cry until they expelled all the pain and sadness that was cloistered inside.

Life would never be the same.

26
REQUIEM

2nd WEEK OF JANUARY 1987, NEW YORK

Susan stood in front of the closed door and listened for sounds. All she heard was the sound of her sister sobbing. She opened the door and sat beside Leslie on the edge of the bed.

"Oh God, Susan. I don't want to live without him. He meant everything to me."

Susan put her arm around her. "I know how special he was."

"He was a famous rock star…gorgeous groupies all around him, and he waited for me. He waited for years until I was ready to have sex because of what happened when I was sixteen. He was the first man that touched me since that dreadful moment. When we finally made love, I was a virgin again. It was pure and new. Our honeymoon, under the Northern Lights was the stuff fairytales are made of. The lights of his beloved Russia in the distance, a place he left and could never call home again. He could have been such a broken man, but he wasn't. Yes, he was mysterious, but he was loving and affectionate. Now…I have to bury him. It's not fair."

Susan took her hand and squeezed it. "I know how special he was. We have to go. Both he and Mike will have a closed casket."

Leslie nodded. "I want to remember him alive and laughing."

Karl entered the room, and he took her other hand. "It's time, Les."

The floor seemed to shake, and the room spun around a bit, but she held on to her sister's and Karl's hands for strength.

She walked out of the house, still holding on to her sister and soon-to-be brother-in-law. The chauffer opened the door to the limo. Once again, that queasy feeling took hold of her and she tightened her grip on Karl's hand.

"You okay?" he asked.

She nodded. The ride to the funeral home was a blur. She and Julienne arrived at the same time. She took a deep breath as she watched Julienne stumble out of the limo, followed by her parents and her brother, Craig, then Mike's parents. Tears misted her eyes and she tried to compose herself, but her body shook. Vlad had no family except the members in the band and their families. She and Mike were the closest family he had. Now, they were together in death as well.

She walked closer to Mike's widow and they hugged. Both sobbing, bodies shaking in grief. They held hands as they entered the funeral home together. The two caskets were being viewed in the same room, so family and friends would pay their respects to both bandmembers.

Her cold hand reached out to touch the mahogany casket. The room spun around, stronger this time, and everything went black. Karl caught her just as she was about to land on the cold, marble floor. He started to pick her up, but his arm was still in a sling. Susan and Michelle helped her up and lowered her to a chair. She opened her eyes.

"I feel so sick," she said as she stood quickly and ran to the restroom. She vomited the only thing in her stomach, a bit of orange juice. Susan joined her; she already knew, suspected for a few days now.

Susan walked her back to the funeral room. Leslie was white as paper. She sat on a chair a few feet from the coffin next to Julienne. They held hands.

Michelle and Susan stood side by side. "I think she's pregnant," Susan said with a loud sigh.

"It may be a blessing in disguise, would give her something to live for. She and Julienne are devastated. It's good that children will be there to take their minds off this *horreur*."

"But with her history. She finally told me she lost a second child the other night when we talked. I don't think she can handle losing another— not now."

"*Merde*. We will just have to make sure she doesn't."

Grandmother Michaels entered from a guest room. She put her arm around Susan. "What's the conspiracy?"

Susan replied, "We think Leslie is pregnant."

"And that's a bad thing?"

"Oh, Gran," Susan sighed. "She's lost two babies."

"Okay then." The older Susan Michaels nodded. "Then like Michelle said, we'll just have to make sure she doesn't lose this one."

Susan hugged her grandmother. "I'm so glad you're here."

♫

Leslie and her family, along with Julienne and her family, were escorted to their limousines for the short trip to the final resting place at Hillside Cemetery, not far from where they died. The remaining friends and distant family members followed the procession to burial sites. Mike and Vlad would be buried in the Evans family plot, at the insistence of Mike's parents since Vlad had no other family besides Leslie. Friends, yea brothers, together even in death.

Leslie stared out the window as they passed homes with people inside going on with their lives. Families, children, couples, seniors…all alive. Life seemed to be going on, but hers ended that dreadful night. There would be no children for her. She missed her husband. How could she ever move on without him? He meant everything to her.

Karl helped Leslie out of the car, and Jim went to help Julienne. The caskets were placed on a lowering device. Both widows knew that once the caskets were lowered into the ground, it was the final moment to say good-bye.

A priest waited for the group to assemble. Leslie and Julienne held hands. They were both widows now, no longer the happy friends of the past. Life was torn away from their husbands by the forces of violence and evil. Sometime during the priest's service, Leslie felt faint again. She didn't want to fall and take Julienne with her. She looked around for Karl. He immediately put an arm around her shoulders to steady her. Michelle and Susan passed out peach colored roses to the guests and handed the widows white roses.

"Does anyone want to say anything?" the priest asked when he was finished. No one dared speak. The events had been too gruesome, violent. If anyone addressed the families, they would surely all fall apart. Karl and Jim hid their puffy eyes behind dark sunglasses. Every time that fateful night resurfaced in their minds, they cried like babies.

Jim caught movement in the corner of his eye, and panic struck. *What if it's another shooter?* He glanced quickly over his shoulder to see the tall black doctor from the hospital slip into a car and leave. *He's the one that took Vlad to surgery. Must feel responsible. Not his fault.*

Jim felt someone at his elbow.

"Who's that?" Grandmother Michaels asked.

"A doctor I saw at the hospital."

"No." She pointed with her cane. "There near that tall monument. He's holding a camera."

"Damn paparazzi!" Jim started toward the man.

The older Susan Michaels, Susan and Leslie's grandmother growled, "Leave him to me."

Not needing a cane at all, the old woman marched to where the man crouched. With one swift swing of her cane, the camera flew through the air. "Next blow will be your head." She poked him with the cane. "Get the hell away from my granddaughters."

In shock, he scurried away like a New York cockroach when lights come on.

Watching, Jim almost broke into irreverent laughter.

♫

Susan asked Leslie to stay with her a few weeks. She didn't want Leslie to return to the home she shared with Vlad. Karl and Jim, along with Grandmother Michaels, made sure his belongings went into storage. The only thing they left behind at the house was the drum set. There was no way they could move them out of the house. It felt sacrilegious.

Two weeks later, Susan accompanied Leslie to the doctor who confirmed Leslie's pregnancy. Leslie rubbed her abdomen. *Please, God, don't let me lose this one. He's all I have left.*

27
LIFE GOES ON

3rd WEEK OF JANUARY 1987, NEW YORK

Dr. Ashley Bennett stood at the nurse's station; her new patient's chart lay on the counter. She was only given one patient to care for, Ron James. The name sounded familiar. She read the chart while trying to see if she could remember why she knew the name. Suddenly, it hit her! She had been to one of his concerts a few years ago. The news of the massacre had been in the headlines for a few days. *You never associate a major rock star you're a fan of as one of your ICU patients*. She turned the pages, trying to assess the diagnosis/prognosis. *Three bullets removed from the chest cavity. Not good at all. Waiting game. Major internal damage, bleeding. Spinal shock with possible initial loss of movement which could be permanent or temporary, time will determine. Pneumothorax. This poor guy doesn't stand a chance. A past heart attack that was caused after a near fatal overdose of heroin. A lifetime of alcohol and drug use.* She closed the chart and picked up a pen and her stethoscope to go see her famous patient.

She opened the door to her patient's room. A tall, handsome young man stood beside the bed. The first thing she thought about was that he was a fan, maybe even the shooter there to finish the job.

"Sir," Ashley said, "Mr. James is not allowed any visitors."

Alex looked at her, worry edging his blue eyes. He noted her name tag. "I'm not a visitor, Dr. Bennett. Mr. James is my father."

Ashley wanted the floor to just swallow her. Why the hell hadn't she noticed that he looked like a younger version of the famous rock star? *Even handsomer, if that can be possible!*

She walked past him and checked the monitors. *Blood pressure, low; heart rate, elevated.* Ashley double-checked the blood pressure manually. She checked his temperature. *Only thing normal for the moment.* No sign of infection was probably the best thing her patient had going for him.

"What do you think, Doctor?" Alex asked. He stood on the opposite side of the bed, and he desperately searched her eyes for a sign of hope.

As a cardiologist, she'd seen the look on so many family members. She remembered having that same look on her own face a few years ago.

"I don't want to get your hopes up, Mr. James. This is not good. Of course, I'm just the cardiologist, but I've never seen anyone in such critical condition make it. He's hanging by a thread. I've been assigned to him because of his history of cardiac issues." She looked at her patient and sighed. She took his pulse again.

Ashley's hazel eyes met Alex's. "Please feel free to stay, Mr. James."

Alex walked out of the room with her. His six-foot-three frame towered over her despite her height, and she was mesmerized once again by how handsome he was. He was tanned, and his clothing, though casual, gave him an air of something she couldn't quite place, regal almost.

"No, it's time to call it a night. My mother will be here soon to spend the night with him. I'm going to pick up a cup of coffee. Can I bring you something?"

"No, I'm fine. You have an accent, Mr. James. Where are you from?" she asked, studying the bluest eyes she had ever seen. His blonde hair was not as long as his father's but not short either.

"Born in Germany, attending Oxford."

Ashley's eyebrow shot up. "Oxford, very impressive."

"And you are too young to be a cardiologist, aren't you?"

"Maybe. I breezed through most of my high school and college years and I took double credits and courses to graduate sooner."

"Why cardiology?"

"I lost someone quite dear to me to a heart attack."

"Sorry to hear that."

"I have to get back to work. I'll make sure your father is comfortable. I think that's all we can do for now."

"I appreciate it, Dr. Bennett," Alex said, holding out his hand and reading the stitched name on her coat.

"My pleasure," she replied softly and placed her hand in his. Her handshake was firm and strong, yet feminine.

The feel of his touch caused her to hold her breath for a second. She hadn't felt that way in a while.

Alex's eyes watched as she returned to the nurse's station with his father's chart. *Wow, awesome!! Certainly not the place or time to connect with a woman, but damn, she was beautiful!*

Since arriving in America, Alex and Niall had managed to visit a lot of clubs and bars along Sunset Boulevard, Spring Street, Olympic Boulevard. Yet, Alex had not encountered a woman like Dr. Bennett.

He watched her from a distance while he waited for the elevator. She towered with confidence over the nurses, almost demanding the respect that went with the fact that she was young, but a cardiologist.

Her dark auburn hair pulled back in a ponytail made her appear almost as young as the nurses' aides. Simple diamond studs adorned her ears. Her hands revealed no wedding or engagement ring.

Alex liked what he saw, trying in earnest to visualize what lay beneath the white physician's coat, white silk blouse and black wool skirt. *She has terrific legs.*

He was so mesmerized by his thoughts that he almost missed the elevator. He certainly was his father's son. Beautiful women unnerved him as well as Niall, but Alex was sure that Niall's days of loving many women were over.

♪

Alex didn't see Dr. Bennett again for a few days. He got into a crowded elevator and she stepped in behind him. When he turned, they were facing each other.

He smiled. "Doctor."

Ashley wondered whether she could turn around and give him her back, but for a moment she hesitated. "How are you, Mr. James?"

Fortunately, the elevator stopped again, and several people got off, giving Ashley some room. In the tight space, he could smell her perfume and his hand almost touched her. Finally, on the ground floor they got out.

"Mr. James, I spoke with your mother this morning. Your father seems to be stable. That's a good sign. He's not better, but he's not worse."

"Thank you, Doctor. I appreciate all you're doing for him."

"I'll stop in later to check on him."

"I was going to grab a bite. Can I buy you lunch?" he asked. Her jade eyes met his sapphire ones, and she smiled. She looked at her watch.

"I have a meeting in fifteen minutes. Raincheck?" she asked.

He smiled. "'Absolutely, Doctor. Dinner?"

"Maybe."

"Whenever you get out for dinner, you know where I'll be."

"Around six."

"I'll be here." He started to walk away but turned. "For the record, legally the last name is Edwards. Alex Edwards."

28
TRYING TO PICK UP THE BROKEN PIECES

3rd WEEK OF JANUARY 1987, NEW YORK

Jim called Michelle a week after the funerals. The music world was still mourning the loss of a famous drummer and bass player. No one knew what was going to happen with the future of The Warriors. Speculation and rumors flew among certain circles, but it wasn't time yet. Maybe not ever again.

"Where's your husband?"

"In London, probably with his girlfriend," she replied.

"Does that mean I get to have you for as long as I want?" Jim smiled.

"Until he returns."

"When is that?"

Michelle sighed. "The end of the week. He wants to be here when Karl and Susan leave. The dedicated band manager."

"Yummy," Jim said grinning. "My place? You haven't been there yet. I need to be with you, Michelle. I just feel lost."

"I'd love to see you. I'm on my way."

♫

Michelle arrived at the address Jim gave her. She looked up at the gorgeous brownstone. He waited on the sidewalk for her.

"Wow," she said. "This is beautiful."

"It's home." He ran up the few steps leading to the front door. Michelle entered the stunning home Jim had completely gutted and upgraded. The foyer reminded her of the one at the Swiss chalet his parents owned. The massive living room was warm with muted tones of ivory and taupe. The only color was from the priceless artwork he'd collected over the years.

"Surprised?" he asked.

"Yes, very." She glimpsed an irreplaceable modern glass sculpture in the center of a carved marble coffee table.

He watched proudly as she assessed his living room. She was a lover of the arts and was quite a collector herself.

"Did your little designer girlfriend do this?" She referred to the young decorator he had been seen with on and off in Los Angeles and who decorated his L.A. home.

He snickered. "Jealousy doesn't suit you, Red. Especially when there is absolutely nothing to be jealous about. Remember Nancy? Well, Scarlett and I fucked."

"I guess I don't have a right, but I miss you so much when you're not with me. I toss and turn all night thinking of you, wanting your touch, craving your scent." She shook her head. "We should have never started this, at least not until Richard and I divorced."

He stepped closer. "This didn't just restart, babe. It never ended. There was never a moment in my life I didn't want you."

"I need you every moment of the day, especially now. Life can end in a second." Her voice turned into a whisper. "What have you done to me? I can't sleep, I can't eat...ever since..."

"I don't want to think or talk about death, not now. Are you challenging me to make up for the lost time and keep you satisfied until we have another opportunity?'

Michelle unbuttoned her top and threw it on the soft suede sofa. She unzipped her skirt and stepped out of it. Her black lace bra and panties didn't leave much to the imagination. Nipples at attention. Her garter belt held up black lace-top stockings. She went to remove her heels and he stopped her. "Don't...leave them on."

He reached out and placed his hand on her waist. He drew her near and took possession of her mouth. Michelle sighed as he slipped his other hand under the black lace to caress her bare bottom. She was on fire, moaning as he slipped his tongue into her mouth. He caressed her navel and slithered his hand lower. She clung to his neck as her legs shook.

"Spread your legs, Red," he breathed, and she obliged feeling his touch. He guided two fingers into her, and he slid his tongue under her bra, searching for her nipple. He felt her orgasm coming; he knew more about her body than she knew herself. She threw her neck back and cried out, her body shaking violently. She gasped calling out his name. He kissed her earlobe. "Before this night is over, you will be begging me to stop." His fingers intensified against her, bringing her to another monumental orgasm.

♬

He kissed her the following morning. "Red, this is bigger than us. Our feelings are just too intense, too perfect. It's frightening, but I'm willing to face the monster head on this time."

She placed her index finger over his lips. "I know," she whispered. "Just give me a little time, wait for me, Jim."

"Of course, I will. There's never been anyone else."

♬

Michelle woke up to the sound of a tender, sad melody in the distance. She put on Jim's black silk robe and slowly slipped down the stairs trying not to make a sound. Her eyes captured him. A glass of wine on the Steinway grand piano, music sheets scattered on the opposite side and a Mont Blanc pencil lying over them. She watched as he concentrated on the sound, his eyes closed. He sensed her presence and turned. He smiled and motioned her over then he patted his lap. "Sit."

She moved closer. His arms curved around her so that he could play her the melody that had come to him just as he was falling asleep. He rested his chin on her shoulder causing the robe to slip away.

"You like it?" he asked.

"It's such a sad melody."

He shrugged. "I am sad and heartbroken."

"It's going to take time."

She straightened her back and placed her hands on the ivory keys. She played the same tune an octave higher and changed the key. It was beautiful, not as sad but full of love and sentiment.

His lips nuzzled her neck. "I forget that you were a musician in another lifetime."

"Write the notes down, Jim. I think you have your next hit."

"Do you think there will be a next time?"

She laughed. "Of course. You guys don't know how to do anything else."

29
BON VOYAGE

1st WEEK OF FEBRUARY 1987, NEW YORK

From the moment Susan stepped into the elevator of the building where she lived after having visited Ron, she put her hands over her face. Karl took her hand when the elevator stopped. He opened the door to the apartment. Susan put her arms around Karl's waist and sobbed uncontrollably.

He placed his good arm around her shoulder and just let her cry. He, too, let his tears flow. They'd witnessed violence at its worst, and to top it all off, one of the shooters was still on the loose. He caressed her cheek. "Hey, we're fine, and Ron's going to be fine, you'll see."

She looked up at him, tears flooding her cheeks. "Do you really think Ron is going to make it?"

"I do."

Stefani and Niall arrived at her mother's house to say goodbye. No one knew when they would see them again.

"We brought lunch." She hugged her mother. "You okay?"

Susan sighed. "I will be once I leave."

"I know you will. You're a strong woman, Susan Michaels."

Michelle and Jim showed up and were surprised to see that Richard had returned. He didn't offer any information, so Karl asked if his "new" significant other had given birth.

Richard nervously responded. "She's fine, still waiting but I wanted to get back to see you guys off."

A small smile touched Karl's lips. "Thanks."

Vera dropped in to see her brother off as well.

Michelle and Vera helped set the table. Ronnie sat at the table with a frown on his face. He didn't know what was going on, but he knew it was serious. He'd been staying with Esmeralda in Los Angeles, and they had flown in, and now he was all ready to go on his trip with his mother and Karl, oblivious to what was happening around the family.

"Niall spoke with his mom a while ago," Stefani said. "The doctors finally think Dad will pull through, but there's a chance he may have some paralysis. One of the bullets might have caused some spinal cord damage."

Oh God, Karl thought, *a wheelchair? Ron James in a wheelchair?* Karl's eyes met Richard's and Jim's.

Karl's hands shook. Richard put his arm around Karl's shoulders.

"Come, let's get some real food into you. Ron's going to be fine," Richard said.

"What's wrong with Daddy? Where is he?" Ronnie asked.

Susan sat next to her son who was maturing too quickly. His hazel eyes expressed concern, and his brown hair shot out in all directions. He liked wearing his hair that way. Unruly. He was indeed the sum of both parents.

She smiled at him. "He's fine, just in the hospital for a procedure."

Ronnie wasn't easily fooled. "Stefani said something about a bullet."

"Stefani was talking about another patient in the hospital." She stroked his hair. "Your father is fine."

He turned back to his lunch. "He promised to take me to a baseball game."

Susan leaned down and kissed Ronnie's cheek. "He will, honey, when we get back from our vacation."

The child shook his head. *Not as clueless as you think, Mom.*

Karl and Susan picked at their food. Although they were surrounded by family and friends, they didn't hear a word that was spoken around them. Stefani served some cheesecake as Michelle and Vera poured coffee and passed the cups around. They sat on either side of Susan. Leslie was going to stay with Michelle. Julienne was just a taxicab ride or a walk away.

Vera took her hand. "You and my brother need to get out of here. Stay away as long as you need to. You know that we are all here for you. Just call us from time to time and let us know you are fine. Take care of yourselves. Love each other as much as you can. Life is short. We were all at death's door a few days ago and one of us hasn't crossed the threshold back into this world. Take care of my brother and 'nephew.' You're a strong woman, Susan. Don't let this shatter the Susan Michaels I met in college. Michelle and I are here for Leslie and Julienne. Leslie will need to go to Los Angeles at some point. Michelle and I will be with her."

Susan tightened her grip on Vera's hands and tried to smile. Michelle pulled her up out of her chair. "Come on, let's get you ready for your trip. You look like *merde*."

Susan had no choice but to laugh. Michelle was always around, to make her smile, laugh, forget her problems. She had done it repeatedly over the years.

"I don't know what I would do without you girls." Susan whispered. Tears threatened to spill.

She followed them to her bedroom. Michelle, the fashion diva, went through Susan's closet and pulled out a red sweater and black leather pants. She knew her friend's taste in clothing and more importantly, knew how Karl loved to see her friend dress. Only Susan knew about Michelle and Jim seeing each other again and couldn't ask how her week went in front of Vera.

Karl and the guys remained in the living room. Jim poured some Remy Martin into snifters and passed them around. He pulled a chair from the dining room table and sat facing Karl. He leaned forward holding his snifter in his hands, staring at the amber liquid. He looked up, sadness and concern in his eyes.

"You take care of yourself and Susan," Jim gave him a stern glare. "Take as long as you need to repair the pain. We'll always be here for each other. We'll stay with Eva until she decides what she wants to do and see what happens with Ron. Michelle and Vera will make sure that Leslie and Jules are fine."

Richard put his hand on Karl's shoulder. "Call us if you need anything. In the meantime, go, get out. Take some time with Susan, heal your bodies and make some babies."

Karl sobbed. It was good that his friends were supportive. Ron's fate was still in God's hands.

Damn, he needed to get away. He couldn't stand the pain in his heart for his friend, his family. Karl couldn't get to the airport fast enough.

Susan began looking through the mail that had accumulated before leaving. There was a thick envelope from her divorce attorney. In it was her settlement agreement and final judgment. She sadly looked them over. *How easy it was to dissolve a marriage! Ten years of a life.*

"Your father and I are officially divorced, Stef. What a fucking couple of weeks!"

Susan abruptly picked up her coat. "Let's go. I can't leave soon enough. Come on, honey."

"Mom, we're going on an airplane again?"

Susan kissed Ronnie's head. "Yes, baby, we are."

"Karl too?"

"Karl too."

Ronnie looked at Niall. "Are you Stefani's boyfriend now?"

Niall laughed. "What do you think?"

"I think you like her. You look at her funny."

Niall, who had never in his life been embarrassed by anyone, felt heat followed by the color red rise to his scalp. Karl couldn't help but laugh inwardly for the first time in days. He thought Ron would have guffawed.

Tearfully, Karl and Susan said goodbye to the friends they loved. Since the conversation about Richard's mistress's impending delivery was such public knowledge, Jim placed his arm around Michelle who started to cry. He didn't care anymore. Richard disrespected him twice in his lifetime and it was over. Michelle was his and would be until death parted them. He was willing to fight for her tooth and nail.

Richard pointed his index finger at Michelle. "You need to talk to your sons about this."

Daggers flew from Michelle's eyes. "Not as much as you."

♫

The limo carried Karl, Susan, Ronnie, and Esmeralda who was going to accompany them. Ronnie sat between Karl and Susan, his head leaned against Susan's arm and his eyes closed.

After the longest, most grueling hours of flight and travel time, Susan and Karl entered what would be their "new home" for the next year or two. A mansion on a private island near Moorea in the South Pacific.

Karl was glad to get away. His doctor in America contacted a friend in Papatee in case of an emergency. They waited patiently while their bodies healed. Their hearts would never heal.

30
A NEW RELATIONSHIP

2nd WEEK, FEBRUARY-MARCH 1987, NEW YORK & L.A.

Alex walked out of his father's room and sighed. Ashley saw him in the distance, and she went to greet him.

"I'm on call, Alex. I'm sorry. I have to eat in the cafeteria."

"I'm okay with that. They're beginning to know me by name there."

"I'm sure," she replied with a smile.

He carried their entrées on one tray while Ashley's tray held drinks and salads. He waited until she sat to slip into the chair across from her.

"I wanted to tell you that I was offered a job on the west coast and I'll be leaving the end of the week. Dr. Weinstein, who is an excellent cardiologist, will take over for me."

Alex looked at her, finding himself drowning under green eyes. "Where on the West Coast? My mom is moving my father back to his house."

"I'm going to Cedars in Los Angeles."

Her cheeks turned warm when he grinned. His eyes held hers and she timidly returned the smile.

"We'll be neighbors. My dad's house is in Holmby Hills," he said.

She explained that it was an excellent opportunity she couldn't pass up. She thought about how close they would be. *Could it be fate?* Time went by too quickly and she had to return to her patients.

Alex stood. "Can I call you when you get out to the West Coast?"

She sized him up cautiously. She didn't like what his presence did to her. She didn't want to be attracted to a man again, not for a long time. She didn't want to face the loss or end of a relationship. It hurt too damn much. She tried to shake the feelings he stirred in her. She really didn't want to give him her telephone number. Once she left the hospital and was in Los Angeles, it was going to be a new life for her.

Not knowing what possessed her, Ashley gave him her new telephone number. *He will never call.*

♫

For an entire month, he continued to pop into her mind from time to time. There was something about Alex. It wasn't the fact that he was a famous rock star's son; there was an animal magnetism that drew her.

She opened the door to her apartment as the telephone rang in the distance. She dropped her things on the couch.

"Hello?" she panted into the phone.

"Hi, is this a bad time?" Alex asked. She didn't have to ask who it was; she knew.

"No," she replied. "I was just getting in the door. How's your father?"

"The same," he said. "No improvement but my mother's moving him into his own home as soon as the doctors allow it."

"Sometimes that makes all the difference in the world."

He sighed. "Are you free for dinner?"

"Yes." *Too quick an answer. What is wrong with me?*

"Seven?"

She looked at the clock. It was 5:30. "Sure."

"Casual, nothing too fancy, okay with you?"

"Y-y-yes," she stammered.

"I'll pick you up."

She gave him her address. Nervously, she straightened the place a bit. She checked her fridge to see if she had anything to mix drinks with, then went to shower.

♫

Alex was right on time. He pulled up in his father's black Porsche, which he used for the time being. Ron was still not fully awake, but he was making some progress and responding to treatment. It was still touch-and-go.

Her heart stammered when she opened the door. He stood tall, wearing sunglasses in jeans and a blue shirt. He held a simple, white, calla lily in his hand.

"Welcome to California," he said, holding the flower out.

She took it from him as he leaned forward to kiss her cheek. "Thank you. Would you like to have something before we go?"

He shook his head. If he went inside, he might never leave. He wanted to devour her!

"Let me get my bag and put this in some water and we'll go."

They went to a restaurant with an oceanfront view in Santa Monica A candle at the table cast a soft glow on their faces. They picked their own lobster from a fish tank.

"Do you want a drink, or do you prefer wine?" he asked her. Unlike his father at that age, Alex was polished, well-bred and didn't lack for much.

"I'll have whatever you're having," she replied.

Identification in hand, Alex ordered a bottle of a local Chardonnay. He put his elbows on the table and clasped his hands together. He leaned his head on them and looked into her eyes.

"So," he said, "how have you been?"

"Fine. It's been a long month with the move and getting adjusted. The West Coast is way different from the New York/New Jersey area I'm used to. How's your father?"

Alex took a sip of his wine. "Holding his own. I'm glad you were transferred out here. I started to miss you around the hospital this past month. It's good to see you again."

She was speechless. No one ever found her silenced, not even...

He interrupted her musings while he looked at the menu. "Did you lose a family member to a heart attack?"

"Yes." She could talk about it now. "My fiancé."

He stopped reading the menu, and his head shot up. He put the menu down. "I'm sorry, Ashley. I didn't know. I didn't mean..."

She placed a warm hand on his. "Hush, apology accepted. Let's talk about something lighter. Someday, I'll tell you all about it, but not now. I'm not ready to talk about that yet. He died two days before our wedding."

He entwined their fingers together and held up her hand so that he could kiss her fingers. "I'm very sorry, Ashley. I hope I become so special in your life someday that you will trust me enough to tell me all your most intimate thoughts and secrets."

She nodded and a warm feeling flooded her body.

"Tell me how it was growing up with a rock star for a father," Ashley said. She tried to change the conversation and lighten the atmosphere up a bit.

"I didn't grow up with him."

"Really?"

"No, I told you that technically my last name is Edwards. Ron and my mother had a short relationship when they were teenagers. They grew up in an orphanage. When he turned eighteen, he set out to find his parents. They never saw each other again until I asked my mother about my father recently. We didn't know how he would react, but it turned out well. I hope he improves. I missed a lot by not knowing him, although my stepfather was a great man."

"I think that if he's lasted this long, Alex, he's going to make it. I can't tell you how well he will turn out, but I think he's a fighter."

"Are you in a hurry to get home?"

"No, I'm on the late shift tomorrow."

"Let's walk along the beach."

She took her shoes off and dangled them from her fingers. Alex casually took her hand. Ashley felt alive again. She let Alex put his arm around her shoulders.

"Are you cold?" he asked.

"No, but just keep your arm where it is. I like it."

He stopped and stared down at her. He placed his hand on her neck. "I'm going to kiss you, Doctor, and when I'm done, you'll have to check my pulse because it will be racing."

His lips softly touched hers. Her tongue met his in a sweltering passionate kiss. She placed her arms around his neck and felt herself floating in a wave of emotions. A long time ago, she dreamt of finding someone who would sweep her off her feet again. She moved closer, feeling the warmth of his body against hers.

His lips caressed her cheek. "Ashley, you are delicious."

He kissed her chin and returned to ravage her mouth again. He awoke feelings she hadn't felt in years. He caressed her cheek, and she sighed.

He smiled and caught her hand. "Where's your stethoscope, Doctor?"

"I didn't think I needed it. I can take your pulse, though."

His lips touched hers lightly once again. "Can you count that high?"

They continued their walk along the sand. They passed an open bar with music and he dragged her in.

"Come, let's have a nightcap." Alex claimed a small table facing the ocean and ordered a scotch on the rocks for himself and looked at Ashley.

172

"Long Island iced tea," she said.

He took her hand and led her onto the dance floor. It wasn't the music he loved, but their attraction to each other was strong. The events of the past few months were put on hold, while he felt human again. He liked everything about Ashley.

She danced way better than Madonna ever did when "Into the Groove" blared from the jukebox, followed by "Don't You Want Me?" by The Human League. An hour later, they still drank and carried on casual conversation.

"I didn't think you liked this music," she said fanning herself and gulping her drink.

"I don't as much as the harder stuff, but the place was here, and the music was calling out to me. You dance really well, Doc."

"You have some interesting moves yourself."

He laid some money on the table and took her hand.

"Shall we?"

When they arrived at her home, she opened the door and faced him. "You have a bit to drive. Why don't you let me make you some strong coffee?"

"No, I'm good," he said. Alex knew that if he went inside, he would stay the night. It was their first date; there was no way he was going to spoil it with Ashley. For the first time in his life, he realized that Ashley was *the* one.

31
RON GOES HOME

END OF MARCH 1987, NEW YORK TO L.A.

Ron's condition didn't change much over the next few weeks. Eva remained by his side, only leaving when Niall and Stefani came by so that she could return to the hotel to shower and change. One of the head doctors entered the room one morning while she read a book to Ron. Even if he was in a coma, she believed the sound of her voice could soothe.

There was a reflective look on his face, but it wasn't negative. "Mrs. Edwards," he said, softly. "I believe that we have done all we can for Mr. James. His wounds have healed. He is going to be slowly drawn out of his coma under medical supervision."

He sat on a chair. "It's time he went home. It may be good for him to be in familiar surroundings even if he is still unconscious."

Eva understood. It was time. She would make sure he was well taken care of and be there for him when he came out of the coma.

"Doctor, I know you've all done your best for him, and I agree that it's time for him to leave. I just have to ask you and his manager to help me make the medical arrangements necessary to transfer him to his home in Los Angeles. I will hire a nurse to be with us twenty-four hours a day. I just need to make some calls."

Richard entered the room after he received a call from the doctor to let him know that Ron was ready to go home. Eva, the doctor, and Richard worked together to get The Warriors' private plane with a nurse on board ready to fly Ron to Los Angeles. An hour later, an ambulance carrying Ron and Eva was on its way to Teterboro Airport. The twins, Niall, and Stefani followed in a limousine. The Warriors' plane took off headed for Los Angeles.

Eva made sure that Ron was comfortable and moved to the front of the plane to be with her son, Stefani, and her two daughters. They had been neglected for weeks.

The twins were in awe of the private jet. "This is so cool," Anneliese said as she tried every seat until she found herself a home on a huge leather recliner. She allowed it to envelope her while the plane took off.

She unsnapped her seatbelt as soon as she could. Niall looked at his favorite sister. She was dressed in black Adidas high-top sneakers with matching leg warmers over charcoal gray sweats and hoodie with a black turtleneck. She crossed her ankles and pushed the recliner back. "Shit, this is heavenly. Have to make sure I marry a rock star." She closed her eyes and sighed. She suddenly jumped back up.

"Have you guys met this doctor that Alex had dinner with at the hospital?" she asked.

Anneke rolled her eyes and looked at Stefani and Niall. "She just can't keep quiet, can she?"

Stefani laughed. "I saw her once or twice."

"He was totally into her," Anneliese added, studying her newly polished nails.

Niall slipped off his shoes and placed his feet up on his sister's footrest. He held Stefani's hand. "Didn't Mom teach you not to gossip?" he asked.

"This is not gossip. This is a family conversation," Anneliese said. "I could tell he liked her. Why do you think he went out to L.A. in such a hurry? I heard the nurses say she was moving out to the West Coast. Couldn't fool me, that guy."

Niall and Stefani sat on a love seat that faced two big leather recliners. Eva sat a few feet behind them. Her feet were propped up, and although she wanted to share some time with her children, exhaustion took over, and she succumbed to a much-needed deep sleep.

The flight attendant brought the girls soft drinks and some chips. Niall and Stefani settled for a glass of Merlot. Eventually, Niall turned the lights off and pushed the back of the love seat so that it turned into a bed. He searched the overhead compartment for some blankets and threw one to the twins before he lay beside Stefani. He slipped his arm over her waist and let sleep take over.

32
BACK IN LOS ANGELES

END OF MARCH 1987, LOS ANGELES

Stefani moved into her mother's house in Los Angeles. Anneliese and Anneke lived with Alex and Niall in Ron's huge mansion that he bought after the split with Susan. They looked forward to going to Stefani's house for dinner and to meeting Ashley. It was time. They were all taking it easy and trying to lie low while Ron was still in such a delicate state.

Stefani cooked dinner for them. She didn't want to "throw a party." Not yet. Still, the girls and Stefani wanted to meet Ashley formally. Stefani put together some pasta with sausages and meatballs on the side, a huge salad and garlic bread. She called Niall to come and pick some food up for Eva.

He still hadn't showered or gotten ready, but he went as soon as she called. He was becoming a real fool around Stefani. He couldn't get enough of her. He was getting ready to leave the U.S. for the meeting he had with Robert Turpin, Interpol bigwig, and he still hadn't told her. He had thought he would be gone a year ago, but he rationalized these jobs required a great deal of background checks. Then, his heart lurched. *What if my association with Ron James is the delay—I mean his past and all, and now this shooting?* Niall didn't know what offer awaited him, just that Turpin had put him off a whole year and then just a couple of days ago, he'd called again. He was in the top five of his class in criminology, managing long-distance correspondence course work. He was a natural. *I would like to be able to help catch the fugitive responsible for assassinating Mike and Vlad.*

Niall wanted the chance to find the person or persons still out there. Perhaps get a medal of honor, which didn't matter to him in the least, and then retire from his profession to move on with Stefani in his life if that was possible.

He was in a pair of jeans torn at the knees, a plain black t-shirt with the sleeves cut off, his muscles and tattoos on display, and flip flops. When she answered the door, he rolled his eyes. "Don't do this to me,

Stefani."

She wore tight, cut-off shorts and a white tank top that was transparent. She was barefoot with bright red toenails. Her hair was up but disheveled, and she had that look as if she needed it badly. She smiled innocently up at him, and he went in and slammed the door behind him. He took her face in both his hands and hungrily kissed her. He picked her up in his arms. His eyes met hers as he rushed into the first bedroom he found.

"The waiting game is over. I really want you too badly not to make love to you. We could have died that night too. I don't want to leave this earth without having you."

Stefani allowed herself to be pulled into his gaze. Her heart still pounded like that of a child on Christmas morning when she saw him.

His lips touched hers softly; she had to open her eyes to make sure he was still there. If butterfly kisses existed, then she had just been a recipient of one. Her body ignited with a strong flame that rushed through her blood. He laid her on the bed and slipped the tank above her head. Her fingers quickly tugged at his t-shirt and she caressed his warm chest. Her fingers fumbled lower to pop open the button of his jeans and unzip them.

He pulled away so that he could tear his clothes off hurriedly, and he slid the shorts over her hips. His hands roamed over her back and her chest. He lowered his lips so that he could kiss her breasts and lick her nipples. Her body responded to every caress. His lips and tongue travelled the length of her. She moved to accommodate every stroke of his tongue. His teeth bit into the soft flesh of her inner thigh and she moaned under his expert tongue which quickly brought her to an earth-shattering orgasm. He moved up on the bed so that they were facing each other sideways and kissed her nose and her cheeks. He took her leg and threw it over his hip then moved his body up so that he could glide inside her. She gasped and he silenced her with his mouth, allowing his tongue to dance fiercely inside her mouth in search of hers. He bit her lower lip as he plunged into her again and again, bringing her to another orgasm and finally to his own violent shudder.

He pulled his head back savoring the moment and her tongue danced circles on his neck. She bit him softly, making him loose control of himself, of who he was.

"Damn you, Stefani," he groaned loudly. He crushed her body against his and he rolled onto his back, pulling her with him. His eyes captured hers and he reached out to grasp her hips and he swayed them toward him and away from him as he became hard again. She tossed her head back and pushed him deep, crying out his name. She could feel every inch of him inside her. She looked at him for a few moments and then laid her cheek on his chest. She closed her eyes and wanted to let delicious sleep embrace her, but she had dinner to finish.

She turned her face up to Niall and grinned. "What was that all about?"

"You should never answer the door for me in that state. You drive me crazy, Stefani. You have no idea. I just broke my promise to your father. You were so worth the wait and the risk."

He dressed hurriedly and picked up the basket she had prepared for his mom. She walked him to the door in her underwear and tank top. He turned to kiss her. "I'll see you in a bit."

♪

Niall got into the car and drove away. His eyebrows furrowed; distress hardened his features. Ron's house wasn't far from Susan's. Niall stopped at a red light and threw his head back on the headrest. His thoughts ran a hundred miles an hour. He sighed. *I am so screwed.*

Alex was leaving to pick up Ashley as Niall pulled into the driveway. "The gals are almost ready. I'll meet you there."

Niall nodded silently. Alex opened the basket of food and peered inside. "Smells delicious. The kid can cook."

Alex noticed Niall's look. His distraction. "You okay? Did you guys have a fight?"

Niall didn't answer for a long moment. "What?"

"Did you guys have a fight?"

"Stefani and me? No, why the hell would you ask that? I just came from there."

"Your mind seems far away."

Niall held the doorknob to the front door and started into the house. "I have a lot on my mind. We'll talk later."

Eva was in the kitchen when Niall walked in. He kissed her cheek.

"Stefani sent you this. I'm running late. Are the twins ready?"

"Almost."

"Yeah, I know, their 'almost' means an hour," he said, trying to shake the feeling of discomfort.

Eva walked up to him and pushed his hair back. "You okay?"

He rolled his eyes. *Why is everyone asking if I'm okay?* "Yes, I'm fine."

Eva opened the basket and the smell of food filled the kitchen. She took Niall's chin in her hand and turned his face so that their eyes met. "Do you know what I think, Niall? I think you loved your lifestyle, and I think you've fallen in love and have no idea how to handle it. You never see love coming when it suddenly hits you. Are mother's always right or not?"

He looked at his mother and bit his bottom lip. He remained silent.

"I have to shower and get ready."

"Am I right?"

He sighed. "Are you ever wrong?"

"Don't fight it Niall, because it's the best feeling in the world."

He nodded and left to shower and change.

♫

When he returned, his mother was back in the room, reading to Ron. He went in search of his sisters.

The fraternal twins' personalities were polar opposites. Anneke was elegant; she wore jeans and a white ruffled blouse with white ballet flats. She styled her hair in a straight, angled bob and accessorized with diamond studs in her ears. Anneliese, on the other hand, fashioned the looks of the times. She was into the whole "black lace and leggings under a tight black skirt" look. She had long and layered wild light brown hair with blonde highlights and wore hoop earrings accompanied by a diamond in a second hole in each ear.

Anneliese whistled as Niall walked down the long, spiral staircase to get them. "Wow, don't you look sexy!"

He smiled at his favorite of the two. "What do you know about sexy?"

"Hmph!" she replied. "I read plenty."

Indeed, he was the epitome of sex. He wore jeans with a white cotton button-down shirt, sleeves rolled up casually. His hair was pulled back in his signature ponytail, giving him a neat appearance despite the ever-present small gold hoop nestled between two diamond studs in his left ear. His wrists were adorned as well as several chains and leather necklaces with a wild array of pendants hanging from his neck.

Living in California now for quite a while tanned his body to a light, golden color.

"Come on, ladies and don't get used to having me as chauffeur. You need to learn to drive."

"Why should we? We have you and Alex," Anneliese said.

"Because you'll get your own car, then."

She clapped her hands. "Do I get a red Ferrari like Karl's?"

"Fat chance," he replied, laughing.

"I can get myself a 'sugar daddy' and save myself the drama of falling in love." She snickered.

♫

Stefani let Niall and his sisters in. She was dressed in a simple short black skirt with a black tank top and flat, gold flip flops that showed off her tanned legs and red toenails.

When Niall kissed her, the effect to their flesh touching, even in a simple kiss overwhelmed Stefani. Damn, they had just had mind-blowing sex a few hours ago, and she was ready to make love to him again. *Could it be possible?*

As if reading her thoughts, he smiled a crooked smile and leaned over to whisper in her ear. "I know, liebling, I'm feeling the same thing."

Her heart pounded. *He called me "liebling", same thing Karl calls my mother.* It made her all gooey inside. She hesitated a moment before turning her attention to the captivating teenagers.

Stefani put her arm around Niall's and frowned. "Are you sure these girls are twins?"

"That's what Mom says. I think she gave birth to one and found the other on the way home from the hospital in a garbage can and felt sorry for her. Care to guess which one she found?" he said, teasingly.

Stefani reached out and kissed each twin on the cheek. "Don't worry, ladies. I love you both the same.

"I didn't want this to be too formal, so can we do the patio?" Stefani asked.

"Sounds good to me," Niall said, holding several bottles of wine. "It smells wonderful, where do you want these?"

"Outside."

Niall went to the tiki bar and took out several wine glasses. He couldn't find an opener, so he entered the house and went to the kitchen. He found one in a drawer, and when he turned to go back outside, Stefani entered the kitchen. She put the garlic bread in the oven to warm. Niall took her hand, and he kissed her ravenously. His fingers stroked her bare arms.

She pulled him closer and ran her tongue over his neck. "And if you stay the night, I promise to run my tongue over each and every one of those little snakes that surround your belly button and try to bite their heads off."

He took a deep breath, his hand slithering over her derrière. "And I will lick and bite every inch of you, Blondie, and do unthinkable, luscious things to your body. I promise to drive you insane tonight because I am beginning to question my sanity around you."

Alex arrived with Ashley in tow and introductions were made. The twins were impressed by the fact that Ashley was such a young and gorgeous doctor.

"You guys have beautiful names," Ashley said as she kissed each twin on the cheek. She handed Stefani a bunch of flowers and a bottle of wine.

Anneliese said, "I know, but since I've been in the States, everyone wants to 'Americanize' my name. God knows they never pronounce it right. You can't imagine what I've been called."

Niall took the bottle from Ashley and read the label. "Great wine to go with this dinner. I like you already. What do you think we should call Anneliese from now on?"

Ashley smiled. "Well, we don't have to totally change it, and she is rather adorable. I would call her 'Annie'."

Alex nodded. "I like that, Annie. You?"

"I guess I will be Annie from now on." She shrugged.

Ashley turned to Anneke. "I bet yours is even more butchered by Americans."

Anneke nodded. "Brutally."

"Would you like us to pick a nickname for you?"

"I already have. I'm Niki Edwards."

"Awesome move, little sister," Alex said.

Dinner was delightful, and they all got to know one another as the wine flowed.

Alex sat back in his chair and rubbed his stomach. "I've heard that Susan couldn't boil water 'til very recently, but Stefani you knocked it out of the park today."

Niall took Stefani's hand and brought it up to his lips. "A good cook..." He looked around to make sure the twins were out of the room. "...and great sex, what else could a man want?"

Stefani punched him in the arm affectionately.

Alex and Ashley promised to take the twins back home because Alex had to pass Ron's house to take Ashley home. They all went into the game room to play pool for a bit. Alex mixed drinks while he and Ashley seemed to win one game and lose another to Stefani and Niall. The girls treated themselves to videos on MTV and Warriors' concerts.

After they left, Stefani began to put the dishes into the dishwasher and Niall took her hand. "I'll help you with that tomorrow."

♬

The aroma of fresh coffee woke Niall. Sunlight filtered through the curtains. He stretched his arm out; he was alone. He stood and stretched. He showered and entered the kitchen with just a towel wrapped around him. He had no idea where his clothes were. They weren't strewn around the game room where he left them the night before. Of course, the shirt was of no use to him anymore. He grinned remembering the sound of buttons popping and hitting the marble floor.

Stefani stood at the counter, sipping from a cup of coffee and reading the *L.A. Times*. He walked up behind her and slipped his hands under her camisole. He took a deep breath and kissed the back of her neck which was still damp from the morning shower. She poured him some coffee. She kissed him, long and hard. He licked his lips as the taste of her tongue mingled with the coffee dulled his senses. *Damn her! What is it about Stefani James?* Could it actually be love that he was feeling?

"Good morning, sleep well?" he asked.

"Of course, I did." Her voice was a whisper and she bit his earlobe softly.

He took her hand and sat on the stool beside her. "Stefani, I need to talk to you about something I haven't discussed with anyone else. Do you think you can keep your hands to yourself for a few minutes?"

She looked at him skeptically. He appeared worried, and concern flashed across his features. He drew his eyebrows together and brought her hand to his lips. He took each of her fingers and put them into his mouth one by one.

"If you're trying to have a serious conversation with me, Niall, that's not going to work. Every time you lick one of my fingers, do you want to know exactly where I feel that delicious tongue of yours?"

He laughed, couldn't help it. He leaned over and kissed her cheek. "I don't know what you've done to me."

She got up. "I'll start breakfast, and you can talk."

He watched her back as she faced the stove. "You've got a great ass, and you are not letting me concentrate on what I have to say in that pair of white lace panties. Maybe we should get dressed before we can have a serious conversation."

Stefani stepped out of the panties and walked toward him. She threw them aside and put her arms around his neck. "If they are distracting you, I can always take them off while I make breakfast, or maybe we could make love before we get dressed, and *then* have a serious conversation."

"Great idea," he said, smiling.

♫

Afterwards, they sat at the kitchen counter having breakfast. "I've been asked to go and interview at the Interpol office in Lyon, France. If I'm offered a job or internship, I am going to take it."

Her heart thumped at his statement. "I thought you were considering heading security for The Warriors?"

"I would like nothing more but, in the meantime, if I can work for Interpol and have access to certain records, I may be able to help find this other assassin. If I'm offered the job, I want you to come live with me in France." His lips touched hers lightly.

"I'll come to you as soon as my father gets out of the coma and is up and around. I need to stay here. Your mother is all alone."

He kissed her, allowing his tongue to pierce her lips and he whispered, "I love you Stefani, and I've never loved any woman before."

"And I love you too, Niall Edwards."

33
RON'S REALITY

APRIL 1987, LOS ANGELES

Eva cared for Ron, gave him sponge baths, moved him around on the bed to prevent bed sores. She fed him through the feeding tube inserted into his stomach.

A week after their arrival in Los Angeles, the doctors eased Ron out of the coma, and he was put under sedation for several more days.

Eva called Karl because she knew he would want to be present. His retreat would still be there.

It took some time for the message to get to Karl and Susan that the doctors were planning to bring Ron out of his coma. They caught the next flight back.

Eva sat on the king bed beside Ron where she spent her days. She never left his side except to shower. She ate her meals in the room and read to him. Her pregnancy began to show, so she told her children that she was pregnant. Neither Alex nor Niall were happy about the announcement, but the twins were thrilled.

Ron remained in a semi-conscious state for almost two months. His vital signs were normal, yet only time would tell when or if he would make a full recovery.

Eva read to Ron one afternoon when she felt the baby move strongly. Eva took Ron's hand and placed it over her stomach. The tiny child moved again as if sensing the touch of a parent. Eva's hand lay softly over his. She felt Ron's fingers twitch. For a split second, she thought she imagined it, but his fingers wiggled again.

She shifted her position so that she lay beside him. She threw her arm around his chest and laid her cheek against his shoulder. Her lips kissed the warm skin, and her eyes became heavy with sleep. A slight movement beside her woke her. Her hands shook, and the first thing she did was touch her crucifix. *Please help me cope with this situation.*

When she looked at Ron, azure eyes focused on her and recognition brought a smile to his lips. *Shit,* he thought, *I am dead and we both ended up in Hell.* He looked at her tear-filled eyes. *Well, at least I'm in good* company.

He felt weak and didn't even know how he got where he was. He tried to move, to get up, but he couldn't! He tried to reach out to touch Eva's cheek, but his arm refused to take any orders from his brain. It fell lifeless beside him.

He felt a slight twinge in his chest. He tried to remember what happened. His hand lay on his chest. *Is blood gushing out of my chest? Why is a warm trickling fluid slipping through my fingers? Is that the smell of gunpowder?* He closed his eyes, exhausted. He couldn't remember! *Tomorrow, I'll remember tomorrow.*

Eva knelt on the bed beside him and took his hand in hers. She smiled down at him, crying.

He could barely find his voice, but he smiled and whispered, "Sister, are we in Hell?"

She cried even harder. "No, my darling, we're still on Earth."

"What happened? How long have I been like this?" he asked.

Eva caressed his cheek and bent down to kiss his dry, chapped lips. "We'll talk later." She stood and called out to her sons, "Alex! Please get the nurse; your father is awake."

Alex hesitated between going to get the nurse or seeing his father. He opted for the nurse. Ron's vital signs were normal. It appeared that he was out of the woods.

After the nurse left, he looked at Eva. "What happened? What day is it?"

Eva smiled down at him. "Hush, there's plenty of time for that. You need to begin getting your strength back. You have been in a medically induced coma for a bit and then under sedation. Because of your past history with drugs, the doctors have been weaning you out of it as safely as possible."

His eyes were skeptical and disoriented. "How long have I been this way?"

"Almost two months since we got back to L.A., two in New York," she replied, sighing and pulling the covers a bit lower.

"I want to get up."

Eva nodded. "Not right now. The doctor is on his way. You have a feeding tube, and it has to be removed."

Ron looked away. His eyes filled with tears. Weakness set in and his eyes fluttered shut. "What's wrong with me, Eva?"

She walked around the bed. "Hush, Ron." She reached out and brushed his tears away.

The nurse returned with a doctor following behind her. "Mr. James, Dr. Horne is going to check you."

During the next few hours, Ron was sedated slightly again so that the doctor could remove the PEG feeding tube. He left Eva with instructions that Ron could begin to have some broth and liquids; he needed to sit up and begin his recovery. The doctor wanted him out of bed the following day.

♫

Alex called Stefani immediately after the doctor left to let her know their father was awake. He didn't go into the bedroom, preferring to give his parents some time alone. From the sounds coming out of the room, Ron wasn't doing too well.

Niall joined him in the den. "What's all the commotion about?"

"Dad's awake," he replied.

"Did you call Stefani?"

"Yes, I caught her as she was leaving. She's meeting us here for lunch."

Niall stood at the French doors that led to the patio and gazed outside. He crossed his arms in front of him. He couldn't really make out what they were saying, but the nurse that had been tending to Ron stomped out of the room in a huff. Niall's mind was far away, and his thoughts distracted all common sense. Ron was a nice guy, and he was Alex's father, but Niall wasn't too sure about a relationship with Eva. It pissed him off that his mother got pregnant, not that she had slept with Ron; that was her prerogative. He knew his parents had not been bed partners for years, since his Dad's stroke. His mother was a beautiful woman and way too young to be the mother of four grown children and a widow. Ron left Eva once before. With his track record and well-known lifestyle, Niall didn't think this child was going to make things any better.

Alex handed Niall a glass of wine. "I know what you're thinking."

"She deserves more than this."

"I know she does. Niall, he may be my father, but I've barely met him. I won't let him hurt Mom."

Niall sipped his wine and continued to look out onto the patio. Stefani entered the den. She stood in all her five-foot-nine glory with four-inch heeled red sandals and crimson toes. Dressed in skin-tight faded jeans and a red long-sleeved sweater that barely brushed the waistline. Her hair was up and messy. She wore large gold hoops in her ears. Her Gucci sunglasses were propped on top of her head. Niall held his breath and felt a stir in his pants. She overwhelmed the space she occupied with her beauty and figure. The scent of Miss Dior filled the room. Stefani could be elegant and trashy at the same time, a perfect combination for Niall's taste. She kissed him causing him to groan inwardly. She unnerved him to pieces. He was shit in her presence. When did that happen?

"He's awake?" she asked.

"Yes, but we've left them alone for a bit. I think he would want a moment alone with my mom," Alex said softly.

Stefani pushed past Alex and Niall. "Fuck him; he has no idea what we've been through." She opened the door and stomped into the bedroom.

Niall's and Alex's eyes met. They hoped Ron would eventually do the right thing and make a commitment to Eva so that they weren't forced to step in. Ron could do no wrong in Stefani's eyes.

Ron was propped up on several pillows. He was pale and weak, but he gave his daughter a huge smile. Eva was on the telephone with a doctor. Stefani practically ran to her father's side and kissed his cheek. Her eyes filled with tears and she sat on the bed beside him, legs crossed under her.

Ron looked at his daughter. *When did she turn into such a beautiful, young woman?* She inherited her coloring from him, but she was gorgeous like her mother. Perfect features, dazzling smile that could conquer the heart of any man. No wonder Niall was out of sorts with himself lately. Ron chuckled to himself.

"What are you laughing at?" Stefani asked.

"Just looking at you and seeing how much you have grown and matured, admiring my daughter, I guess. I'm getting old Stefani, don't pay me any mind."

"I'm so sorry for getting mad at you before the concert when you threatened Niall with what you were going to do to him if he hurt me. I know you meant well."

"I meant every word I said and still mean it. I don't regret saying it, and I don't care if you get mad. I'm here to protect you. I've been like him. I know the drill, and it won't fly with my daughter; you hear?"

She gave him a thumbs up. "I hear you loud and clear. Are you in pain?"

He shook his head. "Not much. I love you so much, Stefani," he whispered with tears in his eyes. She put her arms around him carefully.

When she let go and looked at him, tears dotted her cheeks. "I was so afraid. I thought I would lose you."

"Not yet; still here."

"Thank God," Karl's voice came from the doorway. He strode to the bed and hugged the man he considered a brother.

Susan came behind him, holding Ronnie by the hand. She kissed his cheek.

Ronnie frowned and said, "Dad, you look awful."

Nobody in the room could keep from laughing.

After a short visit, Ron insisted that Karl and Susan go back to their vacation. Eva informed them that she would notify them immediately if there was any news.

♫

The nurse came in early the following morning and checked her patient. It was time to get him moving again. She made certain notations on her patient's chart. "I'll be right back, Mr. James."

A few minutes later, she returned with a wheelchair. "I want to get you out of bed, Mr. James. You've been confined too long."

Ron laughed. "You better put that thing away. I'm going to get up on my own." When Ron tried to move his legs, they didn't respond.

His eyes shot up at Eva. "What's going on?" he asked, his voice a frantic whisper.

Eva took his hand. "There is a bit of shock to your spinal cord, not a lot, but enough to..."

Ron closed his eyes. "No, that's not acceptable." He looked at the nurse, "Please leave us for a moment."

"Mr. James, I have to make sure you get out of bed."

Ron's eyes turned dark. "What is your name?" he asked the nurse.

"Marian," she replied.

"Well, Marian, I'm asking you in a very nice way to please leave and give me a moment alone with Eva. If I have to say it again, I'm not going to be so fucking nice, and please close the door on your way out."

He waited until she was gone and turned to Eva. He reached out and touched her crucifix. "You have to help me. You have always been my guardian angel. You have a direct connection to Him I don't have. He listens to you."

She kissed his cheek. "He listens to you too, Ron."

"I have too much other shit to resolve with Him before He'll give me the time of day."

"Do you believe He has the power to help you?"

Ron's eyes filled with tears. "I certainly don't have it."

"Can you trust Him?"

"I don't have a choice, Eva. Do I?"

"Sometimes He tries to get our attention, and when He doesn't get it, He has to resort to extreme measures. How many times have you been in danger? Yet, here you are. You weren't an abortion because you were meant to be here. You were at the orphanage because someone decided to give you life, and all you've done is feel sorry for yourself and turn to alcohol, sex, drugs, whatever it took to ease the anger and pain. You are here for a reason. You have three amazing children. You married a woman who put up with you and whom you abused. Now you have me. I will not leave you, whether you ever walk again or not. I love you, and I will never leave your side. If you want to walk again, you have to put your faith and trust in Him, and He will give me the tools that I will need to help you walk again. Don't harden your heart, Ron; you've run out of options, you can't do this on your own. You have to do this for your children, for me, and for the new baby that is growing inside me. Someone's giving you another chance to make up for all the wrong you've done, so don't waste it away. It may be your last chance."

Ron covered his face with his hands and sobbed. "Oh, God."

34
GRAND ENTRANCES

JUNE-SEPTEMBER 1987, NEW YORK & L.A.

Six months to the date of her father's death, Michaela Antonia Evans came into the world. Leslie made sure she stayed in New York to be with Julienne when she gave birth. She was a beautiful baby who would never know the great man that died on a stage floor doing what he loved best.

Julienne remained stoic after her initial emotional upheaval. She confided to Leslie, "I'll never love again. Mike was it for me." She caressed her daughter's head. "This new relationship with my child will be my world. I'll make sure she knows about her father. All of you can help keep his memory alive in this child. Will you be her godmother?"

Stunned, Leslie could only nod.

"Good. My brother will be her godfather. She will be loved."

Outside the hospital Leslie rubbed her own abdomen. *Neither will you know Vlad, my little love, but I'll tell you all about your father, and I'll take you to see his Northern Lights. You were his last gift to me. I still love him so.* She could not stop more tears from flowing, but she determined to go back to L.A. immediately after Michaela's baptism.

♫

Eva made it her mission to make sure that Ron received the best therapy possible in order to get him to walk again. She contacted specialists who confirmed that Ron's spine was not damaged, and as a result, the cause of his paralysis was undetermined.

She entered the room and a contraction took her by surprise.

"Alex, call the midwife. Her telephone number is on the refrigerator and help me get Ron into the bedroom. I want him there."

Ron held Eva's hand and cried while she gave birth. He felt so helpless. Two hours later, Monique James came into the world. Eva kissed her third daughter and she placed her gently on Ron's lap. He looked at her, and his tears stopped. *Fuck, a girl who looks just like*

Stefani and Alex! Poor Stefani, what have I done to her! He couldn't help but smile at the tiny creature that was trying to focus her light eyes on him. She looked straight into his heart. Eva purposely named her after Ron's mother; she wouldn't have it any other way.

Eva refused to let Ron feel pity for himself. She bathed their daughter and handed him the baby bottle so that he could feed her when she didn't breast feed her. Eva taught him how to burp a baby. She waited until Monique was soiled and took his wheelchair to the crib and handed him a diaper. She taught him how to change her, how to bathe her. She kept his mind busy. She asked him to sing to her. Every night, Eva would put Monique on his stomach as he lay in bed and asked him to rock her to sleep. They sang German lullabies to the infant.

For the next six months, Eva set aside time every day to massage and exercise his legs and bathe him. Every afternoon, after lunch, she helped him stand as best as he could so that she could get him into a jacuzzi. She'd had a ramp built so that all he had to do was stand for a mere second from the chair supported by her shoulders and the platform of the jacuzzi.

It was a daily ritual he hated. Made him feel helpless, but Eva didn't waver when it came time to care for him.

His hand reached out to hers, and he pulled her close so that he could kiss her softly. He appreciated everything she did for him. It if hadn't been for Eva, he was sure he would have died.

♫

Leslie's due date was only weeks after Eva's. She was still staying with Michelle who had convinced her to wait until her child arrived to return to California, just in case there were complications. Leslie was thankful she had reached a point where she was confident Vlad's child would be born. She got up one morning, and Michelle waited for her to have breakfast. Leslie was still beautiful, but sadness masked her features. She remained quiet and reserved. She stayed home during her entire pregnancy with the exception of visiting Julienne after Michaela was born and going to her goddaughter's christening. She didn't need to work since she inherited Vlad's estate. She and her baby would be well provided for their entire lives, but she missed his crazy, Russian self. He brought her back to life. Made her laugh, taught her what making love was really about and not the violence she had been subjected to at an early age.

"I think we should ask your sister to come back for the birth, don't you?" Michelle asked.

Leslie nodded. "I think they need the time away, but I'd like her to be here. I guess, she'll meet her niece or nephew when she returns."

"Well, you have me. I will be with you when the time comes."

"You have been so supportive. Thank you, Michelle. I'm glad you told me about losing a child. You truly understood my fear." She caressed her protruding abdomen. "This little one is Vlad's legacy." Tears threatened to spill again. She swiped them away angrily.

"Have you thought of names?" Michelle asked, trying to cheer the young woman.

"If it's a girl, Tiana for Vlad's grandmother and Vladimir for a boy. I would never name him anything else."

♬

Michelle called Susan and had to relay the message a half dozen times. When Susan got Michelle's message, she was a little shocked at the vehemence of Michelle's words.

"I don't care what you're doing. Drop everything and get home. I love Leslie, but she wants you. You might not get back in time. She is ready to pop. Move your ass."

Susan kissed Karl. "Gotta go, babe. Be back as soon as I can."

He read the communique and laughed aloud, picturing Michelle's chastising face.

♬

Susan got back to New York five days later, with only two days to spare.

A week after Michelle called Leslie's sister, Vladimir Vavilov, Junior came into the world without Vlad being present to witness the birth of his son but with a mother who was determined to tell her son everything about the man who was his father.

35
LONG-AWAITED WEDDING

JANUARY 1988, MOOREA

Karl opened his eyes and watched Susan sleep. Her head was on his chest and her arm was draped around his hip, the weight and warmth of her arm close to his family jewels. He always wanted her in the morning, and it was hard to decide whether to wake her or let her sleep; it was a tough choice but usually, his roaming hands won. Her eyes opened and she moaned.

"Mmm," he whispered as he kissed her neck. "Can I lick you awake?"

She lost her breath and she climbed on top of him. "You can, but I'm doing the licking first," she said so softly her voice sounded like a cool breeze in the spring. She kissed his earlobe, pulling on the skin ever so lightly with her teeth. She trailed a line of soft kisses down his chest and moved lower. He threw his head back and moaned as his hips moved, wanting more, expecting more. Her lips closed around him and he gasped out her name. Her tongue teased him and when she could feel his orgasm nearing, she stopped and allowed him to slide into her body. His hands reached up to pull her against him, his fingers clutching her hips, biting her lower lip. She moved expertly, quickly bringing them to earth-shattering heights.

She collapsed over him and buried her face in his neck.

"I want to make you my wife, liebling. Let's get married, here, in this tropical paradise. Just you and me," he said.

"I would love that..." she agreed.

The arrangements began; the service would be a traditional Tahitian style ceremony in Moorea.

♫

Susan followed local village women on the morning of her wedding to a ceremonial hut. A large claw-foot porcelain tub sat in the center of the room. The scent of gardenias filled the air, and steam rose from the hot water. Two older women helped her remove her clothes and get into the tub. They handed her a bar of gardenia scented soap. Susan slipped the soap over her shoulders and arms. The hot water made her sleepy and relaxed. One of the women smiled at Susan and softly tipped the bride's head back to wash her long, black hair. They handed her a huge, warm white towel so that she could step out of the water. Her hair was brushed until it dried naturally and gleamed in the light. She was then led to a darkened room where she was massaged with warm fragrant oils that complimented the scent of tropical flowers. She slipped a white native wedding dress over her naked body.

At the same time, Karl was led to a royal floating house where his upper body was temporarily tattooed using a pen as was the custom. He dressed in soft white pants and a white traditional shirt that remained opened, to show off his chest and the fancy handiwork of the tattoos. He was barefoot.

Susan arrived at a nearby beach in a canoe. The white sand felt like warm sugar under her feet. The women helped her out and escorted Susan to the ceremonial grounds where Karl waited with the native priest. Neither could take their eyes away from the other. Their love was apparent to all those that stood on the beach. The ceremony began, translated by an interpreter. The native priest joined Karl and Susan's hands with a coconut leaf and blessed them by pouring seawater from a large conch shell for unity in the marriage. Once that portion of the ceremony ended, two native women placed leis of plumeria, frangipani, and yellow hibiscus around the bride's and groom's necks. Next, a "hei" made from the same flowers crowned their heads. The priest took the rings, two plain gold bands and uttered some words over them. He handed the smaller one to Karl and asked him to repeat his words in English as Karl placed the ring on Susan's finger. There were tears in their eyes by the time it was Susan's turn to place the ring on Karl's finger. They kissed, sealing their vows and commitment to each other until death parted them. The sun began to set on the horizon and the sky turned into fiery shades of crimson, coral, yellow, and purple. It was Shangri-La.

A boat driven by a native carried them to a bungalow that rested on stilts out on the water. Karl took his shirt off and picked Susan up in his arms to carry her to the bed which had been filled with pink rose petals, and he dropped her in the middle of the bed.

"You are finally all mine," he said, unbuttoning his pants.

His bandages were long gone, and he felt like himself away from the madness. Time and distance healed him.

♫

A month later, they sat in front of a doctor who confirmed Susan's pregnancy with twins. As Susan left the doctors' office, she protested, "I looked like an elephant with Ronnie; I'm going to be the size of two elephants!"

Karl kissed her lips softly. "One or two elephants, I will still love you. You see, liebling? You were so upset about not getting pregnant and now we've got two."

She looked up at him and smiled. "Thank God I don't have to perform anymore!"

Kiefer and Veronica Engels named after Karl's late parents came into the world screaming at the top of their lungs, flailing legs and arms in the air.

♫

Karl opened his eyes and looked out over the South Pacific Ocean outside the master bedroom. He stretched and got up from the bed. Susan stirred, and he pulled the covers over her bare shoulder. He quietly went to the kitchen to make some coffee and sat on the patio in the paradise he now called home going through his mail, which didn't come but once every two weeks in the remote area where he built a king's mansion. The entire family was still asleep. He put on round, wire-rimmed glasses and began to open envelopes.

The stack of mail contained more than a dozen royalty checks. There was no way to stop the wealth from pouring in. The fruits of his long, hard labor had paid off so well, it couldn't help but accumulate. Long way from Hamburg, the orphanage, poverty, and hunger.

Life was ironic, though. He remembered a time when all his shoes had holes in them. Now that he had all the money in the world, he walked around his house for days barefoot. Man was such an ungrateful animal.

He sifted through the envelopes, throwing the royalty checks into a wicker basket. He came upon an envelope that looked like an invitation. Curiously, he opened it. Richard Stone's invitation for a long weekend in France to celebrate Christmas and skiing the Alps. The great and anticipated Warriors reunion. He thought for a moment, not realizing that his hands tremored.

Do I have the strength to see them again, to resurrect the past? They no longer spoke to each other on a daily basis. *Almost two years.* He wondered if it wouldn't be better to just leave things as they were. He sighed and placed the cream-colored envelope aside for the moment.

He stood on the terrace and looked out over the Pacific. The sun was rising out of the horizon—a symbol of a new day and perhaps a new beginning. He looked around his surroundings and wondered if he could ever adapt to living in the modern world again. For a whole year and a half, Karl and Susan lived with nothing but bare necessities and he and his family were doing well. He stared out, watching the birds as they announced a new dawn, and the waves crash along the shoreline. He spoke to his sister from time to time and Jim, but the phone calls weren't often.

Jesus, he thought, *I haven't even worn modern day clothes in a while.* He wasn't sure he still owned a pair of underwear. A cold shiver ran down his spine at the thought of seeing his friends again. He smiled faintly because he was sure that out of all The Warriors, it was unusual that he had become the recluse more than any of the others.

He had not picked up a newspaper. He lived with no radio or television, just his books, music, peace of mind, and his wonderful family. He didn't know the outcome of the murder investigation and during the times that he spoke to Vera and Stefani, he asked them not to mention the past, just got updates on Ron.

He poured himself a glass of cognac. It was the first time he touched liquor in a long time. He looked at the clock on the wall and decided to call Michelle. He long ago, lost track of the time difference to California, to New York, and he didn't care. He just needed to hear her voice, French accent and all.

One of the maids answered the telephone, and it seemed like forever, but finally Michelle's voice broke the silence.

"*Bonjour.*"

"This is a voice from the past; how are you?"

She immediately recognized him. Tears came to her eyes. He was fine; they were fine!

"Oh, Karl! How are you guys? I've missed you so much."

"We're good. What's this invitation about?"

"Getting together for the holidays. All of us. I'm dying to see you."

"And Jim?" he whispered into the phone.

She laughed. "Especially."

"When was the last time you saw him?"

"Last night? He stays here a lot, or I stay with him. Richard is aware. He doesn't care, but we will be at the French chalet together. We own the place as husband and wife, and it's time we all saw each other as in the past. It will be the last time I'm anywhere with Richard. The 'old' Warriors, I guess. We'll be divorced before the end of the year. Please say you'll come."

"We'll be there."

"Congratulations on your marriage and the twins. Put that bitch on the phone."

Karl handed the phone to Susan.

When Susan and Michelle hung up, he called Vera. His niece Karla answered the telephone on the second ring.

"Uncle Karl! How are you? We miss you so much."

"Me too, little lady. What have you been up to?"

For the next five minutes, Karla proceeded to inform him on all the details of her young life. School and for the first time, she mentioned a boy in her class who played tricks on her and that she thought was cute, but she liked Ronnie better and she missed him. Karl laughed. Time passed by too quickly. It seemed like she was born only days ago and here she was telling him about a boy in her life and admitting her attraction for Ronnie, his stepson. He cringed. *Ronnie—verging on puberty. God help us!*

"When are you going to invite me to the wedding, Karla?"

"You silly goose, not yet.

"My Dad said he misses you guys. He talks about you all the time. Wanna talk to my mom?" she asked when she tired of talking to him like most children do.

"Of course, I love you, be good."

"Love you too, Uncle Karl."

He could hear her screaming out for her mother as only a young child could, and he was glad that Vera had given him two nieces.

"What a wonderful surprise!" Vera exclaimed. "Is it really you?"

"You know I always try to keep in touch with my favorite person."

"How have you been, Karl?" she asked, concern edging her voice.

"Actually, much, much better."

"I guess the nature of this phone call is because of the invitation Richard sent out."

"Yes."

"Are you going?"

He sighed. "I'm not sure. Any reason why we should come out of seclusion and attend this gala event?"

"Maybe it's time, Karl. We can't hide forever; we're family."

He remained silent for a moment, then, "You're right."

"I'm meeting Jim at Kennedy and taking the flight with him, Leslie and Jules left already. I can't believe you and Susan wouldn't go. We all need to see one another again, Karl. It'll be fun to reminisce about the old times and ski a bit."

"We'll see."

"Everyone has confirmed to Richard that they were attending, except for you and Susan and Ron and Eva. Stop being so mysterious, guys, we all need to see you."

Karl poured himself another drink. "What's this about?"

"Christmas together I guess, and Richard thinks it's time we talked a bit about what we're going to do for the rest of our lives and also be grateful for what we do have and the fact that we lived through the nightmare."

"Work? I have no intention of ever stepping on a stage again. We're missing two major players. I'm not doing it without them. The Warriors ended the day Mike and Vlad died. I won't do it."

"He's concerned about us, Karl. You know Richard has always been a father figure. He's protective of the only professional family he's ever known."

"Too bad he was not protective of his own family, the asshole. I'm not going back to being a Warrior, Vera."

"No one's asking you to. Look, we really should try to spend this holiday together. Michelle and Richard's divorce will be final that same week and it would be nice to get together again. I don't think Ron wants this separation. The last I heard, he was still confined to a wheelchair, so maybe it's time we were there for him. We've all moved on in some way, but he's really the victim who ended up having to face the shooting on a day-to-day basis imprisoned in a chair."

He sighed. "Okay...I guess we'll meet you."

"I won't tell anyone you're coming, and you can surprise everyone.

"Karl? Be grateful that Richard *didn't* take care of his family. Jim and Michelle are back together again, and I'm very happy for them."

Karl grinned. "Me too."

When they hung up, he slipped back into bed with Susan and kissed her shoulder, while his hand became lost under her white lace nightgown. He could see every inch of her under the lace which did not hide much from him. It would be interesting to go back into civilization.

36
PAST LIVES

JUNE-SEPTEMBER 1988, HAMBURG

Trés Haley entered the hospital room to pay his mother a visit, saddened that the doctors said there was nothing else that could be done. She hadn't been sick for long, but by the time she found the lump on her breast for the second time and went to the doctor, it was already too late. The cancer came back with a vengeance a year after the first round of radiation and aggressive chemo treatment.

A wide smile greeted him. Her only son. Other than loving women since an early age, he turned out to be a fine young man who made her proud. Her natural beauty faded in the last month, replaced by the pallor of eminent death.

His big strong hand engulfed her frail one as he bent down to kiss her bony cheek. She'd done much for him as a single mother. He placed his Styrofoam coffee cup on the night table.

"Sit," she whispered. "I have to speak to you about something very serious."

"Mother, just rest. I don't want you to..." he declared with a sigh.

"I need for you to listen to me."

He took his jacket off and joined her on the bed. She could hardly lift her hand to caress his cheek. "You are my entire life. I love you so much."

Her eyes filled with tears. "Right after you were born, I tried to contact your father to tell him he had a son. I bumped into him at the Cosmos, a club we used to go to. You were small, and I tried to tell him about you, but he didn't want to hear me out. He and his friends were drinking, and I don't think it was the right time. I contacted his father..."

His softened voice interrupted her, and he got up to sit on a chair that faced her. He didn't want to jostle her too much. "Mom, we really don't have to talk about this not now and not ever. Thanks to you, I never missed not having a father around. I would like to know him, but you've done a damn good job"

"Hush, Trés. You need to hear this." Her voice came out once again that of the stern woman who raised him. He sat back in his chair, defeated by her no-nonsense tone and crossed his arms.

"I'm all ears." His smile revealed perfect white teeth.

"How would you rate me as a mother?" she asked.

"Ten plus."

She was taken aback. "Really?"

"Yes, you are terrific. A little tough, but I probably needed the severe discipline."

She stared out the window; she would never see the outdoors again. She smiled sadly recollecting a bit of her life. "I may have been a good mother, but I was a bad woman. Too promiscuous growing up...it was the times, and it was all good. I did care for your father."

"Mom, please..."

"I said, hush. We do need to discuss this, so kindly humor this mad woman her last dying wish to have this conversation with her son."

He took a sip of his coffee.

"Your grandfather was the U.S. Ambassador to Germany at the time. I wanted you to have a family. Your mother, being an only child and pregnant at the age of nineteen, thought it was important that you know your grandparents and, perhaps, your father eventually."

She moved on the bed in an effort to find a more comfortable position. He went to help, but she put her hand up. "Your grandfather came to see me. He hated the fact that your father chose a career he strongly disapproved of. He and your father became estranged when your dad told him that he had decided to stop attending the University of Hamburg where he studied International Law. He wanted his son to follow in his footsteps, and your dad was a spoiled, rich American with all the privileges and benefits of any diplomat's son but a passion for music his father didn't agree with. Your father is a great classical pianist, but he chose another path. He travelled all over Europe with the band until he made a huge name for himself."

"Who is he?" asked Trés.

"Let me finish, and I promise I will tell you. 'Grandpa' was pissed about the fact that his son got a girl like me pregnant, especially since we met at a sleazy club in the Reeperbahn. Your father was his embarrassment. I contacted him because I had no idea of your father's whereabouts, and he came to visit us. I thought that maybe things would work out, but they never did. Instead of helping me contact your father, he drew up legal documents; and although he gave you his last name, he threatened me. He told me that if I ever divulged whose son you were, he could make my life very uncomfortable and that he had friends in very high places that could silence me in any way possible. He promised to support us as middle-class citizens, paid for your private school, and sent a hefty monthly allowance to buy my silence. I had no choice than to agree. I couldn't give you a better life than the one he offered and thought that with time he would soften up, but the son of a bitch never did. I'm not even sure he told his wife that she had a grandson. Rest assured, Trés. Your father is one of the finest men I ever met. Highly educated and far more intelligent than he gives himself credit for. He was handsome and a gentleman in every respect."

Tears rimmed his eyes, and he tightened his hands into fists. His blood boiled with sympathy for his mother. He never questioned how they could live the lifestyle she gave him. Thought maybe she inherited money from her parents. Never thought to pry.

"When I told him you had an interest in music, he became furious. It reminded him of your father, and he told me that I should try to persuade you to study something more reliable. Music wasn't going to get you anywhere, and he never acknowledged your father's talent and international fame. He really hated the path your father chose. I knew it was time to speak to you when you sat at the piano and played 'Forbidden Love.'"

Trés remembered that day. His mother joined him on the piano bench and asked him about the song and why he chose to play it. He shrugged and told her that it was an old song he loved. She didn't press him. The piano intro to the chart-topping song was his father's composition and rendering.

She reached out to take his hand in hers, and she whispered, "Go find your father. He is the guitarist and keyboard player of The Warriors, Jim Haley. I may not be around much longer; it may be days, weeks, months. or years. In any event, there is nothing your grandfather could do to me now. I just want you to meet him, and I need for him to know that you exist."

His hazel eyes met hers, and his heart pounded as he felt the sting of tears.

"Tell him you are Nancy Braun's son; he'll know. If not, Karl Engels and Ron James know me as well. Try to contact them through their manager or however you can. Find Karl and Ron and tell them you are my son. If you can't get to them, my cousin Michelle Bujold and he had a long relationship. I'm sure she'll help you. Once your father met Michelle, no other woman existed in the world for him."

"Is he still with her?" Trés wasn't too knowledgeable about The Warriors. He loved them as a band but didn't know about their personal lives.

"No, she married someone else."

"Why?" His frown was just like his father's.

Nancy smiled and shrugged. "You'll have to ask your father that. Go find him, Trés. He's going to love you. He's a good man."

"One other thing, Mom. How the hell did you come up with my name?"

"Because you are the third James Haley. I didn't want to call you Jim because of how much I dislike your grandfather."

"Do you realize that most people don't know how to pronounce it? I was called 'Three' by the Spaniards in my school because it's spelled like the Spanish word for three."

"Well, it's pronounced like "tray;" it's French like my cousin and my mother, and I loved it, just like I love you. It means 'very.' You are *very* much every good thing in my life. Go find your father."

♫

Three months later, Trés Haley buried his mother. His grandfather didn't attend the funeral; he didn't expect him to. In the reading of Nancy's Last Will and Testament, she left the home that she owned outright to her son, and there was a trust with a substantial amount of money that his grandfather funded. In a safe deposit box, he found his birth certificate that did, indeed, say that his name was James Haley, III, as well as the legal documents his mother spoke about. There were old photographs of his mother with the members of the Warriors and some other teenage girls and boys taken in front of a club that closed a decade ago named The Cosmos. He recognized the members of the band. A very young version of their lead singer, Ron James, in a leather jacket stood behind a motorcycle with Karl Engels and Jim, his father.

Trés noticed the similarity immediately. He'd always found something familiar about the guitarist and their last names caused him to wonder, but it never occurred to him to ask Nancy; he didn't want to hurt her.

Over the next few months, he moved into his mother's house, but he didn't want any part of the trust allotted to Nancy by his grandfather.

It wasn't hard for him to find articles at the local library detailing The Warriors, their past and their present. Two of the members were Germany's pride and contribution to rock music since the sixties. He filled a notebook with copies of articles about his father with pictures of him with his ex-partner and two small girls. A smile touched Trés's lips, one of them looked like her mother, blonde with green eyes, the other carried the dark Haley trait and her father's brown eyes. *I have two little half-sisters. Who would have guessed?*

What really confused him was that he found article after article for a time period close to a decade about his father and the beautiful young woman named Michelle Bujold, heiress to the Bujold empire and well-known socialite in European circles. The two were captured by every magazine and newspaper of the time, travelled to exotic locations, rubbed elbows with royalty and famous musicians and actors. The lens caught the love in their eyes as they laughed, looked at each other, and kissed. Damn he wanted to find a woman to feel those things with—yet something had gone wrong despite the magic Kodak encapsulated forever.

He bought a round trip ticket to Los Angeles. America excited him. He didn't ask his current girlfriend to accompany him. He wanted to do this on his own. A young man on a mission. A mission to find his father and the family his mother always yearned he have. He had a few more gigs to play at small clubs and then freedom for a month. He wanted to see what life had in store for him in America with his father.

37
THE ENEMY CLOSES IN

DECEMBER 1988, FRANCE

Richard stepped forward and raised his wine glass. "Let's hold a toast to the fact that although Karl and Susan and Ron and Eva didn't make it, we have a lot to be grateful for. Some of us have taken a long time to heal; I think we've healed in the best way possible."

Michelle turned as she heard someone arrive and enter the foyer. She stepped onto the marble floor while a maid took Susan's and Karl's coats. Michelle ran to hug Susan, and Karl picked her up in his arms as was his usual greeting when he saw Michelle. Stefani joined them. Vera's eyes watered as she hugged her brother. "It's so good to see you again."

"Vera, you look fantastic!" Karl said.

"Yes," she cried, "but look at that damn Susan; she looks better every day."

Susan hugged her dear friend and sister-in-law. "So, do you. The years have been extra nice to you too."

"I hope you brought pictures of my new niece and nephew."

"Of course, we did; they are such a handful. Ronnie's a saint next to these two."

Leslie looked frail. The only thing in life that she looked forward to was raising her child. She was happy to see her sister and the others, but Vlad's absence left a void in her heart, especially around the holidays.

Julienne accepted the invitation as well. After all, she was part of the family. Her brother, Craig, accompanied her.

Craig was a musician also and still unmarried. He dedicated his life to writing music, and although he was a ladies' man, he remained single and waited for the right one to come along, not unlike his deceased brother-in-law who married late in life. Mike was an inspiration to him.

Michelle looked at the simple gold band on Karl's left hand, and she started to cry. "Congratulations on your marriage. Long overdue."

Susan could barely get the words out herself. "Yes, we finally did it. We got married in a beautiful ceremony on a beach not far from our home. Just us and a bunch of natives. We dressed in native costumes, barefoot. I couldn't have asked for anything more romantic or breathtaking. It was so worth the wait." She squeezed Karl's hand.

Everyone applauded at the long-anticipated news and held a toast to the newlyweds. For the next half hour, Karl and Susan became the center of attention. Jim asked Karl questions about their disappearance. Susan stood by a doorway with her arms crossed and smiled as she watched Karl. A few times, he looked in her direction, and their eyes met. He and Jim were now closer than ever. They were the Three Musketeers: Ron, Karl, and Jim. One for all and all for one.

"So, Karl, what have you been up to?" asked Richard.

"Sun and the beach, just hanging out and recovering from the events of two years ago that tore us all apart. Susan and I are the proud parents of twins that are our pride and joy, but absolute killers. I've never seen such energy. Susan has some pictures. We're happy and that's all that matters."

The doorbell rang and they all froze. Stefani and Alex held their breath. She squeezed Niall's hand.

Susan and Karl looked at each other. Could it be? Was it him? No one ever heard from Ron and Eva except Stefani, Alex. and Niall. Susan's heart pounded. *Can we face a crippled Ron? How is his anger now?*

Michelle ran outside. A limousine chauffeur stood holding the car door open.

They all came out of the house to greet him, wheelchair or not. They needed to be together. Eva got out of the car. She and Susan looked at each other. Words were not necessary. Their tears flowed freely as Ron stepped out of the limousine, no crutches, no cane, just his long, thin legs. His long blonde hair caressed his shoulders, and sunglasses hid his eyes. He was so emotional that he couldn't say a word. Tears streamed down his face, and he sobbed. He looked at each of his brothers. *I've turned into such a wuss!*

Karl walked up to him and hugged him. "How are you, asshole?"

Ron removed his sunglasses. "Not as tan as you and with a few dents in my chest, but looks like they don't want me upstairs yet. I can still dance and move my hips, ask Eva."

"Stop bragging," Jim said, laughing.

Karl and Jim embraced him, and they held each other tightly.

Ron let Karl go so that he could hug Stefani and Alex, then he turned to Susan. They faced each other in silence. He put his arms around her. They cried together for a few moments. He pushed her away so that he could get a good look at her. "I owe you and Eva so much."

Susan hugged him tightly. "I'm just glad my children have their father back."

♫

While the help began to prepare the dining room for dinner, Michelle slipped a mink jacket over her shoulders to go for a walk. The full moon cast an azure glow over the mountains in the distance, and she thought of a magical time, long ago. The years passed too quickly. The memory brought a smile to her lips.

She felt an hand on her shoulder. "Hit song for your thoughts, Red."

"We surely had some good times not too far from here."

Jim sighed. "We did. You and that place hold a special place in my heart."

Michelle put her hand over his. "You do too."

They stood silently looking up at the stars in the sky.

"I love you more than ever, Red," he whispered as his lips touched her temple. "We'll never be apart again."

"I love you too, Jim."

She took his hand and squeezed. "My divorce will be over either the end of this week or the next."

"I know. I can't wait."

"Seeing you and spending several days together, knowing you are alone in a guest room breaks my heart. I just want to hold you."

He pulled her closer. "Don't ever think I don't feel the same way. I promise I will make it up to you...very soon. And Red? You just don't want to hold me; you want that delicious kinky sex we have always had."

Her laughter echoed in the night. "You know me too well."

Karl walked out and stood with them several minutes looking up at the mountains in the distance and remembering their times together at the chalet. "What amazing weekends!" A smile crossed his lips, and he whispered, "Come inside lovebirds. Dinner is served."

♫

The group shared a loud dinner and exchanged gifts around the Christmas tree. The last ones to exchange gifts were Niall and Stefani. He knelt down in front of her and handed her a box which contained a beautiful leather jacket trimmed with silver fox. She threw her arms around him, loving her present and kissed him softly on the lips. He smiled and opened his mouth; nestled between his teeth was a diamond ring with a two-carat square diamond surrounded by two rows of small diamonds.

Stefani's eyes opened wide. He took her hand and placed the ring on her finger. "Stefani James, you have changed my life; will you marry me?"

Her eyes filled with tears and she looked down at her hand. The ring was gorgeous! She kissed his lips, lingering a bit too long.

She pushed back a stray lock of hair from his forehead, although his hair was several inches shorter for his internship with Interpol. "Of course, I will marry you," she whispered.

Susan stood by the Christmas tree with Karl and started to cry again. The look of love in Niall's eyes for her daughter was too much to bear. Her baby girl, married. Ron left Eva's side for a moment, and he wiped Susan's tears away. "It looks like my turn to wipe tears tonight."

Karl placed a hand on Ron's shoulder. "Congratulations."

Ron looked toward Stefani whose arms clung to Niall's neck. Their foreheads pressed together as some secret message passed between them.

His eyes teared, and he remembered Susan's visit during his time in prison when she showed him the photo of the precious little blonde creature they'd created.

They returned to the den. Jim went for a walk into town with Alex and Ashley. Michelle and Richard remained with their guests. Susan took her mug of hot chocolate and went outside to sit on the porch steps.

A hand touched her shoulder, and Karl said, "Want some company?"

"No better company than you, babe. I love you."

He leaned over and kissed her lips. "You taste delicious, chocolaty."

He sat beside her, and she stretched her hand out. "Want some? Is that even a word? Chocolaty? You're beginning to sound like Michelle, making up words."

Karl took the mug and chuckled. He noticed her reddened eyes.

"Were you crying?"

She shrugged her shoulders. "Maybe a little bit, nostalgia, memories...stupidity." She laughed.

He took a sip. "He looks great, doesn't he?"

Susan nodded. "Thank God."

Michelle and Richard came onto the porch. "We're going to take a walk into town," Richard said. "There's a great bar with a small dance floor, kind of an upper scale Cosmos for the socialites and the wealthy in the area."

Karl stood. "Probably very upper scale Cosmos. Want to go, liebling?"

"Yes, let's."

"I'll get our coats."

Karl emerged with Susan's coat, and he held it out for her. He was still a gentleman after all the years.

"The others went ahead." Richard said. "You'll like this place; every time Michelle and I went we really enjoyed it. It's probably the last time Michelle and I will go there together. They play a lot of songs from the sixties and seventies. "

"Before my time." Susan said.

"Sure, mine too." Richard snickered. He stopped them for a moment. "Listen guys, I haven't had the time to come clean and talk to you about this divorce. I love Michelle with all my heart, but the love has changed. We had this weekend planned since before the ill-fated tour, and we were not going to ruin it for you guys. I don't know what the future holds for us, but we have to talk about it. Michelle and I will be divorced by the end of the week. I didn't ask Liz to come for the holiday because I wanted it to be just us, like old times."

Karl patted Richard on the back. "No apologies needed, Richard. Life is too short to be unhappy. You are and always will be our manager. You and Michelle have two precious young boys that are friends with Ronnie, Karla, and Jenna. It'll be fine. Michelle will be fine as well."

"I know she will," he replied.

Richard and Michelle went down the porch steps, and Karl took Susan's hand to follow. Ron and Eva decided to join them. They walked hand in hand for a few blocks until they came upon the center of the town full of artsy shops. Michelle strolled along quietly beside her soon to be ex-husband, hands in her pockets. She couldn't wait until this trip was over and she could be with Jim.

Richard sighed a breath of relief. His guys were back and their emotions on the mend. "Sorry I couldn't convince Leslie and Julienne to come. I think Craig wanted to, but he wouldn't leave his sister."

Ron shook his head and he looked at Susan. "Stefani is so pissed. Look at what we've done to her. Always the 'little princess' and now she's surrounded by a full royal court. Alex, Ronnie, Monique, Kiefer, and Veronica. Guys, we need to close up shop; that girl is going to kill us."

They burst out laughing, glad that the sense of humor slowly returned to their lives as well. Snow began to fall as the group arrived at the club, crowded with people dancing, lovers holding hands, and plenty of people out to have a good time after a day on the slopes. Jim, Alex, and Ashley held a table for them.

Vera stayed behind in Richard and Michelle's home with Craig, Julienne, and Leslie. She didn't want to be a part of the couples. She was no longer a couple, and the only one without a partner was Craig. Julienne's brother was handsome and sexy, but she didn't want another musician; she wanted to be alone for a while. She still had hope that John was alive, and she would find him someday. She, Leslie, Craig, and Julienne sat on the floor in front of the fireplace to play poker.

Susan pulled Karl's hand, leading him to dance. They danced to so many songs, they seemed to lose count. Songs they grew up with. "Jumping Jack Flash," "Paint it Black," "Shout," an endless list. "Time is on My Side" came on and Karl took her in his arms. She closed her eyes and was back at the Cosmos, in his arms, safely tucked away under his protection. He kissed her cheek in the dim lights. She swayed, lost in a sea of beautiful music and emotions. He pulled away and said with love dancing in his eyes, "I've missed being alone with you."

"Me too."

She smiled up at him. "I don't want this song to ever end."

"Do you remember this song?"

"It's the first song we danced together at the Cosmos. Thanks to the Rolling Stones."

They held each other close till the song ended.

Richard watched them from afar and knew his babies had been away from music for too long. He watched Alex dancing with Ashley. The

New Warriors could become as popular as the originals. Alex had a strong voice, not unlike his father's. Susan was well aware that music and people's tastes changed over time, and she changed with the times in a most graceful way. The Warriors could be a smash again if they hired a strong drummer and a great bassist. Alex just needed time, the right band members, and the right direction.

Jim and Michelle were phenomenal dancers, and Jim appeared out of nowhere and took her hand and led her to the dance floor. Richard didn't dance, and Michelle was a natural born *danseur*.

Jim placed his arm around her waist and twirled her then slowly brought her close and pressed her to his chest to "MacArthur Park" by Donna Summer. As soon as the tempo picked up, they separated, and the dance floor cleared except for Karl and Susan who followed every inch of Jim and Michelle's moves. During the song, Karl and Jim exchanged partners and continued with "Dr. Love" and switched partners again to end the dance session with "Don't Leave Me This Way" by Thelma Houston.

Jim pulled Michelle close and whispered in her ear. "Will you satisfy the need in me?"

She missed a step and looked at him. "Always. *Toujours*." He let go and continued to dance with a grin on his face.

Finally, they returned to the table, and Karl took Susan's hand and led her to the bar. "Hot stuff, liebling; you gals haven't changed a bit."

"I can't help it; music runs through my veins." Susan began to fan herself with her hand. She took her drink and said. "Karl, I need to get some air."

"Not until you dance with me," Ron said, grabbing her wrist. As they walked to the dance floor, he stopped and whispered in her ear. "Let's show these people that I can still move."

He grabbed her waist and pulled her close. Susan looked like she was about to burst out in tears. He pulled her away and frowned. "Susan Michaels, are you going to cry? Again? We've all been crying all damn day and night."

Susan pouted. "I thought I would never see you dance again." At that, her tears spilled onto her cheeks.

Ron laughed. "I can still dance *and* move my hips."

Susan cried even harder through the laughter. Ron pulled her closer.

"I told you once before, Ron, you are an amazing man, and I'm proud of the fact that you are Stefani and Ronnie's father. Eva is very lucky, and you are very lucky to have her."

They finished dancing and Ron handed her over to Karl. "Let's go outside, I need to cool off," she said, putting her coat on.

Karl took her hand. A blizzard seemed to be in full force. Susan stood on the sidewalk and let the flakes fall on her. She looked up at the lamp post. It was magical. Karl took her in his arms. His lips found hers and they kissed. "We have to get away from all those little monsters more often when we get back. I've so missed having you all to myself." Susan's tongue reached out to caress Karl's lips as snowflakes melted on their cheeks and lips.

Jim and Michelle joined them a few minutes later. Jim felt no pain from the alcohol, and he danced his way out the door still holding Michelle's hand. As they reached the spot where Susan and Karl stood, he twirled her around one more time and pulled her against him.

"It won't be long now, and you'll have her all to yourself," Karl whispered.

By the time Richard walked out of the place, Jim and Michelle safely stood a few feet away from each other. Richard knew about them, but it was all about respect.

Susan went back inside and returned to the table. She announced, "I think we're going to have to sleep here unless we get going. There's a blizzard out there."

Niall stood beside Susan a moment later holding Stefani's hand. He scanned the area, and the hair on his neck stood on end. *There's more than snow out there.* He touched his ankle where he discreetly carried his backup firearm. *I hope to God I don't need this.*

38
TENSE AND TENDER REUNION

CHRISTMAS 1988, FRANCE

Niall quickly slipped on his sweatpants and opened the door to go to his room. As he came out of Stefani's room, Ron walked down the hallway. Their eyes met. Ron studied Niall dressed in sweats, shirtless and no shoes. Whatever might have been going on in Stefani's room didn't appear to require much clothing.

"I spoke to you the night of the shooting, and I told you that if I ever caught your ass behaving inappropriately with my daughter, I was going to wipe the streets with you."

For a moment, Niall stared at him in disbelief as anger built inside him. Niall wasn't a saint, but he certainly loved justice. His blood boiled. *How dare he?*

Before Niall could reply, Ron punched him squarely on the cheek. Not expecting it, Niall fell back against the door to Stefani's room, but Niall punched right back, hitting Ron in the jaw. Stefani stormed out. "Dad, what are you doing?"

"Stay out of this, Stefani. This is between Niall and..."

Before Ron could continue, Karl ran out of his room, and he grabbed Ron's arm just as he was going to belt Niall again.

"No!" Niall shouted, his face red with anger. He felt the heat of his blood rush through his veins. "Who the fuck are you to accuse me? I've made a commitment to your daughter; I love her, and I'm going to marry her. You defiled a nun years ago and had an affair with her; you got her pregnant and took off. Now you're doing the same thing, knocking her up and living with her, not making a commitment yourself, asshole, and that is *my* mother!"

Karl stepped between them and he took the blow Niall lashed out which landed on Karl's good shoulder. Eva ran out of her room. Susan pulled Karl away before he got hurt. Niall took advantage of the fact that Karl had moved away and landed a second punch on Ron's jaw.

Stefani stepped between them. "Dad! Niall! Please!"

Niall took her arm and kept her out of the circle.

Eva took Ron by the wrist and Niall by the hand. She shouted, "Stop it, both of you, NOW!"

Neither one dared to move, afraid to hurt Eva who stood between two men towering over her.

Alex and Ashley ran up the stairs to see what the commotion was.

Niall pointed his finger at Ron. "Listen to me, asshole. This cannot be about who is sleeping with who; there is something bigger looming here! That asshole that shot you and Karl and assassinated Mike and Vlad is in the vicinity. I saw fresh tracks out there that do not look familiar. You guys left and all walked in a certain direction. The tracks are in the back of the house. There were at least three shooters the night of the concert, maybe more. Slugs recovered from the walls did not match those taken from victims. I don't give a rat's ass whether you ever talk to me again or not, but I intend on making Stefani my wife, and no one is going to stop me, not you and not all the punches you throw me. And I will sleep in her room all I want and as long as she'll have me. It's the best way for me to keep her safe. I. Love. Her. Too!"

Niall walked away and went into his room. When he came out, he wore unlaced construction boots and a black turtleneck sweater. He held a Glock 17 in his hand and handed a .357 to Jim. "You know how to use this?"

"Sure do," Jim replied.

Niall walked past the group and started down the long, winding stairs leading to the foyer.

"Niall..." Ron called out.

"Don't fuck with me, Ron, not when I have a gun in my hand and my blood is boiling. You assaulted an officer of the law," Niall said. His anger edged his voice.

Stefani ran after him. "Niall don't, please! I don't want you to get hurt!"

He turned, love in his eyes, and he reached his free hand out to cup her chin. "Trust me, Stefani. I know what I'm doing."

Susan looked at Ron angrily. *How could he ever doubt the love Niall has for Stefani?*

Niall's eyes looked at Alex. An unread message passed between them. If Niall didn't come back, it was his duty to console Stefani and his mother.

"Wait!" Alex shouted. "I'm coming with you."

Niall shouted as he continued down the stairs. "There's another two .357s on my dresser, grab them and give one to Karl."

Alex didn't waste time; he grabbed the guns, handed one to Karl, and they followed Niall. He trusted Niall's instinct, that special gut feeling law enforcement agents have. Niall threw open the front door. Standing behind him Jim, Alex, and Karl followed them down the stairs.

Before closing the front door, Niall shouted, "I don't want anyone opening this door no matter what you hear."

Jim and Michelle glanced at each other for a second, and he followed them. Her heart pounded in her chest, afraid for his safety. Before walking out the door he looked at her and gave her an air kiss. Richard was in his study on the telephone to the police.

Susan hugged Karl and kissed his lips softly. "Don't try to be a hero."

Niall slammed the front door and followed the footprints in the back of the property with Karl, Jim, and Alex trailing behind him. He released the safety of the Glock and bent down to see if he recognized or could match the footprints to anyone's shoes or boots. He shook his head; they didn't appear to match. He stood and looked into the trees, anger and frustration edging his features. He drew his eyebrows together and ran his hand through his hair, pushing it away from his face. He squinted into the darkness, daring the monster to show his fangs. The footprints disappeared. He stood, defeated and stepped deep into the forest area that surrounded the property.

Niall knew that his suspect was long gone, and he sighed. He shook his head. "He's gone. I feel it."

Karl placed a hand on Niall's shoulder. "You can count on me for any help you need with this, Niall. He tried to kill Susan too. I want him just as badly as you do."

Niall nodded. "I never thought he would dare to get this close. I need for him to make a mistake."

Jim rubbed his temple. "For God's sake! Why is someone after us after two years?"

Niall gusted a breath. "I'm not at liberty to discuss it, but if you think long and hard, you'll figure out the answer. This gathering scares the hell out of me because it puts everyone together again. I checked the house thoroughly for a bomb or something when I got back tonight. You make sure Ron knows I'm doing this to protect the women I love—Stefani, Mom, and my sisters."

He looked at Alex. "Don't leave the house without that gun. I'm warning you. You guys either." He looked beyond the wide expanse of snow between the forest and the huge mansion. Snow continued to fall in a steady stream. He took a deep breath. His cheek hurt. They headed back.

Jim caught Karl's arm as they walked a few steps behind the brothers. "Vlad."

"What?" Karl's brow furrowed in confusion before he opened his eyes wide. "Damn."

"He was a child," Jim snarled. "How could anyone think that he could know anything? All he ever told me was his grandparents got him out of Russia, and his parents were in government there. No details. Nada."

Karl took a deep breath. "What if they go after Leslie?"

"I think maybe Niall is having all of us watched. It was easier when we were at separate homes." He jerked his head to catch up with Niall and Alex.

Niall entered the house and left his snow-covered boots at the door. The four men entered the den where everyone awaited their return.

Niall looked at the clock on the mantle; it was almost five in the morning. He took Stefani's hand, pulled her up from the sofa, and looked at Ron with a look of defiance on his face.

"I'm tired, and my cheek hurts. I promised to marry your daughter, and no one on this planet is going to stop me from sleeping in her room tonight. I've had a rough night and I'm pissed as hell, so I just suggest you save the overprotectiveness for another time, Ron."

Ron opened his mouth to say something, but Susan glowered at him. "I dare you to say anything, Ron," she said with her mouth forming a tight, thin line.

He shook his head. "I'm sorry, Niall."

Niall's eyes turned into slits of anger. "Save your apology, Ron. I'm not in the mood to accept it right now."

He tightened his hold on Stefani's hand and led her away. She followed the new man in her life.

Susan stood and poured herself a shot of cognac and one for Karl. "That went really well, Ron. I hate to say it, but the kid's right. You claim you love Eva so much, and you haven't done a thing about it."

39
THE FUTURE LIES AHEAD

CHRISTMAS 1988, FRANCE

Although the lights weren't turned off until past five on Christmas morning, Stefani and Niall were gone the next day by the time the house came to life.

A late brunch was served in the main dining room. Susan came down in a pair of jeans and black sweatshirt. She scanned the room. "Where's Stefani?" she asked. "And Niall?"

Ron put his cup of coffee down. "I thought they were still asleep."

"Everyone else is here; they would have heard the commotion and comings and goings." Susan rolled her eyes. "Oh, Ron, really. I hope they didn't leave because of your behavior last night. I haven't seen her in over a year."

"Relax, Susan. I'll go check on them."

Eva stood. "I'll go. I don't think Niall has ever worn pajamas, and I changed his diaper numerous times."

The door to Stefani's room was ajar. The bed was unmade, but her suitcase and clothes were still there. Niall's bed in his room was still made but there were clothes all over the bed. She smiled, realizing that her son never slept in his bed in the past three days. *Oh, that boy is going to be the death of me!*

Eva returned to the dining room sighing. "They didn't leave."

When she took her seat beside Ron, he placed a hand over hers. "I'm really sorry about what happened, Eva. You have to understand that she's my daughter."

"And he's my son," she replied. "Don't let that happen again, Ron. Niall's a good and responsible kid, and Stefani is a big girl. He's just doing what boys do, don't you remember?"

Ron sighed. "Yes, I do." He was defeated, and he wasn't liking this Susan and Eva partnership one bit. It was a feminine conspiracy against him. Karl glanced at him and burst out laughing.

"Susan, I think they are just out. All their clothes and suitcases are still here."

Niall and Stefani returned just as brunch was being served. "I hope you're hungry," Susan said as she poured them some coffee and tried to promote the peace treaty. She turned, "Ron? Did you want to say something?"

Ron's eyes met Susan's. "I'm sorry, Niall. Please forgive me."

Niall looked at him. "You know that you are a German national, living in the United States, in the country of France for the holiday, and I could have you arrested for assaulting an Interpol agent; but because you will be my father-in-law, I'm going to let that one slide. What I won't let slide is where my mother stands with you."

Ron took a sip of his coffee while Karl smiled at Ron. He put his cup down. "Your mother and I don't need a lot of fanfare at our age. I will marry her before we leave, you have my word."

Niall smirked and he reached behind his waist. He took out a set of handcuffs and held them up. "Good, because I don't really want to use these on you and make sure you get five years for assaulting me."

Ron went to reply, and Susan opened her eyes real wide, caution written all over her face.

Ron looked at Richard. "Do you think we can find a priest somewhere?"

Richard laughed. "I will dig one up, don't worry."

"Karl?" Ron asked.

"Honored to be asked."

"Excuse me, guys, but I don't really think that a priest would marry us. I was excommunicated from the Church twenty-four years ago." Eva stated.

Ron shrugged. "Their loss, then."

"I can perform the ceremony," Richard said.

"How so?" Eva turned questioning eyes toward him.

"I was ordained in the Anglican church a long time ago, but it wasn't my calling."

Jim spewed coffee and gasped, "You're a minister?"

"I do have a license." Richard gave Jim a lopsided smirk and turned to Ron. "When do you want to do this?"

"As soon as possible; that Niall packs quite a punch," Ron replied, rubbing his jaw.

"Ahh, sweet youth," Karl sighed. "I remember a time when you could easily have kicked his skinny ass."

Jim later whispered to Karl, "You know, I was a U.S. Ambassador's son. Don't tell Ron, but Niall has no authority to arrest anyone, and those cuffs looked strangely like kinky sex."

They chortled.

♫

Eva wasn't sure who to pick as a matron of honor, but she felt that she and Susan had been through so much with Ron, it was only fair to ask her. Eva didn't feel jealousy toward Susan in any way, just like Karl wasn't jealous when it came to Ron. There was a past and history between them that couldn't be ignored.

They finished brunch. Stefani and Ashley and the twins pulled Eva and Susan up the stairs to plan the wedding. Michelle got on the phone to her father, the famous French designer in Paris. Vera stood next to her with crossed fingers as they tried to convince Stefano to deliver a dress to Eva. Vera gave Michelle Eva's approximate measurements so that Stefano could find something.

♫

The younger group went skiing all together that day, while the adults preferred to relax in anticipation of Ron and Eva's wedding.

Richard went to make hot chocolate while Michelle set the coffee table in the den with mugs. Susan put a fresh apple pie in the oven to warm. The others began to trickle into the room one by one. The last to enter the room were Karl, Ron, and Jim. As they enjoyed their hot chocolate and sweets, Richard seized the opportunity to tell them why he had reunited them.

"I wanted to be together this holiday because I think we all have a lot to be thankful for. I also wanted to propose a Warriors reunion album and tour."

They remained silent, then Karl spoke softly. "The Warriors are no more, Richard. I don't know about the others, but I am done. I won't step on a stage again."

"Anyone else have an opinion?" Richard asked.

Jim spoke. "Karl, I think we have an incredible chance to make a comeback once more in memory of Mike and Vlad. We always said we would take a few years off and have a comeback tour, then retire for good."

"How can we with two main members missing?"

Leslie interrupted them. "I'll take Vlad's place." Her voice was eager for the first time since that horrible day.

All eyes suddenly turned to her. "You?" asked Karl.

She looked down. "Vlad taught me how to play the drums. I can play exactly like him."

"Seriously?" Karl asked.

Craig joined in. "I would love to audition for you guys. I play bass guitar. I played for a band when I lived in Madrid. It would be an honor to step in for my brother-in-law."

Karl thought for a moment. He was afraid for himself, for Susan, and for his friends to ever be in the public eye again, especially after his talk with Jim the night before. What if the lunatic *was* still after all of them? Hell, he had pointed the gun at Susan, *and* he followed them to France. Richard handed Ron a music sheet. "Susan wrote this song a week before the shooting. I think there's something here."

Ron read the music, humming the tune to himself and passed it to Karl for his comments. Karl put on his glasses and read it. They watched Karl read in glasses for the first time. Jim laughed. "We must all be getting old, Karl. You had the best eyesight of all of us."

"Shut up! I'm giving this to you next. Let's see if you can do it without glasses."

Karl looked up at Susan. The professional kicked in. "This is great. Do you realize that you have written hard rock lyrics and music that almost borders on something hip-hop and danceable? How do you do this? I don't think anyone's thought of this combination."

"I can see the whole thing up on a stage. I figured that if we never recorded it, I would start writing a rock opera," she said. "I even have all the choreography figured out in my head..."

"I have to think this over. I don't know if we want to expose ourselves to more maniacs," Karl said.

"We can give Leslie and Craig a chance," Richard added.

Karl pinched the bridge of his nose and closed his eyes. "Do it then, and we'll see."

Richard was happy with the reply—it wasn't a firm no. He knew Ron and Karl would come around because music oozed from their pores; they wouldn't be complete anything else.

♪

The long and wide spiral staircase was decorated with white roses, white lights and burgundy poinsettias. On every other step there was a white votive candle in Waterford crystal holders that smelled like gardenias. The Grand Steinway piano dominated a corner of the round foyer.

Richard and The Warriors were going to dinner because there was no way they could have a bachelor party with Ron not drinking, nor did they want to tempt him.

Stefani talked with Alex and Ashley about the music for the ceremony. Susan and Michelle were going out with Vera and Eva doing some last-minute shopping in town and then dinner. The twins agreed to meet some friends they met on the slopes that day. The plans were to go to a club that catered to a younger crowd, and Eva would pick them up on the way back to the house.

Annie dressed to the nines as usual in a tight black sweater with fur at the neck and wrists and a short black leather skirt. Her boots sported four-inch heels. Her light blonde hair cascaded down her back in a sea of curls. Niki just wore a sweater and jeans. She was as beautiful as her twin, but Annie was sensuous.

The newfound friends sat at a table in the front of the stage. It was early in the evening, and they knew they had a least three hours before they were to meet Eva and the others to return to the house.

A fairly popular new group out of their hometown of Frankfurt called Hot Embers was playing.

As Annie walked to the table, her eyes fell on the lead guitarist of the band. *Wow! It should be illegal to be that sexy and fine! Tall, dark, and too handsome!* she thought. Her whole body reacted to him. There was a familiar look about him.

He was tall with brown hair and hazel eyes. He wore tight black jeans and a black shirt with the sleeves rolled up revealing well-muscled arms adorned by several intricate tattoos. A few buttons of the shirt were open. Sweat poured out of every inch of exposed skin.

His forehead creased with intense concentration. His body moved slowly in deliberate steps to entice the mostly female audience. He looked up for a moment only to discover Annie staring boldly at him. His gaze held hers for a few seconds then he winked at her.

She flashed a shy but sexy smile that caught his attention in a big way. His eyes strayed in her direction several times until the song ended. He placed his guitar on a stand and picked up a towel to dry his face and exposed arms. He turned away from the audience to pick up a glass of water.

Annie noticed tight, round buttocks. *No man should have such a perfect ass,* she thought, devouring every inch of perfection. Her hormones kicked into overdrive, and she crossed her legs as warmth travelled over the lower part of her body. He pushed his hair back and turned back to the audience. His eyes deliberately locked with hers. He threw his towel aside and began to walk in her direction, a slick smile on his lips.

"Can I buy you a drink?" he asked.

"Sure," she replied.

He took her hand and led her to the bar. He ordered a scotch. "What are you drinking?" he asked.

"Same." She might as well live dangerously. No one was asking her how old she was. *I'm leaving after Ron and Mom's wedding, and he is damn hot.*

"I'm Trés. Do you have a name?"

"Anneliese."

His smile was perfect. "German?"

"Yes, you?"

"Hamburg born and raised."

"Frankfurt. I'm living in the U.S,, but I'm here with my family for Christmas. Everyone calls me Annie now that they've Americanized my name."

He laughed at her sense of humor. "I'm only here for the night. We're playing in Vienna tomorrow night. Care to join me?" His gaze was intense.

"We're leaving the day after tomorrow." Annie knew that it was a one-time meeting with a handsome stranger. It was fun to know she attracted him. She could be as bold as she wanted to be, it was one night only. She would never see him again.

Trés couldn't keep his eyes off the gorgeous creature sitting beside him. Over the years, he learned to play the rock star card with women, but this one was exceptional. Polished and reeked of wealth and education. She smelled heavenly. He placed a hand over hers. It was soft with perfect soft pink nails. It could be a delicious one-night stand. Another band began to play. and he leaned over and whispered into her ear, "I have to play again in about a half hour. Want to go someplace quieter?"

She shrugged and nodded.

He led her to his dressing room. He opened the door and locked it behind him. There was a leather jacket draped over a chair and several personal items here and there. A fresh pair of jeans, sneakers and a t-shirt lay on a chaise lounge.

"Did you have a good vacation?" he asked, making small talk.

"Yes, it was great. My first time in France and Switzerland. My mom has some friends who own a place here." Annie wasn't going to volunteer any more information. She didn't know him, and they were having enough security issues as it was. He'd be gone in a few hours. Still, she wanted to taste his lips, touch his arms. It couldn't hurt. She intended to play with fire, a fire that crept all over her body. It cried out to be extinguished. Their eyes met, and it seemed to be mutual. He picked her up in his arms and sat her on a ledge that served as a grooming area. He took her face in his hands and brought his lips to hers. Her heart stammered, and her arms encircled his neck. His lips trailed a line of kisses down her neck, and she moaned. His hands caressed her back and slid under her sweater. He undid her bra, and his fingers sought out her breasts. He twirled her nipples between his fingers. He pulled her closer and she slid her hands over his chest. He unbuttoned his shirt and threw it on the floor. His flesh was damp and hot to the touch. There was nothing better than a delicious one-night stand on the road. Two animals in heat couldn't have been wilder.

Annie didn't know what came over her. She wanted this wonderful stranger to touch her in places she had never been touched before. He pulled the sweater over her head and slid the bra straps down her arms.

He lowered his mouth to kiss her breasts, and he took one of her nipples and twirled his tongue around it.

His hands crawled in painfully slow strokes over her thighs. He wanted her more than any woman he'd ever met on the road, and there'd been plenty. The soft butterfly bites she placed on his neck drove him mad. Her breath quickened, and a soft breeze of her hands swept over his back. She boldly slid her hand over the front of his jeans, searching and teasing the hardness. He almost exploded from the brush of her fingers.

Annie's hand was bold, seeking something unknown. His big strong hands seared her skin. His teeth softly bit her shoulder and she threw her head back to give him access. His tongue licked her earlobe. He picked her up in his arms and she wrapped her legs around his waist.

He groaned. "What have you done to me?" he whispered out of breath. "I don't even have a condom to make love to you. You weren't in my plans."

He went to the bathroom, and she was dressed when he returned. A knock on the door was followed by a shout. "T, five minutes!"

He pulled her into his arms. "Will you be here for a while longer?"

Annie looked at her watch. "No, my sister and I don't have transportation, and we are being picked up."

His grip on her waist tightened. "Maybe our paths will cross again someday, Tigress."

"I hope so," she said.

Sometime during his set, he watched her get up with a sister who was identical with the exception of the fact that Annie was sure of herself and luscious. She turned as she followed her sister and blew him a kiss. He winked back. *That little girl is trouble all around.* He was leaving that night. As he continued to play, her perfume unnerved him. *Shit!*

Damn he wanted her, but he had a girl that he saw from time to time, and Annie seemed too polished to use as a one-night stand. *She is the type you get serious with, want for the rest of your life.*

♫

"Did you guys have fun?" Susan asked, turning in the front seat of the car.

"The band was awesome," Niki said.

"The guitarist was awesome." Annie laughed.

"Annie, careful," Susan said, laughing. "I fell for a guitarist a long time ago. Care to describe him in one word?"

"Yummy," she replied. "Unfortunately, he is leaving tonight. I wouldn't mind seeing him again, though."

Eva shook her head. "You guys are growing up too fast."

Annie leaned back in her seat. "He was a hot ticket."

Michelle sighed. "Oh, to be young again! Annie, I fell for a guitarist as well. You have to watch out for those guys."

"What was his name?" Susan asked. She loved the twins but especially Annie who reminded her so much of herself and Michelle at that age.

"Trés."

"Very sexy. No last name?"

She shrugged. "I didn't ask, and he didn't offer. He was really, really hot."

All of them burst out laughing.

♫

Trés finished his set and went to the dressing room to freshen up and change. As he was leaving, his eyes caught a shiny object on the floor. He picked up the earring and clenched it in his fist. Her perfume still scorched his skin. He was still hard as a rock. He regretted not having exchanged telephone numbers, but he couldn't. Annie was lost to him. How she managed to crawl under his skin in such a short time was unreal. He couldn't stop thinking about her. Would have wanted to get to know her better.

He and the band members got into a taxi to head for the airport.

As the taxi turned onto the main street, it stopped to let a stretch limousine with darkened windows carrying the members of The Warriors back to Richard and Michelle's house pass in front of them.

Trés had no way of knowing that his father's limo and the car that carried him crossed paths that night.

Two days later, the young aspiring musician boarded a flight from Vienna to Los Angeles in search of a father he desperately wanted to know.

48
fNESCAPABLE UNfON

END OF DECEMBER 1988, FRANCE

As the bride dressed, Niall came into the room. He didn't expect all the women to be with his mother. He wore a black tuxedo and held up the undone bow tie. "You expect me to make a bow tie out of this?"

Eva laughed. Stefani took a deep breath, and she undressed him with her blue eyes. She was fully made up and her hair perfect. She wore a red silk robe; not much under it. He snickered, winked and mouthed the words, "Love you!" She smiled and ran the tip of her tongue over her bottom lip.

He looked away. She killed him. The rest of the girls whistled at him, and his cheeks reddened.

Susan opened her eyes wide. "My daughter's taste in men is damn good. You look very handsome, Niall."

Michelle passed by Niall and placed a warm hand on his arm. She looked at Susan. "Where were the guys that looked like this when we were in the boarding school?"

"We did pretty well," Susan replied, laughing.

"Yes, but the majority didn't look this way. We had to leave the country to find Karl and Jim. Stefani, take care of him. Pretty damn close to perfect." Michelle grinned at Eva. "His brother is not too shabby either. Good job, girl."

Eva laughed as she buttoned the top button of her son's shirt.

Niall blushed and squirmed at all the attention he was getting from a roomful of half-dressed gorgeous women. In a past life, he would have felt as if he had died and gone to Heaven, but all that changed with Stefani James.

"Mom, hurry!" he hissed as she laughed and tightened the perfect bow tie. He couldn't run out of the room fast enough when his mother kissed him on the cheek, and the entire room shouted a loud, "Aww."

Their next victim was Alex, taller than Niall by two inches. His shirt was still open when he entered the room, not realizing that his mother was not alone. He held up the tie and asked, "Anyone know how to do this?"

Vera, Michelle, and Susan all volunteered at the same time.

"Oh, my," said Eva, "I have to keep my sons away from these horny old women. Ashley take him away, please."

"I can't, Eva. I don't know how to tie it either."

♫

Jim took a deep breath and placed his fingers on the keys to play the low, soft introduction to Beethoven's "Moonlight Sonata." Michelle watched him from a distance and realized that Jim could have been a musical prodigy in classical music if he had chosen that path. His fingers moved slowly, and the notes were soft. His forehead furrowed with concentration, eyes almost closed, feeling the notes with his body. The men lined up at the bottom of the stairs.

Niall went to get his mother. She was on her knees in the room. He didn't dare interrupt. Eva always asked for spiritual guidance when a major event in their lives was about to take place. He waited until she was done then entered.

"Ready?" he asked.

"Yes." She gathered her flowers and glanced at the mirror for the last time. Her hands tremored.

Niall placed a hand on her shoulder and leaned in to kiss her cheek. "You look beautiful."

Eva placed her hand on his cheek. "You and your brother are the handsomest men here tonight."

"I thought you would think it was Ron."

"He doesn't stand a chance next to you guys, but don't tell him that."

The entire wedding group assembled on the landing of the second floor.

Susan walked down the stairs first. There was not going to be a traditional "wedding party." Ron and Eva had run out that morning to buy plain gold wedding rings.

♫

Ron watched Eva come down the stairs on her son's arm and held his breath. When he married Susan, he'd been higher than Mt. Everest. Now, he was lucid and in love with a woman that he met as a boy. She'd helped him get his confidential records from the office the day he left the orphanage. She'd given birth to his first son. She'd nursed him back to health and gave him another daughter.

Niall took his mother's hand and placed it in Ron's. "You be good to her, or I'll kick your ass."

Ron reached out and pulled Niall toward him and they embraced. Richard started the ceremony and then it was time for Ron to speak. He took Eva's hand in his, and his eyes filled with tears. *I am turning into such an ass! What a softie!*

"I need to express my gratitude to God for putting you into my life. I am blessed to have found you again and that He has given me another chance at happiness. I am grateful to have found my best friend, and I want to continue to laugh with you, love you, and grow old together with you. I am who I am now thanks to you. I want to spend the rest of my life with you. Long ago, when I met a little tiny eight-year-old, she gave me the hope to face each day at the orphanage. Leaving it caused me to wander into an abyss. Every note I sing from this day forward will be for you."

Eva's tears streamed down her face. "I can't say it any better, Ron. I always knew there was light in you. I always saw the good and looked past the bad. Even though you strayed, I always prayed for you and asked God to take care of you. I love you with all my heart, and I want to grow old with you too."

They exchanged rings, and Ron kissed Eva.

He looked at her. "I love you so much, babe."

"Well, it was about time you made an honest woman out of this nun."

The festivities went on until late, and outside, it started to snow again.

♫

Michelle couldn't fall asleep. She tossed and turned in bed and finally got up. Fortunately, she and Richard did not share a room. She went to the kitchen and got a glass and bottle of wine. She wanted to sit outside and take in the serene beauty of the snow, but it would probably be safer if she sat in the back of the house. The patio was covered by wall to wall windows surrounding a heated indoor pool and jacuzzi. She sat in the dark and hoped they got back to their homes safely—all of them. The image of Jim crossed her mind, and she smiled. The final hearing on her divorce was in a week, and she would be a free woman.

She heard movement in the dark, and her heart started to pound, not from fear but because she had an idea of who it was. After parties and drinking, there was only one other person on the planet exactly like herself. Someone who needed time to wind down from too much excitement and adrenalin.

The dark outlined his beautiful features, and she held her breath. It was like a spiritual apparition.

He smiled. "Hey, Red, fancy finding you here."

"I couldn't sleep."

He took the glass of wine from her hand and sipped. "Hmm, excellent choice. Your own?"

"Naturally."

Jim reached out and took her hand, and he entwined their fingers together and squeezed.

He pulled her close and his brown eyes looked down at her face, capturing her gaze. "I can't wait to have you all to myself again."

Her fingers touched his hair, and she slid her hand behind his neck. "A kiss will have to do for now."

His kiss was soft, lips touching hers, tasting the fine Cabernet. His tongue parted her trembling mouth. His hand slipped over her back and he pulled her close.

The scent of his cologne and his hair was intoxicating. She placed her arms around his shoulders, not wanting the moment to end.

"How delicious to steal a kiss from you!" he whispered while his finger traced a fine line from her cheek to her chin and to her lips.

"Next time we see each other, I'll be free." Her words were barely audible, and she took his hand and kissed it. "I guess I can go to sleep now."

His smile revealed perfection. "Dream of me because I will surely dream of you tonight."

41
CATASTROPHE STRIKES AGAIN

END OF DECEMBER 1988, FRANCE

our limousines pulled up to the front of the house early the morning after Ron and Eva married. Each car would be carrying The Warriors and their significant others plus Ron and Eva's adult children to the airport as they headed in different directions. Most of them to Los Angeles, Ron and Eva would honeymoon in Karl and Susan's home in the South Pacific. Jim was returning to New York. Vera kept the house in Los Angeles, and he kept the brownstone in New York, and the chalet in the Swiss Alps his parents gave him he owned jointly with a secret partner. The help brought out the suitcases and handed them to the chauffeurs who began to put them into the trunks. The family members began to exit the home.

Richard placed his hand on Michelle's shoulder. "You guys go on to the airport. I want to speak to Jim about something, and we'll meet you there." He kissed her cheek swiftly and waited for Jim to exit the home. He had already told Jim he wanted to speak with him.

Michelle glanced at Jim for a split second, and he looked away. Susan and Karl came out.

"What's going on?" Susan asked.

Karl sighed and urged Susan into the car. "I'm not sure. Richard wants to talk to Jim; they'll meet us at the airport."

♬

Jim glanced at Michelle and got in the car with Richard, slamming the door. Karl watched as they pulled away with Richard at the wheel in a Mercedes sedan.

Richard peeled off. "What was so important that you couldn't call me?" Jim asked.

"It has to do with your relationship with my wife, Haley."

Jim looked out the window. *No longer your wife, asshole. Never has been except on paper.* He remained silent; didn't know where this was going.

"There is no doubt in my mind that you and my wife are together every time I'm not around. As a matter of fact, Jimbo, I'm not even sure those kids are mine."

Jim's blood boiled. "Are you fucking crazy? Listen to yourself! Do you really think that Michelle and I have been together all this time? My feelings for her may have never changed, but I would never do that to you, and listen to what you're saying about a woman who has remained faithful to you for many years. How dare you degrade her like this? Do you know how many times we could have had an affair? We never..."

Richard's hands tightened on the steering wheel, and he sped on the icy road.

Suddenly, gunshots rang out from different directions taking out all four tires. Richard lost control of the Mercedes. The car seemed to soar in slow motion. It rolled down a hill, flipping over and over several times before it finally came to a stop.

The acrid smell of smoke filled the air. The window on the passenger side was shattered as well as the windshield. Jim lay pinned between the roof of the car and the seat. Cold metal crushed his chest...he couldn't breathe. Limited air went in and out. He opened his eyes, but blood streamed over his face, and he couldn't see anything but red. He couldn't feel his legs or his arms. He tried to move his arm to undo the seatbelt, but the roof of the car pinned his upper body against the cold leather seat. He needed to breathe. He was dying.

He closed his eyes succumbing to the darkness and peace he felt.

♫

Seven police cars with lights blaring blocked the road, and the limos carrying The Warriors and their families came to a full stop. The chauffeurs moved to the side to let two ambulances through. A tow truck followed by a fire truck screeched to a halt. Smoke came from below the road.

Curious, Karl got out of the limo and walked to the edge of the road. His hands spasmed as he realized it was a bad car accident. The car lay upside down. A thin trickle of gasoline dripped onto the snow.

It was the same black Mercedes sedan that left the house a half hour before the limos. Someone was still moving in the car.

"Shit!" Karl shouted. "Jim!"

Susan and Michelle ran out to see what was wrong. They recognized the car. Michelle's scream pierced the cold air. Karl put his arm around her and turned to Susan. "Take her back to the car."

Karl walked to the police cars, and he saw the paramedics motioning the firemen to run quickly with the jaws-of-life. Two responders stabilized the car. Karl heard a staticky call from the firemen. "There's a strange clicking noise coming from the car." Karl frantically waved Niall over and told him what he had heard.

Niall spoke to the authorities. "Get them out of there as fast as you can. I think there might be a bomb." He flashed his Interpol credentials.

In the distance, Richard's lifeless body lay in a heap, obviously thrown from the car. Karl's stomach turned as he realized that Jim was still in the car, but there was no sign of movement anymore. The firemen raced to cut away metal quickly trying to get away before the car exploded after the supervisor radioed the danger.

Ron joined Karl and watched Jim being taken out of the mangled metal and placed on a stretcher. Paramedics rushed up the hill, slipping on ice and snow. Policemen tried to keep the onlookers from getting too close.

Ron said to Karl, "Did he say bomb?"

"Ja!"

As the paramedics opened the back doors, the sound of the explosion shook the ground. Flames scorched leafless trees. A plume of ominous obsidian smoke rose to the slate sky.

Eva called out to Ron. He turned and put his hand up. "Stay back please. Eva, stay with Susan and Michelle. Don't let Michelle come out of the car."

Eva tried to lock the door of the limo. Michelle started to wail as she saw Jim's bloody and battered body being taken to the ambulance. The only reason she recognized him was because of what he was wearing. Sweatpants and a sweatshirt. He always dressed comfortably for transatlantic flights. His bloodied bare foot peeked from under the cover. A paramedic administered oxygen. She heard the explosion, saw the smoke. She threw herself from the car. "I have to know; I have to see...*merde!*"

She ran down the road as the paramedics came up with what was left of Richard's body in a black zippered bag. She fell to the ground on her knees and covered her face with her hands. Susan and Eva came to her side and tried to get her to stand. The ambulance with Jim readied to pull away from the scene, and she wanted to go wherever they were taking him. Susan and Eva pulled her back. *Is he going to die too? What do I tell the children?*

In the distance, Karl and Ron spoke with the police. Richard never knew what happened. His body flew out of the windshield and landed about 30 feet away from the car. Every bone in his body was shattered and massive injuries caused a swift and painless death.

The police officers recognized Ron and Karl. "You can accompany us to the hospital if you want. Any of these have a wife? Children?"

Karl's voice broke as he replied. "The decedent has a wife who is in the limo behind us. The other gentleman is our keyboard player, Jim Haley. Should we follow you to the hospital?"

"Yes, please," the policeman replied. The first one to respond was Michelle. Her husband was dead, and Jim was all she had left. She pushed past the paramedics and climbed into the ambulance.

Karl clutched a cold hand, blocked her. He didn't want her to see Jim in the horrific state he was in. "Are you sure about this?"

Michelle's lower lip trembled, and she nodded. Tears streamed down her face. "I have to be with him." Her wail broke Susan's heart, and she ran to her friend. She stepped into the ambulance to pull Michelle away, but horror flashed over her delicate features. She couldn't move. Both stood paralyzed.

Jim lay on the stretcher in the ambulance, eyes shut. His nose was misaligned and swollen. Blood covered his face from a cut on his forehead. His left leg was obviously broken in several places. There was a neck brace on. Broken clavicle. There was no way of telling yet what internal injuries he had. There was a gash on his bare foot. His big toe slanted to the side, broken.

Michelle reached out to touch his chin. Seemed like it was the only part of his body not swollen or bloodied. His skin was cold, and he flinched slightly at the feel of her fingers. He was obviously in a lot of pain. She looked at one of the paramedics. His eyes didn't reveal too much optimism, and he shook his head softly.

"Will you be coming to the hospital?" he asked her in French.

"*Oui.*"

Susan climbed in. "Karl and I will accompany you. The rest are going on to the airport; no use in keeping them here. Besides, Vera is going home to be with all the children. She doesn't want them to see this on the news. "

Jim didn't regain consciousness. The doctors kept him in an induced coma until he arrived at Cedars two weeks later. He had internal injuries; a collapsed lung, five broken ribs, and a punctured spleen. He was transferred to Los Angeles in The Warriors' private plane with the rest of the group and a nurse monitoring him. The cut above his eye required several stitches. His leg was put into a cast and his toe was taped. The clavicle fracture required delicate surgery to guarantee use of his arm and hand. A plastic surgeon was summoned to fix his broken nose. He was still on a ventilator and not breathing on his own.

42
THE PAST—AGAIN

JANUARY 1989, LOS ANGELES

Michelle returned to Los Angeles with Karl and Susan. She hadn't said much since they boarded the flight back to the United States, but Susan held her hand on the flight and made sure she ate and was comfortable. Most of the time, she alternated between a restless sleep and looking out the window, tears covering her face.

Susan hugged her dearest friend tightly as they entered Susan's home. Karl suggested that Michelle spend a few days with them while Ron helped make the funeral plans for Richard.

Michelle's blue eyes turned to Susan. "I'm so afraid that Jim is going to die, too."

"Hush, Jim's going to make it." She put her arms around Michelle and led her to the master bedroom. "I asked Stefani to get me some clothes for you to change into. Take a shower and a nap. We'll talk later."

Susan held Michelle tight and kissed her cheek. "He's still alive, and that's all that matters. We'll all help you get through this. You are strong, Michelle. Don't cave in on me."

Michelle pushed her hair back; tears slipped over her cheeks. "Where are my children?"

"They're with Ronnie at Vera's house with Esmeralda and Jim's girls. Gran is also there keeping the paparazzi under control. I'll ask her to bring all of them later, including your father. She's picking him up at the airport."

"Pere is coming?"

"Of course he is, Michelle. He loves you.

♫

A few hours later, Michelle joined her children and Susan and Karl. Antoine hugged her with tears in his eyes. "I'm going to miss Dad so much."

Sébastien joined them. "I'll miss him too."

"I know. Your dad was a good man," Michelle replied softly.

Antoine looked at his mother. "But he hurt you, Mama. You've been crying for a long time."

Michelle blew her nose. "That happens in marriages sometimes. I don't think your father meant to hurt me so badly. I need to talk with you and your brother soon."

They hugged her at the same time. The twins knew about their mom being unhappy for some time before their parents decided on divorce.

Stefano got the boys' attention. "Papy needs help with his luggage." He gave his daughter a subtle wink.

Michelle was glad Susan had gotten him there even if he was only staying two days.

Karla and Jenna clung to their anxious mother.

Karla had tears in her eyes. "When can we see Daddy?"

"As soon as we are allowed to visit him. We're praying he gets better."

Karla touched her mother's cheek. "Momma, is Daddy going to die like Uncle Richard?"

Vera stared at her daughter for a moment, not knowing how to reply. She looked to Susan and Karl. Karla was a tiny, light-brown-haired and delicate girl who didn't quite look like Jim or Vera, but she favored her father's elegant looks and Jim's mother's features. "We need to keep praying so that he will recover."

Karl picked Karla up in his arms and took Jenna's hand to lead her to the living room where they could sit. Susan helped Vera up and held her in her arms. When Susan pulled away, Vera whispered, "I can't do this, Susan."

Susan whispered. "He's still alive, and I strongly believe our prayers are going to help him."

Vera placed her head gently on Susan's shoulder and sobbed.

"I know that we haven't been together in years, but still, he's the father of my daughters, and at some point, I felt something for him. It's just that I was trying to forget John while he was trying to forget Michelle, but it wasn't all bad."

Michelle moved toward Vera and the two women hugged each other. "I'm sure it wasn't, Vera, and I'm glad you have two beautiful daughters."

Vera cried on Michelle's shoulder. "He loves you so much."

Susan patted her dear friend's and sister-in-law's backs and kissed their cheeks. "Hush ladies; this is not the time."

When she thought Vera and Michelle had cried enough for the moment, she pulled them away. "Karl will handle the girls and your twins, Michelle. They're young and sometimes they assimilate these things better than we do. At least for the moment."

All the members of The Warriors and their families were a close-knit family. They shared decades of struggles, good times, bad times, ups, downs. This was another tragedy they would have to bear together.

The nanny took the children to the den while Esmeralda put together something for the adults to eat. Ron and Eva arrived a few minutes later. Karl filled a glass of cognac and sighed.

"Vera, I don't have to tell you that Jim is family to us. He was always there for Ron and for me. Jim is a spoke in our wheel and the father of my nieces. We're hurting badly, and we will stand by you and Michelle."

Karl turned to Michelle. "Richard's body arrives tomorrow, and we have a few decisions to make."

Ron spoke next. "I suggest a small, private ceremony and then we can think of some kind of memorial that will include fans later. We are too close to let others intrude on our sorrow. We'll do the same as we did for Mike and Vlad. As for Jim, time will tell."

Michelle agreed, and Ron and Karl left to finalize arrangements. She wrapped her arms around herself; she wasn't ready to face the fact that Jim's life could end at any moment.

Richard's funeral was set for the following day, with cremation after a morning service.

♫

Vera and Michelle stayed at Susan's house the night before the service was supposed to take place.

Michelle and her boys got dressed for Richard's service. The girls were not going to be there, nor Ronnie. She put on a simple Dior black dress, black stockings and pumps. She ruffled her red curls, and she smiled as she remembered Jim running his fingers through her hair during their lovemaking, pulling on it in passion. The faint smile brought on by the memory quickly turned to tears at the thought of probably never making love to him again, never kissing him, laughing with him...*Merde! What is wrong with me?* She was burying her husband and all she could think about is Jim's condition...guilt set in and made her cry even harder.

A soft knock on the bedroom door interrupted her musings. She dried her eyes with a lace-edged linen handkerchief. "Come in."

Susan opened the door. "It's time. We should go."

Michelle nodded. She picked up a black shawl and bag. Susan and Karl were going to accompany her in the limousine.

When they arrived at the funeral home, there were dozens of people waiting outside. Her eyes filled with tears. Richard was loved by many who didn't know that after meeting the "other" woman, he became a cold, hard, and unloving person. Usually happened when the music died, and divorce was eminent.

Karl took her hand and helped Michelle out of the car. He put his arm around her to hold her steady.

Stefani and Niall's arrival followed. One hand clasped Stefani's and the other hand checked to make sure his gun holster was unsnapped in case he needed to retrieve his gun in a hurry. There was plenty of police protection. Interpol Detective Turpin already stood guard at the entrance, and Niall wanted to blend in with the mourners. There were dark circles under his eyes, so he chose to wear sunglasses and hoped to not draw too much attention to himself in his black suit, black shirt and black tie. He felt like shit. He studied every person and made sure they were people the family knew.

He motioned Ron over and released Stefani's hand for a moment. "Don't go too far, Stefani. Stay close to me."

"I won't," she replied softly, kissing his cheek.

Niall waited until Stefani was with her mother and Vera. "Ron, if anything happens, you make sure you don't lose your head. There's plenty of police presence here. Let the pros handle this; we know what we're doing."

Ron pushed his fingers through his unruly hair and sighed. "You're asking me to do the impossible, Niall."

Niall's eyes met his. "Don't tell me you're packing!"

Ron nodded. "So are Karl and Alex."

Niall remained silent. He couldn't tell them not to attend the funeral armed, but it could become a bloodbath all over again if they all started shooting in different directions. God, he hoped they'd seen the end of the violence! He ground his teeth. *And technically, here in the States, Ron is a convicted felon in possession of a firearm. I'll just pretend I don't know.*

♫

A taxicab pulled up to the funeral home in the early evening. A young man in his twenties wearing a dark suit and tie stepped out. The warm California sun glistened on his light brown hair. Hazel eyes looked around as he seemed to be looking for someone he would recognize. One of the band members.

He straightened his long, lean form and placed his hand on the door of the car. He took a deep breath. He strolled with confidence to the two richly carved double doors at the entrance of the funeral home.

Robert Turpin stood behind a lectern set up to check all the guests against a list that had been provided by The Warriors and the family members of people who would be exclusively allowed to enter the premises.

The polite young man spoke first. "I'm not on any list, Sir. I would like to see Karl Engels or Ron James if that is possible."

"I will have to check your credentials and check your person before I can get any of them to come out and see you."

"Of course," the young man agreed. He waited patiently while he was thoroughly frisked by a young, LAPD rookie. Everything in his pockets was checked. He only had a wallet with a gold American Express card, some cash and a key to a room at the Beverly Wilshire Hotel. The detective then asked him for his I.D. He produced a German driver's license and passport.

"One moment, please."

After several telephone calls to verify the man's identity, Turpin picked up his walkie talkie and spoke into it. "Detective Edwards, please bring Mr. Engels outside. There's a guest here who is asking to see him but is not on the list. He's clean."

"Sure, what's his name?" Niall asked, retrieving his gun from the holster and holding it where no one could see it.

"James Haley, III."

♫

Stefani saw Niall pull his gun out and walk toward Karl. They exchanged a few words, and Karl frowned. Niall whispered something in his ear and Karl nodded then followed Niall out.

♫

Karl didn't smile at the young man that awaited him, but his hands became sweaty. He held out his hand.

"Karl Engels. I'm sorry, what did you say your name was?"

"Trés Haley."

"Thought you said James Haley, III."

"And it is. Trés is a nickname. My mother Nancy told me about my father, Jim, and said that if I ever wanted to meet him, I was to contact him directly, you, or Ron James. I just heard he was in a bad car accident that killed Mr. Stone. I'm just asking you to help me meet him or see him."

There was no doubt in Karl's mind that the man was Jim's son. The kid favored both Jim *and* Nancy; there was no denying the bloodline.

"How is Nancy?" Karl asked.

"She passed away last year."

"I'm sorry."

Karl reached out and touched his arm. "Your father is still in the hospital. It's not too good because infection can set in, but I hope he can get to meet you. I'm so sorry about Nancy."

He shook his head. *Damn you, Nancy! The one time your pregnancy was real, and you didn't try to contact Jim.*

"Come with me. I'll take you inside. My sister is Jim's ex, and Michelle is Richard's widow."

"I know. I didn't come here to upset anyone, Mr. Engels. I just want to pay my respects to Mrs. Stone and see my father. I've seen pictures of my dad and Mrs. Stone, and I see something in their eyes that tells me there is some history between them. I wanted to be here for her as well."

Karl put his arm around the young man's shoulders. "I'm not Mr. Engels. I'm Karl, and if God has sent you into our lives to ease the pain, you *will be* a part of us, just like your father is. And yes, there is beautiful history and chemistry between them, but this is not the time to discuss that."

The pale and shaken young man followed Karl into the funeral room. Everyone turned to the door. Some of the guests gasped. Annie turned white and her hands trembled.

Karl took Michelle's hand. "Michelle, this young man is Trés, Jim and Nancy's son."

Trés just nodded as a tear slid over his cheek. "I'm very sorry for your loss, Mrs. Stone."

"Please call me Michelle. My heavens, you look so much like him! How's Nancy?" she asked.

"She passed away last year."

"She was my cousin, you know. We lost touch over time."

"Yes, she told me." He said and pressed his lips together to keep from crying.

The resemblance between Jim and his son was astounding. He favored Nancy more than Jim, but his mannerisms were definitely Jim's. Michelle reached out to touch his cheek. "You're handsome, just like he was at your age. You look more like Nancy than Jim, but you wear that day-old stubble that drives some women crazy and *that* is certainly your father's trademark. And...you walk and move just like him."

As Michelle and Trés spoke, he took her hand. "Jim doesn't know about me. My mother tried to contact him a long time ago, but my grandfather wouldn't let her. It's a long story, Mrs. Stone."

"We'll talk later. I know your grandfather *very* well," she whispered.

♫

Annie excused herself to go to the bathroom when she saw Trés approach Vera with Karl and Niall.

Niki held her arm. "Isn't that...?"

"Sh! I need to get out of here." Annie ran into the bathroom. Her heart hammered against her chest. *What the hell is he doing here?*

She opened the door slightly and motioned to her sister. "We have to leave. Tell Mom I'm not feeling well and need to go home. I'll meet you outside; I'm not going back in there."

Niki scowled at the deception, but she delivered the message.

Annie got into her BMW and tore out of the parking lot once her sister joined her.

"Annie, what happened between you two?"

"Not only did I fall madly in love with him, we got damn close to having sex!"

"I am so jealous, Annie. I heard them say he's Jim's son. We can't hide and not attend the funeral."

"Did he see me?"

"I don't know. I don't think so. He appeared distraught and out of place. He walked into a funeral home with his father's manager in a coffin and a room filled with a lot of strangers. I don't think he was looking to meet a chick there."

"Oh, shit!" Annie's eyes filled with concern after Niki dropped her off and returned to the service. She called some friends and went to dinner with them.

♫

Much later, Susan and Karl returned to their home. Michelle would be staying with them. Ron and Eva followed as well as Alex, Niall, and their significant others.

Alex and Niall made sure Trés didn't feel uncomfortable. Alex played bartender while Susan put some snacks out. Vera had already taken Karla and Jenna home, so they didn't get the chance to meet their half-brother.

Annie arrived a half hour later. She was emotionally exhausted from watching her family grieve for someone who everyone loved and considered family and the surprise visitor she would have to face the next day. Her heart broke for Michelle and Vera's girls. She couldn't stand her high heels any longer, and she took them off before entering the house.

The adults were in the den supporting Michelle. She strolled out to the patio to join Alex, Ashley, Niall, and Stefani. She yawned and pulled off her black linen blazer leaving her in a black sleeveless shift. She threw the jacket on a chair and plopped onto a chaise. Her dress rode way up, and she unhooked one of her black stockings from the garter belt and pulled it off, then proceeded to begin removing the second one.

Niall shook his head and coughed. She looked at him, "What?"

"We have company. Annie, this is Trés, Jim's son."

She gawked at Trés and pulled her skirt down. "Sorry. I thought it was just you guys."

A faint smile touched his lips as recognition and surprise set in, and he winked. "Nice to meet you, Annie."

"Likewise," she replied. Her eyes studied him. As a matter of fact, other than Karl, she always thought that Jim was the next best looking one of The Warriors but damn, Trés was sexy. Seeing him now in a suit...*damn him! No wonder he looked so familiar that night!*

"I guess it's a bit late, and I should get going. We have a long day tomorrow." Trés smiled and his eyes consumed Annie's. He placed his empty glass on a side table.

"Where are you staying?" Alex asked as he took Ashley's hand in his.

"The Beverly Wilshire."

"I'll drive you, and I'll pick you up tomorrow morning."

"Thanks." Trés turned to the rest of them and said good night, his eyes lingered a bit long on Annie. "I've never gotten over those great legs," he whispered as he kissed her cheek.

Annie took a deep breath as he passed her, leaving the subtle scent of his cologne behind.

43
ANOTHER FINAL GOODBYE

JANUARY 1989, LOS ANGELES

The funeral home was packed to capacity the following morning. The nannies held on to the children while Michelle and the rest of the adults entered the room to say good-bye before having the body cremated. Although it was a closed casket, Michelle allowed them all to stand around the coffin and bid their farewell. She stayed behind, while friends paid their final respects.

Trés watched Michelle, the stunning redhead that was in a lot of photographs with his father. He went to stand beside her. If his father loved her, he would try to do so as well. He really liked her warm personality. Besides, they were blood kin.

There wasn't a dry eye in the room. She stood slowly to leave. Trés placed his arm around her shoulders. He knew Vera had been with his father, and that they had two daughters; but he knew that Michelle played a huge part in his father's life. His mother had told him.

Trés pulled a handkerchief from his jacket and handed it to her. Michelle cried even harder when she saw him standing beside her. He was a *blood* relative. Her cousin's son and Jim's. She had no choice but to love him. She would do anything in her power to make sure the young man got to know his father.

Everyone was asked to leave the room so that the casket could be taken away.

A priest came to say a few words of condolences and hope. Ron squeezed Eva's hand and stood beside the casket. He placed a hand on it and closed his eyes for a moment. Tears streamed down his face and he sobbed.

Richard Stone brought The Warriors to fame, and that was something they would never forget.

♫

The members of The Warriors and their families returned to

Michelle's house. The help quickly served a full spread on the patio while the nannies tried to keep the children quiet. Children were children and they brought laughter with them. Yes, they would miss "Uncle" Richard, but the worst part of the day was over for them, and they laughed at unspoken jokes, bringing with them a touch of joy and delight during a sad time.

Niall took his tie and jacket off and opened the top buttons of his shirt. God, he hated wearing a suit! He looked around to make sure everyone was a familiar face. Three police cars stood outside the gates of the home, and he breathed a little easier. He and Turpin sipped drinks watching every movement.

Stefani, Susan, Michelle, and Vera sat together. Trés watched them, seeing the love they all had for one another and wanted desperately to fit in with his new family.

Annie stood beside him; she placed a soft hand on his arm. "Hey, you okay?"

He nodded. "I guess as good as can be expected. I just hope I'm not too late to meet my father."

"Your father is an amazing man."

"I see that. When I arrived here yesterday, I wasn't sure what I was going to face. I certainly didn't expect to see you again, Annie."

Her smile lit up the backyard but stopped at her saddened eyes as they travelled to the group inside sitting around Michelle, offering their support. "We're a pretty cool clan, you know. My stepdad can be a little nutty and a pain in the ass, but he means well. Can I get you something to drink?"

"Sure." He sat on a stool and watched her put together two drinks.

"Who would have known you were Jim's son? Come to think of it, you resemble him when you play the guitar, same moves. I thought I saw something familiar that night, but I couldn't pinpoint it. You and your band have a different sound, but your body movements are the same." Her hand stretched across the bar to hand him a scotch on the rocks. She remembered what he drank, what he'd ordered that night.

"Thanks," he said and swirled the glass around. "Don't think for a moment that I didn't want to stay a bit longer, get to know you better, but I had to leave. I have a girlfriend."

"Oh?" she said and arched an eyebrow.

"I didn't want you to know. You were a hot chick on the road, a one-night stand, but you managed to haunt me for many nights after that one encounter. I still have an earring you lost in my dressing room. I'll bring it the next time I come to L.A."

So that's where my earring went! Annie thought.

He sighed and smiled at her. "You live in Germany still?" she asked.

"I was getting ready to come to the States to meet my dad when this happened. I know he has a home here and one in New York."

Alex and Niall joined them. They talked about music, which interested both Alex and Trés.

"When do you leave?" Alex asked.

"I couldn't get a flight back until the end of the week," he replied and placed his empty glass on the bar.

"Do you want another?" Annie asked.

He shook his head and placed his hand over the glass as she went to pour more scotch.

"Why don't we get together before you leave and try a few jams and see what we got? That is, if you feel up to it," Alex said.

Trés shrugged. "I'd love it. Just let me know when."

"Ashley and I are having dinner at her place tonight, so I can call you at the Beverly tomorrow around noon. Lunch and then we can come back to my dad's studio."

"Sounds like a plan. I'll stop by the hospital in the morning to see my Dad and meet you after."

Niall and Stefani were exhausted and went back to Susan's house to rest a bit. They were scheduled to go to Paris at the end of the week and settle into Niall's apartment to begin to plan their wedding, and they still had to pack. Life went on.

Before they left, Niall stood in the middle of the living room where everyone sat. "I need for all of you to listen up."

The room quieted down. Niall took a deep breath. "I know that we're all home now, but I don't want you to feel this is over. I need for each and every one of you to be vigilant. Check your surroundings; be careful. No one has been arrested. The one culprit they caught the first time, committed suicide, so he didn't give us any information. Mr. Turpin is on his way back to France. Stefani and I are moving to France in a few days. Trés, you are a part of this family now; I don't want to tell you that you are in danger as well, but I have no choice. Please, everybody, if you see anything strange or any stranger in the vicinity, call the police. The FBI have been informed and are aware of this monster or monsters. I've arranged it so that each home represented here has twenty-four-hour police protection. Michelle, Vera, Ron and Eva, and Karl and Susan, someone will be there at all times. Jim has police protection at the hospital. Leslie has a guard, and so does Julienne. Don't let your children out of your sight, please stay safe and hopefully we can end this soon. Do I make myself clear?

"Do you want us to drive you back to the hotel?" Niall asked Trés.

"No, I think I'll stay with Vera, Michelle and Karl a little longer. I'll catch a taxi later," he said.

"You okay then?" Alex asked.

Trés shrugged. "Sure."

♫

Susan called everyone into the dining room to have a late lunch. Annie ended up seated directly across from Trés. He had removed his jacket and folded his sleeves up, revealing the strong, tattooed forearms Annie caressed not too long ago. His eyes met hers several times. She took many breaths to fill her lungs with air. She placed the napkin on her lap. She reached out to take the pepper mill at the same time as Trés, and their fingers clashed in midair. They both pulled back as if their skin burned.

"Sorry," she apologized in a deep, sultry voice, and he just smiled, speechless by the sexy voice he yearned to hear in a bedroom, in his bed and underneath his body. He needed to be careful, though.

After dinner, they remained at the table having desert and coffee. He tried to concentrate on the conversation, but it was useless. His eyes kept straying in Annie's direction. It was finally time to get back to his hotel; he didn't want to overstay his welcome.

He took his jacket and was about to ask permission to use the telephone to call a taxi, but Annie picked up her pocketbook.

"I'll drop you off at the hotel." Her smile hypnotized him.

"No, don't bother; I'm fine."

She stood in front of him. She felt the warmth of his body. "I insist."

"I appreciate it."

He was attracted to her...too much. He liked her style. He'd been with tons of women; old, young, older, younger and no one compared to how she made him feel.

The little spitfire caught his attention and tugged at his heart. He wanted her, but it was complicated now. He stared out the window as she took the highway.

"L.A.'s a beautiful city. Very different from Hamburg, though I've travelled a bit in Europe. Never came to the United States." He smiled as he looked out the window. He found himself in an exotic city with a beautiful, young woman he wanted desperately. Too bad he didn't search for his father sooner. It might have been different; he would have had someone to talk to about these feelings. He was sure he and Michelle were going to have a strong bond.

"It is very pretty. I like the palm trees," she added.

Suddenly, he became silent and distant. *Too young for me. Too involved with my newfound family. Alex's half-sister. Brother an Interpol agent. No thank you.*

They arrived at the Beverly Wilshire. "Would you like to join me for a drink?" he asked.

She laughed out loud. "Not twenty-one yet. They know I'm Ron James's stepdaughter at this bar."

He leaned over and placed his hand on her cheek. Their lips met, and although he wanted more, it was not the time or place. His kiss was passionate and long. His fingers slid over her neck and slowly down her arm. They continued to kiss and caress each other until Annie realized that she had to move the car.

"Will I see you again?" she whispered, out of breath. She loved the taste of his lips, his tongue.

"Maybe. I have someone I'm seeing back in Germany, my father is likely dying, and now you are threatening to turn my world upside down. I don't live in L.A. I've just met my father's friends and family, and your brother, Alex, wants to get together musically, and I'm trying to make a decision as to whether I'd prefer to be a part of his music or be with you and risk my neck. These people don't know me. It would probably not be too cool for you and me to date each other at this time." His mind made sense, but his heart and body said otherwise...still he wanted to be honest with her.

"You are dangerous, Annie. I want you too much."

"You'll never know how dangerous, I guess."

Trés got out of the car and walked into the hotel. He never looked back, couldn't for the moment.

She bit her lower lip. She was livid. Instead of crying as most women would have done in her situation, she banged on the steering wheel. She was so damn pissed. Her body was on fire. Fortunately, everyone was asleep when she returned.

She went to brush her teeth and looked in the mirror. Her lips were swollen and bruised. *So much for the fun and games of a one-night stand. Fuck!*

♫

The next day, Trés went by the hospital where he found Karl waiting for him. "Jim's still not conscious. He's holding his own, but I don't think you should see him in this condition. Michelle wants you to stay with her, and there's no way you can say no to her. She'll make sure you get in here to see Jim as soon as he's awake. Just be patient."

"Karl, I saw my mother hooked up to all kinds of tubes."

"Another reason not to see your father."

Trés sighed and nodded.

Karl put his hand on his shoulder. "Aren't you supposed to meet Alex for a jam session?"

"Yes."

"Come, I'll drive you."

♫

Trés walked into a fully customized studio, and his mouth dropped open. "Wow!"

Alex pointed. "That is your dad's guitar. Grab it, and let's see what you've got." He handed Trés some sheet music.

Trés glanced over it. "Is this new?"

"Yep, just came up with it last night."

The Haley fingers showed the ancestry when Trés began to play.

Alex thought he was hearing Jim. "Man! You can play!" Alex said.

"Would it be to forward for me to suggest a small change?"

"Like what?"

Trés tapped the page. "Here and here, I'd change the chords." He played the subtle change.

"That does sound better."

For the next two hours the guys jammed. At the end, Alex said, "You have to join Black Ice. It's destiny."

"I'll consider your offer seriously after I meet my father."

44
FATHER AND SON

JANUARY 1989, LOS ANGELES

Jim began to recover, and while he was in the hospital watching television, he saw the footage of the accident that had taken the life of music mogul Richard Stone and left Warriors' member Jim Haley in serious condition. He started to shake. It was awful. *Richard, dead?* With an immense effort and pain, he sat up in bed and looked out the window. He hurt for himself, his friends, yes, even Richard, but most of all Michelle. Tears formed in his eyes. *Shit, it happened again! Niall was right.*

A nurse came in. She put a thermometer in his mouth and took his pulse. She wrote something on his patient chart and turned to him. "You'll be in the hospital for a few more weeks. Just making sure infection doesn't set in."

He nodded.

Trés and Michelle walked down the hall to visit Jim. Michelle opened the door to the room slightly to make sure Jim was awake.

She placed a hand on Trés's arm and whispered, a wide grin on her face. "He's awake. You go on in, and I'm going to speak to the nurses and see if I can speak to a doctor."

Trés entered the room. He was at a loss for words. Now that the moment was here, he didn't know what to say.

The two looked at each other for a few moments. "Michelle told me I could come today. I'm Nancy's son, Trés. She said that if I ever wanted to meet you, I was to contact Ron or Karl."

Jim cautiously sized up the young man; he knew, gut feeling. He shifted his position on the bed and grimaced in pain. "How's Nancy?"

"She passed away not too long ago. She said she tried to tell you about me, but you and your friends had been drinking, and you didn't want to hear her. I'm your son, Mr. Haley. I'm James Haley, III. Trés is a nickname."

Jim sighed. *Seems like I have a dark past as well. I was no better than Ron back then. Hell, none of us were.*

"Come closer; sit."

The young man sat on a chair beside the stranger that was his father, yet a figure loved by millions around the world. In person, he was larger than life.

"For someone who writes lyrics, I'm at a loss for words, Trés. Please forgive me."

"I can leave if you want."

Jim looked at the young man. "Absolutely not. I just need to absorb this. I was just in a horrible car accident, our manager is dead, and I'm still in a lot of pain. The doctor said I will need a cane to walk for a few months. I'll need a lot of physical therapy, not to mention mental."

The door to the room opened, and Jim's mother and father walked in. Jim rolled his eyes. "I guess we are having a happy family reunion."

Lillian kissed her son. "How are you?"

"I've been better, Mother. You?"

"Good."

James Haley, Sr. glared at Trés. "Your mother is going to have to answer to me, young man."

"My mother died, *Grandpa*."

The pieces of the puzzle collided in Jim's mind, and he realized that his father was the biggest obstacle between his meeting his son, his own flesh and blood.

"You blackmailed her, didn't you?" Jim asked. His blood boiled. "You threatened her and told her never to tell me about him. And you probably paid her a hefty price to keep quiet."

In great agitation, Lillian asked, "Who are you?"

"Your grandson!" Jim snapped and flinched with the pain his outburst caused.

Standing at the nurses' station, Michelle caught sight of Jim's parents entering the room. *Merde!* She raced to get to the room before Jim's father could do more damage.

The door to the room slammed open, and Michelle stormed in, her angry cheeks as red as the cascading curls. "He paid her a million dollars and set up a trust for Trés to pay for his education."

Jim's mother looked at her husband, disbelief clearly on her face. "James! Did you prevent me from meeting my own *grandson*? Because his mother and father were not what you expected in life? The family of the U.S. Ambassador's perfect one? Your marriage was never perfect. Your son is an outstanding musician. How dare you!" Her voice became shrill. "I've allowed you to do too much damage to my son and me. I wasted so many years with you. Please leave us."

"I won't argue with any of you. I don't like the path my son took. As for the marriage, I no longer care to be married. The kid? Fuck him. The bastard son of a slut and this thing."

Michelle stood in front of him. "You are a heartless son of a bitch. Your wife should have seen through you years ago. Don't you ever say another word about your son. As far as I'm concerned, he walks on water. Your grandson? Thank you on his behalf for the private education, and for your information, his mother was just a product of the times and my *cousin*. If it hadn't been for Nancy, I would have never met Jim. I'm sure you've had women who were questionable. We were *ALL* questionable back then."

She turned to Lillian. "It was time you grew a backbone and sent this asshole packing."

She crossed her arms and hatred spewed from her eyes. "You don't know the damage you've caused me, your son, your wife, *and* your grandson. Get out of here. You are *le diable* incarnate. There goes your perfect reputation, Mr. Ambassador. If you are not out that door in ten seconds, I'll tell the security guard outside to take you away, and I've already started counting in my mind."

James wanted to slap the arrogant French trollop. He pointed a finger at her. "You haven't heard the last of me, young lady."

"Try it, asshole. I have a ton of French lawyers who would love to destroy you politically. Your son has a few lawyers as well. I'm right here, and I will never go away. I love your son way too much to let you continue to damage this family, and you will never get rid of me!"

"Michelle," Jim called out softly. He sighed. "Let it go; it's not worth it. I've lived with this all my life. It's not going to change."

Michelle pointed a sharp finger at the door. "Get out! NOW!"

James Haley, Sr. stomped out the door in a huff.

She walked to the bed and kissed Jim's cheek, then put her arms around him. "I understand now. I'm so sorry for not having had more compassion back then."

Lillian got closer to the bed. "I'm going to leave now. I have to find a hotel room. I won't stay with him."

"You can stay in my house...or Jim's." Michelle said.

"No, I'll just head over to the Beverly Hills Hotel. I'll take a taxi. I need to be alone for a while. I'll come back tomorrow. Maybe after that, I'll take you up on your offer. I want to see my granddaughters too."

She leaned in and kissed her son. "I'm so sorry." Then turned to her grandson. "I intend to be in your life for as long as I live. I swear I never knew about you."

Lillian Haley turned and walked out. Jim took a deep breath and looked at his son. "I'm sorry you had to be a witness to this circus."

"It's okay. I'm glad you know."

Jim stretched out his hand and the young man smiled and placed his hand in his father's. Jim squeezed. "We have a lot of catching up to do. Where are you staying?"

"With Michelle."

"If I'd known about you..." Jim said. Sadness covered his face.

Michelle leaned over and kissed his forehead. She took his hand in hers. "Just get better, Jim Haley. We need you." Her eyes watered.

"I'm going to be fine. 'Try it, asshole?' Michelle you sounded more American than ever! Did I ever tell you how much I love you?"

It was late, and it was time Jim got some rest. Trés looked at his father. "Thank you."

"No thanks are necessary. You are mine and you always will be."

Trés turned to Michelle. "I'll wait outside for you."

She adored the kid. He was sweet and good natured. Handsome too. Just like his dad but softer. Jim was more cynical at that age. *Had to live with the asshole.*

When Trés left, Michelle kissed Jim. He groaned as her tongue snaked into his mouth.

He placed his hand on her tush and squeezed. He winked at her. "Shit, that feels good. The next time you come to see me, make sure you wear a skirt and no panties."

"Why? You want to see my knees?"

"No. I want you to sit on my dick."

Michelle raised her eyebrows. "Seriously, Jim. I really think the accident jumbled your brain a bit. You were never so crude."

He laughed and then grunted because laughing really hurt. "I've

always been crude, baby; you just don't remember. Kiss me again."
   "Oh, Jimbo, I remember every little thing about you."

45
BACK HOME

FEBRUARY 1989, LOS ANGELES

The minute Jim walked into Susan and Karl's home, Karla and Jenna yelled out, "Daddy!!" He leaned on a cane, but he looked well.

They threw themselves against him, making him flinch. Greetings went around to everyone, the children, the adults. "Not so hard," Jim whispered. "Daddy's still very sore."

Vera hugged him. "I'm glad you're well. I was at the hospital several times."

"I know. Thanks."

"What are your plans?" she asked.

"Go home to New York for a while. I need some time. I have to see what the guys are going to do."

She put a hand on his arm. "You'll be fine. Just take your time and let me know if you need anything."

He stood in front of Michelle. She became lost in his mahogany eyes.

"Come, give me a hug," he said, holding out his right his arm.

Michelle leaned against his chest. "It feels so good to hold you," she whispered.

She kissed his cheek and stepped away. "Oh my, do I smell cheap hospital shampoo and soap? How *plébéien* of you!"

Jim looked into her eyes and laughed. "Red, I've missed you so much! You are such a snob!"

"Likewise."

Much later, it was just Susan, Karl, Michelle, and Jim. Jim took Michelle's hand. "You're wearing this!"

"I've always loved this bracelet; good choice, Jimbo."

"I'm so lucky to have been spared a worse fate."

"We have a lot to talk about."

Michelle stood and searched in her jeans pocket and pulled out two tiny mother-of-pearl buttons. "Put your hand out," she said to Jim. "These yours?"

Nothing in the world ever embarrassed Jim. He was an open-minded, liberal American and a rock star who had seen it all. He looked at the buttons in the palm of his hand, and his face turned beet red.

He turned to Karl. "What am I going to do with this chick?"

"What are those?" Karl asked, though he knew.

Before he replied he looked Michelle up and down. Her jeans were tight, she still had the curves, but she was way thinner than ever. "You are still pretty hot, Red." He returned the buttons. "It's a miracle any of them survived. Never mind, Karl. It's a long story."

"What are you going to do? Are you staying for a bit in California?" Susan asked.

"No," Jim said. "I'm going back to New York tomorrow and get to know my son before he leaves on tour. He tells me you guys are coaching him. I appreciate it…what are we going to do without Richard?'

Karl stood and poured himself another cognac and handed one to Jim. "Ron and I were thinking of managing these young guys and just let The Warriors have a comeback in a few years, then retire. We haven't called Craig in for the audition, and I'm not sure about Leslie, though she says she wants to do it for Vlad's sake. I'm sure she can play, but I don't think she can handle the emotional stress of it. Love her too much to put her through that." He gave Jim a significant look, and Jim knew Karl was also thinking about the added danger Leslie would be in if she became part of the band.

Jim sipped his drink. "I like that thought. I think it's time to take a breather, get to see my girls more and get to know my son. This bachelor wants to start over…a new life." He looked in Michelle's direction and she ran the tip of her tongue over her lips. He looked away as he felt parts of his body come to life.

"Jim, we need to move on," Karl said.

Jim put the glass down. "Agreed. I have to go. My flight leaves early tomorrow, and I have to at least get some stuff packed. I know that Vera and Trés sent the rest of my stuff to New York. He's coming with me, and we'll come back the end of the week, right before he leaves."

Michelle stood. "Trés will probably be home late. I can drive you."

She put her heels back on, holding on to Jim for support. Susan and Karl watched them together once again. Time stood still, and the rekindling of their relationship was inevitable.

"By the way." Susan grinned. "Your tapes are safe."

Jim shook his head. "What tapes?"

"You had a slew of videotapes, and the box was marked CONFIDENTIAL." Karl smirked.

"Which one did you watch?" he teased.

He never expected a quick and positive answer from Susan. "Mykonos," she stated nonchalantly.

Jim rolled his eyes, and his cheeks flamed.

He turned to Michelle. "Seriously? You showed her that tape?"

"Of course not," Michelle replied. "They're just teasing you."

While they were together, Jim and Michelle taped most of their trips and some of their wildest sexual escapades.

She took his hand and pulled it. "Come on, *mon amour,* I have to get up early. My turn to take the kids to school. I can't stay up all night anymore."

Jim followed Michelle to her Mercedes. She held out the keys. "Wanna drive, or should I?"

He took the keys. "I'll drive."

They were silent for a few moments. He took her hand and kissed it. "I know we have a lot to talk about. I'm going to be in New York for a few months. You go on and do what you have to do in the islands. We'll talk on the phone."

They arrived, and he put the car in park. "I agree. I just need some time for my kids to adjust to the loss of their father. I'll go to Turks & Caicos and finish Richard's project." She went to get out of the car, but he pulled her back. He placed his hand on her neck, his thumb against her cheek.

"How did I ever let you go?" He leaned down, and his lips barely touched hers at first.

Michelle reached out put her hands on his shoulders. She moaned as she felt his kiss intensify.

His hands caressed her arms, and he let them slide over her breasts before stroking her neck. He lowered his lips so that he could kiss her earlobe. He slipped open the top button of her blouse and kissed the spot between her breasts, sliding his thumbs over her nipples. Michelle placed a warm hand on his thigh.

Jim broke away, and his eyes penetrated into her. "Good night, Red. I'll call you when I get back."

"Yes, please," she panted.

He drew away and got out of the car to open the door for her. Michelle stepped out of the car and stumbled. Jim grabbed her. He waited until she was steady. "Too much alcohol or too much Jimbo?"

She leaned over and kissed his cheek. "Not enough alcohol and certainly not enough Jimbo."

He smirked. "Goodnight, baby cakes."

♫

Michelle dropped off the children the following morning and went to the gym to meet Susan. They were going to a day spa afterwards.

Michelle entered the gym walking slower than usual. Susan held out some type of green drink to Michelle.

"Pass." Michelle said, plopping her butt on the chair in front of Susan.

"You okay?" Susan asked.

"Didn't sleep a wink."

"I would have driven the kids. You could have called me."

"I was up anyway."

"Heavy night with Jim?"

"Almost. It got pretty heavy in the car. I remembered those Hamburg days in his father's car. His son was at his house, and I think they need some time together. By the time I got home, I almost had to call in the Fire Department. My entire body was on fire, not to mention my pussy was burnt to a crisp."

Susan laughed. "Nice language, Red. Let's just work out for a bit and hit the spa early so that you can take a nap this afternoon. I'll pick up the kids at school."

46
GOODBYE FOR NOW

MARCH 1989, LOS ANGELES

Michelle entered her palatial Malibu home. Dressed in a black and white tweed Chanel jacket and jeans, she sorted the pile of mail before she set out to Susan's. The phone rang, startling her.

"Hey gorgeous, I'm back," Jim whispered, his voice full of melodic tenderness.

"How are you feeling?"

"I guess as good as can be expected. I went for a swim in my pool this morning. Ashley suggested I get some exercise so that the damaged muscles start to heal. I'm trying to use the cane less and less. I feel okay, you?"

Michelle sighed. "*Comme ci comme ça.*"

"When are you leaving?"

"Day after tomorrow."

"Can we have dinner? I promise you'll be better than just so-so."

Her heart pounded. "I'd like that."

"Do you mind if we have dessert and coffee with Susan and Karl?"

"Not at all."

"I'll pick you up in a bit."

"I'm in jeans; I only have to change."

"You probably have on a Chanel jacket and stilettos."

Michelle pouted. "*Cher,* am I that predictable?"

Jim laughed loudly for the first time in a long time.

"I've known you for too long. Don't change; you'll be just fine. Nothing too fancy."

When he arrived, she had to hold her breath. He cut his hair and wore it combed back. Grey at the sides. That day-old stubble was now a beard, cropped close to his face, and the hoop in his ear made him devastatingly handsome.

He kissed her softly on the lips. "Can you get any handsomer, Mr. Haley?"

"And you are like wine…better with age, and you taste even better."

She smiled and put her arm around his as they walked to the car. Once in the restaurant, he ordered wine. He sat back and looked at her features, still exquisite after all the years. *Even better!*

The waiter brought them a bottle of wine and Jim ordered. Michelle took a sip from her wine. "Are we going to sit here all night and gawk at each other?"

Tears came to Michelle's eyes. "What has Karl told you about that day? Getting you to the hospital in that ambulance that took forever. I honestly thought you were going to die. "

He took her hand again and tightened his grip on her fingers. "He told me how close to death I was, and that Richard didn't know what hit him. Died instantly."

"*Non.* He didn't suffer."

She looked down and her features became serious. "I'm off to spread Richard's ashes at the White Cliffs of Dover. I'm asking Susan to come with me. Then, I have to fly to Turks & Caicos to finish the project of the mega recording studio and home Richard started to build for all of us. It will probably take a few months; we're still not even halfway through the project. I would like to spend some time alone. Trés tells me that his mother tried to tell you about him, and you didn't want hear it."

Jim took a deep breath and clasped his hands together, elbows on the table. "I went back to Hamburg, one night twenty, twenty-one years ago. Ron had already left, you girls didn't travel to Hamburg anymore, Karl was somewhere, and I just felt like shit, missed the friendship, the band, the camaraderie we shared. It had nothing to do with you, Red. Vladimir, Mike, and I knew we had a fantastic band, and here it was scattered all over the place. We took a trip back to the Cosmos, and I got so drunk, I could barely stand. I saw Nancy, and she tried to get me to go back to her place. I just couldn't; you were the only one I've wanted to be with since I met you. Then, she tried to tell me something, but I didn't want to hear it. She left the Cosmos, and I passed out after that. I guess she wanted to tell me about Trés."

Jim shrugged and picked up his glass of wine. "It was a dark time for me. The group disbanded, our dream was shattered, and my parents fought like cats and dogs every night. My mom accused him of cheating on her, and he accused her of having affairs with several diplomats."

Michelle reached out and took his hand. "You never told me how much you were hurting," she said softly. Her eyes were full of sympathy.

"I was still hiding from the truth." He brought her hand to his lips. "Let's go have dessert with our favorite people."

As they walked out of the restaurant hand in hand, he placed his arm around her shoulders, and she put her arm around his waist. "I'll miss you."

"And I will miss you too, but I think we both need this. I'll call you while I'm away, I promise. I'm not leaving the planet."

♫

Karl and Susan were thrilled to see them. Miraculously, they were alone. All the children were spending the night at Vera's. They sat outside and Michelle told them about her plans. "I need to get the place finished. He didn't want anyone to see it until it was completed, so I guess I have to go out there and finish the project in his honor. It's the least I can do."

Several hours later, Jim drove her home. He stopped the car and turned in his seat. He slipped his hand over her cheek. He took hold of her parted lips. She wanted him so much, wanted their old life back but it couldn't be, at least for a while longer. She grasped the front of his shirt and tightened her hands into fists, pulling him closer. Their mouths fused and she moaned. The tip of his tongue slid over her neck and his teeth bit down on Balenciaga infused skin. Her fingers stroked his groin, feeling the bulge between his legs. "Hmm, I like this. Come inside, Jim. I think I can make that better."

They spilled out of the car.

The precious Chanel jacket cascaded to the ground in the foyer. He shed his shirt, unbuckled his belt. Her hands caressed his arms, his shoulders, and she bent down to kiss his chest. They stumbled into her bedroom. He slipped the black t-shirt over her head. His eyes fell onto the most beautiful lace apricot-colored bra he had ever seen. The lace was soft, and he unsnapped it, revealing her fleshy globes. His fingers slipped over the soft mounds, his tongue circled her nipple and pulled it into his mouth. He moaned; she gasped.

He slipped his hands over her buttocks and slipped her panties over her soft hips and tossed them to the ground. He picked her up and they fell onto the bed. She caressed his navel with the tips of her nails, travelling lower with deliberate slow circular movements. He couldn't hold out another moment. He took her ankles and spread her legs so that he could plunge into her, calling out her name. A few seconds later she reached her own heights.

Nothing changed; the love and the passion were still there.

47
THE WHITE CLIFFS OF DOVER

MARCH 1989, L.A. TO DOVER

Susan stood by the French doors and looked out to the backyard. Michelle sat on a stone bench. A small smile touched Michelle's lips but didn't travel as high as her sad eyes. Susan went out to her friend and sat beside her on the bench.

"What's wrong?" Susan asked softly.

Michelle shrugged and her eyes filled with tears. "How am I going to handle this? The kids without their father? Jim back in the picture?"

Susan took her hand in hers. "We'll do this one day at a time, just like we've been doing."

Michelle squeezed Susan's fingers. "Will you come with me to spread Richard's ashes? His favorite place was the White Cliffs of Dover. It's the least I can do. I've waited long enough."

"Of course, I will. Whenever you want to do it, I'll be with you."

"I don't want anyone else to go, just you and me."

Susan nodded and she hugged her dearest friend. "Just you and me, Michelle. Just like old times."

"I never thought I would be a widow. One week and our divorce would have been final."

"Liz never showed up for the funeral after the mess she caused."

"I know." She gave a one-shoulder shrug. "She didn't cause the mess alone though."

With a snicker, Susan said, "She probably thought you'd break her nose again."

Susan kissed Michelle's cheek. "Now, hush. I don't want you thinking anymore; you'll drive yourself nuts. You have no reason to feel guilty."

They held hands. "Come, let's have something to eat, I'm starving!" Susan pulled Michelle up.

♫

Susan accompanied Michelle to the White Cliffs of Dover, a place that Richard mentioned many times. It was a place to seek solace and meditate. He and Michelle travelled there several times because Dover was his birthplace. Distant family still lived there, and in recent years, Richard remodeled and modernized the house where he was born that belonged to his parents their entire lives.

The taxi stopped at a small shop so that they can pick up some groceries and wine for their stay. Susan and Michelle arrived at the modest but beautiful house touched by Michelle's warm taste.

Michelle's hand shook when she put the key in the door. Her thoughts flashed back to touching memories with Richard after their marriage and spending holidays there with the twins when they were toddlers. Although she had never stopped loving Jim, the first years of marriage to Richard were not bad.

She carefully placed the urn containing Richard's remains on the marble mantelpiece until their visit to its final resting place.

Susan helped her unpack the groceries. They cooked dinner together, Susan taking tips from Michelle. "Boy, you sure have come a long way from your days of boiling water," Michelle said in jest.

"It was improbable, not impossible. I have to feed my family. Besides, I love your French cooking and learned from the best." Susan refilled the wine glasses.

Michelle rolled her eyes. "That was never your concern."

Both of them laughed and then tears welled in Michelle's eyes. Trying to fight her own tears and stay strong for her friend, Susan reached out and hugged Michelle.

After dinner, Susan and Michelle sat on the couch in the living room legs folded under them, like they had in the dorm room of the French boarding school where they met.

Michelle's shaking hand clutched the wine glass, and she sipped.

"My children are going to miss him. He was a good father. I couldn't have asked for a better man in the beginning. I've been lucky. I had two men who loved me, whereas some women don't even have one in their lifetime, even if he did fuck it up at the end. Do you realize that if Jim and I would have stayed together and he had died, I would probably still be a widow? I guess widowhood was my destiny."

She turned to Susan and chuckled. "Is widowhood even a word in English?"

They both laughed remembering the times that Richard corrected her atrocious use of the English language with the French accent. Although Michelle's English improved over the years of being married to a British man, it was almost as bad as Susan's French. Jim never corrected her bizarre use of the English language because it was one of the precious things he loved about her.

"Don't say that," Susan assured her. "Jim is back and in better form than ever."

Michelle's eyes misted. "Don't I know it."

They opened another bottle of wine with some cheese and crackers. They had changed into flannel pajamas, and Susan started the fireplace in the living room.

"I love him so much," Michelle said. Her tears fell on her cheeks, and she shook her head.

Susan's hand paused in midair, holding her wine glass. "I know, Michelle," she whispered.

She nodded. "I tried to love Richard, but for the longest time after we began seeing each other, I still missed Jim terribly. Even on my wedding day when Jim asked me to dance, my legs shook and my heart pounded so hard, I was afraid someone would notice. I was happy for him and Vera, but there was always a magnetic pull between us I was never able to let go of. I hate myself sometimes when I think of it. Vera was a dear friend but…it never went away, Susan. I never stopped loving Jim. I felt so guilty sometimes."

"I know you've always loved Jim, but you tried to make your marriage work."

Michelle's eye opened wide. "*Merde!*"

Susan frowned. "What?"

"Richard's ashes are right there on the mantel. Do you think he's listening to our conversation?"

Susan laughed. "I think we've had too much wine, and it's time to go to sleep."

Some things never changed.

♫

The next day as Michelle gently spread Richard's ashes along the White Cliffs of Dover, Susan began to hum, "Dust in the Wind."

Michelle glanced at her friend. "*Merde*! Really?"

Susan shrugged.

With a final toss into the air, both women laughed. Susan could see healing take root in Michelle.

48
TYING UP LOOSE ENDS

MARCH 1989, LOS ANGELES

Trés went down to the front desk since he had stayed at the hotel again, sensing his father might want a little time with Michelle. They had had a great trip to New York, and Jim wanted him to stay. He didn't want to leave Los Angeles, but a lot of work awaited him in Hamburg. He had to think about Alex's proposal. Did he want to take the offer and come back only to be near temptation? Annie was worse than temptation—maybe his doom. He kept flip-flopping, but he had told Jim he'd join Black Ice

If he made the decision to move, he would have to tie up ends back home. Sell his mother's home, break up with his girlfriend.

He walked to the front desk to pay his hotel bill.

"Mr. Haley, your bill has been paid, and a limo is outside to take you to LAX, compliments of The Warriors."

Trés smiled and turned to get into the limo. As he walked out the door of the hotel, he swiped tears away.

♬

He returned to his Hamburg house after two weeks in New York with his father. He put his bags down in the foyer and hung his coat on a rack. It was good to be home. He sighed and poured himself some Scotch in a glass. Thoughts of a darling, little blonde crept into his mind. He didn't want her invading his thoughts.

He had it all together. Why was his life taking such a dramatic turn? He was in a fairly successful rock band and made a decent living, was seeing a nice young woman, and enjoyed being out on the road and getting a taste of a groupie here and there. In Los Angeles, everyone commented on how much he looked like his father; and it was true, though he had his mother's coloring. Good looks and a guitar caused women to drop to their knees.

He changed into some sweats and a black t-shirt to call Alex. Their jam session went well, and Trés knew it was a perfect fit, not to mention two sons of Warriors! It was an opportunity he couldn't miss. He refilled his glass with more scotch, sat on the sofa and crossed his legs underneath him.

Annie answered on the third ring. "Hi, I wanted to speak with your brother, Alex"

She suddenly felt at a loss for air. "Isn't it a bit late in your part of the world?"

"Yes, as a matter of fact, I just arrived. Annie, I've made my decision. I will be taking your brother's offer..." He let his words trail off for a moment; his voice dropped a few octaves when he whispered her name. It caused her head to spin.

"I'm glad. I'll get my brother for you."

"Annie, wait!" She paused.

"It was good to see you again," he said.

"I never thought I would see you," she added sarcastically.

"Maybe it's meant to be."

"Maybe not. Hold on. I'll get my brother," she said, not wanting to read too much into his words...not yet, anyway. He was still miles away and with a girlfriend back home.

Moments later, Alex spoke into the phone. "Hey, I was just going to call you to see if you arrived well."

He took a sip of his drink. "I did, thanks, and I had plenty of time to think on the flight here. I've decided to join Black Ice, Alex. There's nothing else for me here. I just have to tie up a few loose ends and I'll be in L.A. by the end of the month."

"Great! We'll keep in touch."

♫

Annie awoke humming one of The Warriors' greatest hits, "Forbidden Love." It was Friday and she and Niki would be returning to school after the weekend and the holiday. Her mother and Ron were out, her sister was still sleeping, and Alex was at Ashley's. She poured herself a glass of orange juice and poked around the massive Sub-Zero refrigerator to make herself something to eat.

Annie remembered her father fondly and knew that he provided a cook and a maid for his household, but her mother seemed to have hit the jackpot with Ron. Annie had never seen a bigger refrigerator in her life, not to mention the fact that it was full. The cook came into the kitchen, and there were two separate maids in addition to a full-time gardener who tended to the outside areas. A nanny for Monique.

"Would you like something, Miss Edwards? Lunch will be served as soon as your mother and Mr. James come home," the elderly woman asked.

Annie looked at Ines and thought. *No, my mother is not the only one to hit the jackpot. I did too.* She smiled at the woman. "Maybe some juice and coffee. I'll be out on the patio." She took a large glass of orange juice with her.

Annie sat outside and looked out over the manicured garden and swimming pool beyond. Ines brought a bowl of bananas and strawberries, along with a silver coffee service set. "Can I get you anything else?"

"How thoughtful of you to bring fruit." She held out the glass. "A bit more orange juice, please."

As Ines turned to go back into the kitchen, Niall exited the house to join his sister on the patio. He bent down to kiss her cheek. "Hey, baby face, you okay?"

"Couldn't be better." She took a banana, peeled it and broke it in half. She offered the half to Niall.

"That sounds too good," he said, taking the offering.

"What brings you here?" she asked adding a bit more sugar into her coffee. Ines poured a cup for Niall.

"Lunch with the family, and then Stefani and I are off to the airport. Our flight leaves at six."

"Cool," she said and brought her cup up to her lips.

"How come you have a crazy glow about you. New guy?"

She shrugged and remained silent.

He sat across the table from her. "Mom said you drove Trés to the hotel when he was here. Could he be the cause of this 'new and improved' Annie?"

She looked away, a mischievous grin on her face.

Niall leaned back in the chair and crossed his arms. "Annie, be careful; we don't know him."

"I know that. He's a nice guy. I met him while we were in France. It was the night before the chaos."

Niall's voice was surprised. "Really? What a coincidence!"

Annie nodded. "He was playing at that club that was too young for you guys," she added, laughing. "What do you think, detective? Is he a nice guy?" Annie stood to go and shower.

"I'll let you know after I do a background check on him."

"He is *not* the person you were looking for that night!" She sighed with exasperation. "Are you going to check out every man I go out with?"

"I most certainly will and Anneke too, young lady."

"Not my father, Niall. Don't act like Ron."

His jaw dropped. She kissed him on the cheek and ran inside to get ready.

Well, what do you know? he thought. *Annie grew up! Anneke, I mean Niki, I don't have to worry about; the guy she dates on and off is in Frankfurt. They call each other on occasion, but it won't survive the distance, not at this age. Annie, on the other hand, is trouble in every sense of the word.* He never thought twins could be so darn different.

Eva and Ron returned to the house, followed by Susan, Karl and Stefani. Ron was nervous about letting Stefani move so far away from her parents and loved ones, but Niall was offered the opportunity of a lifetime at Interpol. Not to mention Susan had reminded him more than once that Stefani had already spent time abroad, with Josh, no less. It was a sad day for both parents, but it was time Stefani spread her wings and fly away from the nest permanently.

Ron couldn't have asked for a better man. Niall adored his daughter, and she changed his life. Damn, if the kid had not proved him wrong more than once.

The help began to serve lunch and the family moved into the formal dining room. "Where're the girls?" asked Eva.

"Running late, as usual. Putting on the Ritz," Niall said.

A few minutes later the twins surprised everyone by entering the dining room on time, like they didn't have a care in the world. Annie's and Niall's eyes met, and she gave him her sweetest smile. *Bitch! She'll play him well, all right!* he thought. A vision of Trés wrapped around the finger of an older more mature Annie invaded his mind and he laughed. He remembered Karl's words. "They are all beautiful until you meet that one who turns your life around. You won't know what hit you." *Trés, you are so fucked, my man! I saw that pathetic look on your face! The same one I had a while back.*

49
A NEW BEGINNING

APRIL 1989, HAMBURG

Trés finalized the meeting with the attorney who helped him with his mother's estate. He had his mother's diary and several nice pieces of jewelry from her safe deposit box. All accounts, what little there was, were transferred to his name. He stopped by his mother's house and picked up his bags. Over the past few weeks, he managed to sell all their belongings and the house. Walking around from room to room allowed him some closure. His mother's death, his father's accident, and leaving the only place he ever called home—so much change in a short time. His first steps down the hallway, his first words were imbedded in the walls.

A young couple with a baby on the way bought it. He hoped it would bring them the same happiness as it brought him and his mother. *Time to move on.* An incredible opportunity awaited him in America. The chance of a lifetime, still he wondered...*is it the right decision?* He was fine in Frankfurt. Hot Embers was a good band beginning to get recognition in Europe. A good woman who loved him. He couldn't return the love; it just wasn't there. They parted amicably.

A new life awaited him. He cut his hair and wore it unkempt, unruly and semi-spiked. He got himself another tattoo of a blue-eyed white tigress on his left upper chest and pierced another hole in his ear so that he could wear two small hoops in one earlobe. Only after he saw the tattoo did he realize what he'd unconsciously done. A daily reminder of blue eyes he wanted to forget at times.

He stood in his old room looking out at the backyard where he'd played as a child. In that yard, he'd been a policeman, a fireman, a knight in shining armor. His lips turned into a smile as he remembered building a tent out of his mother's bedsheets so that he could play "doctor" with a neighborhood girl named Clarissa. His mother caught them both naked, him on top of her and just rubbing against each other, too afraid to put two and two together. They were ten years old.

The next time they decided to play, there were obvious changes in their anatomies. Breasts appeared where there had been two tiny pink circles. When he touched them for the first time, her nipples became more pronounced and harder. They fumbled with their clothes and discovered new hair in certain parts of their bodies. Clarissa was his first, but he wasn't her first. She taught him everything she knew about sex.

The doorbell interrupted his memories. The new owners of the house arrived. He wiped a tear away before letting them in and handing them the keys.

He smiled and wished them luck. The wife, a beautiful, small blonde whose smile reminded him of Annie. It erupted a flow of emotions he wasn't used to. Her protruding belly seemed to be taking its toll on her small frame. The taxi arrived just in time to take him to the airport.

Once on the plane, he asked for a scotch on the rocks and looked out the window as the plane took off, and he left his beloved home to a new life. He closed his eyes.

Her hands and lips were all over him, torturing him, licking, biting; driving him insane. She straddled him and moved expertly. His hips pushed deeper and deeper into her soft, hot folds. He reached out to caress perfectly round bouncing breasts that teased him. She threw her head back, calling out his name, and he could feel her body tremble violently from head to toe. She bit her bottom lip as wave after wave of her orgasm took her to new heights. He felt his own orgasm near, and he felt the explosion building, building and he was about to let go...

Somewhere over the Atlantic, he woke with a start and a hard on that only she could placate.

50
BLACK ICE

SEPTEMBER 1989, LOS ANGELES

Black Ice was slated to go on a yearlong experimental tour throughout the United States and Canada before heading across the Atlantic. Their first single "Atlantic Crossing" shot to the number one spot on all the rock stations. Trés returned to Los Angeles and Jim stayed behind in New York.

Alex and Trés met with Ron and Karl before they went on the road. The older rockers were going to meet up with them as much as possible. The Warriors were still writing music and although they weren't planning on a reunion, it wasn't totally out of the question.

Ron stood against the mixing board in his home studio with a glass of club soda with lime. "Trés, where the hell did you ever come up with writing a song about having a hard on over the Atlantic Ocean?"

"Because it happened for real. I had an incredible wet dream and woke up hard as a rock, on a plane, over the Atlantic. Pretty painful shit, and no one around to take care of it!"

"Anyone we know?" Karl asked, wiggling mischievous eyebrows at the young man.

Trés laughed. "It was someone I met one wild night in France."

Ron, sharp as an eagle asked. "Where did you play in France?"

"It was a small bar in Courchevel called 'le Lieu.' It catered mainly to a younger crowd. Lots of young girls out enjoying themselves while their parents were out on holiday. It was a pretty special night. I never forgot her."

"Sounds like trouble to me. Susan and I were able to maintain a relationship because we were always on the road together; you don't have that. As a matter of fact, Karl will tell you, Susan and I got along better on the road than at home. Jim and Vera's relationship didn't survive the long separations. Stay single and don't get yourself involved till you get older. It's not easy being on the road and having temptation at every turn. Not fair to leave a woman home ninety percent of the year either."

Trés sighed. "I know. That's why I didn't ask my gal back home, to come with me. It wasn't working in Hamburg, and it wasn't going to work now."

Ron picked up his club soda and looked over the schedule. "You guys leave the day after tomorrow. The travel entourage consists of about ten people who are there to assist you and will get whatever personal needs you run out of. They will do your banking, buy anything from underwear to condoms. They will rent you a car if you need one, arrange for tours of the different cities. They will make sure you attend dress rehearsals, sound checks, you get the picture. Karl, you have anything to add?"

"You guys are young, we've been there, and we know where your mind is. There will be hundreds, if not thousands, of women willing to do anything for a chance to get in your bed. You have to be so careful, guys. There's disease out there, HIV, pregnancy...some of you have love interests; don't forget that. No groupie out on the road is worth putting what you have at home in jeopardy. I know I sound like an old man, but I am speaking from experience."

"If you want to play out there, make sure you let go what is here and for God's sake stay away from drugs," Ron reiterated.

♫

Trés left the studio at Ron's house. He saw Annie's car in the driveway out of the corner his eye. He hoped to run into her even if for a second, but it didn't happen.

He arrived at his father's house to finish packing. Everything seemed to be in order, but something gnawed at the edges of his heart. He briefly thought about his life and the turns it was taking. Life could change in a moment. He decided to call Annie. If he was leaving, he had a good excuse to ask her to dinner. She answered on the third ring.

"Hi, Annie," he said.

"My brother's not home," she said with immediate recognition.

"I'm not calling for your brother; I'm calling you."

"Oh?" she said with sarcasm.

He could understand her anger, but he didn't let the tone of her voice bother him in the least. "Since I'm leaving soon, I'd like to take you to dinner."

"Why?"

He held his breath, trying not to get angry enough to change his mind.

"Because I'm not going to see you for a while, probably not until Niall and Stefani's wedding and yes, Annie, because I like you...a lot more than even *I* want to admit."

Grateful the conversation was on the phone and not in person, she couldn't help but grin. "I like you too, Trés. You know that."

"Is that a yes?" he asked.

"What time?"

He looked at the clock over the black marble mantel. "An hour and a half?"

"Sure."

"I'll pick you up. Casual is fine, jeans and a t-shirt."

"I'll see you then."

Annie nervously went to shower. She rummaged through her massive walk-in closet and couldn't find a thing to wear. It had to be perfect, the underwear, the shoes, the accessories. She decided on her tightest jeans with red lace underwear.

He showed up right on time, and the butler let him in. His eyes sparkled as he admired her and loved her "look." The off the shoulder cashmere red sweater showed that she was braless. Her shoes were high-heeled black sandals, and she wore a short leather jacket. She picked up her hair wanting to look older and topped off with medium gold hoop earrings. She wrapped a silk Hermes scarf loosely around her neck and was ready to go.

Annie said goodbye to her mother, thankful that Ron wasn't around to read her a list of the reasons why she should not be going out alone with Trés. She didn't care that he was older and wiser; she was prepared to meet him head on with whatever he unleashed on her.

He kissed her cheek taking in the sweet scent of her expensive perfume. He took her hand and entwined his fingers with hers.

Annie practically fell into the car as he held the door open for her. He shut the door and walked around the car. Why did he affect her so? It was supposed to be a game, a one-time only encounter, and here she sat next to him months later and trembled from head to toe.

He took her hand and kissed her fingers. "Hungry?"

"A little."

"There's a small bistro on Wilshire near my place where I pick up food now and then when I don't want to cook we can go to."

"You cook?" she asked, taken aback.

He laughed. "Yes, I cook. I've always loved to cook and cooked for my mother the last year of her life. I'll cook for you when I get back from the tour. I just didn't have enough time tonight."

"Wow!" She exclaimed. "Here I thought you were just a handsome face with a perfect ass."

He looked at her. "Were you staring at me as a sexual object that night?"

"You were grinding your hips, sweat poured off your body, your shirt was glued to your chest, your arms are perfectly muscled and tattooed...shall I go on?"

"Don't let me stop you." He grinned.

"Your jeans were so tight I could tell you were blessed in *that* department. Your voice was soft and soothing. Your guitar playing flawless."

"I'm so glad you eventually noticed my musical talents." He squeezed her hand tightly as they arrived at the restaurant.

Dinner went well. They mostly talked about their pasts—schools and friends they left behind in Germany, getting used to Los Angeles. His eyes saddened. "I'm just so sorry I didn't go in search of my dad sooner. I was too busy taking care of Mom and even though she told me about him, I didn't want to hurt her in any way. I didn't know how my dad was going to react after so many years."

She reached out and placed her hand over his. "Jim is a special man; he would have reacted as any good father would. You were his first born, a son." She shook her head. "He is a good man, father, friend, and musician. He, Ron, and Karl are inseparable, you know, The Three Musketeers."

She sat back and took a sip of her Coke. "Now as for your grandfather, he is one nasty son of a bitch, or so I've heard."

"I saw him at the hospital. It was an all-out family war. Michelle put him in his place. She is such a tough woman. My dad adores her, and I like her a lot." Trés stood to leave.

"Annie, would you like to stop by my place for a bit? It's still early."

Her breath stopped. She didn't want the night to end. "Sure."

♫

Annie looked around Jim's lavish living room while Trés went to mix some drinks. She lifted the heavy piano cover. Her fingers played a few keys.

"Do you play?" Trés asked from the mahogany bar where he mixed their drinks.

She laughed. "I can't tell a B flat from an F sharp. Don't have a musical bone in my body."

He took her in his arms. "I don't know about that. Your body sounds pretty musical to me when I stroke it."

She looked up at him and allowed herself to be consumed by his gaze. The dim lights of the sconces were like stars in his eyes. She studied him, wonderful lips, unshaven face. He held her tight, and she could hardly get enough oxygen into her lungs. She offered her parted lips. The tip of his tongue traced the outline before taking possession of her mouth. She wrapped her arms around his neck.

He sighed. "I don't want to hurt you, Annie. I'm leaving tomorrow, and I have no idea when I'll be back. We can't have a relationship right now. I don't know what awaits me out there, and it wouldn't be fair to ask anything of you. I don't want you to sit by the phone waiting for me to call because I'm not sure I will."

"I understand," she replied.

He tightened his grip on her. "I know these relationships can work. Karl and Susan have lasted a lifetime together. I know they trust each other. That's what I want eventually, Annie, but not yet. I need to get my bearings straight, see how this is going to work. Vera couldn't stand being married to a rock star. She didn't want to be 'Jim's wife' and sit home waiting for him to return from touring; she also didn't want to travel with him."

"I know, Trés. I just want another taste of you before you go." She whispered and turned toward him to run her fingers under the waist of his jeans. She leaned in close to him in a sexual invitation he was not willing to pass up.

His eyes caught hers. He was about to enter dangerous territory, but he didn't care. She unnerved every inch of his being. The force of his kiss took her by surprise. His hands slipped under her top and he caressed her breasts. He pulled her closer, so their hips met; she was breathless under his power. The palms of her hands felt the warm, hard muscles of his back. He slipped his hands over hardened nipples. She moaned under his touch. Her fingers unbuttoned his shirt, and she ran her hands, ever so slowly up and down the firm muscles of his chest. His teeth drew her bottom lip into his mouth, and he kissed her chin. The heat of wet kisses slid down her neck.

He pulled the sweater over her head. She placed her hands on his shoulders and threw her head back as his lips found her nipple, letting out a sigh.

His fingers slid over her arms, causing goosebumps on her skin. He picked her up in his arms and carried her to the bedroom. He fell on the bed with her, holding her tight, afraid to lose the sensations she brought out in him.

"I want you so bad," he whispered, biting into her neck and flipped her on the bed so that he lay over her. His lips found one breast again as his hand slipped over the nipple of her other breast. Annie wanted to scream out. His tongue licked between her breasts and he moved lower while his fingers fumbled with her jeans.

Her panting drove him insane as his hand stopped for a second leaving her to groan as he began to glide the jeans over her hips and pulled them away, discarding them. He needed to feel her flesh against his. He stood and undressed himself and returned to the bed. He parted her legs and kissed her, invading her mouth with his tongue. His kisses became more demanding and his tongue slipped lower and lower.

"Annie, you can't imagine all that I want to do to you. You drive me crazy. There are not enough hours in a day to do all I want. I need to taste and possess every inch of you."

Her body moved involuntarily as waves of pleasure overpowered her, took her to a new level. She exploded into a million fragments, calling out his name. He slithered over her body and licked her neck, pressing himself against the length of her.

Her hand slid lower to caress him and he thrust his hips against her hand. He rolled over, pulling her with him and she slid lower, licking his abdomen and traveling beyond. His hands became lost in her hair. He wanted desperately to hold on longer, enjoy the moment but it was not going to be possible; she drew away, and her hand took the place of her mouth.

A moment later, he moaned out her name as she took him to heights he'd never come to know until he met her.

That night, Trés and Annie re-wrote the book on how rewarding foreplay could be. They brought each other to thundering orgasms numerous times. Annie collapsed on his chest, drained of energy. His hands caressed her back, and he closed his eyes. He was loath to take her home; but he did.

♫

Trés turned on the coffeemaker and yawned. He certainly was going to need it. He ran up the stairs and peeled off his clothes to get in the shower. He let the hot water pour over him and he scrubbed himself vigorously, trying to rid himself of her musky scent, her perfume. He couldn't, it was imbedded in his flesh. He smiled as he dried himself and remembered her touch. *Damn her!*

He put some sweats on and ran down to the kitchen to get some coffee, sure he would not sleep a wink. Three tour busses were expected to pull out of the parking lot of the high-tech recording studio and office building The Warriors owned at 6 a.m.

♫

Alex Edwards, Trés Haley, Rick Taylor, Steve Jones, and Chris Thomas boarded the tour bus headed to Seattle, the first city in the West to East tour. Eva, Ron, and Jim stood out in the parking lot. Eva's eldest was going on to make a name for himself, like his father. They both hugged him, and Ron slipped him several hundred-dollar bills.

Jim smiled proudly. Surprised to see Jim had come back from New York, Trés embraced his father just before getting on the bus. Jim, too, slid some spending money into the young man's pocket.

"You take good care of Michelle, you hear?" Trés warned his father.

"I will, I promise." Jim fought back tears.

Nancy did a great job, and he was proud of the young man.

Black Ice was ready to take America by storm.

ABOUT THE AUTHOR

A native New Yorker, Barbra Best now makes her home in Miami, Florida, with her husband Gus. Using her real name, her works have been published in *The Magnolia Quarterly,* and her debut novel, then entitled *Forbidden Fruit*, landed as a semifinalist in the Faulkner Wisdom Competition. Barbra is an avid reader, music lover, and the proud owner of a French Bulldog named Winston.

THE WARRIORS CONTINUE THEIR STARDOM IN:

Resurrection of a Rock Star

December 25, 1991 – the Soviet hammer and sickle flag lowered for the last time over the Kremlin.

December 26, 1991 – the world woke to the announcement that the Soviet Union was no more.

How do changing world events affect the dynamic rock band, The Warriors?

They that mourn shall rejoice!